MW00772410

JOURNAL OF HAWAI'I LITERATURE AND ARTS

bamboo ridge

ISSUE 113
40th Anniversary Issue

ISBN 978-0-910043-99-1

This is issue #113 of *Bamboo Ridge, Journal of Hawaiʻi Literature and Arts* (ISSN 0733-0308)
Copyright © 2018 by Bamboo Ridge Press

All rights reserved. This book, or parts thereof, may not be reproduced
in any form without permission.

Published by Bamboo Ridge Press
Printed in the United States of America
Bamboo Ridge Press is a member of the Community of Literary Magazines and Presses (CLMP).

Founding Editors: Eric Chock and Darrell H. Y. Lum
Guest Editors: Gail N. Harada and Lisa Linn Kanae
Managing Editor: Joy Kobayashi-Cintrón
Copyeditor: Normie Salvador
Business Manager: Wing Tek Lum
Typesetting and design: Kristin Lipman
Cover art: *Compass Series IV* (detail), by Noe Tanigawa, encaustic on mahogany.
"Oceans" by Juan Ramón Jiménez and translated by Robert Bly in *Lorca and Jiménez: Selected Poems*
is reprinted with permission from Beacon Press.

Bamboo Ridge Press is a nonprofit, tax-exempt corporation formed in 1978 to foster the
appreciation, understanding, and creation of literary, visual, or performing arts by, for, or about
Hawaiʻi's people. This publication was made possible with support from the National Endowment
for the Arts (NEA) and the Hawaiʻi State Foundation on Culture and the Arts (SFCA), through
appropriations from the Legislature of the State of Hawaiʻi (and grants from the NEA).

Bamboo Ridge is published twice a year.
For subscription information, back issues, or a catalog, please contact:

Bamboo Ridge Press
P.O. Box 61781
Honolulu, Hawaiʻi 96839-1781
808.626.1481
brinfo@bambooridge.com
www.bambooridge.com

Bamboo Ridge Press gratefully acknowledges the donations of the following individuals and organizations in 2017:

Carol Abe
Nancy Aleck
Anonymous (16)
Charles T. Araki
Esther Arinaga
Victoria Asayama
Fred Bail
Barnes & Noble
Dawn L. Baughn
Emily A. Benton
Doreen E. Beyer
Joseph R. Bibeau
Marlene Booth
Sally-Jo Bowman
Amalia B. Bueno
The Cades Foundation
Kay Caldwell
Jane Campbell
Casey Charitable
Matching Programs
Carol Jean Catanzariti
Susan Chamberlin
Stuart Ching
Eric Chock
Ghislaine D. Chock
Sue Lin Chong
Xander Cintrón-Chai
Sara L. Collins
Rebecca L. Covert
Linda R. Cunningham
Cathy Song Davenport
Roger Debreceny
George R. Drick
Ernestine Enomoto
Elena Farden
Foodland Super Market, Ltd.
Robert L. Freedman
Richelle Fujioka
David Furumoto
Alvin Fuse
Karen Fuse
Claire M. Gearen
Stephanie A. Grande-Misaki
Merie Ellen F. Gushi
Carolyn Hadfield
Angela Haeusler
Lynne Halevi

John Hara
Kasumi Hara
Marie M. Hara
Mavis Hara
Gail N. Harada
Jim Harstad
Hawai'i Council for the
Humanities
Hawai'i State Foundation on
Culture and the Arts
Leonore Higa
Craig Howes
Janet Inamine
Ann Inoshita
The Islander Group
Lisa Linn Kanae
Rachel Katsuda
Demetra N. Kaulukukui
Scott Kikkawa
Frances H. Kikugawa
Carol Jean Kimura
Milton Kimura
Joy Kobayashi-Cintrón
Brenda Kwon
Kapena Landgraf
Melanie M. Lau
Juliet Kono Lee
Lanning C. Lee
Sonia Leong
Peter C. T. Li
Michael Little
Russell Loo
Eulalia Luckett
Jack Luckett
Darrell H. Y. Lum
Mae Lum
Tan Tek Lum
Wing Tek Lum
Mark Lutwak
Marion Lyman-Mersereau
Jennifer Madriaga
Annette E. Masutani
Tamara Moan
Lori S. Murakami
Amy C. Murata
Shareen Murayama
Leila S. Nagamine

Jackson Nakasone
National Endowment
for the Arts
Marsha Ninomiya
Angela C. Nishimoto
Ethel Aiko Oda
Carol Ogino
Carol T. Ohta
Frances M. Oliver
Christy Passion
Elmer Omar Pizo
James M. Reis
Daisy Chun Rhodes
Kent Sakoda
Electa Sam
Jui-Lien Sanderson
Keith Sanderson
Suzanne M. Sato
David M. Sherrill
John Simonds
Michelle Cruz Skinner
Sharon D. Smith
Smithsonian Institution
Monica B. Sullivan
Hazel H. Takumi Foundation
E. H. Tamura
Noe Tanigawa
Virginia Tanji
Moriso Teraoka
Jean Toyama
Joe Tsujimoto
Rochelle Uchibori
Julie L. Ushio
Lance K. Uyeda
Amy L. Uyematsu
Western Union
Elizabeth A. Wight
Myra Williams
Rick Williams
Eileen Wong
Illiana G. Wood
Lois Yamauchi
Valerie B.H. Yee
William Yomes
Kristel Yoneda
Nancy S. Young

CONTENTS

BAMBOO SHOOTS

CONTRIBUTORS

FROM THE EDITORS

Why would anyone want to start a literary journal? Why would anyone want to squeeze through the anxiety of grant applications and sales charts? Why would anyone want to be in the business of print in an age when digital publications are practically the norm? Why would anyone spend hours reading hundreds of submissions and interacting with hundreds of creative writers and artists—some really nice, some sort of needy, most brilliant?

This issue marks the 40th anniversary of Bamboo Ridge Press. Since 1978, BRP has published literature and art by, for, and about the people of Hawai'i that reflect Hawai'i culture. Who would do this unless there was a genuine love for this place and its literature? As schmaltzy as it may sound, love sustains Bamboo Ridge Press. It certainly isn't the money, fame, or accolades—and there have been many accolades. It's all about da love—for the creative process, for seeing for the first time a well-chosen cover, for hearing a writer's response to being published, for the undeniable power that words possess, and for seeing our voices in a book. The question is not "Why do it?" The question really is "Why wouldn't someone do it?" Forty years is pretty impressive for a small, independent literary press, so let's raise that metaphorical glass and celebrate that big BRP Four-O milestone, but keep in mind that there are generations of writers and readers who will continue to turn to *Bamboo Ridge* for many years to come.

—Gail N. Harada and Lisa Linn Kanae

Kahakuloa Honey (detail), by Noe Tanigawa, encaustic with Kahakuloa beeswax, 10 x 18.

DEREK N. OTSUJI

FIRST DREAM

For the first dream of the New Year
my uncle pins his hopes on a vision of three things:
Mount Fuji, a hawk, an eggplant of good color.

Seen in sequence, these signal luck
in the coming year. On New Year's Eve, above
the headboard of his bed, he posts a colored print

of all three, exactly as they might appear
in the New Year's dreamer's dreaming head.
"Not one good omen yet!" clucks my aunt.

Here's a man who's seen misfortune:
retirement savings bilked, investments gone bad,
a daughter snatched by illness prowling

the blood, and a grown son whose mind
took flight in the pious 70s on wings
of angel dust. A wife married to a man of such luck—

what else *can* she do. It's the first day of 2015.
We're gathered at my uncle's for the year's
first meal. *Ichi Fuji, ni taka, san nasu,*

he repeats, counting down hours
like rosary beads, murmuring the chiming
words like a mantra whose frequencies

will set superstrings of the cosmic purse
a-humming till, loosened, they open the mouth
of auspices, spilling coins of good fortune,

lining bare pockets of the singing pilgrim
with loads of actual or metaphorical gold.
What he's got instead are goods of more

durable luck, which the coming months
will prove—a knack for loss, contentment in a wife
of fifty years, a mood of rugged cheer.

DEREK N. OTSUJI

A VISIT TO THE HONGWANJI TEMPLE ON THE ANNIVERSARY OF OUR GRANDFATHER'S DEATH

When the priest talks to us of death and life,
we sit like small children at boarding school.
"Life is like a flower. . . ." His voice is cool
as well water, erasing the world of strife.

Beneath the Buddha's feet a lotus blooms.
"This lovely water flower," explains the priest,
"like the meek and humble, grows in the least
promising of places. Yet from a pond's

stagnant depths, where all is murky and cold,
it rises to the surface, blossoms white
and pure, as if burning with inner light,
an emblem of spirit in the turbid world."

The sermon done, the priest withdraws himself
in long ceremonial robes to chant
a sutra for the dead. All attachment
now falls away, the finite self engulfed

in the infinite, as he steadily intones
tuneless verses that like pure rivers run.
We file, beginning with the eldest son,
before the shrine, the urn that holds his bones,

and then in turn, hands pressed in solemn prayer,
bow and offer incense, burning off in plumes,
while from the singing bowl a bell tone booms
—sound and fragrance purifying the air.

The atmosphere is tuned by singing bronze. . . .
Like souls ascending the planes of existence,
incense climbs the stairway of its essence.
The shrine's gold leaf gleams through a veil of gauze.

The sutra dies, the closing knell is struck.
The priest wakes from his trance. With real concern
our aunt inquires about care of Grandpa's urn.
The good priest dispels her fears of bad luck.

DEREK N. OTSUJI

HALULU RUN AT DAWN

Twelve anglers
in a line—
thigh deep in water's
clear sea tones, weak
tea browns
tea greens
teals, steel and
cobalt
blues

Their backs are
to the sun

Straw hats and baseball
caps
Tank tops, bare
brown arms,
colored T's pulled
over white ComfortSofts
with loose long sleeves

Ripples, flashes,
shadows and
specks

what is imagined
what is real

A silver flock

at the surface
breaks
is reabsorbed

flick
from a long wand
calls
a twitching light
from the
sea

LAUREN K. N. PADILLA

WAIMAKA

The sun was beginning to set by the time Maka had managed to bring everything down to shore—The hull, outrigger, and both wooden spars; her rig ropes, paddle, and steering blade. Lastly, arms fatigued, she set the salt urn down on the sand. The canoe looked like a carcass, nothing like *Manu*, the name her father painted on its bow. In front of her, the entire bay swayed with warm wind and the horizon shone. She greeted the sight with deep breaths and began her work.

After starting the rig, Maka picked up the first spar, pinned it across the gunnel with her knee, and wrapped it temporarily to the hull with a thick strip of rubber. She yanked on the ropes till they groaned, secure. Then she threaded them over, through, across, under. Switch. Over. Through. Across. Under. She knew she should have brought more rubber or ratchet straps; the finished rig would be loose and uneven without the extra hands and body weight to hold the finished crosses taut. Kumu taught them that the rig was a job for two people. Kumu was right about a lot of things. She had been Maka's mother, after all.

Hands working, Maka recalled the day her mother asked her whether she was going to join the high school paddling team, for which she was to be assistant coach. Maka hadn't answered right away. That night when she looked in the mirror, she thought of dyeing her blonde hair to dark brown, or cutting it short, anything to hide the fact that she looked nothing like her mother. But she also had father's pale skin, slim frame, and Standard English accent. She would be marked as an outsider. She would never fit in. But her mother had asked. She joined the team that fall.

"This is my daughter Maka," said Kumu. "She will be paddling with varsity starting today."

Maka immediately felt sick. Her new teammates stood around her like a gigantic eye. She didn't hear them with her own ears, but she knew what their whispers were: *haole, who does she think she is?* They proceeded to make it clear that not even being the assistant coach's daughter would earn her any sympathy.

"Seat five, coach, seat five!" they jeered. The fifth seat in the canoe was second from the back, in front of the steersman, reserved for those who needed the most coaching and had the least strength.

Maka felt a glimmer of hope when her mother decided to start training her as a steerswoman. Steering would mean she could see everything, and at the same time not be seen. She could stay out of everyone's way and yet have all control. But of course, the "special attention" made things distinctly worse. And she turned out to be a wretched steer. It was supposed to be simple: poke left, boat goes left; poke right, boat goes right. But even on the stillest, flattest days she could barely manage to keep the nose straight; the boat fought her, turning opposite of her pokes and even sometimes refusing to turn at all. Her crew could execute their part of a race turn perfectly, and she would still lose control of it before the turn was complete. She would run the outrigger over the turn flags in scrimmages, call changes on the wrong stroke, keep her blade buried too long, too short, too deep, too shallow. Maka would lean over the gunnel and wet her face as she reached shore so that no one would see her crying.

Her mother had remained on her side all the while: she would straddle the rear spar during practice, as the assistant coaches often did, and comfort Maka with simple shifts in her expression. Still, her teammates' backs mocked her always. They'd break regatta's number-one rule—to never look backward—just to cast disdainful looks at her over their shoulders. Maka ended up requesting to sit five after all; she wouldn't bother anyone and no one would bother her.

"Why? You don't like to steer?" her mother had asked her in reply.

"No. And no one else likes me to steer either."

"You just started learning, baby."

"I don't like it."

The lights went out in her mother's eyes. "Why not?"

Maka thought to take it back, or lie. But what good would it have done anyone? All she did was use up a steering blade that someone else deserved, that someone else wanted more than she ever would.

"Everyone just *looks* at me," she'd barely managed to say. As she said it, she realized that sitting five wouldn't make any difference. She didn't know if anything would.

Her mother took her hands then. "If you don't think it's worth it, you don't have to stay on the team. I'm sorry for forcing you."

Maka looked at the way her hands crumpled in her mother's, which were broad and sturdy, weathered with experience. She tore her own away in disgust. So be it. She never wanted to be near a canoe again.

"You didn't force me," she replied. Tears were already falling.

"Maka. Maka come here, I'm sorry," her mother pleaded as Maka walked away. Maka didn't think she'd ever heard her mother sound so weak.

Maka went to the head coach and quit the team the next day. Soon afterward, her mother stepped down from assistant coaching to train for the Moloka'i Hoe canoe race. Maka knew it had been her mother's lifelong dream to steer a crew across the channel, but they never spoke of it once. Three times a week, her mother would zip her nylon cover over her steering blade and smile at her on her way out the door. And she would come home with the same smile, dark hair wild with salt water and wind. But they never again spoke together about paddling. Maka hardly knew how to be sorry. She assumed that it could go unspoken.

But one day her mother covered her blade, left for practice, and didn't come back. Instead, she and her father received a phone call: it was an open ocean practice, miles from shore, and her mother had suffered a severe heart attack. The crew's emergency radios were found to be out of working order, and by the time the canoe reached shore, there was nothing left to be done. Her mother would never cross the channel. She would never steer a canoe again. And all those things Maka should have said to her mother, her Kumu, burst out in wails and tears with the weight of all her years.

The funeral was full of people Maka had never seen before, and even people that no one in her entire family had ever seen before. This woman's daughter was once her mother's apprentice, and that elderly man the kumu of her first canoe club. One woman, who had taken turns steering with her mother on a koa boat's first voyage, came up to Maka and asked her who she was. Maka almost bit back, but the woman lifted a crooked finger and smiled.

"Ah. You're her daughter, aren't you? Look at those eyes."

When both spars were rigged to the hull and the outrigger, Maka lay back to rest on the sand with her arms spread wide. Her chest heaved and her palms burned. How long had the rig taken her? The top layer of sand was already cool. An hour? She didn't have a lot of time, but the light and tide promised by the full moon would buy her just enough. Once she crossed the bar and met the channel, she would be safe. She could wait all night for the next high tide if she needed to. A single ghost crab was scuttling about, just close enough the Maka's head for her to hear. Its sound reminded her of the summer nights she'd collected them with her mother in small plastic sand pails. When the pails were full, they would release them all at once. She loved how their legs pricked and tickled her palms, and would delight in watching them disappear into the sand, the waves, the dark, as the moonlight slipped off their backs. But now, alone with the canoe, the ghost crabs and the dark didn't seem so inviting.

Maka stood up, retrieved her paddle, steering blade, and the urn, and stepped over the outrigger to stand beside the hull. She stowed the urn in the bailer, and the two paddles under one of the seats. With both hands braced against the forward spar, she shifted her weight to push *Manu* onto the water. But her arms began to tremble.

Maka checked to see that the urn was still there. Of course it was.

She pounded her fist on the spar so hard it stung, and she watched her own tears fall onto the wood and into the whitewash.

The night they met with the executor of her mother's will, he presented her with an envelope bearing her name. In it was a single piece of paper with her mother's handwriting and signature:

Maka—

When you're ready, bring me back to the channel.

Mom

The executor reminded them that there were no further instructions in the will regarding her mother's burial wishes, and that, since the letter was not part of the official will, it was up to Maka whether to carry out the request. Her father took her hand. The last person to do that had been her mother.

"Mom left her steering blade to you."

"I don't steer, Dad."

"She's asking you to."

Maka continued training with her team as a steersman as the lei strewn around the steering blade wilted and dried onto the mantle. She began questioning her decision to return. She also started doubting the grief that drove her effort—as far as she could tell, she wasn't improving. Maka picked the lei up off the mantle and caught her reflection in the carbon fiber blade.

Ah, you're her daughter, aren't you? Look at those eyes.

Holding the blade and remembering the old woman, Maka found a strength she'd forgotten. Childlike laughter, and bare feet among ghost crabs and sand. The waves. The dark. Her mother's hands. She decided to go in search of the woman who had steered alongside her mother all those years ago.

Maka wiped the tears from her eyes with her forearm, gripped the spar, and drove it forward with her whole weight. The hull scraped and scraped over the sand, then lifted. Her arms faltered when she hoisted herself in, but she made it to her seat, aft. *Manu* bobbed and drifted with her movements, almost as if she were stretching out her wings.

Maka held her paddle at the handle near the base and steadied the blade end at the water line.

Okay.

She buried the blade. *Rip through the water. Recover on return. Reach out and bury. Rip. Recover. Reach.* The nose lifted and fell; the hull skipped forward and gained speed. She took eight strokes on the right, eight on the left. Maka set her pace to her heartbeat, and the shakiness left her limbs. *Pull with your back. Pull parallel to the boat.* The tranquil sounds of the waves climbing the shore flooded her with memories of the regatta. She'd never officially raced, but even from afar the regatta was an unforgetable sight. Bright, immense rows of paddlers, tents, six-man canoes. Eighteen lane-flags wobbling on their buoys. *Keep your body aligned. Keep your top arm straight.*

Maka brought the canoe about five boat-lengths from shore before letting it run. She still wasn't sure she could do this. She might have been wrong about the wind, and as soon as she left the bay it could flip her outrigger over. She could miss the high tide and get stuck behind the bar. Maka picked up her mother's steering blade. This time there was no comforting sensation; the wood was cold and lifeless and the light too dim to see her own face. She put it back under the seat. Maka felt foolish. Of course, there was no old magic, or charm, or fairy dust on the blade. When Maka found the old woman, Malia, again and told her about her mother's note, even she had laughed at her mother's antics.

"Aunty?"

Malia flipped her long salt and pepper hair over her shoulder. "That sounds just like her! So, you want to learn how to steer?"

"N-no! Actually I was hoping *you* would—"

"Ha! You think that Kauanoe would stand for that? No, no. *You* are going to steer that boat.

"Aunty, I don't think I—"

"Did your ma end up keeping *Manu*? That old four-man canoe?"

The water at the entrance to the channel was unpredictable tonight, uneven and sporadic. The closer she came to the baymouth bar, the higher it rose around her, and the longer the canoe would lurch on its crests. She buried her blade over and over, but she could no longer see how far she was moving. Darkness was closing over the boat like a dome. The sun was gone. Her nerve was dissolving. Twice she stalled her blade on one side, tempted to turn the boat back toward shore. Maka was scared. *She couldn't see.*

I'm sorry for forcing you.

Maka made one more vigorous stroke and let the boat run, leaning onto the rear spar to hold the outrigger down on the water.

You didn't force me.

You aren't forcing me.

I'm taking you to the channel.

Where is the canoe drifting? Left. Where are the waves breaking? Twenty yards. The shore? The sandbar? *Okay.* With a loud cry, Maka buried once more.

After teaching Maka how to rig the four-man canoe, Malia trained her to steer for several weeks. Just like her mother did, Malia sat on the rear spar and coached her through every wave, every J-stroke, and every turn. She was sharper and stricter, but she loved the water more than anything.

"You can't make the boat go faster by steering," she would say, voice shrill, "Your job is to stay out of the way. What are you fighting the water for?"

"I'm not fighting."

She crossed her arms. "You're not?"

"No."

She shook out her hair. "Then which way is the current moving?"

"Right. That's why I'm poking left."

"Wrong. The *wind* is blowing right. The current in this bay is going left.

Watching isn't just *looking*, Maka, you've got to—"

Maka threw her blade onto the floor of the hull and shouted, "I don't know what 'eyes' you're talking about! I don't have them! If I did, then my mom would still be here!"

Her cries echoed through *Manu*'s belly for no one but Malia and the ocean to hear.

Rip. Recover. Reach. Bury. Water battered Maka's arms and poured over the splashboard as she approached the mouth of the bay. A freak wave flung her outrigger into the air. She slammed it down with her paddle. It snapped the blade.

"No! Shit! Shit!" She pounded the gunnel in fury and hurled the splintered shaft into the sea. She was pathetic. These waves were nothing compared the channel. The salt air was suffocating her. Someone else should be here. Someone else should. . . .

In a panic Maka locked her eyes on the bailer. The urn was still safe inside. Maka took two shaky steps forward in hull and lifted it out.

Why did you ask me? Of all those people who came to see you, you should have known. You should have known.

She shifted to curl her body up on the seat, and her foot nudged something on the floor. Her mother's blade. She reached down and mustered the strength to close her fingers around the handle. Then she brought it up to cradle it with the urn. Unlike her own paddle, which was—until a moment ago—lightweight and curved at the base and the upper shaft, her mother's steering blade was heavy and angular and straight. Maybe if I'd looked more like her. *Maybe if I were stronger. Maybe if I'd stayed on the team.*

Maka ran her palm over the blade and looked around. The three-mile marker at the sandbar was visible just below the horizon. She put the urn back in the bailer and went back to her seat with resolve. There, she set her mother's steering blade at the water line, and buried it. She adjusted her stroke to its weight and the stiffness of its straight shaft. Maka fixed *Manu*'s nose on the marker, its reflector shining almost as clearly as the moon above.

An immense quiet was blanketing the restless swinging of the ocean around her. Even the combers breaking in the distance ceased to roar. Maka swore that instead she was hearing the moonlight slipping from whitecap to whitecap, shimmering on every capillary far as her eyes could see. Suddenly the waves and the dark before her were a thousand ghost crabs, with no vessel to keep them captive.

Rip. Recover. Deeper this time, and farther. Just an inch farther. Pull with your back. Pull parallel to the boat. Keep your body aligned. Keep your top arm straight.

Manu alighted beside the marker; Maka was over the bar.

She set the steering blade down and took the urn from the bailer, weighing it in both hands. She straddled the spar and planted her feet on the floor of the hull, her knees secured on either side of the saddle. The urn's surface was gritty, and marbled orange and white. It would dissolve within four hours of being submerged.

Maka thought again of her mother's note. *When you're ready, bring me back to the channel. Mom.* She'd surely written it without knowing that she would never make it to the channel in life. But when could she have written it so that she believed Maka would be capable of bringing her in death?

Maka wanted to wonder whether this was enough, but it was too late to believe in anything else. She rotated the salt urn in her hands and focused on the boat rocking gently beneath her.

Maka.

Everything a steersman is was embedded in her name. *Eyes.* But so far she'd seen her whole life through her tears, pointed her gaze down at her knees. What was she looking for? Was she looking at all? Maka swung her feet out over the side of the hull, and let herself fall into the water, entrusting her mother's ashes to the moonlight and the sea's infinite embrace.

When Maka broke the surface again, *Manu* would be waiting for her, perching on the crests of the waves. The horizon would be gathering streaks of violet and dark. The ghost crabs would be watching, waiting, on the sand. 🦀

Oceans: Kaua'i, Hawai'i (detail) 38" x 68". Oil, encaustic, mixed media.

HERE AND NOW

An Interview with Noe Tanigawa

PHOTO BY A.J. FEDUCIA/*FLUX*

Noe Tanigawa interviews others as the Arts and Culture reporter at Hawai'i Public Radio; she is not usually the subject of an interview. We sat down recently with a bottle of wine for a little chat. Here are excerpts of the interview.

Noe: This is a chance to reflect on what writing does for me, why I love to work with writers, tortured though they may be at times. I've found them to be quite fussy about exactness, often able to point out larger patterns or implications. For audio story purposes, writers are the best to interview.

Usually, they've actually thought about stuff. I guess putting words to experience makes us organize it in our minds.

Gail: When we did that Artists/Writers Intersect collaborative project with Robert [Pennybacker], you were doing acrylic paintings. The one we used for the video was this big canvas that you were working on, and I just remember the colors. What were you experimenting and working with at that time?
Noe: I think it's always an issue of wanting to give something for people to hang on to and something for them to make the ground slip off from under their feet. So those elements are still there regardless of what the particular endeavor is.

Gail: I just remember the colors. They felt like they were very clear colors but maybe also reflecting colors that I felt were related to local experience in a way. Kind of reflecting the colors of the landscape.

Noe: That's what I would really hope for, without going to the far end of this really vivid spectrum work where you're doing everything in croton colors. You know what I mean? And then you look at the native Hawaiian plants. A lot of them are kind of those dusty greens, are just sort of those shaded or hooded colors and really interesting. Like think of kukui, right? This sort of powdery green. Not that screaming color. But I like what you're saying about color because it's a choice whether to use color that is transparent or color that's opaque, and I really like transparent colors. They're made more complicated not by being opaque but by having their complement added to them.

Gail: I think also what was interesting about that first project that we were involved with was the question we focused on—the choice to come back to Hawai'i instead of trying to make your art kind of fit the New York scene in a way—in terms of writing for me but also in terms of film for Robert.

Noe: I know. I think that was made into more of a statement when I felt more of a question mark and I always felt that because being here shapes what I think of, right? For example, a lot of people are so lucky to be able to go to another environment and suddenly find their voice. Maybe Grace Jones in Paris or that dancer, Isadora Duncan. They're just moving around waving scarves in America but they move to Paris and they're like fantastic. I don't know, it'd be nice to be like that, but I happen to be back in my hometown.

Gail: But then you did move to New York for several years. So while you were there, how do you think that affected the kind of work you were doing?

Noe: I don't know. It's just I'm really glad that I could just continue pursuing some ideas that I had during grad school when I was in New York. I kind of kept going with these ideas of structure, bones, ligaments, textures, that kind of thing.

Gail: So what started you on the encaustic?

Noe: Searching for a way to get that texture, and then realizing that encaustics were going to be the way. Because I took a materials and techniques class when I was a grad student at UH, with Don Dugal—that's where I learned about it. That's where I learned to gold leaf too—such a useful skill.

Gail: When did you start thinking about the lotus as an image and why the lotus as an image?

Noe: I think it was during grad school. So, that means it was like before 1990.

Gail: So, as an image, the encaustic part. using encaustic to render that image—

Noe: I've always been looking for a way to get that translucent glowing quality. And you can do it with wax and proper lighting. That translucent glowing quality that lotus has, right?

Gail: And it's dimensional too. The lotus image is something that you've worked with for a long time and in the most recent installation at Saks Fifth Avenue, it seemed a little different—to me, it was a more maybe refined image? I love the images before, but do you feel like the more recent lotus images are kind of moving toward what you were hoping to achieve?

Noe: I've always called them *In a Lotus Garden*—it's a series about the feeling being in a lotus garden. And the most recent ones, actually they're not that recent. I had them at a Punahou Carnival maybe like five years ago. They didn't sell and I had invested in frames for them and everything. I said, "Oh my God. These things were terrible. I don't know what's wrong." So I haven't looked at them until I just mounted them there at the Saks show. And I really made peace with them. They were okay all along.

[Noe Tanigawa's paintings have been featured on more Bamboo Ridge covers than any other artist's work. Her art has been chosen for two regular issues (#19 and #98) and three books (*An Offering of Rice* by Mavis Hara, *The Nanjing Massacre: Poems* by Wing Tek Lum, and *Beyond Green Tea and Grapefruit* by Gail N. Harada).]

Gail: So, your work has been used for several Bamboo Ridge covers, and I think the first one was the one with those dancing figures, that sketch, right? For all the covers except for the cover for Wing Tek's book, the editors selected from paintings you already had. For Wing Tek's cover, was it something that you did especially for his book?

Noe: Yes. It was. It was taking lotus for the symbol that it is and putting it in the context of repressed violence. I used Wing Tek's words to plumb the emotions of soldiers, rape victims, moms, missionaries, murderers, all those perspectives he offers. I made four large-scale encaustic paintings and dozens of charcoal drawings based on those poems. The *Nanjing X* installation included a reference table with chairs, where I presented news clippings, diary entries, official documents, photographs, and other records of the period along with the poems. I hope someone had time to explore and in his or her own mind somehow connect those fragments of experience.

I wish somebody will help me one day figure out my fascination with lotus. I've just focused on it, but why? That's the only flower I do aside from night-blooming cereus occasionally. I don't know. I think I've got to take them deeper at this point. Not sure quite how to take them to the next level but that's what I'm going to be trying to do.

Gail: Did you choose a lotus in part because of kind of the symbolism of the lotus in the first place? About rising from the muck and then—

Noe: As well their ultimate just physical beauty. Their hugeness. Their presence. Their smell.

Gail: And the quality of the light kind of that they capture.

Noe: Yes. Those petals are like cups of light.

Gail: You also have the honey series or bee series.

Noe: I love bees because they contribute so much to my work. I couldn't do my work without them. And I like them anatomically correct—just all kinds of bees flying, mating, landing, approaching a flower. That kind of thing. So much fun.

Gail: Those pieces are a lot of black and honey color.

Noe: That's the natural color of the beeswax. I got a beautiful wax from Kona that I was using for a few years there. But I've got a new wax that is a wonderful golden color from Kahakuloa on Maui. So I can't wait to be making more of those.

Gail: The *Compass series* is brand new; it's black wax and burnished mahogany. Do you want to talk about how those came into being?

Noe: I was looking at these 18th-century Japanese compasses. The needles themselves are really, really simple, and then I just sort of started fitting them in a space and then I thought how I wanted to make them, which was by carving them and then using natural beeswax with black wax. So you know—when you're standing at City Mill trying to figure out the most economical way to accomplish this, it gives you certain dimensions and that kind of dictated the shape of the pieces. They turned out to be a felicitous proportion. I don't know how the next ones I do will ever work out. Maybe I'll just stick with this proportion. [Laughs.] They look so simple but it took freaking hours just to get the luster and the texture of the black just right. There's got to be an easy way to do this. Hopefully I'll figure it out next time around.

Gail: Your choice of the compass?

Noe: Well, you know, I'm definitely seeking direction.

[Silence.]

Gail: Do you want to say anything about seeking direction after Uki's passing?

Noe: I guess it's— Well, I thought I'd be taking care of my mom for at least 10 more years. I thought I'd have time to—I don't know—cook a lot more for her, bathe her, take her around, see the cherry blossoms at Wahiawa, stuff. Just do stuff, more stuff. But since I don't have that time with her . . . what do I have the time for? [Laughs.]

Gail: So, where did you find the images of the compass? Was it kind of serendipity that you came upon them or were you actually looking for this idea of a compass?

Noe: I was looking for the idea of a compass. It sort of orients you in space without telling you where to go.

Gail: Is that what kind of attracted you? So, when you were looking for compasses, how did you come upon the Japanese compass? Were you just looking at different compasses or—?
Noe: Yes, I was. I really was. I don't know what's authentic for me as a Japanese-American, yeah, I don't. There was no Japanese-American compass. [Laughs.] I love Pacific navigational maps and stuff.

Gail: It's so interesting—those *Compass* pieces look Polynesian even though you started with Japanese compasses.
Noe: I don't know. It has to be one of those—just one of those leaps that was made. I don't know. It was like a synthesis that just could be made suddenly could be made.

Gail: You also have an *Oceans* series. What's interesting about those *Oceans* paintings is the colors but also that you're using these patterns—I don't know if you call it an overlay or underlay.
Noe: It relates to the organization of the physical universe, really. Working with aerosol paints and stencils allows the layering you're talking about. It refers to the simultaneity of experience. There's a lot going on at any given moment! The period that's spent making art can be used in so many ways—the time I spent with the compasses, for example, I used that time listening to gong meditations and chanting. But in the period that I was making those big blue *Oceans* things, I was listening to a lot more expansive work like these ethnologic recordings from the Solomon Islands with their idea of rhythm which is so much more expansive than our 4/4 or whatever kind of time. They always take me by surprise.

The time that's spent making art is such a valuable time to comb through ideas. It's not just the product. It's the time spent feeling out ideas and the implications of ideas. That's why working with words is so bracing; it's like working alongside someone else who is prospecting the same vein of gold, or awe, or pain.

In the end, I love that series of *Oceans* paintings because of their relationship to the poem "Oceans."

Gail: By Juan Ramón Jiménez?
Noe: Yes, I always want to have a copy of that poem reproduced along with those works. All those blue *Oceans* paintings spin around that poem "Oceans." I guess words are evocative and focusing for me.

I conclude this interview piece with the poem "Oceans" that Noe referred to, written by Juan Ramón Jiménez and translated by Robert Bly in *Lorca and Jiménez: Selected Poems.*

OCEANS

I have a feeling that my boat
has struck, down there in the depths,
against a great thing.
                      And nothing
happens! Nothing... Silence... Waves...

—Nothing happens? Or has everything happened,
and are we standing now, quietly, in the new life?

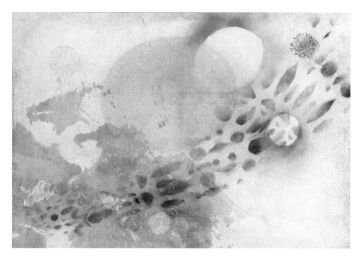

Oceans: Niʻihau, Kahoʻolawe, by Noe Tanigawa, oil, encaustic, aerosol paint, 42 x 54.

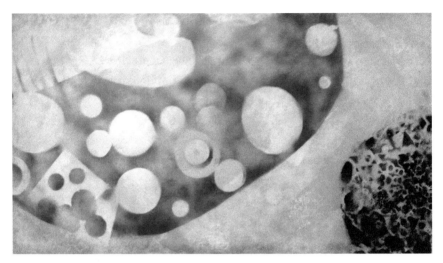

Oceans: Kaua'i, Hawai'i, by Noe Tanigawa, oil, encaustic, mixed media, 38 x 68.

Starfish with Staghorn Coral (detail), by Noe Tanigawa, oil, encaustic, acrylic, on lutrador, 42 x 48.

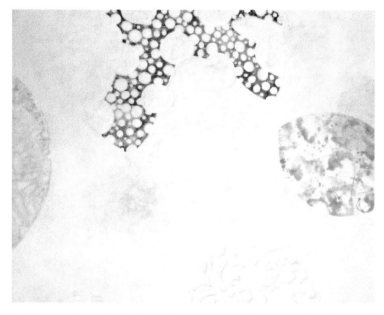

Starfish with Staghorn Coral, by Noe Tanigawa, oil, encaustic, acrylic, on lutrador, 42 x 48.

Limu Moko (detail), by Noe Tanigawa, encaustic, 12 x 12.

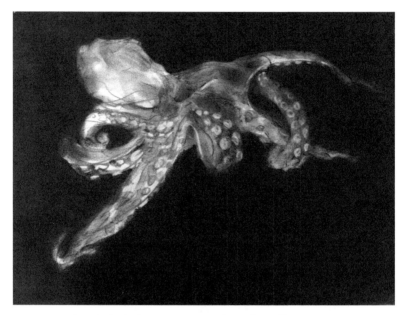

He'e Series #3, by Noe Tanigawa, charcoal on vellum, 14 x 17.

Little Mambo, by Noe Tanigawa, encaustic, 10 x 8.

In a Lotus Garden Series Hindu I, by Noe Tanigawa, oil and encaustic, 36 x 50.

In a Lotus Garden Series Hindu II (detail), by Noe Tanigawa, oil and encaustic, 36 x 50.

Your Crown, by Noe Tanigawa, encaustic, gold leaf, varnish, 9 x 12.

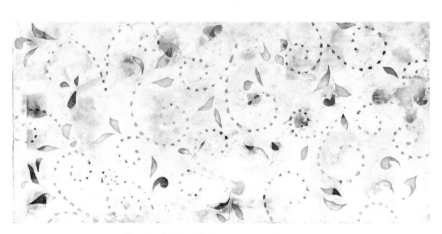

Kwai Fa, by Noe Tanigawa, encaustic, 12 x 23.

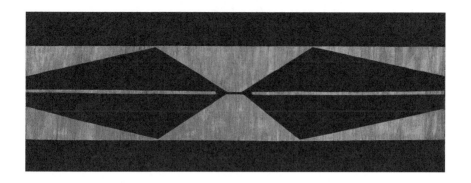

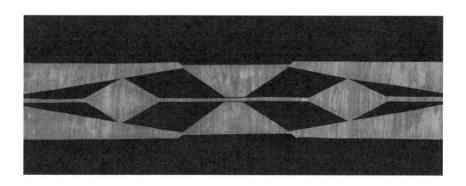

Compass Series II-IV, by Noe Tanigawa, encaustic on mahogany, 18 x 48.

DIVING LESSONS

I arrived at Uncle's house just as the sun came up over Makapuʻu. Uncle was still drinking his Nescafé and canned milk. He was at the kitchen table, which overlooked the back yard that stretched down to the beach. Spence was down at the water's edge, getting the boat ready. I went down to help him check the tanks, make sure all the safety equipment was in place and that everything was working. I followed his wordless orders as we both anticipated a day on the water.

Uncle was not really my uncle. He was my friend's uncle. I met him at a party in Palisades and was drawn to him immediately because of the way he talked about the ocean. When he started talking about picking limu, I got excited. I asked him how he knew where to find the limu he wanted, how to pick the different kinds, and how he used them. I guess he liked this haole girl who wanted to know about all kinds of Hawaiian things and decided to take on the job of teaching me. I started going out to his Waimānalo Beach house almost every weekend to learn about the ocean from him. Usually there was some nephew, grandson, or neighborhood kid hanging out, ready and willing to go out diving or picking, or to throw net.

Spence was a regular. He was my friend's brother-in-law. As we finished our tasks, Uncle finally came down to the water's edge. We pushed the boat into the water, and Uncle got the engine going.

Once we were underway, Uncle turned to me and said, "It's your turn, girl, take us through the reef."

I was stunned. I knew that Uncle's Boston Whaler was not a cheap boat, and the thought of grinding a hole in the hull filled me with dread.

"What's wrong, girl? We've been in and out of this reef half a dozen times. You should know the way by now," Uncle reassured me.

Ashamed, I replied, "Uh, I didn't know you would ever want me to steer the boat, so I'm sorry, but I don't think I paid enough attention." Then I continued, "If you or Spence do it this time, I promise I'll watch carefully."

Uncle made a disgusted sound and shook his head. But then he said, "Go ahead and give it a try anyway. You know more than you think you do." (Note to self—lesson number one in learning from a Hawaiian uncle: watch everything and remember it. Bumbye you'll be expected to do it, and do it well!)

I went to the wheel on shaky legs, feeling queasy. The channel in the reef was pretty far out, so I had an opportunity to get used to the controls. But before I knew it, we were at the mouth of the channel. The tide was going out, so I only had to steer. The current sucked the boat out toward the outer reef and the open sea. Once we were past the reef, Uncle told me to open the throttle and head toward the west end of Rabbit Island.

While we were still some distance off shore, Uncle told me to reduce throttle while he and Spence peered over each side of the bow. After a few minutes, he told me to "cut it," referring to the engine. As I did so, Spence dropped the anchor. Quickly, he put on his fins, grabbed a facemask, and dove down to set the anchor in a way that wouldn't damage the reef. Uncle turned to me, "We're going to scout the reef a little. You wait here, but get your things ready to dive. When we come up, you'll go back down with us." Spence surfaced. Reaching over the side of the boat, Uncle handed him a tank on a homemade "Hawaiian harness," a weight belt, and a net bag.

According to Uncle, the Hawaiian harness was a genius contraption. It was a metal frame that strapped around a diver's waist and held the air tanks. Usually it had two metal hook-shaped shoulder pieces that rested just above the diver's shoulders. However, Uncle had modified the design of his harness by welding on only one shoulder piece. He often said his harness design was one of the things that enabled him get out alive when he was with Special Forces. He had been a reconnaissance diver in the Mekong Delta during the Vietnam War. The reason Uncle's harness was so great was that he could simply release the belt and roll out of the apparatus. This was useful if the harness got stuck on river grasses or submerged branches, or if an insurgent grabbed the tanks.

Uncle thought that most scuba divers were ridiculous to use buoyancy-compensating vests. They were for people who were just too stupid or lazy to figure out how many weights they needed to carry on their weight belt. Besides, vests were dangerous. The diver couldn't slip out of the vest if he got caught on something, or if someone grabbed it. I always wondered why the harness was such a good proposition in the crystalline waters off Waimānalo, where there were no insurgents—as far as I knew. However, I never quite mustered the courage to ask. I just watched and did whatever Uncle did.

Uncle put on his own gear and tipped backward off the boat to join Spence. As they submerged and dove down, I got my mask, snorkel, fins, tank, and belt ready at the side of the boat. I sat down to wait, savoring the beauty of the ocean, cliffs, and sky. The sun began to get hot. Wavelets gently slapped the side of the boat and it rocked gently, tugging at the anchor line. I was a little thirsty, so I grabbed a can of passion-orange juice out of the cooler and chugged it down. I sat. I waited. I started to sweat. Then mild nausea set in as the juice settled in my stomach. Putting on the mask, snorkel, and fins, I dove into the water. I always got seasick on a boat that was anchored, but for some reason, being in those same waves that made the boat rock didn't make me sick.

It was far more interesting to watch the ocean while in it, so time passed more quickly. The reef below was well vegetated with many different kinds of limu and algae. The contours of its surface were being grazed by many different kinds of colorful reef fish. Three hīnālea, sporting tetra-like colors, swam below me, searching amongst the brick-red pencil sea urchins for a meal. In a small sandy spot, a Kona crab must have spotted me. Like an ʻuku burying itself into a dog's coat, the crab plunged down into the sand to hide.

Before long, the two men returned to the surface. Spence hoisted himself on board to get spearing equipment. While he was at it, he handed me my tank in its harness and my weight belt. He handed the spears, a T-bar, and mesh bags to Uncle and fell back into the ocean again. Each of us took a spear and mesh bag from Uncle. We dove down and Uncle placed the T-bar near the anchor. Off we went, skimming over the floor of the ocean, exploring for fish in the overhangs, grottos, and groves of coral. Uncle speared several menpachi and took them back to lace onto the T-bar, which he brought part way back with him. He tried to help me spear some more menpachi, then some taʻape, but I wasn't quick enough.

The spear was another item Uncle had made himself and said was the best. He called it a Hawaiian sling. It consisted of a metal rod with three thick wires at the end that were sharpened to wicked points. There was a loop of rubber tubing attached at the other end. If he hooked his thumb through the loop while grasping the shaft, then pulled back the end of the spear, he could aim, release, and shoot. It was a basic and understandable principle, and I was able to accomplish the aim-shoot-release maneuvers. However, I just didn't have the speed and stealth necessary to be an effective hunter. Uncle got impatient with my misses, so he went off to do some real hunting.

It didn't bother me to be left alone. I preferred being a fish tourist rather than a fish killer. However, I would never tell Uncle that. I lounged around and took in my surroundings. I was in a large depression in the coral. It was a sort of valley. There weren't as many fish as I had seen earlier, but those that I saw were bigger—and probably faster. I was just as happy to hang out, as to continue chasing fish away with my inept spearfishing attempts.

During this time, I was fairly stationary. Out of the corner of my eye, I saw a piece of a rock move. I jerked my head around to look directly at the rock, but it was motionless. This time, I stayed completely still, but focused on the area where I had seen movement. Just like viewing an optical illusion, my focus shifted. I distinctly saw a rockfish where before I had seen only rock.

Slowly and smoothly, as if drifting in the current, I hooked my thumb through the rubber loop on my spear and pulled back the end of the shaft. I floated around into a good position, and released the three-pronged missile. My aim was dead-on. The fish was impaled. I pulled the spear from the reef, took the fish off, and stuffed it into the mesh bag trailing from my weight belt. I positioned myself near another area of reef, cocked my spear, and waited. Soon another rockfish came into focus. I let the spear burst through my grip. Another fish in the bag. I did it one more time then swam off to find the T-bar. Before we went out the first time, Uncle had told me divers should never have more than three speared fish in the bag unless they wanted to be shark bait.

As Uncle swam around a bulge in the reef, he saw that I had speared some fish. He brought over two more: a large kole and a weke 'ula. He threaded his fish onto the T-bar, then signaled me to give him my bag. Looking into it, he shook his head, then pulled the rockfish out, threaded them onto the T-bar, and signaled me to surface. We drifted up slowly, even though we hadn't been very deep. When we broke the surface near the stern of the boat, Uncle handed the T-bar and his spear to me, took off his fins, and climbed on board. He unhooked his tank and weight belt and pulled off his mask. He shook the water off and shoved his fingers through his hair. He then held out his hand for the fish and spears, which I handed up to him. I took off my mask and fins, tossing them into the boat. Then I unclipped my weight belt and harness, which Uncle took from me. Finally, he reached his hand down and hoisted me onto the boat—I had yet to master the art of getting onboard without landing in a pile of limbs on the bottom of the boat. We both set to work arranging the equipment neatly on the deck. Finally, Uncle grabbed two cans of juice from the cooler and handed one to me.

"Whew, girl! You are some kind of rockfish hunter!"

I was mighty pleased with myself, even though I knew that rockfish were easy prey. I was even happier that Uncle was at least amused. I laughed, "Yeah, that's the only thing that stays still long enough for me to spear!"

He laughed with me. Then he picked up the spear I had used and inspected the tines. "You keep this up, and bumbye, I'll have to teach you how to sharpen my spears." He put it back down and sat back.

I was glad Uncle didn't scold me. At that point, I would have sharpened every single one of them to please him, even if it took all weekend. We relaxed in silence for a while before Spence came up. He handed his bag to Uncle, who opened it and pulled out a large, gorgeous, turquoise and teal uhu with coral edged scales. The uhu joined the kole, menpachi, and my rockfish family in the ice chest. Spence handed me his tank and weight belt. He dove down to release the anchor. Uncle brought the engine to life, reversing to create some slack in the anchor line. When Spence came back up, he climbed skillfully onboard. I handed him a juice, and Uncle took off toward Black Island.

We anchored again, about 100 yards off shore. Uncle and Spence carefully checked the air in the tanks. They decided the ones we had been using had plenty of air. Then Uncle turned to me saying, "Now I'm going to teach you how to spear lobster."

I blurted out, "But Uncle, it isn't lobster season."

He made a sound of disgust. Spence averted his head, busied himself with his equipment, and tumbled into the water. "Who makes the lobster season, girl?" he asked rhetorically. "Some guy in an office in Honolulu, wearing a reverse-print aloha shirt that he can't even take the time to tuck in. That's who makes lobster season. Besides, I'm Hawaiian, I have gathering rights."

A part of me wanted to remind him that ancient Hawaiians maintained the sustainability of their fishing stocks by putting a kapu on certain fish in specific seasons. But I knew that it really wasn't my place to tell a Hawaiian kupuna about Hawaiian things. Chastened, I just said, "Oh."

Uncle's mood lightened and he flashed a huge smile. "So, girl, have you ever met Mr. Puhi?"

"Uh, do you mean an eel or do you mean a guy named Mr. Puhi?" I asked.

"Same thing, girl. Either way, you gotta respect him!" He laughed and slapped his thigh. "Anyway, the important thing to remember is that wherever you find lobster, you find Mr. Puhi. He guards every lobster hole there is. So when you spear the lobster and then reach in to grab it, you have to make sure Mr. Puhi doesn't bite your arm."

After a statement like that, I felt somewhat daunted by the task. After pondering a brief moment, I replied, "Well okay, that makes sense. But why can't I just pull the lobster out of the hole on my spear?"

"Because you need to grab the lobster and pull it out with your hand so you don't lose it off the end of your spear," Uncle explained to me, as if I were a dolt.

"I see," I replied cautiously, not at all sure this was the adventure I wanted to have.

"Don't worry, girl. Just watch what I do and you'll get 'em." He started handing me my gear. We went overboard, and I followed him down. The area where we were diving was pocked and pitted with crevices, tunnels, and small caverns. Uncle would peer into a hole, shake his head, and move on. At about the fifth such cavern, he backed up quickly. He signaled me to look and he stuck his arm out. Then he pulled it back quickly. Something long and brown darted out, but pulled back part way. As promised, there was Mr. Puhi—a large eel—peering at us.

Uncle slowly moved on. I followed, giving the eel a wide berth. After passing, I looked back and saw it retreating into the lobster hole. We swam around to the other side of the rocky area. Uncle looked in another hole, made a thumbs-up, and waved me over. I peered in. I could see that it was the back side of the same hole. The lobster was still facing the other entrance. Uncle aimed his spear and released it. He hit the lobster and quickly reached into the hole, grabbing the spiny crustacean. Pulling it out, he quickly backed away. The eel got to the edge of the hole just a millisecond too late. Uncle put the lobster in his mesh bag and signaled me to follow again.

Spotting another hole, he beckoned me to look. I did so rather hesitantly. This cavern had a second opening at the top. With the angle of the sun I could clearly see there were at least three lobsters inside. Uncle indicated that I should spear them this time. I hadn't seen any eels around the hole, so thought maybe it would be all right. I hooked my thumb in the rubber loop, pulled back the shaft, and let go. The spear flashed into the sunlit cave and came to an abrupt halt. I had hit something so hard the end of the shaft continued to vibrate. There was a lot of commotion inside the cave, which disturbed the sediment at the bottom. I couldn't tell what was moving. Uncle was motioning me to reach in and grab. I complied, but hesitantly.

Suddenly, I saw Mr. Puhi. I reflexively started to pull my spear out. Uncle grabbed it, and in what seemed like one fluid motion, pushed the spear back in, reached out with his other hand, and grabbed whatever was on the end of the spear. As I got out of the way, he hauled everything out. The eel bolted out after him, but Uncle spun the spear around and jabbed the blunt end toward the brown streak. Mr. Puhi grabbed at the shaft with his needle-toothed maw, twisting and constricting his long body around it. Uncle wrenched the two lobsters off the spear tines and kicked away, letting the spear drop.

Once the eel realized that all he had was a spear, he let go and glided back to the cave. Uncle motioned me to go pick it up. By the time I got it, the lobsters were already in Uncle's mesh bag. He signaled me to check my tank pressure. I realized that I had been gulping air. Sure enough, the needle was approaching the red zone. Uncle pointed up, signaling me to rise to the surface. He followed.

We broke the surface, and he spat out his mouthpiece and exclaimed, "Damn, girl! Two lobsters, and a puhi in hot pursuit!"

I was beginning to feel the effects of the adrenaline leaving my system. Thankfully, Uncle couldn't see me shaking. I knew that I should have grabbed the lobsters after I speared them, but I still felt good that I had actually gotten two of them. I was also amazed and relieved that I didn't have an eel attached to my arm. I couldn't tell if Uncle was impressed or upset. He started tossing his things into the boat, and I followed suit. He got on board first to take my tank and weight belt before hoisting me up. I immediately started stowing everything properly while he pulled the lobsters out of the bag. The one he speared was huge. Of the ones I speared, one was good sized, but the other was about half the size of his.

Uncle glanced across to me and said, "Well, girl, that is pretty impressive for the first time. But next time, I'll let you wrestle with Mr. Puhi, if you don't mind. That was a little too close for comfort."

"I know, sorry about that," I said sheepishly.

Uncle continued, "Well, don't ever try to pull the spear out like that again. If Mr. Puhi is going to get you, he's going to get you. No sense in wasting good lobster!"

Humbled, I just nodded. I felt bad that I had endangered Uncle. But I was glad he was skilled enough to save the situation.

We waited for Spence to return. The late morning sun was drying my skin, leaving each hair on my forearms rimed with tiny salt crystals. No doubt, I would soon be itchy. Finally Spence came up, holding the anchor and his catch. As soon as his things were stowed, we were off. We circled part way around Black Island, and Uncle cut the motor. Spence dropped the anchor, but didn't dive down after it. When I looked at him quizzically, he said, "The bottom's mostly sandy, so the dragging anchor won't cause too much harm."

Uncle pulled a cracker tin and three cans of sardines out of one of the compartments under the seats. He handed each of us a can, and put the cracker tin on the middle bench, between all of us. I never realized sardines could taste so good. After lunch, we rested. Spence dozed, and Uncle whittled a stick with his wicked-looking Special Forces dagger. I spent the time gazing across the glassy calm water to the dramatic cliffs that provided a spectacular backdrop to the narrow strip of land at their base. After a while, Uncle put away his whittling. Spence roused with a huge yawn and scratched his belly. He rolled off the side of the boat into the water to wake up. He swam a few strokes and climbed back on board.

"We're going to go down to a deep trench out past Rabbit Island," Uncle told me. "Spence wants to hunt ulua. You can stay in the boat, or nearby, but if you would rather, you can dive with tanks right around here. It's safe, just don't go too far and don't spear anything."

"I'll dive," I replied, relishing the idea of just me in the sea. At last, I could relax and enjoy the beauty around me without worrying about damaging equipment or facing vicious creatures.

"Okay then, girl. Suit up."

Uncle and Spence made sure all our tanks had plenty of air. Over the side we went.

I watched the two of them swim off into the deep blue, toward Rabbit Island. Leaving the side of the boat, I dove down toward the floor of the sea. I swam along the bottom for a while, breathing easily from my regulator. At first the bottom was pocked with coral crags and grottos—ideal lobster holes. Gliding by, I imagined Mr. Puhi at each opening. I also saw the ugly, but delightfully easy-to-spear rockfish if I focused carefully.

Rounding the base of Black Island, I was amazed and stunned to see a gleaming white seafloor stretch out before me. The sandy bottom was dotted with a variety of pastel corals where small schools of fish calmly grazed. Involuntarily, I drew in a large breath in awe before I realized I shouldn't suck air out of my tanks that way. The vista sloped gently down to depths that were first turquoise, then a deeper blue.

The white sand sparkled and glistened below. The swells shone above like aquamarine jewels as the waves rolled toward the shallows followed by a broad trail of bubbles. Bulbous domes of brain coral glowed platinum white as if lit from within. Branched corals in lavender, yellow, and pink stood in irregular clumps, suggesting a carelessly planted garden. Yellow tangs the color of buttercups and stripped manini grazed in this garden. Several white weke, or goatfish, were stirring up the bottom with their whiskers. A school of translucent fingerlings swam past me as I floated, equalized, about ten feet below the surface. A small octopus undulated across the gently sloped seafloor below me. Bubbles escaped past my regulator as the corners of my mouth curved up in a smile.

On a whim, I stroked down to the sand and turned over onto my back. My tank rested on the seafloor and I spent the next slice of time gazing at the waves above me. They washed in from Makapu'u Point, past me, and up onto the shores of Black Island. The tune to Ringo Starr's "Octopus's Garden" started playing in my head, followed by the words. As I lay there, the fish became curious. A few even swam over to tentatively nibble at me, trying to figure out what I was. Their inquisitiveness tickled. I felt a bliss that exceeded anything I had felt before so I hugged the scene to my heart and just held it there as I continued to enjoy the moment.

Eventually the sunlight dimmed slightly. I looked at my pressure gauge and my tank was half gone. I rolled over and glided out of my octopus's garden back to the boat. Uncle and Spence were still gone. I tossed my fins and facemask into the boat. I unhooked my weight belt, and pushed it up and over the side. Unclasping my harness, I struggled to hook it on the side of the boat. Next came the fun part. Holding onto the edge of the boat, I raised my left leg up. After several awkward tries, I managed to curl my ankle over it. Somehow, I levered my leg so my knee was hooked. I pushed against the side of the boat with my right hand as I tried to pull myself up. My right leg was flailing and splashing. I eventually managed to roll over the edge and get my whole body into the boat, landing in an ungainly pile. Quickly I sat up and looked around to see if anyone had seen me. Relieved that there were only curious seabirds on shore, I pulled my tank onboard and stowed everything neatly.

The afternoon had grown overcast, so my wait was not as hot as it could have been. Finally, Uncle appeared at the side of the boat. I helped him get his things onboard. He hoisted himself up and into the boat in a continuous, graceful motion. I thought about my own arduous efforts and my cheeks grew warm as I compared his accomplishment to mine.

Spence swam up. As he came to the boat, Uncle pulled out a gaff. Spence held a silvery ulua by the gills. It was the size of his own torso. Uncle gaffed the fish and hauled it aboard. I helped Spence with his tanks and other gear. He hoisted himself on board and rested for a second. After catching his breath, he looked up at Uncle. They exchanged broad smiles and Uncle slapped him on the back. We stowed everything. Uncle reversed the boat a little and Spence pulled up the anchor. He circled the boat around and headed home.

As we approached the reef, Uncle motioned for me to take the wheel. Now knowing better than to object, I took the wheel, feigning calmness. Easing the throttle, I nosed into the channel. About halfway through, Uncle shouted, "Port hard!"

I had no idea what he meant and asked, "What?"

He grabbed the wheel as Spence sucked in his breath then released it. Uncle gave the wheel back to me and said, "Straight in, girl, straight in."

My heart was pounding, but I was triumphant. I knew I had just passed a test. I had used all the knowledge I learned. And after Uncle had fixed my error, I was brave enough to take the wheel again. Both of us knew that I would be able to take the boat in and out of that section of reef from now on.

In the shallows, Uncle told me to shut the engine off. As he tilted it up, Spence jumped into the chest-high water. He held the bow rope as he waded through the shallows. Once on shore, he tied the rope off on a coconut palm. He went up on the grass and released the winch lock on the rope for the boat trailer. He pulled the trailer down into the water as Uncle and I jumped overboard. We positioned the boat onto the trailer and secured it. Spence went back up and started winding the winch. Slowly the trailer slogged across the sand then rolled smoothly up onto the lawn. We busied ourselves with rinsing, cleaning, and stowing all the equipment.

Uncle cleaned the fish, tossing a red menpachi to Popoki, the patiently waiting cat. He turned to me and said, "Next time girl, I'm going to teach you how to dive with sharks."

I smiled and nodded. But inside, I was thinking about Mr. Puhi. I heard myself chirp, "That sounds great, Uncle." Meanwhile, the rest of my being shouted, *Oh hell no!*

Thus ended my diving career.

NALANI MAMOALI'IALAPA'IHA'O ANO

KA'IWA RIDGE

Trailhead sign reads
Pillbox Trail
Trail?
It's a Climb
Thirteen minutes
To the top

Bunkers
Pillboxes
No matter
I run past
Running along
The Sky
High up on
The Ridge

The View
Waimānalo on my Left
Kailua on the Right
Enchanted Lakes
Straight Ahead

Running through
Pockets of Breezes
On craggy rocks
Branches grab
At my hair
Clothes
Legs
Scraping my face

Dry heat of the
Burning sun
On my shoulders
Thankfully
A Pocket
The breeze
Cools my
Stinging skin

The momentum
Takes me faster
I'm flying
Now
Among the brush
Under the canopy
I am an 'Iwa
My arms lift up
And let the
Wind carry me
Nimbly over the
Rocky, dusty path
Gliding

Gnats swarm
I run through
With my
Mouth and nose
Shut tight

I make my way
Up
Down
The gulches
Of the Ridge
I know this

Ground
I can run it
In my dreams
For
The mountain
And I have
Become One

Now when I am

Apart
I will miss it
It has become
My Friend
When I need
One
It will always
Be there
When I need it

No one
Can move
A mountain

This poem is about my XTERRA Training across Ka'iwa Ridge where I ran from Kailua to Enchanted Lakes, and then back over the mountain again.

RAINBOW EUCALYPTUS
or *The Woman Giving Birth Standing Up*

The following sculptures rest at the bottom of Corkscrew Swamp in Naples, Florida.

Eagle

The eagle wasn't always headless. Sixteen inches from wing to wing, it sank with the tail holding the bulk, plunging its feathers deep in the muck. Kaili's first visit to the Sullivan County Wildlife Preservation was when she lost her first tooth, fleeing the talons of an uncaged eagle, tripping on her mother's shoelace before tasting asphalt.

After the boa constrictor escaped into their kitchen cabinets, her first husband would not allow Kaili to buy another exotic animal. Instead, he suggests she return to sculpting.

Four years pass before Kaili's suicide attempt.

The following fall, she begins a high dosage of experimental antidepressants, designed to relieve night terrors within 24 hours, the ultimate goal being complete eradication of sleep paralysis. Afterward, waking in the morning is like walking out of an empty room in her head. She doesn't believe the medication works.

Her first husband discerns little from her descriptions of the world: *Look for the photons with yellow eyes dancing between us on sunrays.* A cold, black, twenty-cubic-inch block of clay is placed in the study for Kaili to mold or massacre. In the empty room in her head, where those dreams of passing between universes disappear each night, she sees only the shapes of animals as shadow puppets on her eyelids. An eagle perches there in prayer, or famine.

So begins the scaling back of clay corners into feathered wings. The aquiline shaping of the beak takes her only hours to perfect. The swamp breath of Florida morning oscillates in and out of the room. Her husband had cracked both windows in the study to save on the electric bill.

He says, "Look here, I could kill this woman now, or give her a long and happy life filled with the tonics of love. Why does she deserve either? Moreover, if I write here that a gazelle were set loose in the public library, would it be my burden to decide the fate of the librarian? Do you see, K, how stories are a big responsibility? Of course you don't. You are a stupid, sad woman."

Footstool

"Why a footstool?" asks her grandmother. Kaili rotates the statuette so that its tilt is visible.

"Cattywampus," Kaili says. "I thought I messed it up the first time around. Then I just kept making it smaller and smaller. Now it's three inches tall and the angle is still off."

At this moment, her grandmother dies.

The air outside the hospital tastes of pine needles. Kaili grips the miniature footstool tight against the shock of cold wind. This is the last week of her fifteen-year life spent in Missouri, as custody passes from grandmother to aunt, a hapa haole tour guide working on O'ahu.

It was the statuette of the footstool where Kaili found her love for oblique angles and exotic animals (although on the plane ride over she told the soldier with a window seat that the world feels more rigid from heaven, and that to truly make sense of physics it's better to get as far away from things as possible). This footstool was imperfect and therefore (for Kaili) animalistic.

Twenty-seven years later, in a violent outburst, her third husband steps on the footstool, breaking two of its three leg pieces off. While Kaili glues the pieces back together to obscure the legs, he applies pressure to the hole in his heel. The next morning he puts his gym shoes on to water the lawn and his foot becomes infected. At the same time, in the living room, she unfolds newspaper across the coffee table, positioning the sculpture for maximum obscurity. The remaining leg piece is now stained red from his blood.

"Why a footstool?" he asks from the hospital bed.

"Have you ever thought about how small you can make the world? How far away you can get and if that would make things any clearer? My first husband was a writer. Not a great one. He didn't drink. What kind of writer doesn't drink? And still beats the shit out of me? He asked about my sculptures once and I told him I think they're cursed but they're mine and I shouldn't have to give them up."

"This is the guy who wrote the story about a kid with twelve assholes?"

"Yeah. Riveting stuff, I know," she says.

Kaili does not believe her husband has been faithful because she has not been faithful to him.

"If I die, will you remarry?" her third husband asks without tears.

"You're not going to die. It's just a minor infection," she says.

"Every time I'm in a hospital I feel that I will die."

In the waiting room, Kaili discusses her affairs with the janitor mopping up a child's vomit. She tells the man about the hole in her third husband's foot and about her first husband's dive off of the balcony and how bits of his skull were coming out of his ears and about the smell of her grandmother's hospital room and the taste of ocean air over the Pacific and before she is finished the janitor hands her a picture of his daughter as a young woman at a school dance.

"She passed last year," he says.

When he lifts the mop, Kaili wonders if that pile of vomit could have been his own, or that it wasn't vomit at all but the sludge trail of someone passing through the floor to another space, somewhere behind this room where translucent bodies build an armature or scaffolding to repair those broken things about her past that she can no longer reach.

"I'm sorry," she whimpers, not because she cannot think of anything better to say, but because the photograph reminds her that she is barren.

At this, the janitor begins his quest for proof of men passing between dimensions, or for strangers to befriend over a pool of child's vomit.

Rainbow Eucalyptus or *The Woman Giving Birth Standing Up*

In the garden, a business of mongooses chases after the same green anole lizard. The mountains steep over from Kamehame Ridge down into the Kamilo Iki Valley. These rises and falls feel to Kaili like the most honest retelling of history, as if the folds in each pass, even down to the particles of red dirt, had been carefully detailed by nonhuman hands. There is no way for her to describe a more peaceful salting of the air than to breathe in the island.

The aunt's garden is unkempt, although the wild mongooses seem to enjoy the chaos and debris. Here, the fallen rainbow eucalyptus from a nearby park was dragged and propped up against a wooden terrace. It was her aunt's idea in the first place and the whole island was talking about the lightning strike. For months, locals visited the garden often asking Kaili to photograph them next to the felled eucalyptus. Her aunt would explain eventually that this is the closest most of them would come to holding lightning in their hand (each lied about finding God there).

On her seventeenth birthday, Kaili slowly ascends four thousand stairs made of plywood and scrap metal. The hike is known as the Stairway to Heaven or Haʻikū Trail, depending on whose God is calling the shots. Kaili is not especially worried about falling, although her friends tell her she is taking too many breaks. When they reach the top, it is still twilight and a teenage boy drips the acid onto sugar cubes. By dawn, the yellows and oranges and blues and pinks of the island spin around each other and reveal to them all the nature of this universe. Each division of color seamlessly hues Kaili into a silhouette of the pieces of life she will never understand: departure, stardust, cocooning, shark-fin soup, etc.

Eastward, she sees shadows of buildings waning with the rising sun. And these shadows begin to stretch backward toward her, like her mother's fingers before a feeding. There, a line of hotels on Waikīkī Beach, well-oiled tourist machinations taking on the shape of spreading thighs. Kaili cannot help but think of the tree in her aunt's garden. She wondered about the poetry, and when her mother was tying off her arm on the thirty-eighth day of rain, did the island give her some strange new language? Had it strapped her down to the mattress in her sleep and stalked around her bedroom in the dark?

When Kaili arrives home that evening, she asks her aunt if it is all right to make the rainbow eucalyptus into an art piece. It has been months since the lightning strike and the locals have lost interest.

The following morning, her aunt asks, "How long do you think before it rots away?"

"Years, I hope. But I'm going to sculpt it regardless." She molds this out of clay and chicken wire.

The mongooses will make the rainbow eucalyptus tree into their new den. The sculpture, *The Woman Giving Birth Standing Up*—oil paint on ceramic—is placed on display in the University of Hawaiʻi Art Gallery for nine months while Kaili works on her graduate degree.

While she unwraps it out of newspaper and slides the dolly from under its base, a young man asks if this work is hers. In a year, they will both finish their Masters in Fine Arts (hers for sculpting, his for creative writing) and get married on Makapuʻu Beach. Before her first husband accepts a teaching position in South Florida, Kaili asks that her aunt spend time each morning with the mongooses, and to call immediately in case of another lightning strike.

No such call has been made.

Period

Of the seven sculptures thrown into Corkscrew Swamp, the ball she calls *Period* is the easiest to move and the hardest to sink. As Kaili rolls it off the truck bed, she swats at the swarm of mosquitoes near her face. Hollowed and buoyant, she ties a rope horizontally and then vertically around the circumference of the orb, which is connected to a duffle bag full of bricks. At sixty-two years old, she pauses frequently to catch her breath and weep about these pieces of her lost at the bottom of the world.

Her third husband died the previous week from esophageal cancer and now she is sure she would have to remarry, or worse.

When Kaili is twelve years old, the doctors diagnose her with menorrhagia (heavy menstrual bleeding) and tell her grandmother it would likely continue without hormone therapy. Her grandmother sees the therapy as a serious risk to Kaili's wellbeing and chooses not to disclose the information to her. Thus, Kaili spends the entirety of her teenage life ashamed of her frequent excuses to use the restroom, and avoids showering in the girls' locker room, dating boys, dressing seductively, or allowing herself to feel wanted. Instead, she makes friends with a gay couple at a skate park in Hawaiʻi Kai and acquires a healthy marijuana habit to complement her sculpting.

As she hoists the bag of bricks into the water, it becomes grossly apparent to her that she hasn't had a period in twenty years. *Period* was designed after she opted into hormone therapy and her cycles stopped for good. Although she never read the list of possible side effects, Kaili associates this treatment with her violent shifts in mood, her erratic urges to pray, and her dreams spent in a liquid forest.

She thinks about most of this that night as she is held down by monsters and eaten alive, forced catatonic by her sleep paralysis and the accompanying hallucinations. Kaili is not asleep, but she is certainly not awake. To her credit, she no longer fears these monsters (usually they look like porcupines with tentacles, or a blanket covered in oil then wrapped around a young boy).

Over time, there are no things more familiar to her than an empty room.

Coral

Her second husband works underwater. While Kaili loves the ocean, her worst fear is being attacked by a shark and surviving (if she died she does not think she would care that much). For three months, the entirety of their marriage, the couple only speak at night before bed. On the evening before his drowning, he gives Kaili a piece of coral and tells her about the rise of ocean temperatures across the globe and describes the process of coral bleaching, in which algae is expelled because the water is too warm. Because this is the only remnant of their life together, Kaili buys a block of white marble out of which she crafts the sculpture of this memorabilia.

The piece is sold at auction for a large amount of money, but is returned to Kaili by an anonymous collector years later. Kaili never found this suspicious. And so it stands in the study until her third husband walks in on her with a man half his age. In the chaos and embarrassment, her third husband reaches for the closest projectile, which happens to be the coral reef sculpture (not an easy feat as the piece weighs in at over fifty pounds). Items are knocked to the floor in the cuckolding (trinkets, statuettes, jewelry, pill bottles, etc.). Fashioned with incredible durability, the coral reef statue does not break.

As her third husband chases her lover out of the house, Kaili begins cleaning up the blood. She imagines the tracings of each man, apparitions running about in the study. She thinks that if her second husband hadn't drowned she would never have ended up in Florida again (in thought it was clear that this was selfish of her). A tidal pull from the Atlantic (or the Gulf maybe) seemed to keep her from moving back into her aunt's house on Kamehame Ridge. Each life short lived on the island was answered with some seeming damnation back to the muck of South Florida.

Gazelle vs. Librarian

The morning started with thunder in a clear sky. The novel he describes to her involves characters with little depth, although her criticism has always fallen upon deaf ears. Most of their conversations start and end with his contemplations on the mundane and (in Kaili's opinion) frivolous intricacies of their life, how small the potatoes need to be diced for the perfect hash browns, or the synchronization of the oven clock with the grandfather clock in the hallway. What was once endearing had slowly become to her the worst part of him.

And so after a long, one-sided conversation in which her first husband attempts to explain the significance and evolution of the antler in the animal kingdom, Kaili decides to have a go at suicide. And to explain to him where he had gone wrong, and because of the way he says sculpting as if she were a child throwing a tantrum, a plan is hatched to complete her final sculpture.

The sculpting lasts nearly a year, during which she solidifies her decision to kill herself. Careful attention is paid to the antlers, particularly how they enter and exit the librarian's stomach.

A letter in an envelope sits on the plinth of *Gazelle vs. Librarian*. Her first husband reads the letter and studies the statue, contemplating the end. Kaili waits for the bottle of Prozac to guide her into the lulls of death, but she awakens in a hospital bed with a tube down her throat, unaware of any happenings in the interim. The knowledge that this sculpture would not actually be her last fills her with spite.

"Where is my husband?" Kaili asks the nurse.

"No visitors since you came in," she says.

After being held three days in the facility, Kaili returns to an empty house. She does not see her first husband again until the following summer when he throws himself from the third floor balcony having never finished a novel.

"You're back," Kaili tells him as he lifts his foot to the ledge.

"Not for long," he says.

"What did you think of the statue?"

"Perfect," he says, leaning forward into gravity.

Room

"Did you do anything today?" he asks.

"No," Kaili says. "There was no rain."

"Oh you can only work when it's raining?"

"It helps a lot. Walking in the rain puts me in the right headspace."

"I'm sorry," he says.

"Why?"

"I don't know, I thought that's what I was supposed to say."

"Well what about your day?" she asks, rolling onto her back and pulling the covers to her chin.

"Sea turtles, a moray. Had a guy flip his shit underwater and had to do an emergency ascent. But got a sweet tip out of it so that was nice."

"Do you ever worry about drowning?" She touches his earlobe with the tip of her finger.

"Nah."

"I need to talk to you about something," she says.

"Okay."

"I don't love you and I never will."

"That's fine," he says.

"I've never loved a man. Or anyone for that matter," Kaili says this with a distance in her voice.

"What about your aunt? Or your grandma, you talk about her sometimes."

"I'm cursed," she says.

He chuckles and falls asleep.

After her second husband drowns, this conversation she commits to memory. She makes a list of quandaries about that night:

- Were the monsters inside my walls listening?
- If the air turned green, how fast was I moving? Or, if blue, how quickly should I have disappeared for him to survive?
- Did he know the distance from the bed to the walls, or if they had shifted during their conversation?
- Have my sculptures been designed by the same architects, and how many of them are covered in the same sludge?
- What does it mean to die? To drown?
- How many mongooses are left in the garden? How many are in this room?

The sculpture, at its widest point, stretches five feet. Each epoxy-coated ribbon juts in a black and random direction around a splintered staff, a chaotic re-imagining of the sleep-creature she could never name. When viewed from above, these ribbon fingers twist to form a perfect corkscrew. After lowering it into the swamp, the tip of the staff is still visible above the surface.

"What do you do?" asks the barfly as Kaili contemplates escape, the island and the mountains, lightning, the sound of a creeping night-lurk, folds in a sunrise, blue and green, unread and unwritten novels, skull bones, mothers blessing and damning their daughters with bloodlines unexplored, ghosts and shadows repairing the background, infidelity (or virility), marriage, despondency, creatures with amorphous skeletons at the bottom of the Pacific Ocean, mopping up the insides of your children from a hospital floor, heat shimmers on asphalt and the search for new points of view, the tearing apart of uterine walls, empty rooms and the porcupine mutants hiding under the bed, her grandmother's yellowing fingernails, sulfur in the swamp, lying and loving, senility, birds of prey in a fog, husbands without names, the smallest parts of the universe (quarks, neutrinos, protons, electrons, spirits, explosions, etc.), how her smile feels to a stranger in an unfamiliar place, cornerless walls, diced potatoes, alligators or boas, what life would be like without eyes or hands, lava rock scarring the soles of her feet, pill after pill after pill, lucid nightmares and conversations with translucent men, plywood stairway toward faithless conversations with God, passage. It's all a whisper.

"I'm a sculptor," she says.

"Any good at it?" He finishes his drink and moves one stool closer.

"Not really," she says.

"Don't say that, I'm sure you do great work." She tastes the gin in his breath.

"Do you want to see?"

FITZIE

My stomach didn't feel so good that day, Labor Day 1952. I was not quite twelve.

In those times so long ago girls still wore dresses to school and boys in second grade pulled up their skirts from behind and shouted, "Puka pants! Puka pants!"

During recess we jumped double-eye rope, and the boys played marbles. After school at home we played outside all the time, because there was nothing to do indoors. We went to bed before 9 p.m., because there was nothing to do indoors or outdoors. On Saturday mornings we each got a quarter, if we'd been good during the week, to cover admission to the Mickey Mouse Club at the theater, with a dime left over to buy popcorn so we had something to keep our hands occupied while watching Mickey himself, a chapter in the serial, and a Tom Mix western.

That summer when I was still eleven my parents deviated from the usual routine and dumped me at Girl Scout camp at Paumalū for a week. I spent the first two days being homesick and the next several hobbling around after slicing the inside of one ankle with a hatchet while sitting on a step husking a coconut I held between my feet.

Then, on Labor Day, a new wave of homesickness came over me. My parents had dumped me again, for a lot longer. They tried to soothe me by saying I was growing up and it was time. Everyone else in the family for two generations had gone to this school. I could come home at Thanksgiving. And maybe I'd see Brother at some all-schools event that included both boys and girls.

After they left me in my dorm room, I fingered my dresses hanging in the closet and my sheets and blanket folded in a stack on the bottom bunk. I wandered to the bureau. In the wavy glass mirror, I seemed as small as a first grader.

The longer I stood in front of the mirror, the more I felt I would throw up. Just as I was wondering where the bathroom was, a voice broke through from the doorway.

"Eh! Kuaʻāina! You no like da top bunk?"

The big voice boomed from a small, compact body. Oh no. This must be Gerald Ann Fitzpatrick. That was the name on the roommate notice. How could a person with such a haole name speak such Pidgin? How come a Fitzpatrick looked so dark?

"Where you from, kuaʻāina? Da sticks?" She carried two suitcases into the room. One had a rope for a handle. "You evah come Honolulu befoʻ?" She moved into the middle of the room and eyeballed the twin bureaus and the side-by-side desks.

"Sometimes." I backed partway into the closet as she advanced. "I guess you're Gerald Ann."

"Ha!" She stretched her left arm out stiff until the elbow bent backwards, made a fist, and rotated her arm. Her elbow cracked.

"Gerald Ann! You call me dat one mo' time, you sleep da top bunk forevah." In case I might not understand, she made stink eye.

My roommate had been in Honolulu once before, but her parents were with her. This time they had put her on the plane in Hilo, hoping the school would have a bus at the airport. It hadn't bothered her a bit.

She opened her two suitcases and began stuffing things in drawers. She hung her school dresses on the wooden hangers she'd brought—they were on the list: twelve wooden hangers with name in indelible ink—but the dresses were so crumpled the hems hung cockeyed.

"Girls!" Another doorway voice. This one was tougher than Gerald Ann's. No bluff.

"Girls. I'm Mrs. Chu. The assistant housemother. I believe Mrs. Van Dyke checked you in. I am here to inspect your bureaus."

Gerald Ann's bureau drawers all were open, towels and socks and pajamas cascading.

"Is this yours?" Mrs. Chu stared at me.

"No."

"No, MA'AM."

"No, ma'am."

Mrs. Chu faced Gerald Ann.

"Remove your things from this bureau. Then put them back in. Towels in the bottom drawer. Sweaters and pajamas in the middle. Underwear, top right.

Handkerchiefs and socks, top left. Every name tag must be showing. And in that closet: every dress and blouse facing to the right, name on each dress and each hanger visible. Church dresses at the extreme right, outing dresses next, school dresses last. Shoes lined up in pairs on the floor. Laundry bag on the hook. And closet door closed at all times, except at night to air out." She turned in a way I'd seen at an Army parade.

"And these beds. Girls. These beds are to be made tight, with hospital corners. Top bunk spread tucked, bottom bunk spread left loose but not touching the floor. No wrinkles. Don't ever sit on the bed. It makes wrinkles."

Mrs. Chu clumped out of the room. We could hear her next door saying "Girls" to some other misfortunates.

"Gerald Ann," I said. "What's a hospital corner?"

"I give. And no call me Gerald Ann, I wen' tell you already. Can call me Fitzie, like at home."

"So what about Mrs. Chu?"

"Fut on Choo Choo," Fitzie said. "Come."

She led me to the library on the first floor, where there was a very dark, very tall piano.

"Sit," she said, pointing at the bench. She sat next to me and taught me the bottom part of "Heart and Soul."

Mrs. Chu, it turned out, had given us just the tip of the iceberg of regulations that froze our lives for the next six years. And Mrs. Chu, we saw shortly, was the only faculty member who wasn't haole. She might as well have been. They were all alike. Maybe it was the proximity to the military program for the boys' school. Or old-maidism, or widowhood. Whatever it was, they had the attitude of fundamentalist missionaries and the power of drill instructors.

Something was even wrong with the one married faculty couple. They were young, but the wife was pale and puffy, and the husband was so, you know. Ete. One day he backed the school bus up against a mango tree, branches and leaves flopping through the open windows. All of us tittered, and the girls in the window seats picked little green mangoes.

Fitzie was one of them. The pickers all got extra detention, fifteen minutes for arms out the window. Everybody got fifteen minutes for tittering. That was a Tuesday. When Mrs. Van Dyke posted the detention list on Friday after school,

Fitzie's name, as usual, was at the top, since it was arranged numerically by length of detention. Her sins were numerous. Late to breakfast. White shoe polish on black part of saddle shoe. Wrinkles in bedspread. Wrinkles in skirt. Food left on plate. No name tag on pink sock. Wad of paper in wastebasket. Wearing cardigan sweater without blouse under. Water spot on sink faucet. I got fifteen minutes for that too. We shared the sink.

But with fifteen minutes for the mango tittering and fifteen for the water spot, I was still free on Saturday by 9. Fitzie's sentence put her past the last bus down the hill.

"Fut," she said. "But I can go home Thanksgiving."

Detained girls did penance only until noon on Saturdays. I guess the school didn't have the old maid power to ride herd on them all day. Fitzie spent almost all Saturdays on campus, the mornings scrubbing and raking and the afternoons roaming the ridges behind the school, in the forest where the Koʻolau mountain winds rustled the saber leaves of koa and eucalyptus. We heard the winds at night on the sleeping porch. Once, when we were all up in our pajamas pushing the beds around so we could all be in the moonlight and become beautiful, Fitzie told us there were baby kangaroos way back in the mountains. She shut up when we heard Van Dyke tiptoeing in the hall.

"What are you girls doing? It's past lights out." The dark housemother silhouette stood for a moment adjusting its eyes. When it saw our beds ferried to the one window like barges in the harbor, it spoke: "Fifteen minutes. All of you. Now get those beds back."

We rolled them back into hospital ward layout. When Van Dyke's form retreated, Fitzie whispered, "Fut on Van Dyke." The rest of us tittered.

"Fifteen more minutes." Van Dyke must not have heard "fut."

By our second year, Fitzie quit calling me kuaʻāina, except on rare occasions. I was no longer a country yokel in her eyes, but the alternative name was worse. Blondie. My hair was actually brown, smooth and fine like my dad's. I was as much Hawaiian as most of the girls, but I was as conspicuous in the sea of dark heads as a white cap on a calm sea. Fitzie's hair was coarse and black, the result of a little Chinese and a lot of Hawaiian. Irish from her dad's side could hardly affect it. She had me cut the unruly hair into a V that reached between her shoulder blades. Every night she wound it into big pin curls around the neckline, slicking her bangs down on her forehead with water. She even got detention because of her hair. One Thursday, hair-washing day, she checked her wet head in with a new housemother, but had forgotten to wash her brush and comb. Fifteen minutes.

None of us really expected Fitzie to ever get out on a Saturday. She herself took to stocking the high shelf of her closet when she returned from vacations, like a Mormon preparing for Doomsday. She usually had Spam, assorted crack seed, and preserved lemon or plum, and once she had stewed prunes in a jar. Those she forgot at the back of the shelf and when she found them weeks later, we decided they were fermented.

"Eh Blondie," she said. "We j'like da boys, how dey put hooch inside hair tonic bottles."

"How do you know that?"

"I heard from Rags," she said.

Rags. Beads of congealed hair oil always dangled from the pokey ends of Rags McIntyre's haircut. Fitzie thought it made him cute. I'd heard about Rags from my brother. They were a year older than us. The first time Brother met Rags was in the boys' dorm bathroom. Rags was sitting in a stall practicing "The Stars and Stripes Forever" on his Martin. Good acoustics, he said. You need an echo for a really good effect with a uke. Later Rags discovered the acoustics also were great for magnifying farts, and he tried to wait until the gang shower was full of guys so he'd have the biggest possible audience.

You da champ, the boys told him. Da Fut King. Gotta be.

Rags enjoyed being the informal champion, but he wanted undisputed status. So he engineered a contest for study hall, the other place with reasonable acoustics, with its smooth cement floors and walls in the dorm basement. Three nights a week Mullageek presided over its library-like stillness.

Mr. Mulligan taught English literature at the boys' school and directed the mixed choir that practiced Thursday nights. Choir membership was always at a maximum since rehearsal was the only weekday chance of boys seeing girls and vice-versa. Fitzie and Rags had met because she was a last-row alto and he was a first-row tenor.

Mr. Mulligan was blue-eyed and pointy-nosed, ruddy-faced by nature, more than middle-aged and fond of recounting his service to the King in British India. The boys knew him best for his perfectly monotonous poetry reading, but the girls fixed on his music director style: He looked like a Thanksgiving turkey trying to escape slaughter. He danced up and down on the balls of his feet, his arms flapping like distressed, desperate wings. It didn't take Fitzie long to convert his name to a squawk: Mullageek! Mullageek! On "geek" she rose on her own toes and flapped her elbows.

So she became particularly fond of Rags when she heard what he did to Mullageek in study hall.

The fart contest had only one rule: Whoever got the biggest reaction out of Mullageek would win. About 40 boys were in the hall; hard to say how many planned to enter the contest. The first two or three explosions were minor enough to escape much notice, except for those immediately around. About eight o'clock two sophomores in the back row detonated respectable volleys, and Mullageek looked up from his desk on the platform. Ten dull minutes went by. One or two other boys made random efforts. Then a salvo. Mullageek was turning his head as if watching a tennis match. When Rags fired what turned out to be the finale, Mullageek turned redder than they'd ever seen him, and wormy blue veins writhed in his temples.

"Boys! Boys!"

By now the boys were laughing out loud and punching each other in the shoulder. They could barely hear the turkey voice above themselves.

"Boys! Boys! This is a quiet study hall! There is no place here for this kind of unseemly behavior! Dismissed! But you! McIntyre! I want you up here. Now!"

The next Saturday the whole bunch spent the whole day breaking down their M-1s and polishing their brass. And Rags got busted back to private.

After that, Fitzie loved him.

We girls never were so brave or brazen, but we had our ways. The best part of each new year was coming back to school to new teachers.

"FOB," Fitzie said.

"Hah?"

"Fresh Off da Boat, kua'āina."

We took our places and waited for roll call, faces impassive. Over several years we'd come to the theory that the paler the skin, the more the embarrassment.

At the beginning and end of the alphabet were the English, Irish, Scottish,

German, Chinese, Japanese, Filipino, and Portuguese names of those of us whose mothers or grandmothers had married foreigners. The Hawaiian names were in the middle, because almost all of them started with K. The first part of roll call lulled a new teacher into thinking it was going to be a good first day. Nothing to it. Ah Nee. Chun. Dawson. Fitzpatrick. Fong. Hughes.

About then Fitzie cracked her elbow. It was a signal.

Next up was Ka'ana'ana. After that came Kane'ai'akalā, and Keli'iaua. We laid in wait behind those treacherous multi-syllables like a guerilla gang. Every year we let the initiate stumble to full blush before the girl in question pronounced her name, soft and fast.

At the end of the first day of every school year Fitzie said, "Eh, Blondie! Too good, ah?"

In reality, the teachers were unaffected by this or anything else we did. They gave us information they thought proper, and when it pertained to individual girls, that meant none at all. After Christmas in tenth grade, Claire Ka'ana'ana didn't come back. We never heard why.

The next year, Christine Manuel didn't return after spring vacation. The subject came up one afternoon after school. Those of us who weren't supposed to be washing or ironing were in Fitzie's room eating Spam and saloon pilots.

"I heard she wen' get hāpai," Fitzie said.

"How do you know?" I always seemed to ask that.

"Just heard."

"How could she get pregnant?"

"No be one doodoo head, ah."

"I just don't see how people do it," I said.

"You lie down, put your legs up," Fitzie said. "Li' dis." She rolled back on the bottom bunk and hoisted her legs. Her feet touched the flat springs of the top bunk and she bounced the two girls up there until they begged her to stop.

"Not!" I couldn't believe it.

"Yeah," Fitzie said. "And den da guy get on top you. . . ."

"Not!" I was nearly screaming. "It's supposed to be nice!"

"Awright awreddy," Fitzie said. "You going see. Someday."

"Not me," I said. "I'm not doing that."

After that day the subject surfaced only now and then. The whole idea was pretty remote, as we seldom even saw boys. Yet even the school acknowledged that we were growing older. In eleventh grade, we were permitted to wear lipstick to dances, and nylons for special functions. We began to worry about straight seams and runs, and garter belts. The deal on the lipstick was that every trace must be removed by Sunday breakfast. Of course, Fitzie got detention for lipstick outline.

The teachers laid heavier and heavier work on us, and we factored equations, acted out the parts of Bottom and Peaseblossom, and spent half a year reading one fairy tale in Spanish. All that came out of the year of Spanish was that Fitzie took to saying, when you called her, "Una pimento."

The biology teacher, Mr. Ware, decided a field trip to collect specimens would make his specialty more interesting to us, and he took us to a rocky tide pool area at the far end of Waikīkī. All of us immediately swam out so far that Mr. Ware looked like a dwarf ete on the sand, waving his stubby dwarf arms wildly, trying to get us to come back. He waded knee-deep, cutting his feet on the coral. He waved and waved, and eventually we swam in.

"Back to the bus," he ordered.

"But we don't have our specimens. We can go back out and get wana."

"I'm cancelling the assignment. You disobeyed."

So all of us got a whole Saturday morning of detention. Some of us were assigned to scrub the laundry on hands and knees with stiff-bristled brushes and Bon Ami. Others were to Bon Ami all the dorm windows, then wipe the chalky powder off with old newspaper. The last few were on the grounds, picking up dead plumeria leaves.

In the afternoon Fitzie rounded up some of the group for a trip up the ridge. "Come," she said. "Going be good fun."

It had been raining the last couple of days, and the path was red and wet, the mud curling between our toes in a satisfying way. The spiny ridge grew narrower and steeper. One of the girls stopped and picked a lehua.

"Eh!" Fitzie barked. "No pick! You make rain."

In an hour we reached the top, where our ridge came to a T with the backbone of the Koʻolau range. Fog swirled, and we all got chicken skin in the damp. In moments the tradewinds blew the fog behind us, and we could see Kailua and Kāneʻohe bays sparkling green in the afternoon sun. Two thousand feet below were wet forests we knew smelled of rotting guava. It gave me the creeps, being so high and so exposed.

"Let's go back," I said.

"You scared, Blondie?" Fitzie said.

"Well."

"You gotta say *nah*." She made it sound like a bleat. "Then you come brave."

On the grade down, it was lots easier to slip. My toes spread wider than usual, trying to gain a hold. At a curve in the trail, Fitzie pointed to the right, back toward the summit. "'Ass where da small kine kangaroo live."

"Who said?"

"Rags. They saw one when they wen' pick tī leaves."

Just as she said it, both my feet lost their muddy grip, and I shot over the side of the ridge. I shrieked.

About twenty feet down, I lit in the forky feet of a hala tree. One of my legs tangled in the roots, and I hugged the trunk tighter than any Catholic has ever hugged a cross.

"Eh! Blondie!" Fitzie called. "Come!"

I looked up, expecting to see her on the trail sweeping her arm in an arc in case I hadn't understood the word "come."

But her right hand was within inches of me, and with her left arm, she gripped a guava bush. I grabbed her hand and she jerked me out of the hala roots. I stumbled up the tangled bank back to the trail and collapsed, crying and gasping. Fitzie held me until I stopped. She spit on her hand and tried to wipe the mud from a welt on my bare thigh.

"Eh, Blondie, no fall no more."

We went back to the dorm, cleaned up, and ate Fitzie's entire supply of crack seed.

For once, no one found out about the misadventure. But even at that, Fitzie still had so much detention, she'd given up on ever getting a citizenship award. In the last week or two of eleventh grade sewing, she and Nani Souza were sharing a machine, masters of wala'au while Nani ripped out the section where she'd caught the collar in the armhole seam.

"Girls." Miss Smythe rapped her ruler on the machine cabinet. Fitzie and Nani both looked up.

"Would you like to share your gossip with the rest of the class?"

Fitzie said, "No."

"All right. Both of you go to the office. Miss Marsden will want to speak with you."

This might have been the spark for the way Fitzie started our senior year the next September. The first day of school—the day of the ritual roll call—Fitzie appeared in black and white. Stripes ran around her horizontally, both blouse and skirt. We weren't permitted to wear pants to school, or she would have made pants. On her head was a straight-brimmed striped hat about the height of an angel food cake pan. She'd spent most of August sewing.

By lunchtime, she got sent to the office. Before meting out detention, Miss Marsden asked why Fitzie had made the prison suit.

"That's what I think we should wear at this school," Fitzie said.

Later, to us, she said, "Fut on Mars."

But she didn't really do a thing to Marsden. Yet, for all her failure at citizenship, such as the school defined it, she was a huge success at schoolwork. In fact, she was by far the smartest girl in the school. The minute she hit class she would switch from dorm Pidgin to the King's English. It was easy for her to remember rhymes of the Ancient Mariner and theorems for geometry. She could recite the periodic table. She even thought medieval France was interesting.

She and I dreamed we'd go to New York after we graduated. I'd go to art school and she would enroll at Columbia. We would share an apartment, maybe find a couple of other girls to join us. Of course, we would have barely any money, so in the middle of the year we started gathering provisions. In the back of her closet, Fitzie stashed the toilet paper she swiped when she was on bathroom duty. By March, she had enough that I could see we were going to have a shipping problem. When school let out for spring vacation, she stuffed the toilet paper in her suitcase and took it home to Hilo.

When she came back ten days later, she was sick. Her brown skin had a yellow look to it, and her eyes didn't flash. She hardly got detention. One afternoon I offered her Oreos.

"Nah," she said.

"Sushi? Cone kind?"

"Nah."

"What's the matter with you? That's your favorite."

She made a little swallowing motion, like she was trying not to throw up.

Then she whispered, "I think I'm going to have a baby."

"Fitzie!" Then I said her name again. And again.

After the third time, she said, feebly, "Fitzie. That's me. Christmas time Rags told me it would be okay."

The middle of the next week Fitzie disappeared. So many girls had the Asian flu, the infirmary was completely full. Everyone but me thought she had gone there, but the girls on junior nurse duty confirmed she wasn't there.

By the weekend she still wasn't back. As usual, the teachers told us nothing. The memories of Claire and Christine attacked my mind like wild pigs slashing dogs. I sat on the bed, wrinkles or no. Fut on this school, I thought. Fut on this goddamn school.

But a week later Fitzie was back, with a scar to show for it. Appendicitis. The kind that brews for a while and then blows up. She'd been in Queen's Hospital.

The year before, Fitzie had invented a huge bubble machine for the prom, so she was a natural to work on the senior skit. Usually the few girls interested in drama devised some inane act in which they played both male and female roles. Fitzie decided that every girl in the class should have a part, and she wrote a talent show/travelogue script that incorporated an astounding miscellany of things we'd learned in six years: archery, modern dance, typing, tumbling, piano. She herself did a pantomime to a recording of "What's Behind the Green Door?" Her muscular, acrobatic body gyrated in front of a stage-prop green door, her black hair flying wildly. The top part of her costume looked stripedly familiar. The song was jazzy, and the underclass girls began to clap in rhythm as Fitzie did a back bend, holding one arm out and the other one in front of her mouth, as if guzzling from a bottle.

The guzzling did it. Detention on the very last Saturday, the day before graduation.

On Sunday, she gave the valedictory speech. But when Marsden announced the school scholarship, the name she called was mine. I never expected it.

I only saw Fitzie from a distance after the ceremony. Her long wavy hair was tangled in a pile of lei that reached just below her eyes, and her family surrounded her, holding stacked boxes of gifts and food in their arms.

In the mob scene, I lost her, and before long everyone had disappeared not just from the auditorium but from campus entirely.

Two days later she called me from Hilo.

"Fitzie!" I shouted through the crackling connection. Something must be on her mind. Long distance phone calls were only for tragedies.

"What you mean, what wen' happen?"

"About the scholarship," I said. "You're the smartest person I ever met."

"I knew I wouldn't get it," she said, choosing the King's English. "Remember when we had college counseling at the beginning of the year? Marsden told me I'd never make it. I wasn't college material."

"What!" This time I shrieked. We'd given up the New York plan but she'd been talking about colleges in California. I'd chosen a public university in the Midwest that had low out-of-state tuition.

"Yeah," she said. She didn't sound like Fitzie at all.

"Fitzie, will you write to me?"

"Yeah, Blondie. Okay. I gotta go."

"Fitzie?"

"What you like?" She slipped into Pidgin, but she sounded strange.

"You're the one who taught me 'Heart and Soul.'"

She never did write to me. While I was in college, I heard from another classmate that Rags had joined the army and got killed in a car accident on a highway outside of Fort Ord. Later I heard that Mullageek married the sewing teacher and moved to Kansas. Marsden retired but was named "administrative adviser." After we'd been out of school about fifteen years, Fitzie became a lawyer. I moved to the West Coast, and then home. I called her shortly after I heard about her passing the bar. I hadn't seen here since graduation day. We met at Ciro's downtown. "Eh, Fitzie!" I said.

We hugged. "Blondie! You still look like one haole."

"T'anks, ah," I said.

"Ho, nevah know you can talk da kine." She smiled.

"You're a lawyer," I said.

"Yeah," she said. "I finally found out I was smart."

"I knew that," I said.

"I didn't. Marsden told me I wasn't good enough. She really meant I wasn't haole enough."

"I never thought of that. But you're right, that's what she meant."

"Kuaʻāina." She reached over the table and punched my jaw gently." She stretched out her arm and cracked her elbow. Then she picked up her drink.

"ʻOkōle maluna," she said. "Bottoms up." We clinked our glasses and she added, "Fut on Mars."

THE CURSE

It is believed that a curse among Filipino families takes on a life of its own. The necklace was cursed. Or so the Peralta clan gossiped once upon a time. And even now—many moons since the gold in the ancient necklace was forged in the Cordillera Mountains—the necklace still haunted the family. And every time there was an unexpected mysterious illness, they believed the wayward necklace caused it. An unexplained death? The necklace did it. A physical deformity in a newborn, from a harelip to soft carabao horn protrusions at the temples in some second or third cousin—did they blame genetics? No, they invoked the necklace.

The "cursed necklace" tsismis started when Kathy's grandmother, her Lola Perla, announced she was about to die. "I am ready to leave the world for good now. But do not tell anybody, espess-shally your mah-dere," she enunciated dramatically to Kathy on a lazy Saturday afternoon. "It is our secret," her grandmother's dark tone belied her playful, twinkling eyes. Kathy decided to play along.

She narrowed her eyes and sneaked a sideways glance at her 92-year-old lola. Dressed in a blue and white, aloha-print dress and shuffling along in red velvet house slippers, her lola was a comforting sight. Her lola had outlived her husband, most of her friends, and her only child, Kathy's father. She's going to live forever, Kathy thought. Kathy was going to humor her.

"Nah, I don't think so, Grandma. You're going to outlive all of us with your spunk and bossiness. When it's time, you're going to boss Death around so much, he'll give up on you and go on to the next person."

Her grandmother held back a smile. "Don't argue with me," she said, bringing her pointer in front of Kathy's face. "You the one getting sassy nowadays. One year in Nueva York University galah-banting with your Americano casinsins. You come back and think you know everything about Pilipinoz everywhere," she said, fake frowning.

"Listen to me, ah. I cannot die until I get all the things I want to be buried with. And I need your help."

"Ay, not that again," protested Kathy. "Filipino funerals are the worst when it comes to rituals and superstitions."

Lola Perla shook her head and waved her palms around as if shooing imaginary mosquitoes from her line of sight. "Toothpaste, toothbrush, dental floss, dentures, extra clothes, don't forget two panties, my half slip, my white cotton camisole, a leelo bit money, needle, thread, and so on and so on. You know what things need to be there. You make for your Dadi, so you know already," she said, frowning again, for real this time, as Kathy rolled her eyes.

"I really need your help with finding something. I need to find my necklace. Not my expensive ones, but my lingling-o. My grandmother gave it to me on my wedding day. I looked for it everywhere. In the underhouse, in the parador, in the fridedaire. I cannot find it anywhere."

"Grandma, did you look in your jewelry box?" asked Kathy, knowing she was risking her grandmother's wrath. Or doting behavior. She never knew which direction her lola's mind would take—a linear one, an unexpected swerve, or a ballistic missile path. One could never tell with Lola Perla. Because at 92 years old, her extended family attributed her shifting moods to a slight case of undocumented, undiagnosed dementia.

Lola Perla's face suddenly lit up. Her wrinkled face with its full, tobacco-stained lips changed from a frown to a warm, wide smile. "Ahh! I took it out of my jewelry box the day your grandfather died!" she exclaimed, a little smug. "And I untied it into three separate pendants," she said in a dreamy voice. Lola Perla gestured with her pointer for Kathy to come closer. Kathy brought her ear near her grandmother's mouth as she whispered a final wish, "I want all the pieces back so it can be buried with me."

She remembered the day Lola Perla told the story to her family, out of the blue, at the breakfast table, between bites of pan de sal and coffee. She said her husband had always been bothered by the lingling-o. As Lola Perla fingered the imaginary necklace around her neck and delicately swallowed the last bite of her breakfast roll, she regaled them with the tale of the cursed necklace. Her husband believed it was a pagan artifact. Downright un-Catholic and cursed, he said. He respected its symbolism of fertility and abundance, but believed it was powerful and haunted once he learned about the necklace's resemblance to a woman's female parts from Lola Perla, who said she told him he needed to lighten up, that it was only a representation of the calacuchi and the womb. He got irritated whenever she wore the necklace, Lola Perla said. He said he could feel the necklace mocking him for being afraid of it.

When she would tell the story of how she received it pure and fresh according to her Ifugao traditions, my grandpa would start to squirm in his seat, Lola said. "Your lolo said that our Mountain Province, our Igorot roots and traditions were better left in the past." Kathy remembered her dapper, light-skinned grandfather believing in the American dream of hard work and economic success.

"He would get angry when I talked about what the necklace could do."

"Like what, Lola?"

"Oh, purify water. Cleanse the blood. Ward off the evil eye. Bring families together. Break families apart. Make ladies pregnant."

"What?" Kathy said, laughing.

Her mother said, "You never told any of us about this. Dadi was a devout Catholic, but I never knew the necklace bothered him," her mother interjected giving Kathy a dirty look. Her coffee cup in mid-air, her lips pursed, as if poised for a kiss, she turned her attention to her elderly mother and expected further explanation.

Lola Perla shrugged. After her husband died, she said, she decided to give the necklace away. That was 22 years ago, in 1992, when Lola Perla's favorite song was Eric Clapton's "Tears in Heaven," she said. And then she made the sign on the cross on her forehead. She had given the necklace away in memory of her husband. Lola Perla was convinced he was in heaven crying copious tears over losing her through his unexpected death of being run over by the #2 bus on School Street as he was jaywalking to get his monthly haircut from Lanakila Barbershop.

She had untied the black leather strips holding the three-piece necklace together and separated it into individual pendants. "This is a symbol of good luck, fertility and creative energy," she had told each of the designated recipients of a single lingling-o.

Strange things started happening after Lola Perla shared her desire for the return of her necklace with Kathy. It seemed like one eerie, unusual, or unexplained occurrence happened every week for the past eight weeks. Now, every time the necklace is mentioned in casual conversation, Lola Perla makes the sign of the cross. Whenever it is whispered that the necklace caused a strange event, Kathy's mother lights a candle and sets out a bowl of rice on the family altar. Kathy tried to dissuade her family from believing a curse of bad luck and infertility existed. But Kathy knew that Filipinos and superstitions went together like dinuguan and puto.

Kathy finds Daryl at the 24-Hour Fitness on Kapi'olani Boulevard. He is doing chin-ups, awkwardly, as he struggles to lift his body up to the bar. He is sweaty, shiny, and happy to see her. She greets him with "Wassup bruddah dude!"

"Hey, Girlie Katz," is his return greeting, as he lowers himself too fast, relieved for the distraction. They bump fists and hug.

Daryl is big and tall for a Filipino, as his family likes to boast, about 5'10" and 250 pounds. He lifts weights, does cardio, and is covered with Hawaiian and what he thinks are ancient Filipino tattoos of the Cordillera Mountain region, where his Ifugao family is from. Daryl's great-grandmother is Flora, one of the original recipients of a piece of the necklace. Flora is the aunt of Kathy's grandmother, Lola Perla. Whatever their blood relations are supposed to be, Daryl and Kathy called each other casinsin, the Ilocano word for cousin, which was good enough for both of them.

"What brings you to my turf, casinsin? Need another reference for a tattoo artist?" Daryl asks, taking a sip of water.

"Nah, it's family business this time. But thanks for asking. I really like the tattoo I got from Keola."

"Cool. Take a look at mine. It's new. It's Igorot. I found the design on the Internet at a Filipino tattoo website. There was a picture of an old woman who had this design tattooed on her bare chest. She was wearing traditional Igorot clothing and I thought it looked cool," Daryl says. He lifts his shirt, proud of his large, snake-like tattoo surrounding one side of his chest. It was like he discovered a new continent or became part of uncharted territories.

Kathy reaches out to touch his right pectoral muscle. She peers closely at the tattoo and traces a part of the design with her pointer. "Interesting," she says, while shaking her head. "Do you know what it means? What the combined symbols represent?"

"I have no idea what it means. But check this one out—the lingling-o, this one here." Daryl pointed to his extended forearm. "My co-workers believed me when I told them the lingling-o design made me bulletproof. Three days after I said it, I survived a bullet wound that would normally be fatal. They all wanted a lingling-o tattoo like this after that."

Kathy looks into his smiling eyes, sizing up his foolish talk. She remembers seeing the incident at Hālawa Prison in the news. There was a riot over food. The inmates had enough of undercooked rice. They complained to the warden for weeks, but they had had enough. Someone started a food fight and someone grabbed Daryl's gun. In the ensuing struggle, the gun went off accidently and a wayward bullet grazed Daryl's neck. "Oh, I see. Well, you do work in a prison, so believing the lingling-o design makes you bulletproof would come in handy. But you shouldn't play around with something as old as the lingling-o. This lingling-o binds you to our ancestors. Don't exaggerate or capitalize on it."

"Look at you. All serious, li' dat. I figure as long as I treat it with respect, it's okay. How you know all this stuff?"

"From Lina, of course. The studious one. To quote her, Filipino tattoos, especially the ones from the Cordillera region are done 'to increase attractiveness, promote fertility, record accomplishments, bestow honor and protection, as well as its symbolic binding of the individual to their ancestors and posterity,'" Kathy recites, deadpanning it for emphasis.

"I can't believe you remembered that word for word," says Daryl, amused at his cousin's detached delivery.

"Well, you know her. What fifteen-year-old spends the summer studying for the PSATs that are a year away? Only our good old Lina, the wannabe CSI forensic scientist in the family."

"Yeah, science was always her thing. Remember when she conducted an experiment on your Barbie doll? Your grandma gave you folks good lickens on that science project. You folks almost burned down the underhouse."

"Hey, hey, hey! I was the older one, but it was her bright idea. She wanted to see what would happen to Barbie's plastic skin under boiling water. If it would melt or it would only get soft. It was her fault."

"Yeah, and as the older one, you should have figured out all that flattened cardboard box pieces you girls used to light the fire would fly around on a windy day." Daryl snickered at the memory of his cousins. As stories go, they were just playing with boiling water. After it got put through the coconut wireless in their extended families, the story transformed into the girls wanting to burn down the house. Daryl and Kathy both laughed heartily at the thought of flying cardboard and ember showers. Kathy interrupted their bonding moment.

"Hey, you need to find out what your new tattoo means. That snake one that you copied from the old woman whose picture you found on the Internet." They make more small talk for several minutes.

"I'll get to the point of why I'm here, Daryl. I'm on a mission for Lola Perla. Do you happen to know where the original lingling-o is, the one that your great-grandma Flora passed on to your mom?"

"Yeah, I remember that. My mom passed it on to my sis, who thought it was primitive and crude. Sis gave it to me. Years later, the lingling-o symbol became a cool item for those going native."

"Do you still have it? Lola Perla wants it back," Kathy explains.

"Is this because of the curse?"

"What curse?" Kathy asks. Here we go again, she thinks. She decides to play dumb.

"You know, the reason Sistina has been sick," Daryl responds. Kathy nods in sympathy.

"Daryl, the necklace is supposed to bring good luck and enhance fertility. What happened to Sis was a fluke. Doctors can't explain why, but it's not because of the necklace. I'm sure there there's a logical explanation for it statistically."

"Well, everybody's talking as if it's payback for Sis calling the necklace primitive and ugly. I mean, she's only in her late 30s. What disease would make her face look like that? What the hell? The doctors tell us her skull is shrinking, so the skin around her face is going to continue to sag. There's nothing she or her doctors can do about it."

"How's she holding up?" Kathy asks. "You know how sensitive she was about her looks in the first place."

"From so-so, to badly, to in denial. Aunty Minda, who's a nurse, told me it's a miracle that her brain size and the fluids in there are adjusting to the shrinkage. Other than her face looking like an old woman, she seems to be physically okay. But she doesn't leave the house because, you know, she's embarrassed about her looks. She quit her job and she's sad all the time." They sit in silence until Kathy broaches the subject again.

"You know, it's real important to Lola Perla that she gets the necklace back."

"I brought it to Keola at Native Ink about five years ago so he could design my first tattoo with it. Keola wanted to buy it from me afterward, but I just said he could have the necklace if he gave me the tattoo for free. It's been hanging in his shop's display case ever since. He won't sell it to anyone."

"Do you think you could get it back? For Lola Perla?"

"Why? He might charge me for the tattoo now. Is it really important?"

"Yeah, it is."

Daryl looks befuddled. He starts to run down possible scenarios. He could probably get Keola to give it back to him for the price of aloha, free. He thinks, yeah, Keola can mālama him, braddah-braddah kine, for their friendship, for the 'ohana. But it could work the other way. Keola was a businessman. If Keola did give it back to him, he would never ask for cash. But he might, could, maybe ask Daryl for a favor in return. Or he might want something material, an equivalent price of the gold in the necklace. He had done this before with his boys.

"I wouldn't ask if it wasn't necessary," says Kathy.

"I have to think about it."

"Okay. Lemme show you my new tattoo in the meantime," Kathy offers. She lifts her sleeve to show him the Sanskrit-based, pre-colonial, script of her name. "It says Kathy Peralta using the baybayin syllabary." She wonders if Daryl knows the definition of syllabary.

"Wow, I want one, too," Daryl exclaims like a child, his voice excited and a little whiny.

"I'll design one with your name. I learned to write in baybayin."

"K den. When you need the necklace by?"

"How about tomorrow?" said Kathy.

"You got any money?"

"Eh, you da adult here. I'm in high school, remember? You can donate? For the family, dude. If can, can. If no can, no can." Kathy knew Daryl's correctional officer job was giving him lots of holiday overtime now. He also dealt in commodities, which he bartered for services as needed. A little weed, perhaps a bit of muscle-building steroid doses, maybe contacts in the construction industry for a rock wall, things like that. Although Daryl was not too bright, he was enterprising and he worked hard. It was no secret among the Peraltas that Daryl had powers of persuasion, a knack for mathematics, and a long memory.

"K den. For you, cuz. Can do." Daryl hugs his cousin and stands up to continue his challenge with the chin-up bar.

One down, two more to go, she thinks. She will have Daryl's piece tomorrow. As she walks to her car in the parking lot, she turns back to look at the gym. She feels a tinge of regret. She did not have the heart to tell Daryl that his new tattoo was a disaster. There was a good reason he found the design on the chest of an elderly native woman. The snake, the stylized arrow, river water, setting sun, and symbolic man beneath the earth. "The widow of a brave warrior," she says aloud to herself. Poor Daryl, she thinks. She wasn't going to be the one to tell him what his tattoo really meant.

"And here is the second part of the mission," says Kathy to no one in particular. She is in the kitchen listening to the women gossip as they made Sunday dinner. As far as she could tell, and based on what the women were saying, she needed to pay a visit to Aunty Minda, whose husband had recently complained of rice grains in his head. Apparently, Uncle Pablo had refused to drink any more water because he could feel rice grains growing into seedlings inside his nasal cavities. Only one of her aunties scoffed. The rest of the women listened intently. She did, too, trying to translate the deep Ilokano in her head:

He refused all liquids.

He said it was so the seedlings wouldn't grow into stalks and come out of his ears.

You could actually see small tufts of green just emerging from his ear canals.

Then he stopped eating just when you could see small leaves form around his ear lobes.

He had gone a week without eating.

His childless wife, Aunty Minda, consulted with our neighborhood babaylan. The shaman told her to fill a small brown paper bag halfway with rice and to place three uncooked eggs on top. She was to put the bag under Pablo's bed. In the meantime, she was to take her piece of the necklace—Uncle Pablo had given it to her as a wedding gift because it traditionally symbolizes good luck and abundance—and stick it in Uncle Pablo's ears. Aunty Minda alternated putting the necklace piece in his left ear, then his right ear, every other night. After two weeks, she buried the bag under the mango tree in the backyard as instructed by the babaylan.

"Did it work?" Kathy shouted from across the room. They all turned to look at where she sat on a stool, off in the hallway because she did not want to get in the way of the elaborate preparations for the Sunday late afternoon early dinner that all her relatives were invited to.

"Of course it did. Rice stalks grew out of Uncle's ears because the bulul who guards the rice granary thousands of miles away in the Cordilleras wanted Lola Perla's necklace back" was the reply from the babaylan herself, a wizened elder with a hunchback due to her bending over her all-purpose cane when she walked throughout the neighborhood visiting families, walking to Tamashiro Market daily, or waving with her cane from her front porch to passersby on Pālama Street.

Getting the lingling-o from Aunty Minda was as easy as taking a serving of white rice from the huge aluminum tray at the beginning of the buffet line, Kathy told her sister Lina.

"Two down and one more to go," she said in a singsong cadence as she stuffed a hot lumpia in her mouth.

Kathy spotted Faylene amid the crowd at the Art & Flea event in the Fresh Café parking lot in Kakaʻako. It was late November and nippy, with the evening air bringing some pre-Christmas coldness. Customers milled around the featured vendor of the month, Yarnage, a fiber arts supplier who was conducting an Ugly Sweater Contest. Faylene's jewelry stand was right next to Yarnage, so she had a crowd of people interested in her trinkets.

"Katz! Over here. Here! Come over and help me," waved Faylene to her cousin. Kathy made her way to Lingling O Loverlicious, Faylene's jewelry company. She had been recruited to help Faylene in several prior instances, so she knew her job: to just greet and smile, refer potential buyers to Faylene. She kissed her cousin hello and gave her the once over from top to bottom.

Faylene, as usual, was overdressed. She was stunning in a formal black sheath with a deep vee cut down the front. She flipped her long straight black hair at strategic moments, like when handsome white dudes glanced at her cleavage. Her stiletto heels were a natural match to her delicate pink-painted toenails.

"By any chance, are you from Los Angeles?" one of the many attractive white dudes who made up her marketing demographic asked Faylene, flirting. His neon white teeth glistened in the subdued lighting.

"No, but these pieces were made in Los Angeles especially for you." Faylene flashed him her artificially-whitened teeth and a winning smile. Her eyes were perfectly made up to minimize their almond shape, creating an illusion of a deep eyelid fold and prominent under-the-browbone arch. Mr. Attractive White Dude's eyes moved to Faylene's necklace, a glittering gold lingling-o dangling precariously on leather between her breasts. On cue, Faylene picked up the necklace and fondled it between her fingers.

"This necklace will do wonders for your sex life," she said, using the overused opening line as her marketing pitch. Kathy always thought the statement was disingenuous, if not an outright lie. She had told Faylene how she felt, but she continued to use it as her sales angle anyway. "Eh, if they confuse fertility with sex, not my problem" was her rationale. "It says right here in fine print. Fertility, yes. Sex appeal, yes. But nothing in writing about sex."

Faylene worked her Lingling O Loverlicious sales magic and, only three minutes later, the enthusiastic customer walked away with a $300 piece of gold-plated trinket. Kathy thought it was a clever rip-off. The designs were awful. They incorporated other non-Filipino elements on the outer circle, such as extraneous points emanating from the center of the pendant made to look like the rays of a sun. Other designs had what looked like crow's feet scratches, making the pendant unaesthetic. Another one of her designs put a pearl in the middle of the circle where it was supposed to be empty to symbolize the uterus. Faylene liked to say the pearl represented a baby, a sure-fire charm that encouraged fertility for couples having trouble with conceiving, she added. She often sold two of them at a time, one for the woman and another for the man. As far as Kathy was concerned, it was all commercialized shibai. She felt the bullshit exaggerations were a misuse of the cultural value of the artifact. It felt like a touristy gimmick, one that emphasized the necklace as a sex aid and downplayed its fertility-encouraging properties.

This was ironic, since Faylene, at 26, had already decided not to have any children. Kathy thought she was a bit hypocritical. Faylene had unsuccessfully tried to make her two abortions a secret. One last year, and another this year. Nothing was ever secret when it came to the Peralta wireless network.

At 10 p.m, the event came to a close. Kathy helped pack Lingling O Loverlicious merchandise into Faylene's car. They sat in the front seat, talking and debriefing among gift bags, promotional visors, and plastic water bottles imprinted with the company logo.

"You know I have a problem with some of your promotional tactics, but I must admit you are a great salesperson," Kathy said.

"I know what you think I'm doing is tacky. I know you're not here to support my jewelry sales. Yeah. I hear you're looking for the original lingling-o that my grandmother gave me."

"Yeah, your Lola Linda was my Lola Perla's cousin. Lola Perla gave your grandmother a piece of the original necklace. My lola has it in her head that she's going to die any day now. She wants to put the necklace back together," Kathy explained. "Do you have it?"

"Of course, I do. It's my good luck charm. It's in a safety deposit box at First Hawaiian Bank on Ward Avenue. It's mine, though. My grandmother passed it on to me."

"With all due respect, I think you've gotten a good run from it. Maybe it's time to let it go now. You know, with the fertility thing, and all," said Kathy, hoping Faylene would catch the veiled reference. Faylene got pensive. She bit her lower lip and looked straight ahead.

"Perhaps. Two uncanny pregnancies in two months. I know what you're thinking. Of course, I used protection. First two pregnancies ever. First two abortions ever. Who would've thunk it. Me, of all organized and conscientious people."

Kathy let the implications of what she heard sink in. In high school, she heard rumors of classmates being pregnant because of unprotected sex. Faylene knew better, especially since children were not in her future plans. "Are you okay? Did it hurt?" Kathy thought her questions were stupid, but they just slipped out.

"I'm fine. And yes, it did." Faylene said with a solemn and quiet expression. The silence that followed between them was okay, like they were sharing a bonding moment between females, cousins, Filipinos, and just plain human beings.

"I'll get you the necklace tomorrow," Faylene said slowly.

"Do you have all the pieces?" Lola Perla asked Kathy. Kathy sat down on her lola's bed to show her.

"Yes, Grandma. The first from Daryl, then one from Aunty Minda, and the third from Faylene," answered Kathy. "Daryl's been telling people his lingling-o tattoo protects him from bullets. Faylene's been selling this design as a sex aid, far from what it's supposed to be."

"I don't think those are bad things. Culture is not meant to stand still. It doesn't need to be preserved," said Lola Perla. Kathy almost fell off the bed when she heard her grandma.

Kathy was flabbergasted. She put the photo down and sat up to face her grandmother. "But Lola, don't you want these traditional beliefs to continue? For the sake of our heritage and ancestral practices?"

"I want you folks to be happy with your lives. Whether or not you carry old traditions or make your own new ones."

Kathy couldn't believe her grandma carried such modern thoughts. "I thought you were an old-fashioned grandma. But you are just a wise one."

"Oh, I am old-fashioned in many ways. Did you bring the other thing?"

Kathy reached under the bed and pulled out a white plastic bag. She opened it and retrieved a small jar filled with red liquid. She wondered if she would lie to her grandmother and say it was human blood.

"I don't want to know," her grandmother said, as if reading her thoughts. "Goat's blood will do as well."

Lola Perla had set up several items as a makeshift altar on her dresser. She lit a tall white candle and placed it near the betel nut pieces she had arranged in a semicircle around a wooden bowl. "Do you have the spoon?" she asked Kathy, who walked over with the opened jar.

Her grandmother took the jar and spoon and opened the jar lid. She pulled out a hand-rolled cigar made with imported Ilokano tobacco from the pocket of her housedress. She dipped the tips of the cigar in blood and placed the cigar on top of the betel nut. She took a spoonful of blood and sprinkled some of it on the betel nut and the base of the candle.

She chanted, "In the name of Somilge, goddess of childbirth. In the name of Sehana, goddess of love. In the name of Kuntalupa, goddess of all that is creative and dynamic, we ask you to restore everything that is good and right." She bowed her head, said one Hail Mary, and made the sign of the cross. She picked up the first piece of the necklace.

"Come, I want you to do it," she gestured to Kathy. "Please do the honor of restoring the potency of the lingling-o. Banish the bad luck that has come of it."

Kathy walked over and to the dresser and picked up the spoon.

"No, not with that. With your hands. Bathe each lingling-o with blood," she instructed.

Kathy held each piece, felt its heft. Its weightiness moved through her fingertips, up her arm and into her chest. She began the ritual as instructed by Lola Perla, careful to coat each piece thoroughly with blood. As the blood ran over her hands as she washed the third and final piece, her grandmother sighed. She made the sign of the cross and kneeled before her bed. Then she got into bed and pulled the covers up to her chin.

Kathy looked forward to stringing the necklace together to adorn her grandmother's neck. It was only a necklace after all, a talisman meant to bring families together if they fell apart.

DONALD CARREIRA CHING

THE LAST TIME
I SAW HER

Excerpt from *Who You Know*

Until she disappeared, I never cared much about Jorden Freitas. To be fair, I
didn't really know who she was. I mean, I knew her, but I didn't know her-know
her. I knew her like when the teacher calls a name and you recognize a face
below a hand. Or like when you see someone you know at the mall and aren't
sure if you should wave or keep walking. True story, I always keep walking.

That's not completely true though. I mean, we went to Castle together,
so there's that, plus, we both live in Kāne'ohe, which means someone I know
knows her or her family. But we never talked story or anything. In fact, the one
time I did say something to her, it was like, "What, bitch?" I was skating in the
parking lot behind the science building and fell on my ass. My friend Kalena
laughed at me, but she could, I laughed at her all the time. When I got up to grab
my board, Jorden was laughing at us from the doorway of Ms. Y's class on the
second floor. So yeah, I let that bitch know that I saw her, and I reminded her
again the next time I did.

We had found out about the party that afternoon from Kalena's cousin,
Chelsea, a senior at Kalāheo. Some military brat's parents were out of town and
lacked the parenting to take him with them, which wasn't entirely surprising.
Plenty of people think Kalāheo is a class above Castle and Kailua, but it's really
just more white and less local. One thing's for sure though, the drugs are much
easier to cop.

Not that I did much of that anyway. I smoked weed once—Kalena stealing
one of her brother's joints from his dresser drawer. We sat in the bathroom
frantically trying to figure out how to smoke it, Kalena watching the door while
I tried to figure out how to inhale more than my own spit. Needless to say, we
maybe got one toke each before I dropped it in the toilet when the lit end singed
my fingertips. We spent the rest of the day going through her brother's shit,

convinced we were high, laughing at the endless clippings of women that he kept folded away in his bookshelf.

Kalena's cousin though, she told us stories. Once at the Winter Ball, one of her friends bought a couple tabs of ecstasy from a chaperone and ended up jumping off the DJ table and onto the dance floor. Broke her collarbone and her shoulder, and was still rolling all the way to the hospital room. Not like that's the worst story we've heard, just one of the funnier ones. The others are more of the usual health class lectures and teenage angst, with kids ODing on oxy from their mom's medicine cabinet and smoking ice while their dad's on deployment. It's not like we didn't see this shit at Castle, but whenever Kalena's cousin invited us out, it was like that's all we saw. Once, Kalena had even gone shrooming with Chelsea and a couple of her friends. She came back talking like it was the high of the year. Like it was the most memorable night of her life, ignoring the shit that was still stuck under her fingernails.

So maybe that's why I wasn't sure what to say when we got her cousin's text. I half-wanted to just flat out tell her no, but Kalena admires her cousin, looks up to her even if she doesn't have a good reason to. "Be ready," she read the last text out loud.

"Be ready," I repeated back, digging into the lilikoi yellow of my shave ice, mocking the dramatic tone of the text. "She thinks she's so hardcore, you know?" I mused to Kalena from the curb fronting the crack seed store down the road from our houses. "Be ready," I shook my head. "Bet it's just going to be a couple of losers and a bottle of Boone's Farm."

"At least it won't be the *same* losers," Kalena replied, letting her rainbow soften while she tapped out a response on her keypad. "Plus, this isn't a Kāneʻohe party. If she says there's going to be alcohol, there's going to be a shitload of it."

I smiled a sugar red smirk. Kalena couldn't drink for shit. Most of the time, she stood around nursing the same bottle of Heineken until someone noticed and put another one in her hand. By the time she got to the bottom of the second, she'd be signing karaoke to whoever was drunk enough to listen, half a song away from emptying her brains out in the bathroom. But I didn't say shit. Instead, I sucked up what was left of the syrup with my straw and played with the chunks of white at the bottom of the paper cup. "Well, I still think we should just forget that shit," I finally told her. "Plus, how the fuck are we going to get there? Your mom was pissed the last time we took her car."

"Because you puked in the back," Kalena pushed me.

True story: hards fuck me up. "I'll stick to soda," I joked.

"You better." She gave me one of her half-smiles, her lips curling just below the dimple in her cheek. "The last thing I need is you embarrassing me."

"Please, your cousin is going to be on every guy there."

"She is a ho," Kalena laughed. "But so's her mom, so, you know."

I took her cup and threw it in the trash with mine. "So what, we busing it then?"

"Nah, Steph is going to pick us up."

"That's something, I guess."

For the most part, I can't stand Chelsea and her friends. They think they're hot shit because they wear Forever 21 and rock fake Coach bags and have idiots kissing their skeleton cheeks "hello" every time they run into one of them at the mall. That's the exact reason I hate going to these parties because most of the time it's just a bunch of idiots like them, listening to rave music and dropping X until the bass falls out or the cops show up. At least in Kahalu'u, you can get stoned and talk story. At least you can sit back and fucking chill. Steph is the exception. She's the only one of Chelsea's friends that actually talks about shit and makes sense, and she doesn't turn the radio on to some trash station. And, she's Mormon, so she usually doesn't drink enough to kill us all when she's driving us home, which is a plus. Though the religion thing gets tired pretty fast. I get enough of that at my house.

"She's going to come grab us at eleven, so come over like ten, okay?"

"Keh," I told her, knowing I couldn't let her go by herself.

By the time Kalena texts me at 10:15, I'm already outside her house. *Where you at?* I don't bother to respond. Instead I sneak around the back, jump the fence, and head through the screen door, which is almost always open even when nobody's home. Security isn't really an issue here. Like most people on the block, I've known her and her family a long time. Her parents and mine moved to the neighborhood when it was nothing but weeds. It wasn't long after that I found her playing naked in a muddy puddle near the side of her house. I didn't hesitate to join her.

When I'm right outside her door, I text her back, *here*, and jump out from the hallway.

"You stupid bitch," she cackles, throwing an eyebrow pencil at the door. "But perfect timing."

"For what?" I throw a confused look at her and cross my legs on the floor.

"You know," a smile as pointed as her eyebrows crosses her face. Once she called it "prettying me up," now it's usually something like "you gotta at least look like you got a vag." I guess it's difficult to tell with my jeans on.

It's not a choice, of course. She grabs my arm, I pull back, but I know how this game goes, so I just sit there and make faces while she does her best to tame my eyebrows and apply whatever concealers and colors to my skin. Before, she used to make me choose outfits from her closet—whatever she thought would somehow make a shape out of my lanky frame. Thankfully, we don't have the same hips anymore. Still, there are some parts I like. When she's done with most of my face, I take her eye liner and trace just above my lashes and down, letting the black line fall further than it should. Sometimes I draw stars or lacey flowers or peace signs. I know Kalena's going to be way too into tonight, but for her sake, I decide to curve the bottom up to meet the top, making what I think are wings.

She looks me up and down, evaluating her effort. "You'll fuck 'em with your eyes," she finally decides. Then, she takes the eyeliner out of my hand and settles for a few flicks of flair on her own. "We both will," she says into the mirror, throwing me a wink.

We don't wait for the call from Chelsea. Instead, we head out the back and around the house, using the gate this time. Neither of us is surprised to find Steph's Tercel parked two houses down. 11:00 pm, right on time, Blink-182, coming out of the windows. "Ladies," Chelsea waves to us from the front seat. It's dark, but I can see her face glittering in the streetlight. She looks like an art project gone wrong, all sparkle and paste. We get in the back, Kalena pretty much pushing me in.

"So, good news and bad news," Chelsea tells us, cracking her gum and turning the stereo down. "Marshall's got shut down, so that's off the table."

"What happened?" Kalena asked, clearly concerned about the prospects for the night.

"Neighbor called the parents," Steph filled in the blank, correcting the volume. "I don't know what he was expecting."

"Shit was lame anyway," Chelsea added.

"And the bad news?" I joked. Kalena nudged me.

Chelsea threw a glance my way. "The good news," she cracked her gum for effect. "One of my friends who was there called, there's something better."

"Party at the crack house?"

Steph laughs. I see Kalena smile in the dark. "No," Chelsea says flatly, "but we'd be more than happy to drop you off."

Kalena's smile disappears. "I'm alright," I reply.

Chelsea lets it go. "It's not a kids party, I'll leave it at that."

"We don't have time for little boys, right?" Kalena parrots.

"Exactly," Chelsea rewards her.

"And what about you, K?" I ask Steph, "Does God have time for little boys?"

She doesn't take the bait. "I'm just dropping you guys off."

"What?"

"She's got shit to do," Chelsea interjects.

"But I'll come pick you guys up at one."

"We'll call you," Chelsea tells her, ignoring the curfew.

"Chill," Kalena whispers to me, so I keep my mouth shut.

Chelsea doesn't tell us where the party's at, but I keep track of everything I see out the window. I can't see the street signs, but I note the right at the shopping center, the left at the pineapple mailbox, the ten seconds between that and the next right. I've seen enough *SVU* episodes to know to keep track of these things. Steph turns at a "Dead End" sign and stops before she heads any further down. When we get out, I can see why. The street is lined with cars and groups of bodies between them. People talking and smoking and drinking—people on their way to the party or taking a break from it. I can hear the low vibration of music coming from where the road ends.

When Steph pulls away, I realize I'm the only one left at the corner, so I jog to catch up with Kalena. She's a few cars down already and a step behind her cousin. "It's going to be cool," she tells me again, turning to take my hand. I take hers in mine but then she pulls it back, leaving a small tab in my palm. She sticks her tongue out, showing me hers. I mouth *what the fuck?* to her but she's not paying attention to me anymore. She's laughing with Chelsea, chatting nonsense. I slip the tab in my pocket. Later, I'll wonder why I just didn't drop it in the dirt.

For me, the party was like one of those Magic Eye books that my mom used to buy me when I was a kid. It started out as one thing and became something else, with the in-between mostly a blur of color and sound.

When we first got there, it seemed pretty tame. Even Chelsea seemed unsure if it was going to be worth her time. She stopped at the front door—exchanging glances, inventorying bottles and red cups, sizing up the possibilities—and then stepped inside, with Kalena on her Havaianas. One of the first things I noticed was how much older the crowd was and how out of place Chelsea seemed. Usually, within the first minute of one of these outings, she's crowded with hugs and hellos, and her giggle becomes something of an earworm that keeps ringing in your skull. This time, the giggle was still there, but it was met with side-glances and cautious smiles, each one asking, who are you?

Maybe it was our fault. Maybe we looked our age and maybe we were acting it too, sophomores out of place. Chelsea was her usual ho-ish self and Kalena was doing an awkward imitation: following too close behind, trying to make too much conversation with her, echoing every laugh and every wave. Honestly, I didn't want to have anything to do with it. I slid my hands in the front of my hoodie and eyed out anyone who bothered to notice me. But still, in a crowd of twenty-somethings, you could tell we were out of place.

Finally, Chelsea stumbled upon someone she knew near the back of the living room. She did the introductions, but I don't remember the girl's name. Ashley maybe, Ashlynn, some shit like that. She had just opened a beer, so she gave it to Chelsea and then got two more for Kalena and me. "Should you be drinking that?" I asked Kalena.

"She definitely should," Chelsea replied. "Makes it last longer," she added. I didn't have to ask what. I put my beer down and settled in.

Not long after, I noticed that Kalena started to drift away from the group. Maybe drift isn't the right word, bob maybe, bounce. Chelsea had already started to dance in place, dipping and nodding, laughing with Ashlee or other randos that came and went. But Kalena was doing something else. It started when she handed me her beer, the bottle nearly empty. I was happy to take it, but then she started to mutter something about her skin and the way it felt. She started to rub her arms and her neck, her stomach and under her top.

Then she started to move away. Someone turned the music up or maybe it was always that loud. She started dancing with herself, laughing and vibing out.

Chelsea finally noticed. "That's it, girl," she yelled over the synths.

"She's fucking tripping balls," Ashleigh laughed.

I started to feel something turn, pulse. I picked up my beer and tipped it back, trying to remain cool. I leaned over to the person next to me. "What time is it?" I asked. They showed me their phone, but I missed it.

When I turned back, Chelsea had joined Kalena; now they were touching each other. Kalena looked at me and gestured for me to join them. I just shook my head, *we should go*. But she was determined; she came over and grabbed my arm, started to pull. I pulled back, trying to get her to sit down, to chill for a second.

"Come on," she insisted, letting me pull her towards me, "be cool." I let go and she started to dance again, smiling at no one and everyone.

I grabbed her. "Relax."

"You." She pulled back hard. It wasn't anger on her face. It was frustration, impatience. And that was it. Chelsea was waiting for her, this time, with a group of guys who had no problem with what they saw.

"Fuck it," I said to myself.

I got up and headed out the front door. Jorden was posted up near the stairs, a drink in her hand. "I'm sorry about your girlfriend," she slurred to me. Maybe she didn't mean anything by it, maybe she did, or maybe she was actually concerned, I don't know. Sometimes, I'm not sure if she said anything at all. But I remembered that she had smiled, that I had seen that smile before, and I wasn't having it.

"What the fuck did you say to me?" I pushed her. "What the fuck did you say?"

"Cool it," a guy that was with her stepped between us. "Or get the fuck out."

"No problem," I told him, staring Jorden down.

I slapped open the front door and started walking. I didn't have time for this shit. I didn't need this shit. I should have just stayed in the car with Steph and had her drop me off at home. I got to the corner and started pacing, and then I sat down, trying to calm myself, but I couldn't get the thought of Kalena out of my head.

And then I noticed a guy leaning against one of the cars on the road. "You okay?" he asked.

I turned around. He introduced himself, Nick I think he said, or maybe he didn't and instead just reassured me that he wasn't some pervert that had followed me from the party. He was smoking a cigarette. I don't remember what I told him exactly, but it was probably something like, "My friend is just acting like a fucking idiot."

He listened and then said something like, "You sure you're not the one acting like the fucking idiot?"

That made me pause for a long time. I remember that. "No," I told him.

"Yeah, that's usually how it goes." He put his cigarette out on the ground and left.

I remembered thinking that he was right. That maybe I was the one being the idiot, that Kalena probably was looking for me. And then I thought maybe she was right too, maybe I should just chill, be cool, enjoy myself for once. I reached in my pocket for the tab she had given me earlier. At that point, I'd like to believe I just wasn't thinking straight, or maybe I was just thinking too much about the wrong things, maybe I was just being jealous and insecure. Either way, I put the tab on my tongue and swallowed hard, not wanting to think anymore.

The next few hours were bright and black, sharp and spotted, with the colors blending at times. Some of it I would remember, some of it I'd hear about later. It happened quicker than I expected it to. I had waited until I had calmed down before I went back in. I was standing at the door, looking around at the faces, the music washing over me, and suddenly I felt like one of those plasma balls you see on TV or in museums. The ones where you touch the outside and then there's just electricity.

I had no idea how long I stood there covered in chicken skin, letting every sound and movement and breeze hit me like tiny fingers, but at some point I moved. And then I fell, someone bumped into me, I bumped into somebody else, knocked over someone's drink, ended up on the floor and on one of those shag rugs with the tiny wisps that tickle everywhere. I laid there for a while, running my body over the carpet and staring up at the lights, electrified.

When I finally got up, my throat was so dry I thought it was blistering. I started searching the edges of the downstairs, wanting to tell Kalena about the feeling, wanting to share it with her too. There were more people outside, but the dark scared me all of a sudden. And then I realized I didn't know anyone there, none of the faces looked familiar, and then I laughed, or I think I did. Kalena would later tell me that Ashlei saw me, that she gave me a bottle of water, and that I downed it in a single gulp. I told her I loved her and talked to her about flying.

I don't remember that, but I remember zooming around the room and then up the stairs, wanting to get higher up. I fell at the top, tripping on the rug. The sudden surge of pain cleared my mind. I heard voices: a girl's and a guy's, back and forth, back and forth. One got louder, the girl's I think, then I heard something else, or maybe it was just the music from downstairs, the bass hitting the floor.

And then I saw red on the carpet. I could taste it on my lips. I got up and shuffled to one of the open doors—the bathroom. The faucet was on already, I think. No, I turned it on and stood there, watching the blood drip and disperse in tendrils. I felt like I was watching watercolor come to life. The whole thing was too much. I sat down up against the wall and just let the wall vibrate against my back.

It was dark in the bathroom, but there was still light in the hallway. I remembered a shadow passing, crossing over the puddle I had made in front of the sink. Maybe two. I got up, remembering Kalena—it could have been her I heard. All the doors in the hallway were open except one. I opened it. There weren't any lights on but I could see the shape of someone in the bed.

I laughed, I don't know why. I walked over to the bed and crawled next to the body. Maybe I thought it was a game. That Kalena was hiding there for me to find her. And then I saw Jorden's face and I felt a part of me empty. She was breathing, I think, though sometimes when I try to picture it, I'm not so sure. I crawled back, down on to the floor, and that's when I heard voices again, quieter this time. I looked around. The closet door was open. I crawled to it and pressed myself into the corner. I could hear footsteps in the bedroom. I saw shapes pass by through the slats. I tried to control my breathing, but my chest was pulsing, my mind was filling with blood and air, and my jaw was incredibly tight. I wanted to scream but I couldn't. I couldn't get out a word.

I woke up to the sound of fucking. I burst out of the closet doors, suddenly shocked to life, to find two drunks from the party humping awkwardly on the same bed I had seen Jorden on. I stood there, trying to make sense of it. They didn't even notice me.

Right then, I wasn't sure if it had happened. Chelsea talked to me and Kalena all the time about bad trips, and I thought that's probably what it was. Jorden had probably gotten drunk, come upstairs, and passed out. She was probably too wasted and didn't want to fool around, and that's what the argument was about—some dick pissed because his balls were blue like that's an excuse.

I went downstairs to find most of the party had cleared out. The cops had finally shown up to break up the party. Chelsea would tell us later that the guy who was hosting it knew one of them and that's why it took so long. No surprise there. I couldn't find Kalena, I couldn't find Chelsea, and someone told me that Ashlie had left even before the cops had come. I tried to call them both but it went straight to voicemail. Their phones were probably dead.

I remembered there was a bus stop near the shopping center we had passed, so I started walking. I figured I could wait there a few hours until the buses started running again. The bus stop was in sight when my phone rang. "Oh my god, where are you?" It was Kalena.

"What the fuck do you mean, where am I, where the fuck are you?"

"We're with Steph."

"Where?"

"Right down the road," she replied. "We were looking for you." I told her to pick me up at the bus stop and hung up the phone.

It was almost three. I was surprised my parents hadn't called. Surprised too that I hadn't been out that long. My body was aching and I felt a little dizzy, I rubbed the pain in my jaw. My throat felt like sandpaper. "Where the fuck are they?" I asked under my breath, searching the street for any sign of Steph's Tercel. I turned to look down the road and saw a car approach the stoplight from the direction of the party. I recognized the driver, the guy that Jorden had been with, but he was alone. His stare was fixed on the streetlight, his car inching forward, waiting for it to turn green. I thought he was going to run it. He probably would have, but then it changed and he was gone, a pair of taillights speeding into the distance. Where was Jorden? I wondered. What the hell had I seen?

JACEY CHOY

MAKAIBARI ESTATE DARJEELING, SECOND FLUSH

I like second flush best,
she had announced as we
entered the tea shop, Bengali
accent barely hanging in the air.

I didn't know second flush,
or first flush, or any flush
of tea leaves. Flush? Verb? Noun?
Or adjective? My mind swirled as
I nodded agreement, feigned understanding.

Smell that one, she said as she pointed
to the jars of tea on a wall with hand-
written names so small that
when I tried to focus on one, she
had already moved to another.
And another. She knew their names,
their places in the line-up.

Could we smell the Makaibari, she said
to the young woman behind the
counter. A friendly clerk opened
a jar, held it under my nose as I drank
in pungent aromas evoking smoky,
fragrant blossoms from another world,
stirring my imagination. *Which one
do you like*, brought me back to murmur:

MAKAIBARI ESTATE DARJEELING, SECOND FLUSH

All of them, you choose.

We sat together, side by side,
like two aunties under a vermilion
shower tree, animated, laughing, she
adding milk and sugar to my
cup, deciding when to stop while
I sat, smiling, feeling ten or ninety.

Yet it felt familiar. A silvery thread
tugged from the weft of memory.
The pouring, the spooning, the stirring.
I stepped into a universe,
both near and far, alive with a world I once
knew, a world I had forgotten,
as my mother feared I would
when I boarded the plane
to leave the island.

SUNSET'S BURNING

Sunset's burning through these thin motel curtains.
Somewhere in America, west of the Rockies, i think.
Just wandering around to wear out my last pair of issued boots.
Rough suede scoured smooth by diesel and desert sand
familiar and comfortable.

It's gotten to where i'm not so sure anymore
of the things i used to depend on
to make it through each day
now that i've come home.
Each day bleeding into the next
Blurring together at highway speed.
And the used to be important things
Have begun piling up as roadside debris.

Fishing out a cigarette from the half empty pack
of Marlboros, i put a flame to its face
with the easy metallic click of my Zippo
remembering to breathe as the smoke wraps
and caresses me like a lover.
While the last few oxy rattle in the bottle
God's playing dice again.
Shake out a few of the round pink pills
pop them in and wash them down
with what's left of the pint of five-dollar tequila
to take the pain
and make it small enough
to walk out the door with.

going to pack it all in and call it a day
step out in the fading sunlight,
glittering with settling dust
past the 60hz hum of the street lights
just starting to turn on
head out into whatever's out there
run my hand in the currents of the night air
to find something to hold on to.
And see if I can find the stars that will bring home

It's all psychobabble anyway,
Another day adrift in an unfamiliar America
Shuffling through the remains of a life left behind.

" O "

Die, Mrs. Okahara. It is time.

You are so small. A brown, withered body curled like a dried shiitake mushroom on the stark whiteness of hospital sheets. Smudges of red and blue, barely masked by freckled skin stretched tight over the angles of your skull. Sparse wisps of straight gray hair. Eyes closed. Head to one side. Toothless mouth forming the wide "o" of a scream.

Are you breathing?

Yes. I hear you throughout the night from my side of the striped curtain dividing our room. Our heads are not four feet apart. When I cross to the bathroom, I try to pull my IV stand past you without making a sound. The night nurse wheels in a cart. Not to worry, she says. Mrs. O. can hear very little. Needs her hearing aids. Refuses to wear them. Can't stand her dentures. They're back home. She doesn't look like she is breathing, does she?

I hear you throughout the night, each breath exhaled with a sigh, a word, a cry, a rattle, a whisper. Once, a high shriek. *Obake!* Ghosts pressing against your chest. A girl seized by large hands in the woods nearly a century ago. Suffocating Hokkaido spirits lurking beneath layers of snow, leaping up as your *geta* raise the crust that has held them down. Circling, strangling *obake* from your childhood. Tonight, they slide out from under flat hospital sheets.

Ghosts vanish. Low moans now, one with each breath. New visions summon a girl with a sweet voice:

"Sister? Sister. Your hair is so pretty. All of your children, so pretty! Sister."

The nurses bring you tenderness. Clean and change you. Roll you off your broken right arm. Rush in when your left arm bends so that the IV pump's alarm sounds. Whisper to you in the near darkness.

"How are you doing, *obasan*? Let's check to see if you are wet. There now, grandmother. We'll get you more comfortable, O.K.? *Itai*? Where *itai*? Where do you hurt? Your back? Let's give it a little rub. Sorry, grandmother. I can't understand. Ah. No, sweetheart, you are in the hospital. You fell again. Hurt your arm and your ribs and your pelvis. What? Drink? Are you thirsty? Good. That's good. But I need to make your water thicker. Stir in the powder so you won't choke. The choking, probably from when you had pneumonia last time. Remember?"

Towards morning, you sleep. I hear breathing, sometimes a single word from your side of the striped curtain. It's barely dawn, but the corridor squeaks and clatters with wheeled carts. I doze until straight shafts of sunlight move from between the vertical window blinds. They cross the curtain divider, warm my face, the light waking me.

Morning voices. "Good morning Mrs. O. Let me just get your pressure. Won't hurt now. You sleep again, then we'll feed you a nice breakfast."

I feel for the cold tile with my toes, step down, and roll the IV stand along on my journey to the bathroom. You sleep, mouth an oval now. A cast stretches around one thin arm like the metal rings clamped around palm trunks to stop rats from climbing and making nests above. Where your blanket has slipped, the sheets' whiteness illuminates your bones like an X-ray. You don't see me pass by the foot of your metal bed frame. For this entire day, we do not meet. You sleep.

Were you, then, a picture bride? Lurching across the Pacific in the hold of a wooden ship, weeks at sea? The Hawai'i groom who sent for you sending no picture of himself. He had your photo, of course. Put the sepia print, matted with ivory cardboard, in an enameled box he had carried with him from Fukuoka when he was fourteen. Was he cruel, your new husband? Was he tall? Even in those days, you could not have been much over four feet, posing for the black camera, straight forward, mouth primly closed, eyes large and searching, hair coiled into a neat ring by your older sister.

Did *obake* follow you to Hawai'i, weaving themselves between Waipahu palm fronds, laughing low and buzzing curses from under the red dirt, from deep in the shadows cast by tall spikes of sugar cane?

I will make for you a different past. A gentle husband, short but powerful, eyes crinkled at the corners from smiling. His laughter scattering the cane field spirits. I give him a small, square plantation house, painted dark green with white trim. Within its whitewashed walls are hand-hewn tables, chairs. In a drawer, a *shakuhachi* which sounds like a clear shiver of wind when he plays for you on warm evenings, just before the stars pull up into the night.

A small corner shrine offers up ripe oranges, *sake*, rice, a branch of stephanotis, a single yellow ginger blossom to the beneficent spirits that haunt this house.

And in your bedroom, a cradle with fine white netting draped from the ceiling to its edges. Inside it, a *futon* no bigger than your husband's palaka shirt, but thick, soft, and warm when trades blow a taste of winter into the small window. You gaze at him, the baby son whose cheeks are so plump your friends must reach out and touch them, like ripe peaches or the most precious of their gray-pink mangoes.

You do not grow plump, but there is a fullness now, beneath the cloth of your work garments, under the simple muslin shift you wear to bed. The baby sleeps, so close his breath can almost brush you. His lips smack. "He dreams of milk," you tell your husband. "He dreams of you," he answers.

He turns the handle on the lamp and touches the nape of your neck. His fingers pull you toward him, guide you to the place where you fit against his body as perfectly as a candle in a mold. A barred dove murmurs one last call from a distant branch and you fall asleep.

"Good morning, Mrs. Okahara. Are you hungry? Good. We have pancakes today with good guava syrup. You can chew? Yes, of course. Easy for you to chew. I'll give you tiny little bites."

You are awake today. When the aide leaves, I cross to your side of our room. Your eyes are open and you see my shape passing, maybe even the gown flapping against my legs. You are awake and alive, and we meet. You are Fumiko Okahara. You have two adopted sons. On Wednesday, you will leave here with one son and his wife for Maui, where there is someone hired to take care of you until you are better. Someone to keep you from falling and to help you once you are able to walk to the bathroom.

In the afternoon, I hear your daughter-in-law's low, pleasant voice and a higher voice. A grandson? Yes, a grandson.

"Something is the matter with *obasan*'s face," he says.

"She doesn't have her teeth in, Kevin. That's all that's wrong."

"Can she hear me?"

"Not now. She's gone back to sleep."

I push the curtain over from the end and introduce myself to the visitors.

"This is Kevin, my son," says your daughter-in-law. The young woman tells me that your sister died forty years ago. "She told you *what*?" she asks. "No, no, she is Fumiko, but she never had any adopted children. No. She will not go to Maui. We don't know anyone on Maui." She sighs and peers at you over her glasses. "She is in and out now, in and out."

I nod, give a wave to them both, then return to my bed.

Kevin asks, "When will she come home?"

"I don't know. Nobody really knows for sure."

"God knows."

"Yes, yes, of course. God knows."

Only God knows. When it is time to come and to leave. To die. Not doctors. Not family. Certainly not me. Another night is here. I pull my pillow over my head to block out your noises.

I slide the pillow off. What do I hear?

Silence. Not a moan, not a whistle of breathing. I slide off the high bed and look at you in the dim light. No movement. No lifting or falling of your gown, of the sheet. Have my night wishes caused the spirit inside you to circle, to curl itself out from your round mouth, to spiral like stirred smoke, floating away from your shell?

I am shaking. Afraid to touch you. The nurse comes in as I stare. "Mrs. Okahara?" she calls. Then louder. "Are you O.K., Mrs. Okahara?" You move a brown hand and I jump. The nurse chuckles quietly, then whispers, "Sometimes I come in and she looks exactly like a corpse. No, like a mummy. I have to go over and put my fingers on her neck. There's always a pulse, though. This lady is amazing. Really amazing."

You call my name when I open the window blinds at dawn. "Yes, Mrs.

Okahara? Yes, Fumiko?"

"Good morning, teacher." The words are a melody, a song sung in a long ago classroom. "Good morning, teacher!"

You call again. "Teacher? Teacher? *Teacher!*"

"Yes, I'm here," I answer.

"Can I go to the bathroom? I have to go *shishi*."

"You are not in school, Mrs. Okahara. You are in the hospital. You can go in your bed and the nurse will come to change your diaper when you're wet. She'll change your sheets if she needs to. It's all right."

"Ah . . . thank you, teacher."

I have on my own clothes. I wait for an attendant to come with a chair to wheel me away from you. I do not pray for you to die. You are very old, but yes, you are amazing.

I have leaned over you, cut the potatoes on the cream-colored plate into pieces the size of sand grains. I have fed you, then helped you feed yourself and drink your thick water. We have talked when you were there inside your body. We talked when you were walking to school with your sister holding your hand. I heard you swear at the nurse when she turned you over to bathe you. You have told me why you hate your teeth. Why you were afraid of the icy blackness deep, deep beneath the snow. Of the man in the woods. Why you do not care for our new mayor. Why all of your adopted children have cars with trunks that don't latch properly.

You are alive, Mrs. Okahara. Though I leave here before you, I hope that you might go home, too. Home to a small, square house painted green and white, to a floating *shakuhachi* melody and an evening of rising stars. 🍃

A MAN INHABITS HIS BODY

A man inhabits his body. The only rent he pays is the daily bill for wear and tear. A suntan, for example, costs more than a mile run, a steak less than cocaine, and indifference more than a suite at the Ritz.

A man inhabits his body. He tries to keep the walls clean and painted, but, over time, forgets. He rarely makes the bed, though his sheets are almost always clean. The path from his kitchen to the bathroom is direct, with few obstacles. In the center of his living room, there's a hum and a song, but no boom box or radio in sight.

A man inhabits his body. At night, he travels far, seeks new beaches, new women and men, but is sure to leave the door unlocked; if he doesn't, he knows he'll have to rely on uncertain neighbors or continually climb through broken windows. One night, he stayed at someone else's place, and in the morning, when he returned home, a lock appeared, rusted, and fell off. He went in. Breakfast was ready, and he breathed a sigh of relief, but he knew it might not always be so.

A man inhabits his body. It is the only home he has, for now. When it's gone, he will become a traveler on a new road, roaming until stars light the way to new rental units, a complex by the sea, with a pool, a sauna, three meals a day. Even then, a man must inhabit his body. Even then.

NĀWILIWILI STREAM

By mid-afternoon,
the morning rain
is forgotten.

As the tide rises,
the brown river
seems to flow

back upstream,
reflections
of the bridge

shimmering
like a school
of fish jumping

for food.
Was that rain
a dream,

a fantasy,
another day?
How hungry

the fish seem,
how bright
the sun.

THE DANGLING BUTTON

What happened here?

A small uncertainty: the crumpled shirt scrunched in a heap by the steps

     The nights have been too hot.

Sudden rainstorms manage to cool us down.

We edge away from slow drowsiness in the after dinner routine of cleaning up

     to the endless TV patter of voices.

The clock marks bedtime coming up.

Late but not too late.

Tomorrow will be a full day.

     Upstairs we go.

We stop to talk a moment.

We laugh at some odd thing.

Your hand, my hand move in a flutter.

It's been a while, I think, remembering.

Upon the steps, in the dark.

Somehow something noiseless makes a weightless clip at the air,

But it hangs on anyway.

A button dangles by a thread attached to a tiny ripped hole in the blouse

I pull open.

     The sound of rain fills the rooms of the old house.

We sleep so well.

We get up even earlier.

JENNIFER HASEGAWA

VILLANELLE ON
LOS ANGELES 1992

She was half his size, but her arm was light years long.
He was straight-backed and strode in never-been-wet boat shoes.
How his soft honey hair jerked when Schoolgirl knocked him down.

Dookie braids escaped gravity on her head made strong
by the verdict of twelve strangers. No change of venue
as her fist to his face broadcast the news light years long.

Our heads bobbed against hazy bus windows all along
the route from Slauson to downtown, but as her fist flew
at McClintock, we all knew that Schoolgirl knocked him down.

The driver whistled low and switched his radio on
as the motor moaned to damns signaling corner coups
that would reveal a city, burn down blocks light years long.

Shopping carts rattled, careened unboxed TVs sidelong.
Out store doors flattened shoeboxes bloomed their grey pulp hues
while men on roofs held rifles 'cause Schoolgirl knocked him down.

Hair trigger, DUI, orange juice, and truncheon wrong
into law of brick and fire. Oh pyriscence, you cruise,
burn through resins, put a spit-shine on fear light years long.
Kam sam ni da. How you like us now? Schoolgirl knocked him down.

TO ANYONE WHO CAN'T GET HOME
(Including Natives, Immigrants, and Extraterrestrials)

The false harbor of home:
washed ashore and alien
again.

This belongs to you.
It does not belong to me.

Before: the steamship
that delivered great-grandfather.

Before: the brigantine
that brought coffee and the first Bible.

Before: the double-hulled canoe
that arrived to find it was not the first.

Slice the water:
the instinct to take up space.

Trace the trajectory:
the instinct to connect points.

From *Hawaiki*,
the place from which we came
and the place we will call home
when we die—back to Babylon,

where there was a tower built
by people speaking a common language.

From the urge to remember
and be remembered—
the *confundation* of language and meaning:
agents of the first
and eternal voyage away.

In darkness,
we pluck the gourd
from which we fling
pulp and seeds into light.

From the bloody mouth
and the destroyer,
we pluck
calamondin thimbleberry mountain apple
and delight
when we mistake the red fur of the tree fern
for a wild boar.

Every birth
is an act of colonization:
mongoose
born to mouse
born to grain.

In defense, we leave places
in exactness:
a typewriter on a desk,
chicken bones in a sink,
an empty bottle of perfume
on a nightstand.

But return
and return again
to these places
only to find ghosts
clicking keys,
touching bones,
and inhaling the last traces
of home.

JENNIFER HASEGAWA

THE ANCIENT HISTORY OF DAVID BOWIE

When my cousin Dean was sixteen,
he had his psychotic break.

He believed he had to pick up David Bowie
from the airport.

I wanted to believe him.
I wanted to go with him.
I watched my uncle wrestle him
to the floor.

Dean would've driven David
and me down Banyan Drive,
like all the older kids do
on a Sunday afternoon—

>   blasting Cecilio & Kapono
>   mascara
>   tight jeans
>   pocket comb
>   feathered hair
>   gold chain
>   *pakalōlō*
>   cherry lip gloss.

We'd check David in
to the Hukilau Hotel
where Dean's mom cleans rooms
and spends evenings

in the laundry room with Kimo,
who is missing an eye,
but says that the remaining one
is sweet on her.

We'd take David downtown
where the *māhū*
bravely wigged, strong-legged, and hot-lipsticked
adorned the alley
between the barber shop
and the movie theater.

If a family has five sons, the sixth may be raised as a daughter to do the work
of women.
And so his mother said, you, the sixth, the boy closest my corpse, will be the
next noble woman.
Sequential hermaphrodite, *māhū*, *aikāne*: The bridge back to the garden.

Her brother lay with the king, as lover and counselor, chanter and spokesman—
aikāne.
She saw the people with golden books arrive and the infinite sexes became two.
If a family has five sons, the sixth may be raised as a daughter to do the work
of women.

These days, she sleeps on satin. Nights, she cruises the street between the
barbershop
and the movie theater. Tonight, she swears she saw David Bowie.
If a family has five sons, the sixth may be raised as a daughter to do the work
of women.
Sequential hermaphrodite, *māhū*, *aikāne*: The bridge back to the garden.

My dad went to that barbershop
for 50 years, until his barber died.
Toward the end,
he'd come home with lopsided cuts.

"Dat buggah goin' blind!"
my dad mock-complained
as he looked into a mirror
and ran a comb down
the side of his head.

Dean and I went to that movie theater
whenever my mom could spare a few dollars.
The movies were rarely
more interesting than the fireflies
hovering in damp corners.
They danced amongst dust,
illuminating their partners
with ferocity
and a sly vengeance.

RELIEVERS

I was tired of losing, so when they shipped Chun Ho's uncle off to Vietnam, I took it upon myself to find us a new coach for the summer to lead us out of the basement of the Honolulu Little League. All spring I had been working on my slider and rising two-seam fastball, and my dream was to walk into ninth grade proceeded by a reputation as an aggressive inside hurler who couldn't help but bean a few knees and elbows when the situation demanded.

I didn't blame Coach Ho too much, and didn't think of him as a "loser" as some of my other teammates did. Although we didn't quite understand what a draft number meant, even on Muliwai Lane in those days, all of us knew that the announcement of another death of a brother, father, or son was just an Army green sedan away. So I held my tongue on game days when Coach would have us close our eyes, turn our faces to the sun, and have us imagine it was our last day on Earth, playing the last baseball game we would ever play. "What position would you play on that day?" he would ask. Sometimes this exercise was too intense for the younger kids, and I could hear them start to sniffle, but most of us would clamor to play the undeserved positions we only daydreamed about: pitcher, catcher, first base, or shortstop.

As a result, our team specialized in walks since our pitchers could not throw pitches that reached the plate, stolen bases since our jittery catchers were afraid of the ball, and errors since our shortstops were slow of foot and poor in judgment. But if we players were seeing that calamity before us, Coach Ho seemed to be watching another game entirely as he leaned back on the team bench with a broad smile on his face and a dreamy look in his eye.

Most of our fathers were not in the lane that year, some of them, like my dad, were already in Vietnam, and others were working double shifts at the hospital or at the bases to support the troops. No one seemed to have time for baseball except for us kids, and that is why I knew I would have to find a woman to coach our team.

"How about our moms?" Shortshit suggested. Although he was the smallest on the team, he was still our best shortstop. "We could ask one of them."

Dawkins snorted. "What do they know about baseball? They never come out to the games." That wasn't really true, but we overlooked his sentiment because we all knew he hated his mom. She was young so she wore tight bell-bottoms with macramé belts and belly-baring T-shirts, and made everyone call her Julie instead of Mrs. Dawkins. She was much younger than all the rest of our mothers and while that was enough to make Dawkins hate her, for the rest of the team, we were all sort of half in love with her.

"No, we're not looking for baseball knowledge, anyway. We have enough of that already here among us," said Fleabag, our catcher and team philosopher, as he pointed to some of us. "What we lack is someone tough enough to make hard decisions that will turn us into winners."

We all nodded at his sage advice. Could any of our moms be considered tough? There were some like my family whose dads were not around and moms had to go it alone. But even then, these same moms would later look at us a certain way and suddenly crush us with their hugs while they murmured something about high school and just four years from the draft. We all agreed that this latent sentimentality disqualified them from the tough category.

Someone mentioned Shane's mom, and we all turned to look at him. His mom had gone from housewife to Big Boss when she took over the house painting business that Shane's dad had to abandon when he got arrested and convicted for trying to liberate several cases of liquor from the back of Chun Hoon Supermarket in the middle of the night. But he just shook his head, "She paints during the day and cries at night," he said. He looked at his shoes and kicked at the dust. "I think that's all she can handle."

His admission stilled us and we quietly looked away from each other. That is when I saw my grandmother stride out of the lane and jaywalk across the street, gliding along with an orthopedic cane in each hand pumping like a dryland cross-country skier as she propelled herself into the breach that the rest of us called 7-Eleven.

—

I was already in the 7-Eleven by the time the Boy caught up with me, but I couldn't see him because the overhead lights in that place had immediately blinded me. I tried to tell him to watch out, that the lights were too bright and that he was too young to go blind, but all I heard coming out of my mouth was, "Augh, augh, augh."

"Grandma! What are you doing?" I heard him say behind me.

I swung around at the sound of his voice and my right cane struck the doorframe just over his head. It reverberated in that empty store like a gunshot. "I can't see! I can't see! It's like looking into the face of God over here!"

"What are you talking about?" he said. I could feel him push my back trying to get me further into the store, so I spread my legs and locked the left cane. No way was I going further into that phosphorescent maw. In that brilliant glare, I could just make out the registers, and noticed that the teen clerk had already crouched down and was peering at us from behind the safety of his counter.

"At least get out of the doorway," the Boy said. A second shot was fired as I banged the other side of the doorway with my cane while I was bringing it around. Couldn't he see that the lights were too bright? I tried to jab my cane toward the ceiling but the newspaper rack was placed too close to the door. Somehow, I caught the corner of the newspaper rack, which sent it keeling over and vomiting its load of newspapers all over the floor like a drunk.

I could hear the clerk talking to someone on the phone, either corporate or the cops, and before I could bang the doorway one more time and get another shot off, the Boy grabbed me around the waist, pinned my arms to my sides, and wrestled me out of the store. All I could do was beat on his shins with my canes until he released me in the parking lot. Even then, I noticed he stood between me and the store entrance.

"Every week they find some new way to kill me, and you do nothing," I said.

"They are not trying to kill you. . . ."

"Oh, yeah? Why the bright lights this week? They're trying to blind me. . . ."

"All the 7-Elevens are like that. . . ."

That could be true. I hadn't considered that. There was only one conclusion. "Then they're trying to kill all of us."

"Us?" said the Boy.

"Yes, us. All of us old people."

He just looked at the ground and shook his head. It was children like this Boy in front of me that was the problem. If Old Man Tamura had raised his kids right, when he went and died, his kids would have come back from the mainland and taken over his place, not end up selling the entire corner lot to the 7-Eleven Corporation. But 7-Eleven, by bombarding every mailbox in the neighborhood with a coupon for a free half-gallon of milk, was the really nefarious one. How could I get the Boy to understand that the floors of the new 7-Eleven were not the sticky, comforting floors of Tamura's Superette, but a too shiny and too slippery modern substitute that spoke of the Corporation's plot to rid the neighborhood of old people by breaking their hips?

Sirens in the distance seemed to grow louder. "Let's go," he said pulling my arm and leading me out of the parking lot. "Why you gotta wage war with them every week?"

"Because I still want my free milk," said I, shaking my coupon at him.

—

We entered the first week of the season without a coach and to say we lost the first game would be to understate the magnitude of our defeat. Molasses, the slowest player on the team and our first baseman, had forgotten his glove, and so for the first inning, the infield was rolling the ball to him to try and make an out. When that didn't work, I gave him my glove since I was the only other left-hander on the team. But since I was pitching, I couldn't hide my grip on the baseball and the other team was able to read my pitches early and hit me deep into the outfield. Because the outfield was so busy running down fly balls and home runs, our centerfielder Salty Meat started getting sick, so he sat in the grass behind second base and started throwing up the beef jerky he was constantly chewing on. Dawkins and Carter, the remaining outfielders, saw that Salty Meat was allowed to sit down, and sat as well, only rising when the ball was hit to them. Only Shortshit at shortstop was able to make any plays, and even then he had to field the grounders and then run down the batters and tag them, because as he said, "I may be Shortshit but the rest of you guys are just shit."

The umpire stopped the game in the third inning after the other team was up by fifteen, and awarded the win to them because "by the nature of our play" he determined that we would never be able to catch up. The other team volunteered to spot us 10 points so that we could continue playing, but Fleabag picked up the baseball threw it over the fence into the street and walked off the field. The umpire shrugged and declared, "I guess I'm done here," and left the field as well.

The other team started to pack up their gear, but since this was our home diamond, we just left our stuff on the field and made our way to the water fountain to console ourselves. After jostling myself into a respectable place in line at the water fountain someone said, "Hey, Lefty, isn't that your grandma?" and we all looked to where he was pointing.

Sure enough, there was Grandma wading out into the busy four-lanes of Nuʻuanu Avenue. Like Moses parting the sea, cars stopped suddenly around her as she slowly crossed over to the far gutter to retrieve Fleabag's angry baseball before waving it over her head at us and making her way back. Stillness gripped Nuʻuanu Avenue until Grandma hoisted herself back onto the sidewalk, and the cars roared back to life, flooding the avenue with motion once more.

We watched Fleabag join her at the sidewalk and then engage her in a lively conversation. I knew the only reason Grandma had gotten the ball was because she couldn't stand to see anything go to waste, even if it was a game she really didn't understand. Still, their conversation seemed to go on longer than any I had ever had with her, and when she handed the ball over to Fleabag at the end of their conversation, I could swear that he had also shaken her hand.

—

I walked over to the water fountain where they had all gathered and cut to the front where I pushed Shane off the pipe. "What the hell, Fleabag," I heard him say. I bent my head down and took a long draw. The water tasted like it always did: gritty with a strong iron tang and as hot as a fresh cup of coffee. Why do we always drink this? I kept my head down there longer than usual, then dunked my whole head into the flow, letting the water stream all over my head.

I had their attention now. I wiped my mouth on my sleeve, turned around, and let them have it, "Well, boys, I found us a coach."

"No," Lefty said, a little too loudly, I thought.

"Yup, your grandma," I said pointing at him, "has agreed to coach the team for the entire season."

Lefty crumpled over as if my words were a foot into his groin, "Oh, God," he groaned.

It was a brilliant idea, but when I looked around, the rest of the team looked as puzzled as pop quiz day during math class. I couldn't believe it, not one of them could see the potential of this pairing. "Look, guys, she's perfect. She's just what we need." I looked at Lefty who was shaking his head like a fighter recovering from a body blow. "Just ask Lefty."

They turned their quizzical faces to Lefty, and to my surprise he did a sort of dance like his feet were on fire. I knew exactly what I was seeing, all those hours spent watching Saturday morning cartoons had prepared me to witness a person wanting to run but not being able to be move forward. Maybe Lefty was really waiting for the bank vault or grand piano to fall from the sky on top of him. I don't know. In the end, all he did was point accusingly back at me.

I sighed. Had he forgotten? "Your grandma is an expert on taking on lost causes and turning them around, right? That's what my mom told me."

He nodded. At least he couldn't deny that. So I explained to the team how before us, Lefty's grandma had been babysitter who specialized in taking care of kids whose mothers had just died. She would swoop right in after the death of a young mother and stay with the family for about nine months or so, by which time dad and the kids could usually hold it together. "Mom told me that a job like that might weaken a person over a time, but Lefty's grandma seemed to draw strength from it. All those years, she would work from family to family, substituting for the dead, propping families up and putting lives back on track." I turned to Lefty to address him directly. "And what are we, if not a lost cause? This team could use someone who knows her away around bringing the dead back to life."

Shortshit started nodding and pounding his glove and the rest of the team soon followed. I smiled when teammates started happily slapping Lefty on the back, but nothing seemed to dislodge his gloom. "I don't understand," he said. "What does she get out of it?"

"Eh, she did say something about wanting to borrow my catcher's gear when I'm not using it," I said. My gear was really dirty, so I started pounding my chest protector with my palm and years of dust started rising from me like puffs of smoke. The guys started backing away from me and soon only Lefty was still standing next to me. When I was done, he was covered in a veil of smoke like a demon just summoned from the underworld. "She even wanted the shin guards."

"What?"

I shrugged. "I don't know, she said something about needing more protection when she goes to 7-Eleven."

—

The Boy eyes me at dinner. He thinks I don't know that he doesn't want me to coach his team. What he doesn't know is that I don't really want to coach his team, either. I know losers when I see them. But that fat boy's equipment is a wondrous thing. "What's that fat boy's name on your team?"

"Which fat boy," he says.

"You know, the one with the equipment."

"Fleabag?"

"Yeah, that's it." Even though he had a lousy nickname, that kid could drive a hard bargain. "How come he's the only one who gets to wear all that?"

"He's a catcher, Grandma," the Boy tells me, "they all have to wear that equipment." I watch him shovel more food on his fork and throw it back into his mouth. Even when I was cooking for all those unfortunate families, the appetites of teenaged boys always amazed me. Where did it all go? Not to their brains, I would think. "You know," he continues, "that's why you shouldn't be coaching our team. You don't even know what a catcher is."

"I do," I tell him.

"What?"

"The catcher," I say, "is the one who catches the ball."

"From who," he says accusingly.

"From the thrower, obviously," I say.

"The pitcher, you mean," he sneers.

"That's the problem with your team, too many pitchers, not enough throwers."

"What? What does that mean?"

Sometimes when you are swimming in the ocean, you will hit a patch of water where the tide suddenly gets more powerful, much stronger than area around it. And you have to stroke much faster and more deliberately to fend it off for a little while before you can move forward again. I could feel myself entering those waters now. "Your team could use a little more raw energy and a little less by-the-book."

He just shakes his head and says, "You know, Grandma, I'm the team's pitcher."

I nod my head like I knew that. "That's what I mean, you and Fleabite out there, thinking all these thoughts, these baseball thoughts, instead of just going out there and letting your enemy know you know what's going on and you're here to vanquish them and win." I bang the table with my fist for a little emphasis and catch the end of the fork. It flips end over end in a slow arc over the table before the boy grabs it in mid-air and returns it back to the surface. I think, maybe there is hope for his team after all.

He just snorts a laugh out and says, "Whatever, Grandma. Just remember that as the coach you need to be there in the park when practice starts at 3:30."

"Every day?"

"Every day."

—

At first, I didn't know what to think about this old lady coaching our team, I mean, instead of running the practice like he normally does, Fleabag spent most of the first practice explaining baseball to the old lady. I mean, when I walked behind them to get a drink from the water fountain, I could hear him explaining real basic stuff like outs and walks and shit. Then, the next practice comes and she doesn't want to talk to anyone. Fleabag offers to work with her again and even her own grandson, Lefty, tries to get a few words in, but she sort of waves both of them away like they were annoying mosquitoes. She just watches us the entire time, and I don't mean with the bored expressions our parents watch us with, but like how a cat watches a bird for twenty minutes before pouncing and tearing it to pieces.

The whole time, I am thinking how is this supposed to make us better? I mean, she's not offering us any suggestions, not saying anything when we make some boneheaded mistake, and definitely has no advice when we go up to bat. But all practice long, for almost a week, she just watches with those steely eyes of hers, taking it all in like a prison guard minding the cons. Then on Friday, after our last practice before our second game, she sits us down to "make a few announcements."

First, she points at me with her cane and says, "This little kid here is the only one who is in his correct spot. So he will continue to play Shortshit."

"I'm Shortshit," I say to her.

"I know," she says, "that's what I just said."

"I'm Shortshit," I say again pointing to myself. Then I point out to the field. "And I play shortstop. Short. Stop."

She just rolled her eyes. "Whatever you say." Then she turned to the rest of the team and waved her cane at them and said, "The rest of you are all playing the wrong positions. I don't know who told you kids that you should be playing those positions, but come Saturday all of that is going to change."

Stunned silence was followed by an immediate uproar. Rather than being alarmed, the old lady seemed to enjoy it, basking in it like high praise.

"For example," she said loudly pointing at Lefty, "This one here, my own flesh and blood, will be moved from the throwing mound to deep center."

Lefty looked stunned. We all knew he considered himself our ace. Before he had a chance to say anything though, ex-centerfielder Salty Meat asked, "What about me?"

"You, Salty Meat, have no arm to speak of. Out there, you can barely throw the ball back to the infield," she said. I started to think that maybe she was paying attention. Although Salty had speed, she was right about his arm, he threw like an off-balance duck. "So I'm moving you closer to the action." She pointed to second base. "Maybe over there by the middle base."

We all looked at second base and then at each other. Lefty had a look on his face like he had just drunk sour milk, but Fleabag was nodding his head. "Well, at least you'll be closer to second base in case you need to throw up again," he said to Salty Meat.

Cries of "where am I playing, where am I playing" rose from the team but the old lady just raised one cane like a conductor's baton and motioned for silence. "All will be revealed tomorrow," she said, "all the changes."

"Except for me, Shortshit," I said. "Right, Coach?"

Coach nodded and winked at me. Lefty just glared at me. But like I said, I think this old lady knows what she is doing. At least she got one thing right.

—

One thing about baseball, too many goddamn rules. I still don't know anything about the game, even though that kid Fleabite spent a day trying to explain it to me. At the end of the day, I figured if he knew the rules so well, maybe I should focus on something else. So, I moved everybody around, what else was I going to do? They can't keep doing the same thing and expecting something to change. Sort of like with that damned 7-Eleven. All my neighbors agree that the floors are too slick, the lights too bright, the music too loud, etcetera, etcetera. But they say they don't know what to do. Really? They don't know what to do?

"We have to take the fight to THEM," I told the kids before the game.

My grandson, who is miserable I took him off the mound, scoffed, and said, "What does that mean?" And I don't really blame the Boy for being upset, but really, I was tired of him tracking that mud and dirt from the mound onto my porch. Let someone else deal with that for a change.

"We get out early, we score some points," I said.

"And we don't look back," said Fleabite. I was beginning to like that kid more and more.

So the start of the game got delayed because I couldn't tell the two haole boys apart. You tell me, two tall white boys with short hair and ball caps, and I was supposed to figure out who was who? It was like I was seeing twins out there, Dawkins and Carter. I just had them play next to each other in the outfield so I could keep my eye on them. It wasn't till after the game that I figured out that Dawkins was the one with the hoochie-mama mother but by that time it was too late.

Watching the game was an education. The armor that the catcher wears seems pretty impervious to any kind of knockabout. Balls in the dirt bouncing up and banging into the shins, direct shots to the chest, even a few ricocheting off the helmet, that Chinese boy Chun Ho didn't even cry once. I had him play catcher so I could learn how to don the armor. Every inning Fleabite had to teach Chun Ho how to put it on: First, shin guards strapped up in the back, followed by the chest protector over the head and cinched on the sides, and that glorious helmet over the top. By the third or fourth inning, I knew that I would have no trouble getting it ready for my needs this coming Sunday at the 7-Eleven. I was even thinking of uses for that round padded glove he was wearing when the game seemed to end.

"Okay, we didn't quite win this game," I said to the boys after it was all over. "But this time at least we got to finish the game."

Some of the boys were nodding their heads, but some of them seemed skeptical. The Boy, especially, looked dismayed. "When fighting a faceless enemy, sometimes you lose the early battles before you figure out how to win the war," I explained. "So what do we do? We pick ourselves off that cold, slick floor, check ourselves for injuries, and finding none, we vow to return next week to battle again."

More boys were nodding their heads now. "Yeah, no one got injured," said Molasses.

"That's because you dodged practically every hard hit that came your way at third base," said Shortshit.

"At least he moved," said Shane, "When he was playing first base, it was hard for him to even bend down to get the ball."

We all agreed that movement was an improvement for Molasses. More boys stepped up and offered that Salty Meat did not throw up this time, Fleabag seemed less itchy since he moved to first base and was out from under the catcher's equipment, and even Shane suggested that he was better for the team at pitcher because, "pitchers aren't expected to hit well" and he had a natural talent for missing the ball with his bat.

By the time they left the field, I felt things were looking up; At least the team was leaving with a better attitude than the one they came to the field with. Only the Boy looked downcast as I made him carry the catcher's gear back to house so I could clean it up and try to remove the teenage-boy stink.

—

My breakfast was ruined when Grandma stepped into the kitchen wearing Fleabag's gear. She looked like a scarecrow in slipshod armor, like the whole thing was trying to pull her down to the ground. She strutted into kitchen, the shin guards flapping against her legs creating a ripple of applause every time she walked. Her face was radiant inside the catcher's mask and her eyes sparkled with new vitality. It was like she had been invited to a Costume Ball for the Insane.

"Well, what do you think?" she asked. She turned to give me an eyeful and I noticed that she had somehow managed to tie the round catcher's mitt to her hips, like a leather bumper for her backside. "Of course, I'll be holding the cane in this hand," she said, holding up her right hand.

"Umm, I. . . ."

"Yes, eyes. I'm well protected there." She swung her cane up toward her face where it hit the mask and bounced off, leaving a delicate tone in the air. "All I need now is a shield for my other hand."

"A shield?" I suddenly imagined my grandmother as the lone samurai in all those Japanese movies I had seen, surrounded by a circle of bad guys as she battles each of them to death until she was the last one standing. In a 7-Eleven. "What do you need a shield for?"

"To get milk," she said, waving the coupon as she skipped out the door.

—

I found the perfect shield on my way out the lane, sitting there on top of Old Man Wong's trashcans. I grabbed the handle of the metal trash can lid and held it in front of me. Light, not too smelly, and not really my concern if it gets a little smashed up. Who's going to notice? Old Man Wong was in his 90s and could barely see anyway.

I had to admit, that fat boy's helmet was a little too big for me, so my head rattled a bit inside of it. I couldn't really look up either, so it made it hard for me to see the traffic light. But that didn't seem to matter because as I approached the corner across from the 7-Eleven, the traffic seemed to slow down and stop for me. There was a kindred spirit in one of the cars because I heard him say to his companion, "That's why I don't go the 7-Eleven anymore," and I raised my cane and shield in agreement with his assessment of the dangers that lay ahead of me. He gunned his car engine in affirmation.

I crossed the parking lot and straightened my fanny protector before stepping onto the automatic doormats. The door opened with a hiss and a blast of frigid air-conditioned air tried to bowl me over. I put my shield up and pulled the chest protector tighter around me and fought back this wintry attack, making my way to the sales counter. Again, the group of people at the counter stepped back, awed by my outfit and sense of purpose. The young man behind the counter stared at me. I lowered my helmet to protect myself from the bright lights and battled his wordless challenge with my own formidable gaze.

Eons seemed to pass as the tick-tick-tick of the Slurpee machine metered out the time. Finally he broke down and said, "Ma'am is there something you need?" I scoffed at his attempt to belittle me with his "Ma'am" putdown. "Milk," I growled.

With a shaking hand, he pointed to a row of refrigerator units at the back of the store. Shiny metallics and bright colors sang their siren songs from behind the glass doors, trying to distract me from the solid sheet of ice that was the floor, which reflected white glare here and there from the unforgiving lights above. I slapped the coupon on the counter. "Challenge accepted, little man," I said.

As I moved forward across that frosted wasteland—cane forward, then shield, cane forward, then shield—my confidence began to grow. Just then saxophones began to wail from some music just on top of me, but I ignored their distracting lament and continued on my perilous journey. When I reached that refrigerated gateway, I could see the half-gallons from every species eyeing me—two percent, skim, even the heavy whipping—but I opened that portal and grabbed me a whole. The smoothness of the carton surprised me, and I tucked it into the crook of my left arm behind the shield for safekeeping. Its heft, I figured, would give me comfort on my journey back.

I blame the Boy for what happened next, for as I was about halfway back to the counter, a full three-quarters of my mission complete, the entrance doors slid open I saw him bound into the store and look wildly around. Again, the minion at the counter pointed his shaking hand toward me, and just as the Boy saw and started advancing in my direction, the floor beneath me started to shift. Already off-balance on my left side from my half-gallon load, I felt the world starting to tip so I swung my arms out for balance and prepared for ground impact.

—

The next thing I see is an explosion of Pringles as Grandma's cane beheads a row of cans on the shelf, followed by the dull thud of the half-gallon of milk hitting the floor. The trash can lid flies out of her hand like she was Captain America, and she slowly turns and bounces on the carton of milk which erupts in a fountain that sends milk all over the candies on the lower racks, before hitting the floor in a clatter of catchers gear, milk, and Pringle shards.

For a moment, none of us move, dazzled by Grandma's performance. It's only when the clerk whispers, "Is she dead?" that we come to our senses. I rush over to the aisle and roll her over. Her eyes are closed and I start to think the worst while I pat her down beneath the equipment, feeling for broken bones. I can hear the clerk on the phone already, calling for an ambulance.

"Quit feeling me up," she growls as her eyes snap open, "I'm not one of your floozy girlfriends."

"Oh, thank God," I hear myself say, much to my surprise. Grandma raises herself up to a sitting position and starts to struggle with her helmet. I unsnap the straps in the back and take it off her head.

"Everything was fine till you got here," she informs me. She gazes at the chaos around her. Rivulets of milk escape from the aisle, carrying boats of fake potato chips along with them. "If it weren't for you, I would have made it."

The sirens approached loudly and suddenly cut off. There was a bustle at the door as the paramedics wheeled in a gurney before reaching me and pushing me aside. I stepped back and watched my grandmother sit in a pool of milk and calmly answer their questions. I even found myself feeling a little proud of her as she slapped their hands away as they tried to remove the shin guards and chest protector from her body.

"This is the only thing that saved me," she told them. "You think I'm going to take this off?"

The paramedics retreated and lifted her onto the gurney, milk-soaked equipment and all. I led the parade of onlookers into the parking lot as they loaded her into the back of the ambulance.

"Don't forget my coupon," she yelled from the ambulance before they closed the doors. "It's still on the counter."

"Okay," I yelled back. "I'll make sure to tell him you didn't use it yet."

—

Instead of practice, Fleabag suggested we all go and visit Coach in the hospital after school on Monday. When we got there, everyone was talking about her because she refused to take off Fleabag's shitty equipment, and so she was laying in bed, starting to stink up the place. I've always been proud of my Korean heritage mainly because of their development of the world's first biological weapon—kimchi—but I can say without reservation that two-day-old rotten milk is the new stinky champ. I mean the smell was so bad that some of us who were standing around her bed were starting to tear up, as if the stench had tired of assaulting our noses, so it started attacking our eyes.

Coach noticed and patted my hand and said, "Don't worry, Shortshit, the girls here are taking good care of me."

I didn't know what to say. I was afraid of opening my mouth and ingesting more of that odor, so I just wiped my tears.

"I know you need this for practice," she said to Fleabag as she reached next to the bed and pulled out his helmet. Fleabag drew back like she had pulled out the head of the opposing pitcher.

"Uh, no, you can keep it," he said. "I don't think we can wear that anymore."

"That shit smells like road kill," I said, "I don't think anyone can wear that anymore."

Then, Lefty says, "Maybe you should take it. In fact, maybe we should take all of it. For PRACTICE, like she said."

Fleabag shook his head like he was trying to shake off lice. But I understood where Lefty was going with this. "Yeah, Lefty's right, Coach. We should take it all home so we can PRACTICE." I looked around the bed at the rest of the team, but they still stood there like dumbasses. I sighed. "Yeah, we can spare everyone and take it all now and just get it out of here." I accepted the helmet.

That seemed to get everyone going and they helped Coach remove all of her rank gear. It was like skinning an animal, removing all the outside layers till there is just bones underneath. They piled it all on top of me, and I wasted no time trying to get out of there. As I was leaving the room, I could see the nurses mouthing silent "thank you's" to us as we walked past their station.

I was just planning to shitcan the whole mess in the Dumpsters by the parking structure but Lefty said, "I have a better idea," and he took everything from me. We followed behind our putrid Pied Piper as he walked from the hospital to the 7-Eleven, where he stepped inside of the store and dropped the whole mess on the floor in front of the counter.

—

So, Grandma was home from the hospital only a few hours when 7-Eleven started sending these guys to the house trying to make up with her. She didn't let them in the house, she left them pleading on the porch.

"A lifetime's supply of milk," the first one told her through the screen door, a freckled face young man with red hair. He didn't say it, but I could see it in his eyes and the way he fidgeted. They are afraid of a personal injury lawsuit.

"Why would I want that?" she told him. "I'm lactose intolerant."

He looked at her, then at me and frowned. "Why were you using a coupon for free milk, then?"

She closed the door in his face. "If he doesn't understand why people like free stuff, I can't help him," she told me.

Successions of young men like him came to the house but each seemed stupider than the one before. They offered her free lifetime delivery services ("Goodness, you mean from all the way across the street," she said before closing the door), free cigarettes ("I quit smoking decades ago, are you trying to kill me?"), and even a free 7-Eleven emblazoned vehicle that they drove up to the house ("If that car is designed like your stores, you really are trying to kill me.") Each of them left empty-handed until they sent an older woman in high heels who told Grandma that she was the "Corporate Counsel."

"Is that supposed to mean something to me?" Grandma asked as she closed the door.

Corporate Counsel stuck her foot in the doorway and the door bounced off her expensive pump, "Only that I am the boss and am authorized to make any deal I need to," she said.

I didn't know whether it was her words or her foot which made an impression on Grandma, but she considered Corporate again. "There's nothing I need from you," she said.

"We need a new set of catcher's equipment," I reminded Grandma from across the room.

"Except new catcher's equipment," she told Corporate. We watched her write something onto a memo pad. "Make sure it will fit a fat boy."

"Done," Corporate said, "What else can I do for you?"

Grandma looked at me. I shrugged. I was thinking maybe a lifetime supply of soda, but Grandma said, "I'm tired of coaching those losers. Maybe you can get them a real coach."

"No problem," she said, continuing to scribble. "We can sponsor them, get them new uniforms, find someone to make sure they aren't an embarrassment to the brand."

"Yeah, yeah, yeah, that's enough about them. What I want are sticky floors, dim lighting, and silence in your stores," she informed Corporate Counsel.

A couple of hours of haggling later, Grandma settled for changes at our corner 7-Eleven. Rubber mats on the floor in high-traffic areas, a free pair of prescription sunglasses, and Japanese music played between the hours of 1:00–3:30 p.m., the hours most likely for Grandma to shop, "After the wretched single men who had to buy their lunches at a convenience store," she said, "and before the damn after-school kids."

The ceasefire agreement with the 7-Eleven Corporation lasted as long as she lived. And while she didn't live long enough to see us kids from the team graduate and go our separate ways, whether that be draft-mandated or volunteer, she would have been proud to know that I did earn a reputation as a centerfielder with a cannon for an arm that served me well during my tours, that Shortshit continued to not grow and was found lacking by the Review Board, and that Fleabag became a bulkier backstop during his high school playing days and used that experience to shield his squad mates during an attack and came back home to be buried as a hero. 🥢

ANN INOSHITA

I STAY ON DA PHONE

Sometimes me and my sista playing wen our madda talk on da phone.
We make big noise, and our madda cover da phone wit her hand and say,
"I stay on da phone!"
Den she talk into da phone and say stuff like,
"I'm sorry. Could you repeat that again? Thank you."

She take da pen by da end table and write down notes on one paper pad.
Afta dat, she hang up and tell us,
"You guys! You know, I on da phone. No fool around. Hard fo hear, you know."

I ask my madda, "Why you talk li'dat on da phone? Sound fake."
She explain to me, "Sometime, you gotta talk like dat wen you talk to people."

I neva understand. I must look confused cuz my madda tell me,
"You going see. Later, wen you work or gotta do errands, you going talk to all
kine people. Most of dem going talk like how I talk on da phone. Das how."

I watch my mom pay bills.
Boring, so me and my sista tink of one nodda game fo play.

PLATES ARE FO FOOD

Afta my bachan passed away, we still get her Singer sewing machine.
Gotta press down da metal plate wit your foot each time you like sew.

We get da washboard dat she used fo hand wash clothes,
and we get da wood safe wit da screen door fo store food.

We use da big metal pot wit handmade metal wire handle
wheneva my madda make turkey soup
cuz no can find big pots li'dat anymore.

We use da plates stamped wit "MADE IN OCCUPIED JAPAN"
in red letters on da odda side of da plate.

I hold da plate in my hand and sound like Indiana Jones
wen I tell my madda, "Dis. Belongs. In. One. Museum."

My madda no answer, and she grab one bottle tsukemono from da fridge.
For dinner, I put rice, tonkatsu, and tsukemono on da plate,
and I eat cuz plates are fo food.

ANN INOSHITA

WAIPAHU GET EVERYTING YOU NEED

Fo grocery shopping, get Daiei and Times.
Get fabric fo make clothes at Cornet
and senbei at Ishiharaya.
Need one new fridge? Go Midtown Radio.
I bought my first Hawaiian ring from Arakawa's.

Wheneva had field trip, my madda orda bentos from Hamada's Okazuya.
Sato's Okazuya get ono fried noodle wit barbeque stick.
Everybody know Highway Inn and Tanioka's.

Befo time, my madda used to work Tawata Saimin Stand.
I thought da place was like da saimin stands in Japanese movies.
Turns out, was one regular eating place in one building.
She used to make vanilla cokes and any kine sodas while going business school.

My bachan was one fry cook at Country Inn.
Every time she asked my madda wat she like eat befo she left work.
My madda always say, "Cheeseburger and fries."

My jichan was one machinist fo da plantation,
and my fadda was one installer/repair man fo Hawaiian Tel.
Only my madda work in town, as one bookkeeper.

Waipahu get everyting you need
except wen you gotta go Cinerama Theater
fo watch *Star Wars*.

SABRINA ITO

NIGHT FLIGHT

En route from Japan, stretched out for sleep
across three empty passenger seats,

I am wearing my yellow pyjamas
with brown soldier stripes on the sleeves.
I hate them. They are too big for me.
There are no bottoms.

As I pretend to sleep,
I grate my bare toes
against the tight tucked sheets
I am wrapped in—
the only thing that now,
smells familiar.

Not like the plumy scent of American-style coffee,
or the wispy veils of Marlboro smoke
that tap, tap, tap from thin, silver ashtrays.

There is strange music on this plane—
the engine rumbles like an upset stomach
I hear the whispers of my parents,
hushed and sad.

I remember how I pressed my cheek into the metal armrest,
preferring the sting of its cold, the hardness of it.
Anything was better than what was to come.
The word was, "immigration,"
though I did not know that yet.

LOVE RUN DRY

To measure love in any way
is gonna be a challenge.
I think I am run dry,
way past the dregs
at the bottom of the barrel.
Hurot na.
Used up.
Nada mas.
Hele wale.
Zero.

Love that use to pull taut
through my every fiber of being
with electric passion
and mother-bear strength of mind
and blade-sharp purpose
has now, at best,
morphed into comfort,
compatibility,
contentment,
ease,
humor,
and endurance.
These things on a good day.

Yet lately
there is even less —
merely scratchy irritation
and a desire to leave it all behind,
to vanish into some cave,

maybe rent a condo for myself alone.
I don't want to love.
I just want to breathe,
and think,
or not think,
as long as I'm alone.

And it nags at me,
this shift in perception.
Is love dead to me?
Have I become stone woman?
Do I even care about people anymore?
And worse,
do I care that I don't care?

Then last night, another responsibility to fulfill.
A gathering down Hilo side,
in an old carport
beside a backyard stream
that tangles its way toward Wailoa ponds.
We sat at long tables, twenty or so of us,
acquaintances, friends who rarely meet,
sharing shoyu chicken,
roast turkey, beef stew,
chili rice, purple potato,
leafy greens, beany nachos,
potato chips, ice kūlolo,
chocolate cake.

And after the food came the music.
A dozen ukulele, a few guitars.
Songs we knew, or sorta knew,
or wanted to know.
Mostly Hawaiian,
Or hapa haole,

Or little bit rock 'n' roll 70s.
Sing along. Hum along. Harmonize.
Or get up and hula.

A pause. Get a can of guava juice from the chest.
Mound another paper plate with rice and stew.

Our host tells stories of this old house.
Him a kid, rode his cow down the hill
to the old Safeway,
tied it out front, bought candy,
and rode that wide old cow
back up the hill.
A real cowboy he was.
We laugh, picturing it.

More music. More food. Night rain.
And folks start to drift away.
Here, take stew,
chicken, rice.
enough for family.
Get plenny, take more.

By the time I was packing up my guitar
saying aloha to these old friends
and thinking of my comfortable family
and warm home,
I'd rediscovered love.
Simple. It was there all along.

The event describes a gathering at Keoki Kahumoku's house on Ululani Street in Hilo in 2015.

EVERYDAY MAGIC

The gift of everyday magic
showered upon us
like the fat drops
that pelted thick
from Hilo's darkening skies.

It was the end of a day
of music—old style, new style
lickety-split ukuleles
and deep throat guitars
that dipped or roared
or twinkled or plunked
with heartbeat rhythms.

The master was into
the second song of his set
when the sound system quit.
Just like that,
room-blasting reverb
froze to sudden silence.

But not quite silence after all,
for there remained
the soft acoustic tenor
of his old Tacoma guitar.

Without amplification,
his voice was lost,
overwhelmed by rivers
of rain on the tin roof,

yet, just barely, we heard
the pulse of the old guitar.

It was the crowd,
a hundred of us,
who picked up the song,
voices like whispers
of the sea itself
"He leo, no ke kai, ē"
never overpowering
the faint kī hō'alu
of the master.

The voices of many
sustained the song
and my skin prickled
from the strength
of that collective voice,
carrying,
gently,
simply,
softly,
naturally.

The master
tilted his head,
lifted a shoulder,
and played on.

It was a Hilo moment.
No big fuss when the power fails.

It happened like that
and the story of Hōlei
never faltered
that rainy Hilo eve.

The everyday magic
of this land
comes with surprising ease
when a hundred whispers
carry the load,
sharing the gift.

The event depicted occurred at the 2015 Big Island Slack Key Festival, when the power went out as Cyril Pahinui performed "Hōlei."

FROM: "IN COMMUNITY — OR — LETTERS TO TAZ"

(in response to a poem by Taz Ahmed, titled
"If Our Grandparents Could Meet")

Dear Taz,

I'm trying to read about the concentration
camps outside of Lahore that held
your grandfather

I comb through the internet
I curse it for being a storyteller
without a soul

I find bits and bytes of information
that build a shell of a structure
too sterile to house your family's truths

Where are the voices that interlace
the iron gates with
records of trains that move
past the point of what maps are drawn
and their stories and their stories
and their stories

We are left to imagine the holes
and fill the memory
and surmise the blankness

I find myself in wonder
with each word I read
of the poems on your family—
What would it have been to
introduce our grandparents?

Would they have endured the summer heat
to dance in honor of our ancestors
and pick apart the proximity of
meaning to tradition?
Would they agree to disagree or
would they nod and say less
in order to hold the
future between us?

Or of the simplest exchange
The same hearty laugh?
The last drunken toast?
The first to begin to sing?

It would've been fun to see them squat
against the sun
and share the shade
of their fleeting respite

And exchange bits of wisdom
in meditations, chants, and duas

And take in the wine
of better memories

And yell toward the devils
of another man's heaven

And trust their memories
would rattle the bones
of their granddaughters

And speak of grandkids who
would someday make them proud

And know that their future
really did have something to
look forward to

Love,
tkk

THE TESTICLE

You know, they say that pets have a kind of telepathy. Like, they can tell when their owners are coming home or something. Normally I'd say that kind of stuff's all bullshit, but if I'm being honest, I buy that theory. After all, I think only children have a kind of telepathy too—only it's for when their parents are splitting up. I know I felt something the day my Dad told me the news. Before it happened, you know? I heard him coming up the stairs to my room, and I could almost tell from the way he was walking. I mean, it was as if just from his footsteps, I could tell that it was time for "the talk." Funny how that works, huh. Four years of sleeping in separate bedrooms, and I was none the wiser. Then five seconds of footsteps on the stairs and I'm fucking, Billy, from *Kramer vs. Kramer*. But I guess that figures, beginnings are always harder to see than endings.

My Dad put in twelve-hour days back then: 7:00 a.m. to 7:00 p.m., seven days a week. I remember he had a ritual in the morning before he left for work, and a ritual when he came home. In the mornings, he'd iron the clothes he'd be wearing for the day into crisp lines. As a kid, I used to think it was like he was putting on armor to protect him from the stress of his job. If the wrinkles and sweat stains he'd come home with were any indication, he was fighting a losing battle. He never complained about work, but I knew that it was hard on him. That's where the second ritual came in; you could always determine how my Dad's day at work had been by how long after he got home his work pants came off. The Johnson report was finished a week early and sales numbers were up? He might make it all the way to his room before peeling them off. The board of directors was on vacation and he'd been asked to personally lay off an entire department? Those pants were gone before his shoes. I guess you could say it was habit, but I always liked to think of it as a kind of defiance. Almost as if his job could take away his free time, his marriage, and his relationship with his kid, but he'd be goddamned if it forced him to wear chinos for any fucking longer than he absolutely had to.

Like I said before, I suspected something was wrong from the way he came up the stairs.

I felt a kind of cold come over me. Maybe it's a "deer in the headlights" sort of thing, I don't know, but it was definitely *something*. So, I guess I should say ahead of time, on that particular day my friends and I had met up after school to get crossfaded—you know, being drunk and high at the same time? I'd started smoking weed earlier that year, once we moved into our new house in Mānoa. There was this sort of covered patio near the stream that ran through the property. My parents never went down there, so my friends and I started using it to smoke. Looking back, there's no way they didn't know what was going on, but they never said anything at the time. Anyway, the point is I'd been out of sorts since around 4:00. My dad came back around 7:00, and if you know anything about getting crossfaded, you know it sticks with you. Three hours in and I was functional, but certainly not ready to go on any kind of elaborate father-son emotional journey.

So when my dad poked his head in, pantsless, and dropped a "Zeke, we need to talk" on me, I was understandably unprepared.

As was our tradition in times of obvious emotional tension, I used humor to hide my true feelings.

"Don't tell me," I drawled, "you're breaking up with me?"

My father sighed.

"Well, you're half right. Can I come in?"

I motioned for him to come in, and he crossed the room to sit on my bed next to me.

Now, I'd like to tell you that we had a real heart-to-heart here. Like the kind you see in movies? All childhood montages and Elliot Smith. I'd like to tell you that this was a real pivotal moment in my life, built up by everything that preceded it and responsible for everything that would follow.

But that's when I saw it.

The testicle.

Sitting on my bed in front of me, his work pants long since discarded, an intrepid nut had managed to fall out of one side of his boxers. It sat there as he spoke, pulsating slightly in time with his words.

"Look, Zeke, I know the last few years . . . well, things haven't exactly turned out the way I'd planned. This stuff at work, I mean, I don't know how much you've picked up on, but . . . well, it's not going well. We really overextended getting this new house, and to be honest things between me and your mom . . ."

He trailed off. His eyes sought mine, but I remained transfixed. Words washed over me like the "wamp-wamp" of Charlie Brown's adults. Like Proust with a madeleine, I had been consumed by some strange avalanche of emotional realization.

"The truth is that your mother and I have simply grown apart. We hardly see each other anymore."

I used to live in a testicle.

"With me at work all the time, and your mom's work with the Board, we've become separate people."

The improbability of my birth flashed through my head. I imagined untold millions of adventurous sperm cells crowding in droves all around me as I sped through my father's epididymis. My comrades and I raced through coils of urethral tubing until bursting into cervical "No Man's Land." It must have been like the Somme, for my would-be brothers and I. Death all around us, even when life has just begun. From all those millions of possible lives, mine was the only one lived. All those senators, businessmen, hard workers . . . all lay dying, unfulfilled potentials splattered on my mother's uterine wall. And here I was, crossfaded and useless at 7:00 on a Tuesday.

I used to live . . . in a testicle.

"I know it sounds cliché, but we want you to know that it's not your fault. In fact, you've been a big part of why we've stayed together for so long. . . . Is anything I'm saying getting through to you?"

I looked up, and held his gaze.

"Do you think our beginnings matter as much as our ends?"

My father raised his eyebrows, and, as if connected by a string, the testicle retreated back into his boxers. "You mean, do the ends justify the means?"

I shook my head. "No, I mean, does the way something starts determine the way it finishes?"

My father looked at me with a face I now know must have been fear. Whatever he was expecting, a question about the fundamental nature of our teleological intentions and results was pretty low on the list.

I'm sure he answered. I could see his lips moving after all. But for some reason, his words didn't mean anything to me. I'm sure I could have understood them intellectually if I'd tried, but the vision of the testicle had awoken in me some strange sense of . . . mortality. It had made real for me the understanding that this life, this fragile, meaningless, luck-dependant spurt of existence was fleeting. That we all start off in someone's ugly wrinkled testicles, and that there are no guarantees. I wanted to run away, to shout from the rooftops, "we all came from someone's balls!" I wanted to grab my father and shake him and make him believe that being 50 and divorced is a gift because in so many possible worlds you died before you could ever even live.

Instead, I nodded.
We hugged.
And we went on with our lives. 🐚

SCOTT KIKKAWA

ITSUMADEMO

Whoever said time heals all wounds had not lived as long as Hideo Takashima nor suffered as much. His elusive picture bride had entered his life back in 1920, a rare sixteen-year-old prize from Yamaguchi for a thirty-year-old fisherman, whose last glimpse of the ken was when his new wife was a snot-nosed child. He had been too busy and too poor to marry before then, only taking the plunge into arranged matrimony when he had scraped up enough to buy his own sampan and a modest house on Ilaniwai Street. The place wasn't much more than a shack with a crude outdoor furo, but it was all his and he didn't have to share his bath water with the rest of an entire camp. When she came down the gangway at Pier 14 from the big steamer from Yokohama, the queen of his Kaka'ako castle had arrived. Sachie. Pale and pretty and delicate like an errant pīkake petal drifting slowly earthward on a lazy breeze.

Hideo Takashima had come to turn himself in for her murder.

It's 1951 and he said he killed her back in '21. Thirty years ago. He showed up in the morning at the receiving desk with his shabby lauhala hat in his hands, eyes milky with tears of regret and cataracts. The desk sergeant called a couple of flatfoots to escort him to a small room we used for "soft" interrogations and interviews, one with a sunny view of Merchant Street through the venetian blinds and a koa-bladed ceiling fan. It was a friendly little room, where we talked to grieving new widows and high-priced haole lawyers, not one of the scarred interior torture chambers, where we beat confessions out of hopheads and rapists and hired guns. The flatfoots seated him like he was some kind of honored guest and even went to fetch him a cup of bad coffee.

Then they called me: Detective Sergeant Francis Hideyuki Yoshikawa. Frankie to my friends, The Sheik to my fellow cops. The only homicide dick that spoke Japanese. Lucky me. The rest of the division was finishing reports and eating malasadas. I got to talk to Hideo Takashima, self-confessed perpetrator of a thirty-year-old homicide.

I entered the little bright room and introduced myself in Japanese. I showed him my gold shield with my eyes down and I bowed at the waist and offered him a business card with two hands in my best onegaishimasu fashion. He gave me a sad half-smile and bowed reflexively and said: "Come, sit down." Like he was the host. He said it in English, to boot.

I thought about the box near my desk being full of grease stains and loose sugar and no malasadas when I got back and how I really didn't need to be missing out because the man spoke English. I also thought about how I was supposed to talk to a witness way outside of town and that this little talk would make me late for that little talk. I pulled a chair out and fished a pack of Lucky Strikes from my coat pocket. I offered him one and he pinched it out with a calloused thumb and forefinger and nodded thanks. I pulled my own out with my lips and lit us both up. I loosened my tie and shrugged off my jacket; I had a feeling we'd be there for a while. We puffed in silence for a few heartbeats before he said something.

"I killed her, you know," he said. He looked out of the window at nothing.

"Killed who?" I asked.

"Sachie. My wife. Thirty years ago. 1921. Exactly thirty years today. That's why I'm here. Anniversary."

"Congratulations. That's sweet and sentimental. How'd you kill her?"

"I choked her in her sleep. Then I took her out on the sampan and dumped her body fifteen, sixteen miles out."

"Efficient," I said. I blew more smoke in the air and stared at his bald, brown pate. "Now the big question: why?"

Hideo Takashima put his cigarette stub out in the black ashtray next to his coffee cup. I pushed the pack of Luckies across the table to him and he took another out. I lit him up and he told me why.

He spoke in a mild, clipped fashion and punctuated the end of each sentence with a sleepy little smile and a bird-like nod. In this way, he told me of Sachie's highly anticipated arrival from Japan, like she was something shiny and expensive with chrome fixtures out of a Sears, Roebuck and Co. catalogue he had ordered months before. The wedding was a small but heartwarming affair in a little teahouse in Kalihi with just a handful of well-wishers and some sake she had brought in her steamer chest for the occasion, part of the modest dowry from her parents. He took her betrothal photograph out of his pocket, crisscrossed with little lines and worn around the edges from years of handling. She was an attractive girl with a small round, pale face and a delicately pointed chin. He rambled on a bit about the evening, especially dwelling on the kimono she wore, like a blazing sunset fading to a snow-white field. There was the long silver pin in her hair, with tiny silver blossoms at the end. There was wistfulness and a longing in his voice, though his eyes remained as bleak and lusterless as a civil servant's career. He never touched her, not even on that wedding night of theirs, though he ached to do so. She was a prize to remain unwrapped and in mint condition, to be polished before being put on display on special occasions then gently repackaged. He was content with possessing her in this way. Then somebody spoiled her.

Takashima woke one night, a year into their new marriage to animal grunts and squeals as large, obscene lumps writhed under her futon in the middle of his modest parlor where she slept. Sachie was with a man, an interloper who sullied the delicate prize awarded to him for years of hard labor at sea, a prize he dared not touch himself.

Burning with shame and rage, he stole back into his room and waited until the intruder was gone. Then he smothered her under the futon until she stopped breathing and bundled her up and loaded her into the bed of the truck he had been borrowing from the neighboring camp to haul fencing lumber. He spirited the blanket-wrapped body to his sampan and cast off in the dead of night from Kewalo Basin. He sailed until the lights of Honolulu were like tiny candles in paper lanterns cast adrift on a sable stream. Then he tied a couple of ballast stones to the futon bundle and dropped it over the starboard side and watched it descend into the cold, black depths of hell. The last he saw of her was the moonlight catching the silver hairpin as it drifted down with the rest of Sachie.

I sat in the chair across from him and burned three cigarettes, as he waxed nostalgic about his fresh new shiny bride, her defilement, and her disposal.

"Thirty years is a long time not to get caught," I said. "Didn't anybody miss her? Didn't anybody ask any questions?"

"We kept to ourselves. Nobody knew. Nobody cared," Takashima said. He smiled and nodded his bird-nod.

"Why come forward now—I mean other than the anniversary thing?"

"She haunted me. All this time. I see her sweep the floor, wash rice in the basin, sit with her hands in her lap on the zabuton in the parlor. She talks to me, too."

"What does she say?"

"What she said to me that first day. She'll care for me forever. Itsumademo."

"Do you drink?" I asked. I thought to myself that I certainly did, and that I could use one right then. I could feel my day slipping away into an early grave covered with futility. There were fresher corpses out there made by harder, meaner people than Hideo Takashima that required my attention.

"Once in a while," he said.

"But you see her every day?"

"Every day. And I'll see her every day, always."

"Always?"

"Itsumademo." Another smile. Another nod.

My cigarette was almost out and I was determined not to ruin another in his presence. I thanked him for his time and told him that I intended to release him pending further investigation because I knew where to find him and did not consider him to be a flight risk. I didn't tell him that my decision was based on the fact that I thought he was certifiably nuts. He insisted that I take him into custody because he couldn't bear another moment in his little house with the ghost of Sachie. After arguing with him for a bit about procedure and having nothing but his confession and the impracticality of holding him indefinitely while I verified his statement and getting only a "please" and smiles and birdy nods in response, I decided I'd humor him and advised him that we'd put him on a "24-hour hold." This really meant we'd throw him into the drunk tank and release him the next morning. He told me he was grateful and I felt more than saw the smile and nod as I walked out of the room and summoned the flatfoots to book him.

I spent the rest of the day out in a plantation village past Wahiawā Town interviewing a witness to a knifing at a cockfight. It was a lot of "Yes, sir" and "No, sir" and not a lot of anything useful. At least he hung around despite the fact that I had been delayed by an hour. On the way back to town, I grabbed an early dinner of something dead covered in brown gravy at a coffee shop and doused the fire it made in my stomach with the contents of my hip flask. I had a couple of Lucky Strikes for dessert and headed home to my sweatbox apartment in Kaimukī. I took a lukewarm shower, had a couple more drinks from a glass like a civilized man, and went to bed.

When homicide dicks dream we dream the worst dreams of all. We don't dream of the tortured souls of victims crying out for justice or their broken corpses suddenly animating like they do in the pulps. When we dream we dream of reports with carbons in the typewriter and overflowing ashtrays and green desk blotters ringed with coffee cup stains. It's the same dream night in and night out. Paperwork. There is no escape. The unfinished report abides in waking and in slumber.

When I got to the station in the morning, I was summoned into the office of my boss, Detective Lieutenant Gideon Hanohano. Gid wore his 300 pounds like they were only 250 but he still made his desk look like dollhouse furniture when he sat behind it. He was usually in the habit of limping out to see me if he wanted to talk, so an invitation to his office usually meant bad news. I entered with the all the gleeful anticipation of a convict crossing the threshold into the gas chamber. I was all caught up with reports past due, so I couldn't imagine what it was he was going to tell me. That always makes it worse. Gid was reading the morning paper when I knocked on the doorjamb.

"They got free lei making classes at Kawaiahaʻo Church on Saturday mornings. Not just the limp plumeria kind. The fancy ones the pāʻū riders wear in the parades," he said without looking up. Gid always read the paper cover to cover and every last column inch of it. It was his daily ritual in getting the "lay of the land." He told me every good investigator should do it.

"That's nice," I said. "Maybe you can make a few strands to lay on my early grave."

"Sit down, Sheik," he told me. He folded the paper neatly, following the creases and artfully returning it to its original bundle form before laying it on his blotter. His hands were graceful for something the size of boxing gloves. I pulled out the uncomfortable steel-framed chair with the forest green faux leather cushion and parked my ass on it.

"What can I do for you, Lieutenant? I'm guessing you didn't have me come in so we can talk about lei making or a sale on SPAM or anything else in a little sidebar under the headline."

"Hideo Takashima," he said.

"Who?"

"Your interview yesterday."

I thought back to the lunatic fisherman and his wild story about smothering his wife twenty years ago and how he had made me late in getting out to Wahiawā.

"Did they release him?" I asked. I remembered the plan to let him go in the morning.

"Yeah," said Gid.

"So? Did he go back home to his haunted house in Kaka'ako?"

"No," said Gid. "He's at the morgue."

"What?"

"He's dead, Sheik."

Shit. There went my morning. What the hell happened? Gid told me: just prior to talking to me, he swallowed enough sleeping pills to put down a bull elephant. He took them with the coffee the flatfoots brought him before I entered the room. He curled up on the cot in the drunk tank and dozed and nobody thought about it until they opened the cell to release him and he wouldn't wake up.

The next thing I knew, I was headed for Kaka'ako for some answers.

Takashima had been so adamant about not returning there. Why not? He could have just as easily taken his pills there. Maybe there was something uniquely Japanese about coming to turn himself in before doing himself in. My dad used to talk about shit like that: giri, honor, saving face. One last necessary thing to do before ending it all, before leaving the world behind after all the shit you did to turn it upside down to turn it right side up again. Or maybe he really was crazy. Maybe he really thought the ghost of his poor dead wife really did putter around the house and talk to him and it drove him nuts. Itsumademo. Well, so much for that. All it took was some pills put an end to forever.

Ilaniwai Street was crowded and hot and full of stray animals and children darting in and out of ramshackle camp buildings. Hung laundry moved lethargically in the faint breeze and delivery trucks kicked up yellow-brown clouds of dust that lingered over the street in a thin miasma giving everything the appearance of a sepia daguerreotype.

Finding a place to park was a near impossibility, so though I hate to be the kind of jerk cop who uses his badge for accommodation, I pulled into the corrugated tin garage of a tofu maker and told him it was official business and I'd be out as soon as I possibly could. He bowed and gave me a smile that was a thin veneer over his surrender and disgust. I crossed the dirty street and narrowly avoided being flattened by an old Packard and a manapua cart.

Takashima's house was almost ridiculously tiny for even one person;

imagining two people coexisting in the glorified shipping crate without sitting in each other's lap was nearly impossible. Still, it was whitewashed and only marginally grubby and the little lawn was well-manicured with concrete paving stones in a walkway from the pine gate leading up to a lanai the size of a postage stamp. Toward the back, behind a couple of hibiscus bushes were a toilet shed and a furo house of tin.

I undid the rusty hook on the gate and entered the little yard.

Apparently Hideo Takashima had been something of a gardener as well as a fisherman. There were several flowering shrubs of all kinds and red torch ginger up against the pine fence that ran around the perimeter of the tiny lot as well as cucumber and squash vines, eggplant, kumquat, and taller mulberry, which served to shield the house somewhat from view from the street. The lot's neighbors were a Japanese camp tenement and a small electrical supply warehouse. Across the street were the tofu maker and more tenements. The little garden was quiet for the neighborhood it was in, probably owing to the tall mulberry. Takashima had created his own private little world in the middle of bustling Kaka'ako.

I took the two little steps up to the lanai, feeling the boards creak under my weight as I stepped toward the front door. I looked in through the screen as my hand moved to try the knob when what I saw within the little parlor made me freeze with a thrill of terror. There, in the middle of the parlor on a dark zabuton before a small, low table was a woman in a kimono. The kimono was a deep tangerine at the neck and shoulders, slowly melting into a pale peach to pink and finally to white. It was adorned with cranes in flight and snow covered black pine with fantastically twisted trunks. She suddenly became aware of my presence at the screen door and raised her head to look at me. It was the same pale, round face with the little pointed chin from the old black-and-white photograph. I staggered, missing the little step with my heel, and pitched backward. My head struck what was probably one of the concrete paving stones and I plunged into a deep blackness mixed in with cool green and hot red at its periphery. I dove a long way down into the dark until I became aware of a faint but persistent buzzing and something cool against the skin of my face. The falling sensation ceased and was replaced by a floating one. I was adrift on a warm, black sea under a Stygian sky scattered with a million tiny gold stars. Slowly, I became aware of the fact that it wasn't all of me that was floating. It was only my head. I peeled my eyes open with Herculean effort and a soft, perfumed blur came into focus as a face. The same face that sent me staggering backwards off the lanai. A small but strong hand moved a damp cloth slowly across my forehead.

The face spoke in a clear, feminine voice: "How are you? Are you okay?"

I grunted in what I thought was the affirmative. I squinted at the light coming from behind the face and made an attempt at speech:

"Where am I?" My mouth felt like it was full of dry sand.

"In my house," said the face. I blinked a long, lazy blink and the face came more into focus. It belonged to a woman, and so did the kimono below it. She was pretty in the same way porcelain is when it is feather light and translucent. When I concentrated on her features, they seemed very much real and more mature than those in the photograph Takashima had shown me. I guessed that this woman was in her forties, though she could have easily been in her thirties. She was a well-preserved specimen.

"Who are you?" I rasped.

"Sachie Takashima. Who are you?"

"Detective Sergeant Francis Yoshikawa. Honolulu Police. My badge is in my inside coat pocket." I tried to reach up to indicate to her where that was, but my right hand flopped uselessly on my chest and slid back down to my side. Sachie Takashima, if that's who she was, reached one of her small hands into my coat pocket and pulled the leather wallet out and inspected my badge and credentials, then gently slid them back into the pocket and smoothed out my coat over it. I laughed and it made my head hurt like it was being pounded with a claw hammer.

"You're not supposed to be here," I said.

"Why not?" she asked. "It's my house." She looked at me calmly but there was bemusement just under the placid smile.

"I was under the impression you'd been dead for thirty years."

It was her turn to laugh and she did so as heartily as such a small, delicate mouth could, and it didn't look as if it hurt her head the same way it had mine.

"Where did you get that idea?"

"From your husband."

"Who?"

"Hideo Takashima."

"Oh," she said. Her laughter stopped and her face became clouded with what appeared to be genuine confusion. "Have you seen him, then?" she asked, her voice unsure with puzzlement. "He didn't come home last night."

"I did. He came into the station yesterday to turn himself in—for murdering you thirty years ago. He insisted we take him into custody, so I put him into the drunk tank overnight. The intent was to release him this morning pending further investigation of his confession, but he had taken his own life by overdosing on sleeping pills before making his confession and being placed in the cell. He was found dead this morning. I'm sorry."

"Oh," she said. Her hands came up to her face and she stared past me blankly.

"Are you alright?"

"Oh. Oh, my. I don't know, but it looks like there's been some mistake, Detective."

"Obviously. You don't look as if you've been dead for thirty years."

"No, I haven't . . . I mean, there's been a mistake. Hideo Takashima is not my husband. He's my brother-in-law."

"I'm sorry—what?"

Sachie told me her story.

In 1920, the former Sachie Kawamura had crossed the ocean as the teenaged picture bride promised to one Kunio Takashima, also originally of Yamaguchi-ken as she and her family were. Kunio had been in Hawai'i for a couple of years. He had gone over to assist his older brother Hideo, who had acquired his own boat and needed the help. Kunio's photograph revealed him to be a handsome man with a pleasant countenance, though his face was darkened and creased by the sun and sea. Hideo was ten years older than Kunio; their family had been fairly well-to-do in Yamaguchi-ken, their father an army officer, his commission a reward for his family's role in the Choshu uprising. Their father was killed in action during the Russo-Japanese war when Kunio was just a teenager. The family had fallen on hard financial times thereafter, so when he was able, Hideo went to Hawai'i.

Sachie padded about almost silently while she told her tale, wrapping ice from the icebox in a kitchen rag and sitting me up so she could apply it to the baseball-sized lump on the back of my head. Sitting up just then wasn't the easiest thing I had ever done, but I could feel the ability to do such things slowly come back to me. The ice burned on my throbbing scalp and the sensation made me a little nauseous. Sachie's voice remained clear though, and she continued to talk while she sat next to me holding the ice to the back of my head with one hand and stabilizing with the other on my forehead.

She told me of the poignancy of leaving her family, whom she was certain she'd never see again, and her voyage over in steerage, days and nights of sheer hell as part of a herd of human cattle. Upon arrival, she bathed in cold water on the main deck behind a makeshift canvas curtain and donned the kimono she was presently wearing. It remained her only fine garment; all of her family's modest wealth was in that kimono. She wore it only on special occasions, and the special occasion of the day was an anniversary. That family was full of anniversaries.

"What's today's big deal?" I asked.

"This is the anniversary of the morning Kunio disappeared," she said. I chewed on this while she told me more. My head was beginning to feel a little less detached from the rest of me. Sachie talked of descending the gangway and recognizing Kunio's face in the crowd as he shouted an exuberant greeting. She also remembered the strange, quiet man at his side, watching her in intense silence. This turned out to be Hideo. She was whisked off to immigration and quarantine and released the following morning. Kunio picked her up in a borrowed jalopy and they were married that evening at the teahouse in Kalihi. The only guests there were a cousin of hers and his wife, a friend who crewed on Hideo's boat and his wife, and Hideo.

They came back to the little house on Ilaniwai Street we were sitting in. Hideo had his own room, and she and Kunio slept in the parlor on a futon on the floor that was folded up and stored in a small closet at the start of each day. Sachie did all the housework and prepared all the meals for the two brothers. She recalls that Kunio was cheerful and outgoing, and Hideo was the opposite— withdrawn, reticent, and embarrassed to address her. In those first few weeks, Hideo spoke to her only when he absolutely had to, and when he did so he seemed hopelessly flustered. They managed to coexist rather comfortably, though in almost absolute silence.

Then came the first anniversary of Sachie and Kunio's wedding. The brothers had saved a particularly big aku for sashimi from their catch, and some beer and sake were purchased from the Wong Market a few blocks away. The same guests at the wedding were in attendance for the anniversary dinner. It was a festive evening, full of laughter and drinking. Except for Hideo. He always ate in silence and excused himself immediately following the meal, declining any drink except for a single cup of tea and retreating to his room; this even happened when they had company over, and the anniversary party was no exception. When all the guests had departed and the cleaning was done, she returned to the parlor to find that Kunio had put out the lights and spread the futon out. Sachie felt as though she needed another bath before they became intimate, but Kunio couldn't wait. When they had finished, Sachie got up and went outside to the furo house and took her overdue bath. It was already past two in the morning. When she returned from her bath, Kunio had gone. Sachie did not think this strange as he and Hideo often left the house very early to get out on the water, but did find it odd that the futon had also disappeared. Sachie never saw Kunio again. "He didn't go fishing with Hideo?" I asked. I could now move without sending daggers of pain through my head. I could smell the camphor of Sachie's kimono and the Ivory Soap on her skin. I was almost a hundred percent.

"No," she said. "Hideo was very upset. He stopped talking altogether after Kunio ran off. I think he felt hurt and betrayed. He did everything for his brother."

"You continued to live here with Hideo all this time?"

"Of course. He had nobody to keep his house, to cook his meals. And I had nowhere to go. Hideo had been so good to Kunio and me, so generous. I would often tell him, though he would not talk, that I would always look after him, always care for him."

"Itsumademo," I said.

"Yes," she said. "Itsumademo."

I felt I could take my leave now that I didn't sway more than a few inches on my feet or feel like vomiting on the zabuton I had been sitting on. I thanked Sachie, offered awkward condolences for her brother-in-law and told her that I would be in touch. I managed to unhook and open the gate on my own, cross Ilaniwai without ending up under wheels and bought a couple of blocks of tofu from the tofu maker as a conciliatory gesture of gratitude for having commandeered his garage. I drove a couple of blocks makai and parked at Kewalo Basin, where I watched the sampans cast off and filled myself with the bourbon in my hipflask. The flask was empty about the same time Kewalo Basin was and my headache had disappeared with the bourbon and the boats.

I thought about an early morning three decades earlier when a single sampan sailed out under a hazy moon with a corpse in a blanket, or not.

The remainder of the morning was spent digging up stuff to corroborate or disprove what I had heard over the past twenty-four hours. I went down to the Vital Statistics counter at the Territorial Department of Health and obtained a Photostat of a marriage certificate for Kunio Takashima and Sachie Kawamura. There was no marriage between Sachie and Hideo. His "marriage" to her was a phantom in his head—something he ironically reduced the real-life Sachie to. I found out that of the wedding guests, only Sachie's cousin's wife, Tomoko Kawamura, was still alive. I drove back to Kaka'ako to a tenement camp on Cooke Street where she was supposed to be living with relatives from her side of the family.

I sat in the cramped little box of a parlor with Tomoko Kawamura on the second floor of a rickety firetrap. Laundry hung on a line outside the front door helped to obscure the burning afternoon sun. I fanned myself with my hat as I listened to the old woman talk. Tomoko had married Sachie's cousin Hirotaka in 1915 through a mutual arrangement by their families. She made the boat trip to Honolulu and they lived in a Waipahu plantation house until Hirotaka found a job as a fish cutter in town. It was there that he met Hideo Takashima and later Kunio when they would bring their catch in to auction. They were all from Yamaguchi-ken, and Hirotaka eventually brokered the marriage arrangement for Kunio with his young cousin back home. He made an offer to do so first for Hideo, who politely demurred several times.

Tomoko complained that Kunio was a good-for-nothing, a braggart and womanizer and gambler who continued his bad habits even after he was married to Sachie. He helped his brother on the sampan when he wasn't sleeping off a hangover and was rarely home after sundown. Still, Hideo adored his younger brother and doted on him. Even after Kunio ran off, he took care of Sachie out of obligation.

"She should've married that one, the older one," she said.

"I thought she did," I said.

"No. She should've, but he went crazy after the brother ran away. Stopped talking to her. Stopped talking to everybody. Just go fishing, come home."

Went crazy. Coming down to the Police Station and taking a fistful of sleeping pills before confessing to the murder of a wife you never had and never murdered sure fit the bill. Thirty years of silence and yearning might do it. Maybe.

I didn't have any more to ask the lady and she didn't have any more to say, so I thanked her, bowed and went back down to my car. I turned the radio on and heard some Duke Ellington and took my hip flask out of my pocket. Remembering it was empty, I put it back and started the engine and drove back to Ilaniwai Street. It was still hot, still dusty, still crowded.

I had one more question for Sachie.

I parked in the tofu maker's garage again and crossed the street again, oblivious to the traffic. I knocked on the door and she let me in.

I asked her my question: "Where's the hairpin?"

When I came out, she came with me, wearing her magnificent blazing kimono and my handcuffs.

The next morning, I got my fair share of the malasadas and I even got it before it turned cold. Gid Hanohano shuffled out to join me at my desk, pulling up the battle-scarred chair usually reserved for witnesses in shock with scratchy wool blankets over their shoulders. The chair creaked under Gid's frame but managed to hold its own.

"So what question did you ask her, Sheik?" Gid crammed the entire malasada in his mouth. He said it was neater that way; the sugar didn't get all over the place.

"I asked her 'where's the hairpin?'"

"The hairpin?"

"Yeah, the silver hairpin she wore on her wedding night with the fancy kimono. As soon as I asked, she broke."

I explained to Gid that it didn't make sense to me that Hideo Takashima cracked the way he did just because his brother ran away. He knew Kunio better than anyone, and the way Kunio was, running off with some haircut girl wouldn't have surprised anyone. The elaborate fantasy of having married Sachie and killing her, then living with her ghost for three decades was the stuff of something more severe. It was guilt for something heinous. It occurred to me that Hideo's and Sachie's stories superficially resembled each other, but the cast of characters was all screwed up: who married Sachie, who disappeared after the anniversary party. Only the props were consistent—the kimono and the futon. The kimono stayed with Sachie, the futon disappeared with a body. Only the hairpin was missing from Sachie's story. It turns out that went out to sea, just like Hideo said it did.

Sachie admitted that she had really fallen in love with Hideo despite the fact that he was twice her age and that he wasn't as comely as his younger brother. It was his competence and his sense of responsibility that attracted her. Hideo had been smitten with Sachie, too, from the moment she descended the gangway at the harbor. They had a secret affair, spending intimate time with each other in the little house on Ilaniwai Street while Kunio was out whoring and gambling. Sachie wanted to divorce Kunio and marry Hideo, but his love for his wastrel little brother would never allow him to consider it. Sachie asked Hideo: what if Kunio went away? Hideo responded with uncomfortable silence pregnant with unspoken pondering. She took this as an affirmative response.

After the anniversary party, Kunio was exhausted after their sudden, rough coupling and succumbed to the sake and beer. He was snoring almost immediately. Sachie took the silver pin from her hair and drove it into his neck at the base of his skull. It was clean. Kunio never even stirred; he just stopped snoring.

When Sachie told Hideo what she had done, she thought he'd be happy. He was mortified. He loved her, though, and to protect her he took Kunio's naked corpse with the hairpin sticking out of the back of its neck out to sea. Sachie may have killed Kunio, but Hideo killed any possibility of a life with Sachie, and, in a way, Sachie herself in his mind. She was dead to him, a lingering ghost of his guilt. He bore it for three decades until he couldn't any more. He swallowed his pills with resolve and gave his testament as he saw it to the first convenient confessor the law provided: me.

Sachie Takashima shed no tears when I put the cuffs on her. She bowed and smiled and thanked me for listening. In that moment, she was as absolutely beautiful as only resignation and longing for a life that could never be could make a woman. The cranes on her kimono faded into the flaming sky as their flight carried them to their inevitable destination. Sachie was as much a prisoner of herself as Hideo was. Both of them decided thirty years was a long enough sentence.

I found out that though she was practically a child when she killed Kunio and could have successfully thrown herself on the mercy of the court, she had secreted away a handful of sleeping pills in her kimono sleeve and had swallowed them after I uncuffed her and left her on the receiving bench to await booking. She curled up on the bench between a hooker and a wino and quietly went to sleep and died.

"I like the part where you thought she was a ghost," said Gid. He smiled his crooked little half-grin that was barely a grin at all. "I thought you don't believe in ghosts, Sheik." He shoved another whole malasada into his mouth like it was a breath mint.

"Only when they remind me I have work to do," I said. I lit up a Lucky Strike and watched the ceiling fan disperse its smoke.

"Well, your ghost is going to be asleep for a long, long time."

I said: "Itsumademo."

There's no time longer than that.

MILTON KIMURA

EXCERPTS FROM
"TALE OF TWO CITIES: WE'RE
NOT IN KAIMUKĪ ANYMORE"

Do you approach a new issue of *Bamboo Ridge* the same way I do? After glancing at the cover, I crack the book to the table of contents and scan the contributors. If I see a Lum or a Kono or a Kanae, I go to the page and start reading. If I see a Chang or a Smith or a Kimura, I go to the bios to see who the writer is. So if you're like me and didn't recognize my name and checked my bio, you already know that I live in Pittsburgh.

You: Why would *BR* accept work from a mainland guy, even if he once lived in Hawai'i? And why would anyone in his right mind move from Hawai'i to Pittsburgh? Maybe to San Francisco or Seattle or Santa Fe, but Pittsburgh?

Me: Read on and find out.

So Why the Big Move?

As a 65-year-old retiree in March of 2012, I should have had only one more big date in front of me, the one that I couldn't predict and wouldn't need to remember, but it turned out that I had a few more to handle before death. On April 17, my partner Donald and I left Hawai'i after living there together for nearly a half century. Not for a two-week vacation but for good. On April 18, we landed in Pittsburgh, Pennsylvania, our new home. On April 19, we went into contract on a townhouse in the North Side of the city, the first time either of us lifelong renters had ever owned real estate. Three years earlier, we thought we'd live out our lives in Honolulu, so how come the big move? It occurred to me that I was missing something: I was passing up the plate lunch special with extra gravy and settling for the single patty burger with lettuce and tomato but asking them to hold the patty and the mayo. And the bun. Life in Hawai'i was pleasant with a benevolent climate, a familiar culture, a coterie of close friends, and a welcome routine of exercise, reading and writing, and tutoring that provided a framework for my life. But something was definitely missing.

No, not totally absent because I got whiffs of it on our two or three trips per year
to San Francisco, New York, London, and other centers of culture. I realized that
my moments of greatest pleasure had come in the San Francisco War Memorial
Opera House hearing Leonie Rysanek send the Empress's vocal line soaring in
Die Frau ohne Schatten; marveling as Ángel Corella at Lincoln Center embodied
Prince Siegfried's *puissance* in *Swan Lake* by pausing for a moment at the end
of multiple pirouettes before gently setting his working leg in textbook fourth
position; standing open-mouthed at Richard Wilson's *20:50* installation at
London's Saatchi Gallery wondering, "What is this and how did he do it?" The
memory of moments like these carried me through the weeks and months of my
pleasant but mundane life in Honolulu.

Choosing a New City

But let me get back to how we ended up on the North Side of Pittsburgh.
Once we embraced the possibility of moving to the mainland, we began a three-
year research and reconnaissance project guided by urban studies theorist
Richard Florida's book *Who's Your City*, an invaluable reference for anyone
contemplating a move within the United States. What struck me immediately
was that Donald and I lived in Hawai'i for the three principal reasons Florida
cites to explain why people live where they do: they were born there; they went
to college there; or they found work there. In other words, most people live
where they do by happenstance. We, supposedly the most rational creatures on
Earth, don't *choose* where we live; we just let it happen. Absent was the reason
that would become the driving force for our move: a place that would allow us
to pursue our passions. With retirement incomes we could take with us, with
no dependents to support, and with both sets of parents deceased, we were now
free to grasp this reason firmly and run with it. I should add that *Who's Your City*
came to me serendipitously. I volunteered as a tutor for the University of Hawai'i
Athletic Department. I was assigned a basketball player in his senior year who
was taking a sociology course, among whose required texts was Florida's book.
Doug, the player, noticed and commented upon the interest I showed in the
book, so I explained to him that I was contemplating a move and found Florida's
ideas helpful. At the end of the semester, he wanted to give me the book, but I
reminded him that NCAA rules prohibited the exchange of gifts between tutor
and student. I was surprised a few weeks later to get a text asking me to meet

him on campus. When we met, he thanked me and handed me Florida's book, which I could accept now that he had graduated. A nice guy. Most of the time. Whenever I encountered Doug in the narrow hallway of the Nagatani Academic Center or elsewhere on campus, he'd stand right in front of me as we chatted, forcing 5-1/2-foot me to look straight up at 7-foot him. He'd smile as he paused a few seconds before honoring my request to step back because my neck hurt.

Putting in the Grunt Work

We began Florida's recommended research by assembling an eight-page spreadsheet comparing our initial six candidates: Baltimore, Philadelphia, Atlanta, Chicago, the East Bay, and Pittsburgh with familiar Honolulu as a touchstone. Criteria included cost of living; median home and condo prices; number of symphony concerts/operas/ballets per year; repertory that ventured beyond Mozart, Beethoven, Brahms, Puccini, and Verdi; an airport with direct flights to cities with major cultural offerings; average annual snowfall; number of hospitals ranked in the top 100 (all the cities under consideration had at least one; Hawai'i had none); walkability score of different neighborhoods; sales tax percentage; size of gap between rich and poor; the proportion of Republicans and Democrats in elected positions; museum holdings; cost of a kilowatt of electricity and a cubic foot of natural gas; and many more. As Professor Florida recommended, we visited all six cities, staying at least four days in each one. Prior to each visit, we contacted realtors in each city to show us representative properties. Absent from our list were criteria that might loom large on others' spreadsheets, for example, quality of schools, professional sports offerings, and unemployment rates. We omitted them because we have no children, we don't watch games, and we are retired. We footnoted information like the Chicago Symphony being designated one of the top five in the world, Philadelphia's Academy of Vocal Arts being the most successful training ground for opera singers, and Pittsburgh being named the most livable city in America, but we didn't create criteria for honors like these. In order to account for the varying importance of these criteria, we gave each one a multiple of 1, 2, or 3, depending on its significance to us. Thus, a vote for Pittsburgh's high percentage of doctors accepting new Medicare patients would add up to 3 points while a vote for O'Hare's extensive array of nonstop flights would add up to 2 points, and a vote for Philadelphia's superior downtown-airport public transit would retain a value of just 1 point. In tallying our prioritized ratings and determining a winner, we adopted a scoring system like that used in golf: the lowest score wins. Using as an example the criterion above of the percentage of doctors accepting new Medicare patients, Philadelphia's third place finish would give it a score of 9 (3 x 3), Chicago's second place finish would give it a score of 6 (2 x 3), and Pittsburgh would emerge with the winning score of 3 (1 x 3). After the points were tallied, two cities rose above the others on both our ballots: Chicago and Pittsburgh.

Doubts along the Way to a Final Choice

In the back of my mind was the realization that one of our choices, Pittsburgh, had lost population since the 1980s, mostly due to the closing of businesses connected with the steel industry. According to U.S. Census statistics, Pittsburgh was America's 9th most populous city in 1970; by 1990, it had dropped to 19th place; by 2000, it had dropped off the list of the 20 largest cities. And growth had been non-existent or slow since then. On a personal note, we two were part of the increase of 885 in population from 2012 to 2013. We hoped, as did the city's boosters, that the makeup of that population reflected the rise of replacements for heavy industry: education, medicine, technology. Recent figures bear this out. According to the Pew Charitable Trusts, Pittsburgh's adult population declined 9% between 2000 and 2014, but, in that same period, the percentage of young graduates grew from 10.5% to 16.8%, making the city third in the nation for growth in this segment.

Back to our move: in February 2012, we scheduled a second visit to each finalist and continued gathering additional data for our spreadsheet. We chose February purposely in order to savor a taste of these cities in mid-winter. Again, we spent time with our realtors who showed us properties that had come on the market since our first visit. When we returned to Honolulu, we talked and pondered and then voted, independently. It was ironic that we found after our decision that we each had thought the other preferred Chicago; we were both wrong. Pittsburgh emerged victorious, not by a landslide but by a comfortable margin. For me, it was that intangible referred to by author Florida: Visit and explore each city and don't hesitate to reject a place based on your gut feeling, no matter how it ranks on your list. It wasn't so much that Chicago didn't measure up or didn't feel right but that it was so big with such a fast pace and so many options. Perhaps we were too old for such an abrupt change. On the other hand, Pittsburgh seemed not only manageable but quite a good fit. As Florida recommends doing, I could visualize myself living here, walking these streets, shopping in these stores, listening to this symphony orchestra, attending this ballet, contributing to this community. With both of us in agreement, we planned and executed the move in two months and arrived on April 18, 2012.

Mission Accomplished?

So have we realized the prime reason for our move: to experience the arts for which we were so hungry? A decisive Yes. And many times over. To list a few: Natalia Osipova channeling Nureyev as she executed *La Sylphide*'s diagonal exit of consecutive jetés across the expansive stage of the Metropolitan Opera House, each leap eliciting astonished gasps from the audience; Christine Goerke's soprano voice pushing back the walls of Toronto's Four Seasons Centre as she sang Brünnhilde's music with conviction and ease, recalling the words of the early 20th-century critic who compared Ernestine Schumann-Heink's voice to nearby Niagara Falls: she was a force of nature; Christian Tetzlaff playing Dvorak's violin concerto with the Pittsburgh Symphony as though it had been commissioned for him, every note cleanly in place yet linked to the string of those that preceded and those that followed; Frank Lloyd Wright's Fallingwater, seen so often in photographs but now less than two hours away: the rhododendrons along the paths in prolific bloom, the cantilevered stairs from the living room to the murmuring water below, a Diego Rivera drawing on a wall in the small guest bedroom where the Mexican artist himself once slept; Alban Lendorf of the Royal Danish Ballet dancing Act III of *Napoli* and making this 1842 ballet seem freshly conceived, as though it had just been choreographed by Bournonville to suit Lendorf's easy jump, quick beats, and engaging personality; Jonas Kaufmann's assumption of the role of the innocent knight *Parsifal* opposite Peter Mattei as the leader of the Knights of the Grail in the Metropolitan Opera's heralded production of *Parsifal*, both fulfilling the demands of their roles in voice, bearing, appearance, and musicianship and proving conclusively that exalted Wagnerian singing did not die with Lauritz Melchior and Friedrich Schorr; Evgeny Kissinn negotiating the Waldstein sonata with a natural spontaneity and liquid ease that made this, one of my least favorite of Beethoven's sonatas, a delight, and he did so in the presence of a sold-out Chicago Symphony Hall with chairs added onstage to accommodate as many devotées as possible; Jonathan Pryce's Shylock in *The Merchant of Venice* imported from The Globe by the Lincoln Center Festival, his being and body recoiling from the cascading baptismal water as though it were hot oil or searing acid. And this list continues to grow. No, definitely not in Kaimukī anymore.

Moving Is Hard Work, Especially at Our Ages

When I think back on those last two months in Honolulu and on our first two months in Pittsburgh, I am amazed at what we accomplished and appreciatively relieved that we survived. Here's a list of some of the things we had to get done before leaving: notify landlord, utilities, post office, friends, family, banks and credit union, magazines, and several more parties of the impending move; pick a new bank in Pittsburgh and open accounts prior to arrival; arrange a UPS box to serve as a forwarding address in Pittsburgh; find a moving company that would pack our belongings in Honolulu, ship them, and then store them in Pittsburgh for an indefinite period until we bought a home; sell or give away our furniture, housewares, books, and other items, and pack what we were taking with us like CDs, art work, autographed LP albums, bread maker, and summer clothing; arrange a farewell luncheon for dear friends; find a short-term rental in Pittsburgh and alert our realtor to be ready to start house hunting the day after arrival; donate my 11-year-old Honda Civic to KHET public television and arrange for it to be picked up on our very last day, specifying that the picker upper would need to handle a manual transmission; make plane reservations and arrange for a rental car for a week but renewable as needed; refuse as gently as possible invitations to farewell meals as we could never have completed the listed tasks had we accepted; snap photos from our living room of the sunrise and sunset views of Waikīkī and the Pacific; buy and learn how to use a Garmin; and polish the shoes we were taking with us.

Our New Abode

About our new townhouse. First of all, it was cheap, compared to Honolulu. Not surprising, considering that Sperling's Best Places website reports that home prices in Honolulu are 650% higher than in Pittsburgh. So the mortgage, insurance, and property taxes for our new home add up to less than what we paid in rent for the Kaimukī house we occupied for our last 30 years in Honolulu. Located on the north side of the city in what was originally Allegheny City before it was incorporated into Pittsburgh, our neighborhood sits just across the Allegheny River from the Golden Triangle, the downtown area. We can get there with a five-minute car ride, a four-stop bus ride, or a 20-minute walk that takes us down to the river and across one of three bridges called, collectively, the Three Sisters, that connect these two parts of the city. I like the people they named these bridges for: Roberto Clemente, Andy Warhol, and Rachel Carson. Not a politician among them, but people who actually accomplished something worth remembering. The bridges are "sisters" in appearance, having all been constructed in the 1920s and now painted an identical bright yellow. On the way to these bridges, we can pass a large park called the Allegheny Commons, the Children's Museum, the National Aviary, PNC Park where the Pirates play, and Heinz Field where Steeler Nation resides in the fall. Back to the house: it's a newly constructed, three-story townhouse with three bedrooms and two and a half baths, a deck in the back off the kitchen, and an attached garage.

Lucky Luck Would Approve

A digression of sorts though sticking to housing: Remember the *Lucky Luck Show* on Channel 2 in the 1950s? Oh, you weren't born yet? Well, one of the musicians featured was Pua Almeida, who often switched from his lilting tenor to falsetto for the last note of a song. Once, after he finished a song, Lucky smiled and enthused, "Hooo, no can beat that second-story voice, yeah?" I didn't yet know a metaphor from a simile, but Lucky's phrase already resonated beyond the obvious reference to the effortless high note. In plantation Waipahu, there were few houses with more than one story, so any home with a second story must belong to someone rich or privileged. All of my dwelling places in Hawai'i had just one story, even the apartments located above the ground floor in multistory buildings, so living in this three-story townhouse was a new adventure. We worried about the coming time when we might not be able to negotiate stairs, so we made sure that any stairs were straight flights rather than switchbacks. It would simplify installing a chair lift. The prime advantage for us was the isolation provided by multistories: although the house has only 1600 square feet, sound doesn't travel well between floors so it's easy to forget that someone else is in the house cooking or web surfing or doing a load of laundry or listening to Sirius Radio or watching television.

My Mother Was Right, Again

On the first night we spent in the house, I recalled the words my mother had spoken when she moved into the then newly built Waipahu Hall Elderly apartments for senior citizens. Like us, she had lived in a succession of rentals all her life: a shanty—I'm not sure it was, but I like that word—in Waipahu's stable camp, a three-bedroom no-indoor bath house in Nishi Camp, a three-bedroom one-bath on Managers Drive, a two-bedroom one-bath on Makaaloha Street with—get ready—maid's quarters attached to the garage, and a two-bedroom house on Renton Road in 'Ewa between whose wall boards we could see the glow of her living room light as we drove off after a Sunday visit. With all of them, she had had to scrub at the dirt left by previous occupants and bear with what she couldn't erase, but now she was the first to live in a brand new one-bedroom apartment with all new appliances and wall-to-wall carpets. Just before we got ready to leave after helping her move in, she said, "You know, this is the first time I lived in a new house." She was in her late 60s, and she had waited a long time for this. Like her, I rented until I was in my 60s: a one-bedroom apartment on Walina Street in Waikīkī, a two-bedroom apartment behind Jefferson Elementary, a two-bedroom apartment on Wilder, and finally a three-bedroom house on Paula Drive in Kaimukī. Like my mother, I always spent the first days of occupancy scrubbing and painting and disinfecting. So our Pittsburgh townhouse was the first time I had ever moved into a place where no one else had turned on the oven, sat on the toilets, worked the garage door opener, or set the security alarm before locking up for the night. I now knew why my mother got such pleasure from the thought of being the first occupant. Perhaps my happiness went a bit further than hers because not only was I the first occupant, I was also the owner.

Working in Retirement

After retiring in 2005, I accepted my former boss's invitation to volunteer at the Salvation Army Adult Rehabilitation Center in Iwilei. Once a week I worked for two hours with a recovering addict in the residential facility, guiding him through the Salvation Army's 12-step workbook to sobriety. I enjoyed these encounters and, as the cliché proved true once again, I learned as much as I taught. I learned about the desperation of working in a factory in South Carolina assembling cardboard boxes while sweating through the summer, about growing up on a mega-dump outside Manila and finding a dead body while walking home after the first day of kindergarten, and about returning to this program for a second—or third or fourth—time after being dropped for infractions. I felt a need to do more but with clients who wouldn't add to my emotional drain.

Helping the Team

One day while walking to one of the UH classes I took after retirement, I saw a notice in Kuykendall seeking tutors. I applied online, submitted my resumé, and was interviewed. A week later, the athletic department accepted me. One small hiccup was easily overcome: they paid their tutors but agreed to accept me as a volunteer. For five years, I worked with athletes from football and basketball on courses ranging from sociology to English 101 to ethnic music to math to the first required course in the graduate public administration program. Full disclosure: the math was too much for me—I could do it but I couldn't explain it—so we found another tutor after the first two weeks. My hours expanded as I sometimes met with students three or even four times a week. And if a paper was due, we could go far beyond a session's customary two hours. And if the athletic department's Nagatani Academic Center was closed, we met in Sinclair or Hamilton. Once, when a student's paper was due on the Monday after Thanksgiving, I met with him on Black Friday in Kāhala Mall. It was then that I, a non-sports fan, got first-hand evidence of how popular UH athletes can be, especially in a city without professional sports. While we sat with a laptop at a table near Starbucks, we were interrupted several times by passersby calling out to my student. Later he said that he didn't know them and reluctantly told me that it was probably because he had made a key play in a game against Fresno State. Long story short: we finished the assignment and I didn't have to give up Saturday and Sunday. I wrote above about the basketball player who introduced me to the book, *Who's Your City*, which helped us plan our move, but that wasn't the only thing I learned from these athletes. One student and I figured out African polyrhythms by tapping them out on a desk top. It's easier with two people; with one, it's like rubbing your tummy, tapping your head, and doing polka steps at the same time. Another student and I drew an ever-growing timeline to keep track of key events in modern Hawaiian history. Unfortunately, these were pre-selfie days, so I can't share a shot of what a passing counselor called the funniest happening she'd seen taking place in her office. We had borrowed the small room so I could help four basketball players cram for their mid-term. They occupied the four chairs we squeezed into the room. I should mention that the shortest of these guys was 6′ 8″. So I was left to perch on her desk because their four sets of very long legs took up all the rest of the space. Oh, most important: they all passed.

Life Lessons Continue

I didn't escape completely from the emotions that arose out of my Salvation Army tutoring. A student who would be the first in his family to earn a degree—one of several I tutored who fit in this category—had to write a mini-autobiography for English 101. As I interviewed him, he revealed that he had attended a Los Angeles high school that had no computers, that his football coach picked him up each morning and fed him burgers for breakfast on the way to school, that the same coach allowed him to use the computer at his home to complete college applications, and that he was the only child in his family who hadn't been incarcerated. Humbling. Here was I trying to figure out whether our next trip should be to Chicago for a Muti-conducted opera or to Prague for a first hearing of two Smetana operas. I am blessed.

Sometimes Things Just Don't Work Out

Okay, off the soapbox and back to my Pittsburgh students. They have been even more varied than my students in Hawai'i. On one end, I have had my share of disappointments. There was the woman in her 50s whose mother had yanked her out of eighth grade after her husband had died, because she didn't want her daughter to earn her diploma, get a job, and move out, leaving her alone. This student applied to the Greater Pittsburgh Literacy Council, my "employer," two years after her mother died. Unfortunately, her circumstances had left her without the discipline to stay on task and complete assignments, and she used our sessions as a time to vent her disappointments and frustrations, of which she had many. After a month, my coordinator and I agreed that tutoring was not doing the student any good, so we ended our sessions. Then there was another student, a young woman from Burundi who lived with her brothers and their families and who came to the library in her wheelchair. She was intent on getting a GED and moving on to community college, but what she really needed was basic instruction in English, her third language. However, I couldn't get her to see this. She continued to ask when we'd be moving on to geometry and algebra, but she didn't have a firm grasp of the multiplication tables. She wanted to try a GED practice test in reading comprehension when she was missing questions on readings at the eighth grade level. Her frustrations caused her to be late for sessions or to miss them completely without alerting me. Following GPLC's guideline of ending tutoring after three unexplained cuts, we removed her from the program. At several points during my work with these two, I found the energy to persevere by rereading a text message I had received a couple of months earlier from a student who had passed the GED writing sub-test: "Thank you milton you have no idea how much you helped.i felt great about my writing Thanks again" No, I had not performed any miracles. He just needed someone to point out what he did well and what he needed to improve and show him specific ways to go about improving.

Gratifying Successes

Thankfully, most of my students fall into this second category. They have moved towards achieving their goals and, in the process, have brought me deep satisfaction. Prime among these students is a medical doctor from Syria who wanted to work on her oral English while waiting to start her residency at Allegheny General Hospital. She was remarkable, an expert at how to learn. Building on a firm foundation in language acquisition (she spent her early years in France so grew up knowing French and Arabic), she absorbed things heard or read and noted them immediately in a manner I'd never seen before: on the same line of her notebook she'd begin at the left with English and then lift her pen and move it across the page where she'd add notes in Arabic moving from right to left. She asked hard questions. She relished difficult exercises, perhaps because she completed them so handily. She even asked for work in the subjunctive mood. I supplied appropriate exercises after warning her that Americans, especially in conversation, rarely used the subjunctive. Now these were oral exercises so she had no time to think them through or research them. Needless to say, I was sad when we ended our meetings so she could begin her residency. I have a dream of her meeting with a patient who's a grammarian and who expresses astonishment and extends congratulations when my student trots out the subjunctive! What silly dreams retired English teachers have. Oh, and here's one for "small world" collectors. This student told me that when you encounter a too inquisitive Syrian relative or friend who insists on knowing where you're going, you can reply, "I'm going to Honolulu," which gives them no information but lets them know that they're too *niele*.

Remaining Friends after Tutoring Ends

This student referred my second Muslim student, also from Syria and the wife of a resident at AGH. We worked together for a year and stopped only when she gave birth to her first child, a daughter. She was enthusiastic and responsive and had a bear-trap memory, which helps in learning a new language. She was also hospitable and invited Donald and me to dinner at their apartment. She prepared every dish herself including the entrée: lentils, eggplant, and rice cooked separately and then combined in a molded mound. A few months after the birth of her daughter, we were invited to what I believe is a custom in certain regions of Syria: a first tooth party. Again, she prepared all the food on her own, and we joined some 20 or so people, the majority of them her husband's colleagues from the hospital as well as other professionals. We were easily the oldest people there and could have served as grandparents to most of the others. This student's sister-in-law was my third Muslim student. From Saudi Arabia, she was in Pittsburgh to take an intensive English course at Duquesne University and wanted some tutoring on the side. I saw myself in her: when I had struggled with Russian and French and Italian, both in undergraduate classes and then after retirement, my language skills couldn't keep up with my ideas. Too often, my talk was like a line of children bumping along in single file, and sometimes the lead child stopped suddenly and all the others stumbled and collapsed behind her. But what was important was the drive to continue, and over the course of our two months working together, I saw dramatic improvement in both fluency and correctness. I vowed what I've vowed so many times in the past: If my own second languages are to improve, I've got to plant myself in St. Petersburg or Paris or Florence and deal with whatever comes up. Maybe next year.

I hope you can see why tutoring continues to be a central part of my life here as it was in Honolulu. It's something I do well and something that repays me for my efforts. And now you know that if I say to you, "I'm going to Damascus," you should back off and mind your own business. Nah, just joking.

Tallying the Numbers

In 2015, we attended a total of 75 performances: 35 operas, 11 symphonies, 16 dance programs, 5 plays, and 8 other (recital, multimedia, competitive audition). On average, we attend 1.5 performances a week, but this "average" is a statistic that, like many, provides a false impression. There are weeks, especially when visiting other cities, when we see performances on consecutive nights for a stretch of four to seven days, sometimes both a matinee and an evening performance; then there are other times in residence in Pittsburgh when two weeks or more may go by without attending anything; these are made up for by, for example, a recent span of ten days during which we saw a Thursday performance of Shakespeare's *The Winter's Tale* set to music of various Baroque composers and performed in the theatre on the tenth floor of the downtown Union Trust Building, a Sunday Pittsburgh Symphony Orchestra concert with Daniil Trifonov as soloist in a concerto he himself composed, a Tuesday preview of the upcoming season of Resonance Works, a company whose productions we've attended with pleasure since our second year in Pittsburgh, and a Sunday train departure for New York for four Metropolitan Opera performances.

You Can Take the Guy Out of Hawai'i, But . . .

Of course I miss Hawai'i. No, I don't spend part of every day dreaming of the view from our former home on Maunalani Heights or recalling how easy it was to step outside in a T-shirt and shorts and flip flops—excuse me, slippahs— any day of the year. But it shows up now and then. That former student of mine in conversational English, the doctor from Syria, invited me for dinner a few months after I started working with her. She and her husband would be vacationing in Hawai'i, and they wanted to pick my brain. I described the bliss of snorkeling at Hanauma Bay in the early morning, the almost-like-being-in-Tokyo experience of picking out bento on the top floor of Shirokiya (I learned that many Middle Easterners have a high regard for Japan because of its recovery after World War II and its global influence despite a small population and scant natural resources), and the sliver of eternity you glimpse from atop Haleakalā while watching the sun's rosy fingers stretch toward you from Mauna Kea.

She looked at me with a wistful smile and said, "You miss it, don't you?" She had caught me. Yes, I do. Sometimes the realization comes without words. A couple of years ago we took a visitor through the extensive greenhouses of the Phipps Conservatory. As we walked along a hallway linking two greenhouses, I sensed the ghost of a familiar scent. There, just around the next corner in a large planter, was a specimen of white ginger with a single blossom. I am proud of my forbearance: I did not pluck it. I didn't even have to dip this involuntary memory in hot tea to savor it, madeleine-like. I just stood there and inhaled. At our Honolulu home, I purposely planted white ginger in the bed bordering the front door, so the trades would waft the cleaner-than-clean fragrance into the living room throughout the summer. I can't do that in our current home. Well, I could bring back one of those plastic-encased, pre-inspected plants from ABC Drugs and plant it outside our front door, but the fragrance would not penetrate the door's double-paned glass panel, and the first frost would kill it. Another fragrance-induced memory came during a visit to the Philadelphia Flower Show, a botanical extravaganza of epic proportions. Among the entries on display in the orchid section were two honohono plants. Now, this show is held in February, and even in Hawai'i honohono don't come into bloom until high summer. But there in mid-February were blossom-lined stems cascading from the parent plants, one white and one lavender. A guard rail prevented me from getting close, but I used my program to fan the air towards my face. Ah, yes, definitely honohono. No, not as powerful as the Aokis' flowers in Kaimukī whose fragrance drifted down our driveway and perfumed our living room on still summer nights. But, hey, for Philly, this was a near miracle. Then again, in a kind of attempted reverse weather sabotage, I recall potting hyacinth bulbs back in Hawai'i, covering the pots with foil, and placing them in the produce drawer of my refrigerator in order to force the blooms. A lot of work; I did it just once. Here, they just come up, year after year, along with daffodils, crocuses, and forsythia. And primary school teachers don't have to order packets of dried autumn leaves for bulletin board displays; they're all over the ground outside the classroom.

Song of the Islands

The memory trigger can be pressed even in the unlikely waiting area of one of the gates at Chicago's O'Hare Airport. Waiting there one evening for the last flight to Pittsburgh, I occupied myself reading email and occasionally touching-checking the boarding pass in my pocket. But something tickled my ear. What was that on the Muzak soundtrack? No, couldn't be. Yes, it was "Na Lei o Hawai'i," deprived of lyrics and arranged for electronic instruments. But the melody was enough. It time-machined me back to Waipahu Elementary, seventh grade, to be specific. Learning all the verses because the seventh graders were traditionally the chorus for the May Day entrance of the eighth grade princes and princesses and attendants. I could even remember some of the words, especially for the Big Island, O'ahu, and Maui; lehua, 'ilima, and roselani. I don't think I ever memorized the words for Lāna'i and Ni'ihau, especially since the courts for those islands were the last selected, the Miss Congenialities of May Day. Oh, those elementary school politics. But that was now irrelevant, and even via Muzak this melody could make magic.

When Residence Becomes Home

About six months after settling here, I was on a plane returning from the West Coast when I caught myself smiling inside at the comforting thought that I was going home. I watched as downtown's Golden Triangle passed below, succeeded by the gentle hills surrounding the airport. I anticipated negotiating the light rail from air side to land side, turning left to get to United baggage claim, hailing a Yellow Cab, and saying, "James Street next to Allegheny General Hospital." Pittsburgh had become home. There were other signs to come. About that same time I found myself, while away on trips, looking online first at the *Pittsburgh Post-Gazette* and then at the *Honolulu Star-Advertiser*. Peduto's latest pronouncement demanded my attention more than Caldwell's; the opening of Kevin Sousa's latest restaurant in Braddock was more relevant than Ed Kenney's; the Pirates' games-behind stat held my interest more than the Wahine's RPI. When shopping for clothes, I would automatically consider the varied weather conditions that I would need to cope with rather than blithely selecting only for fit and color from the year-round-the-same offerings at the Kāhala Macy's. My weather sense had evolved from cold weather/hot weather to a graduated spectrum encompassing subtle degrees of cold and, in all seasons, the chance that there could be a shift of as many as 30 degrees from the time I left the house until I returned hours later. So hanging in the closet are the all-out blizzard-challenging Columbia parka with zip-out Mylar lining next to wool peacoat with quilted polyester lining next to navy blue and bottle green quilted Italian jacket to black leather bomber jacket to five hoodies of various thicknesses to rain jackets to sweatshirts to . . . Well, you get the idea. And this is a learned behavior. On our second pre-move reconnaissance trip in February 2012, I brought my winter coat. *The* winter coat. Living in Hawai'i, I had only one to take along on any trip between November and April. Well, it was unusually warm during our five-day visit, and I suffered. Even removing the lining and leaving the coat unzipped didn't completely solve the problem.

A final example of successful transference of heart as well as household is doubly meaningful because I'm not a sports fan: while ambling along Cooperstown's Main Street, I paused in front of one of many shops selling baseball memorabilia in this Baseball Hall of Fame town. What caught my eye was a 20" x 24" framed collection of baseball cards placed front and center in the display window. The subject: Roberto Clemente, the Pirates Hall of Fame right fielder in the 1960s. Not being a baseball fan, I didn't know of Clemente before moving here, so why was I hoping someone would walk up and start a conversation about him? Simple, he's part of my city. Like me, he moved here and made it his home though, unlike me, he has a bridge named after him and a larger-than-life statue in front of PNC Park. Oh well. It's still our home. 🐾

JULIET S. KONO

AT YOUR AGE

You've locked yourself up.
Refuse to see me.
You no longer answer my calls,
but I guess it doesn't matter.
I learned you're doing this to everyone.

The relatives talk—
say you owe money all around town.
You owe us money, too, but that's
not the point, *we're family*, so we let it go.
We're stupid, anyway, for giving you money
when you demand it:
Hey, I like borrow some cash!

You're gambling again.
Your poor sisters—they want to help you
but they old already,
live on small plantation pensions and Social Security.
Every penny counts,
so to them, at least, pay back!

The last time I saw you—was Pearl City Longs—
in the parking lot, your hair all white,
long to your waist and wild
flying in the breeze,
your shorts all hammajang, your legs kakio.
You tried to walk away
when I grabbed your arm
and stopped you to ask: *Hey what's up?*

You yanked my arm away,
nearly took me down.

At eighty, you're still strong,
but inside, you're a broken-down house,
plumbing busted,
porch sagging,
roof leaking,
gutters hanging, grass growing in the troughs.
But what bothered me most,
you didn't even look to see if I was okay.
You hurriedly made your way through parked cars,
and while you ran away, I saw you trip once,
losing control of your slippers.

JULIET S. KONO

HEʻE

We lift cold-morning seawater to splash our wetsuits,
rinse out goggles, adjust snorkels, slip on swim fins, check spears,
and attach waist-side sacks for octopuses we'll hunt
in the glass of ocean we shatter, then glide across in diamond cuts.

Out in the bay, we move from silence to silence;
for a moment stop our bickering about my hoarding.
It's easier to give each other space in water,
clean, clear, and neutral, none of my junk
lying around us. Our bodies sway in the movement
of water, opaque, a filmy freedom from the books
and paper strewn on the floors we must step over.
It eases the pain of drowning in the vast sea of our unhappiness.

Here, there's no need to speak or look at each other
when we scan the bottom. It takes a good eye to spot
the telltale signs, a grouping of coral and rocks,
an octopus's camouflaged lair. I jab my three-pronged
spear in its entrance to tease it out, its prehensile arms,
twisting and slithering, reaching upward the length
of the spear head, like the span of years that has us entangled.
I pull the octopus's spineless heft toward me,
grab its head, and rip resistant suctioned arms off the spear
and my wetsuit. I hold it out in my hand; leave it writhing
before it shoots a jet stream of black ink, clouding our sight.
Treading water, I let a tide stream clear the blue darkness—like
I could the house, but can't, not ready in the clutter of my mind.
I open my waist-bag, rip off the octopus's arms from my own,
shove it in without mercy, giving sad acquiescence to displaced anger.

Barely out of water you begin. *The next time you should* . . . about
how I caught the octopus. But it's just a transition to rant
about how I've shut you out because of my hoarding.
It's like you love another man, and I can't compete!
you shout in the running current of your jealousy.
You should know it's not your fault. *I* am *trying to change.*

I'm not going to eat the boneless octopus.
I'm a practitioner of catch and release.
Before going home, I peel its arms from
the insides of my pouch, haul it out to let it go.
But, before I slide it back into water,
I hold it up in the air, its arms, squirming like snakes
of Medusa's head, while I wish the mana to turn you to stone.

JULIET S. KONO

IN DA BOWL

Some guys,
no mattah how much mangoes
dey get in da bowl,
dey
still
stay
climb
the
tree.

ONCE, GOLION

The sea shacks' dim lights speckle the island.
Our early-evening signal, two blinks of the car's headlights
for our friend, an old squatter, to pick us up shore side,
is answered with three swings of a lantern to say he is coming.
He poles his way to where we are waiting at the boat ramp—
teetering as he steadies himself and moves toward us on his
weathered flat-bottom and materializes in a circle of street-reflected
light-tagging water: shirtless, tall, bronzed, sweat shiny.
He spits an arc of dark tobacco juice into the water.

Slicing through the water we quickly reach Mokauea Island.
Incoming waves soft-lap the underside of his shack
built on stilts—stilts heavily barnacled, black ʻaʻama crabs
scattering in our light—one of them shackled by a long rope
to a chicken-wire fish trap he pulls in, shimmering
with dagger flashes from silver fish he nets severally
and flips into an often used, fish-smelly burlap bag.
Take um home. Take um all home!
Tomorrow, they going burn down my house.

A dull desperation passes over us in the wing-beats of seabirds,
as they head out toward dimly lit buoys tolling in the channel.
On the mountain side, the twilight grows dimmer; a falling
sky of thunderheads, lowing distress, further darkening
the head of the mountains and its drop to shore. I can no longer
see Sand Island across the way and wait for rain to come.

In gaslight, we brace ourselves against the railing,
watch the slow tinsel of elongated drops of rain,
and Golion rubs his white beard, looking as if he had left us

and is far out at sea. He lights up his cheroot and takes a few puffs,
the smoke smelling earthy and of life, as it rises, and mixes with
the thick salt-sea air. He turns away from us, and, as if in a shift of tide,
jumps, suddenly, into the penetrable water's darkness,
dissolving past our shouts, the sweep of searching flashlights.

JULIET S. KONO

HOMING

In boyhood antic,
you withheld water from your pigeons
till they bobbed their heads forward
in thirst and circled like old men,
the cage-floor grates.

They gulped the vodka you offered
in water bottles with lifted beaks
and broken cries from sluggish throats,
as if to toast you in a walkabout,
crossing their legs and feet,
angling their wings
in poor attempt at lift.

You opened the cage
and coaxed your birds to fly out.
Flying drunk, they crashed
into each other,
missed rooftops, the brace
of ironwood pines up valley.

But they always came home, you said,
every last one of them.

Letting the birds go would have been the natural
end to your adolescence,
but one day, hurrying home,
hungry for your favorite butterfish
dish, promised by your mom,

you failed to negotiate
the off-ramp from the H-1.

Crashed into a tree in the median.

Later, your mother let go the pigeons
from their cage to find new homes;
encouraged the directionless
young neighborhood boys
to absorb your flock.

Neighbors stopped hanging laundry,
picking mangoes, tinkering with cars,
to watch the birds circle overhead,
but the birds,
once aloft,

kept going back,
kept going back.

BRENDA KWON

CELESTIAL SWELLS
—for Brock Little and the Little ʻOhana

One week after you say goodbye,
I find myself driving to your mother's place
trailing a car whose back seat hosts
a dog stoking on sticking his head out the window
in the way only a dog sticking his head out the window can stoke,
his tight brown fur coat sleek, slick, and unruffled
but his ears—
oh, those ears,
flapping like the flaggiest of flags
like parachutes rattling in the sky,
like windbreakers in counterforce gusts
like drying bed sheets when all four corners are pinned to the line
or the way your curls became jazz hands when you took to the waves.

One week after you say goodbye,
mountains of water pound Waimea,
each lip ending in a crash of thundering foam,
and in the mist lifting off the tubes
I think I see you dancing,
airborne like a maverick,
commanding droplets beneath your feet
because who needs a board when you've got wings?
And my hand shoots up to say hello,
except in the way things come and go
suddenly it's just water to water,
sand to sand.

Sometimes a blink feels like a lifetime.

Back in the days of Bishop Hall,
we learned how nothing that exists is ever destroyed,
how la mariposa could make it shower in Central Park
through the delicate quiver of its wings.
We played our lives with the bravery of youth
invincible and convinced
that we would live forever
and it was nothing but believable that we could never be destroyed.
But in living our years we likewise learned well
that pain could shape-shift into what we create
that sometimes the best of intentions pave the road
to skin wrapped in scars,
hearts cast in plaster,
and something as elegant as a butterfly's wings
can result in the blows of a hurricane.
And in turn,
who knows what distant beauty brought our pain,
drenched in patience as we dreamed of the break.

So once upon a time in Hollywood
you made what seemed impossible real,
leaping tall buildings in a single bound.
You gifted us with the suspension of disbelief,
tallying casualties far out of sight
like Superman hiding kryptonite beneath his skin
so we could believe that nothing could take Superman down.

Except that one thing took Superman down.

And so one week after you say goodbye
I chant mantras of science to keep you here
the way your mother says she goes nowhere without you.
Nothing is created nor destroyed;
everything changes one form to another—
but in the quietest moments of my regret,

I wonder if it's too late to say I'm sorry,
for the delusion and luxury of saying "next time."

Where do I go to cash in on "tomorrow?"

But like you knew we would need the proof
that nothing connected can disappear
one week before you said goodbye,
scientists announce that Einstein was right,
that in this web of the universe, time and space bend,
contracting, expanding to any movement of matter.
Each time we wave our hands in the air
we tug at the net that holds us in place,
and in moving we change the very space
that cushions and cradles all heavenly bodies.
So with every kiss,
stars crest in the sky
and with each embrace,
the planets bowl.
Each time we dance, we shake the cosmos,
the power of Superman in our own hands.

So one week after you say goodbye,
when I find myself driving to your mother's place
I imagine you laughing among the stars
tickled by the current of a dog's flapping ears,
and in honor of you, I conduct space
if only to imagine you paddle vibrations,
tubes as far as the eye can see,
the endless ride of which you'd always dreamed,
and the gift of swell upon swell of celestial waves.

KAREN AN-HWEI LEE

MEDITATION ON NATIONAL SORRY DAY

Sorry for bloodshed on southern hemisphere nights
        when star-fires glow lower than colonial torches,
  than rum-poured shame in a monoxide garage.
Sorry for slash-and-burn. Sorry for small pox. Sorry for genocide.
                Sorry for stolen generations.
Sorry for eugenics. Sorry for bad orphanages,
        for IMR, a high infant
mortality rate. Sorry for endosulfan insecticide.
                Sorry for rotten healthcare,
        for lost languages flaming to sherry-colored oblivion.
                Sorry
        if sorry is inadequate
once a month, once a year—a ritual of xenophobia,
                signing names in a register
        of whiteness lying
                in whiteness of lies.

National Sorry Day occurs on May 26 in Australia.

QUQU NOT QUA QUA

Ququ is onomatopoeia in Mandarin
for crickets chirping,

a chorus of nocturnal song. Pastor
said *crickets* with a question mark

in English. No *ququ* in a chapel
where a summer fan whispered

in the largest room where we sat
together. No one spoke in tongues.

No one questioned the blessings
of double provisions,

not double capacity of *qua qua*
in Latin for a capacity of *being*,

nor *ququ* in Chinese. When I ask,
crickets? This cricket is not

a lawn game confused with croquet
nor a signifier of silence.

Rather, I lift my right wing
at an angle,

grass-green violin of stridulation,
psalm of ascents.

JEFFREY THOMAS LEONG

PUTTY

And when the detainees penciled their calligraphy of sorrow
upon the barrack walls, brushed in with
hair of the meek rabbit,

the powers-that-be painted the scribblings over,
redacted, boards erased to the plain
cream of nothingness.

And when again they charted in imitation
of Wang Wei's outrage against T'ang betrayal,
an emperor's unjust, white-washed again

by building maintenance.
So with kitchen table knives they cut,
traced an outline of strokes, deeper

slit into tiny valleys, ridges,
culverts of meaning for verse coursing
protest until the partitions became a relief of

nights bled away from loved ones in San Francisco
Chinatown or the village.
The officials' response: putty the words,

each wound thickened flat, pack clay like a poultice,
mudcake seal above the scar.
But ninety years later, where that plaster compact

crumbles to powder, as eventually it must,
a truth so long concealed,
revealed,

even sharper than before.

DIASPORA

(dī-ăs′pər-ə) n.

   a. a dispersion of a people from their homeland.
   b. the community formed by such a people.
                    —American Heritage Dictionary

At the Marin Lunar New Year's celebration, my daughter sticks
a pastel plastic pin into a wall map of China,
like the other girl adoptees marking origin
in clustered points.
Her press solo, Taizhou, Jiangsu,
inches from any other,
though I'm surprised by proximity, just north of
Shanghai and East China Sea, to a draw of dots emptying into shape.
And too, the tiny nubs across the vast rub that's Inner Mongolia,
spaced so perfect, evenly,
as if nomadic trails were
gaps between settle and settle.
All of this press in and pull out for placement,
my desire to discern pattern
in *diaspora*,
the word for being spread wide and thin, a living skin,
so that when layered thicker still,
its shadow might become
evidence of
her body.

JEFFREY THOMAS LEONG

EIGHT-COURSE
CHINESE BANQUET

So easily they are swallowed like shark's fin soup.
One year chatting across a round table like
clods of rehydrated scallops,
then next, an empty porcelain spoon.

Where's Tyler, my gay Chinese cousin,
devoured by disease, his name never wetting
his parents' lips even after three years?
They slip chopsticks into the next dish,

rich mayonnaise curled prawns,
or meaty sweet-sour pork chops with pineapple chunks.
And too, Aunt Alice squared away at home,
her Chinese year of wifely grief begun last January,

and though unmarried, her attorney youngest beside me,
chit-chats, eyes fixed on a hefty chunk of
Chilean sea bass, pungent,
its oily flesh masked only by black bean.

Every relative set at table for this eight-course Chinese
banquet, even the missing flavors,
my father gone 7 years, mother even more,
and my wife's grandmother too.

Some fortunes already played,
before we split to see
the lucky lotto numbers on reverse.
In this ritual sumptuousness,

eldest cousin serves red egg and ginger for another birth,
her first grandson, also named Tyler,
as memory begins anew.
It's what I must eat, and more of,

not a first name redux, restaurant label, nor even the lost space
where I parked, but that taste of roast squab,
its slightly bitter salt,
served at meal's end like a flayed-open earth.

AUNTIES AND UNCLES

Auntie Nemmine

She stay Auntie Nellie, but Russo call her Auntie Nemmine, 'cause she always tell, "Nemmine," when you ask her something.

"Auntie I like one Popsicle."

"Nemmine."

"Auntie, I like watch TV."

"Nemmine."

"Auntie can change da radio to KPOI?"

"Nemmine."

We gotta go her house cause Daddy gotta go fix stuff fo her. She no mo kids or husband la dat. Even when Daddy tell, "You gotta get new washing machine."

"Nemmine."

"When you going trow some stuff away?"

"Nemmine."

We go 'cause Daddy say we gotta go and dat Auntie going buy us ice cream. But when Auntie tell us we can go outside and wait fo da ice cream man, I seen her ask Daddy fo money.

Russo say she one old maid and I tink she kinda look like da witch-lady in the Old Maid card game. I no can win dat game 'cause if coming to da end, and I get da Old Maid my hand start shaking when Russo almost going pick um. He can tell, so he pick someting else. He know. Every time. So every time I lose. So I no like play. Make me nervous. Auntie Nemmine make me nervous.

Auntie grow aunt-too-riums outside. Aunt-too-rium one ugly flower if you ask me. She no like da big red kine wit da middle part dat look like one dick wit one yellow tip. She like da funny color ones: green, purple, pink, white, and all mix up color j'like nevah grow right. Da white ones kinda spooky, she call um obake. Ghost.

Russo said one guy at da YMCA get funny kine skin, all white, little bit pink, he no can get one tan Russo said. He one albino. His skin nevah grow right and most times he gotta stay inside da house or go outside wit one big hat.

Albinos no can go outside 'cause den dey going come all itchy itchy their skin.
Den dey rub um and scratch and das da part where come red or brown. J'like
da obake anthuriums. I donno if das true or not but den make me tink, maybe
Auntie Nemmine coming albino j'like her anthuriums: her face getting brown
spots little bit. Every time look like getting bigger even if she try hide um. She
put plenny powder on her face so much dat, more, she look obake. Her arms
always itchy. She scratch until she bleed but sometimes she don't even know she
scratching or bleeding. Red, red. J'like red anthurium.

We gotta go around da hothouse and hold da rubbish bucket while she pull
off da dead leaves from da orchids. We no can touch nutting except fo pull
weeds, but even den before we pull, we gotta ask if das one weed. Like we no
can tell one weed from da orchid plant? She tell da big orchid, da catteleya, stay
da va-jay-jay flower and da anthurium get one boto. "You know what is dat?"
she ask me. And I say, "Yeah." But I donno what she talking about so stupidhead
Russo tell, "So what Auntie, dey going make one hibiscus?" and he laughing
laughing, so I start laughing laughing. Of course Auntie not laughing. But I neva
know what he stay laughing about. Russo look at me and tell, "You know, if da
two flowahs *do* um dey going get hibiscus babies. Das da birds and da bees."
Somemore boo-shet I tink.

He show me one dead flowah from da bucket, "Of course Auntie's one stay
like dis, all dry up and sour." I still no catch, I jes tell, "Yeah, no?"

No can sit anyplace in Auntie Nemmine's house witout her watching you.
Like you going bus someting or steal someting or put your feet on top da coffee
table and mess up da half finish one-thousand-piece puzzle. She get mad and
tell, "Nemmine, nemmine," if you try put in jes one little piece. She tink you
going bend um and once you try push um in da wrong place, j'like you went jinx
um and no can finish um. She get plenny half-finish puzzle put back in da box
'cause SOMEBODY went try put one teeny weeny piece in da wrong puka and
da ting came funny kine and now not going fit anyplace because once it come la
dat, not going fit right. I donno why she was looking at me. You supposed to only
look wit your eye and find where supposed to go and den you can pick up da ting
and hold um over da spot fo double check. And den, *only den*, you can try put um
in but no press hard 'cause if wrong, poho. If right, going go right inside. No can
force um. Even if fit by accident, gotta fit perfeck.

Shet, so we go her house no can even make puzzle. What da hell. So I grumbo, grumbo, grumbo to Russo and you know what he did? He went take one piece from da half-finish one on da coffee table and hide um in da couch way down inside where sometimes he find money. I know 'cause das where he check fo money in everybody's couch. Next time we went her house, Auntie was looking all ovah: undah da couch, sweeping wit da broom way back in da corner, shaking da cushions. I went ask what she doing and she said, "Nemmine," and den I went see um, da whole puzzle finished except fo one piece. Ho was kinda funny and I wanted fo laugh. Russo came and said, "Ho Auntie, junk your puzzle, dey nevah you give all da pieces."

She tell, "I no tink so. Maybe fall down. Try look fo me." When Auntie went shishi, Russo went get da piece and when she came back, he told her, "Look Auntie, dis da one?" She was all happy and try grab um but Russo, he fast, he went "psst" put um in da puzzle. Da las piece. Pau. He dust his hands j'like da cowboys on TV, "Yee-haw! Whoa Nellie!"

Auntie look like she was going cry. She happy dat da puzzle pau but she sad dat wasn't her dat went finish um. I was rolling ovah, laughing, "Too good, Russo. Too good." No good say dat too loud so I made like, "Ho da nice da pickcha: mountains and trees and one lake. Too good!" Was one hard one 'cause da colors all da same: everyting green and da sky almost da same color as da lake. Must have been tree months for Auntie to finish, I mean *almost* finish um.

Too good, Russo. Too good.

Uncle Good Enough

Auntie Nemmine always call Daddy or Uncle Hung fo fix stuff. Daddy not so good at fixing stuff and I not too sure if Uncle any bettah but at least he try. Daddy always scared: scared someting going bus, scared someting going leak, scared of electricity. Me I scared even fo watch. When he like me help him, I gotta 'cause das my job fo be da helper, but I help from far away. Jes in case.

Uncle Hung, Ah Hung, he no scared him. If he bus da pipe, no worry. Can fix. Only ting most times da fix not so hot, so when I da helper, I help from near 'cause I like see how he going bus stuff. Fix da leak means da leak went move to one nudda place. Fix da light switch means you gotta remembah one switch gotta be on and den da uddah one gotta be off so da light go on. He went draw one arrow on da switch for remind you dat da light not broken, jes da switch gotta be in da right position. Toaster not broken, jes gotta go one time, turn da bread around and go again. Russo call him "Uncle Good Enough" cause das what he always say at da end, "Eh, good enough."

He fix all da stuff half ass, Uncle Good Enough. Until da next time broke, he fix um good enough.

Shame go store wit him. He wear his puka pants and bus up tank top: Suck Um Up on da front but he no suck up his stomach so can see his belly button. He wearing his good enough rubbah slippahs, da one he went fix wit one soda bottle cap. You know da middle part dat go between your toes? He fix um with one soda bottle cap and wire. For real! He sew da rubbah part to da bottle cover wit one piece wire, j'like one button. Can tell when he coming 'cause you hear: tak, slide, tak, slide, tak, tak. J'like he get taps on his slippahs . . . you know, Mistah Bojangles kine. But you know what funny? He always bus da right side so he get one whole collection all left-hand side.

So last time I went Times wit him, I pushing da wagon back to da car and right outside get da basket wit all da plastic bags dat people bring back to da store fo recycle. Uncle, he grab one whole bunch from da basket.

"Uncle, whachudoing? Das fo bring your old bags back fo recycle."

"Yeah, I going recyco. Pretty soon da store no can give plastic bag. What I going use fo line da rubbish can? Fo pick up dog doodoo? Help me grab some. I going recyco."

I grab some and push da cart fast. Da wheels going donga, donga, donga. Uncle going tak, tak, tak. Da bags from all diffrent stores: Longs, Foodland, Safeway, Times waving at me.

Avocado's Numbah

When I get to his house after school, Uncle singing while he weed da garden, "Don't come around tonight . . . Bound to take your life . . . Dere's da batroom on da right . . . ."

"Bad moon on the rise, Uncle."

"Huh? Yeah, yeah, Creedence song . . . Dere's da batroom on da right," he sing again and point to da right.

Ever since I started wearing thick glasses in the fifth grade, Uncle Hung call me "Professah." I walk to his house after school and wait fo Daddy come pick me up aftah work. I supposed to do my homework but sometimes Uncle like read my books. He say he going help me wit my homework but mostly he jes like read my science or my math books.

About once a week Uncle test me, "Professah, how you figga da circumference of one circle?"

"Pi-r-squared," I tell, trying fo do my homework.

"Wrong!" He slap his leg and tell, "Pie are not square, dey round! Hee, hee, hee." And he hop around laughing at his own joke. Me, I heard um befo. Mo den once. From Uncle.

"And whachucall it when you catch bus and end up 'Ewa Beach instead of Waikīkī Beach?"

"I donno, Uncle."

"You went catch da rhombus! Get it? Wrong-bus!"

Uncle read from my geometry book, "Tree point one four one five . . ." He keep reading da digits, "nine two six five tree five. . . . Why dey gotta have so many numbahs?"

"Non-repeating decimal, Uncle. Neva going stop."

"Da numbah no end eh? Da bugga go on and on?"

"Yup."

"Non-repeating." He stay quiet, must be reading da book.

"But how dey know fo sure if da ting no repeat?"

By now, I no can do homework 'cause now I tinking about it too. How dey know fo sure? What if some place down da line da ting repeat? What if dey jes neva go far enough?

He read somemore, "Da book says cuz pi one irrational numbah. No make sense."

"Yeah, Uncle, das irrational, no make sense." He no catch.

When I went McKinley, same ting. Catch bus to his house and he still like help me wit my homework. Uncle work at Waldron and sell animal feed and fertilizer. He keep telling me about fertilizer, "You know what is 20-20-20? What 15-30-10 good for?" Maybe das why he like chemistry so much.

Uncle neva take chemistry in high school. He said he was too dumb and dey put him in ag classes. Agriculture. He said das fo da guys too stupid to study so dey gotta work outside and grow corn and cabbage and green onions. Den dey go to all da classrooms and sell corn la dat once a month. Maybe das why he sell fertilizer nowdays.

He take da chemistry book from my hands, "You not using dis eh?"

"Guess not."

Uncle Hung like read my books only ting, he skip around and ask me stuff that we neva learn yet or he ask me stuff that we went learn long time ago, so I went foget awready. So I gotta read and explain to him.

"So Professah, Avocado's numbah, what kine numbah dat?"

"Six point zero two times ten to da twenty turd."

"Das one big numbah."

"Twenty tree zeros big," I tell him.

"Biggah den uku-billion?"

"I guess."

"What dat fo? Avocado numbah?

"Avogadro. Fo measure gas."

"Oh, like gallon gas."

"Mo like your fut-gas, Uncle."

"Who like measure my fut-gas?" He stop and tell, "Pull my fingah, pull my fingah." He pull his own finger, fut, and go, "Ahhh ... vo ... cado!"

"Avogadro, Uncle. Avo-ga-dro."

"Yeah, yeah, Avocado. Too good, him. So what he went invent? One mole? I thought one mole was one animal? Mainland get dat. Moles. Ovah here no mo. No mo moles. Get mongooses. If one local guy went invent dat numbah maybe would've been called mongoose instead of mole." He put down da book, tinking about da idea, "Uncle Hung's Numbah, fo measure Mongooses. Sound good eh?"

I stay cracking up even if I no like encourage him 'cause now, even when I go home I still gotta do homework.

"Rational or irrational, Uncle Hung's Numbah?" he ask me.

"Irrational Uncle. Gotta be irrational." No use study awready.

"I thought so. We go eat ice cream."

He get da ice cream, two scoops in a bowl for me one scoop for him. We sit by da altar. I do the usual first before eating, bow three times and pour a little tea and gin in the pan. Bow three times again. Uncle look at da picture of Ah Po and Ah Goong. Da incense burning behind da five teacups, five small cups liquor. Small statue of Kwan Yin.

He tell me, "Plenny tings irrational. Numbahs, dis kine Chinese stuff. You donno fo sure if true or boo-shet. But still yet you do um 'cause, you know, jes in case. Ah Po used to go to da temple and pray fo everybody, especially you. She trow da fortune sticks and if no come out good, she jest trow um until come out good. She no come home until she get one good one fo each grandchildren. She used to say you guys smart because she went temple and pray. And mo bettah you guys go to temple too."

"I know. Nobody like go wit her 'cause get all incense smoke and da big gold Buddha, kinda scary, and da bolohead monks and Ah Po's friends, all da old ladies, like pinch your arm and your cheek and tell 'Marry Chinese gurl, okay?'"

Uncle laugh and eat. "She was always tinking about bumbye when you get older. She check out which of da old ladies get granddaughters!"

"Aw man. . . ."

"Yeah, from when you was small kid awready, she was setting you up! Now, how long awready but I still do dis kine," he point to da altar. "I donno if Ah Goong or Ah Po know if we still praying fo dem. No can be sure. Not like one theory dat get proof. Not like Avocado's Numbah. Maybe all fo nutting eh? Poho. Maybe when you die, dat's it. Pau. Nutting awready. Except us stupidheads burning incense."

I eat my ice cream, scrape my spoon on the bottom.

"But Professah, you turn out okay. I tink Ah Po know what she was doing, eh? Maybe bumbye you going get one numbah named aftah you."

Auntie Kat

Saturdays Ma and Daddy go grocery shopping and either I gotta go wit dem or I can stay Uncle and Auntie's house until dey pau. I supposed to help Uncle Toong but mostly we watch TV and he gimme Popsicle *before* lunch.

My bruddah Russo told me dat Uncle Toong is one fut checker.

"What? One fat checker?"

"Fut checker."

"Fack checker?"

"Try ask him. I dare you." Russo such a punk.

So when I went their house I went ask, "Uncle Toong, Russo said you one fut checker? Ass true?"

"Yup."

"How you check fo futs?"

"Smell." And he laugh, laugh, laugh. "I work da refinery. We make gasoline, jet fuel, diesel fuel, anykine. If get anykine leak or if somebody no close da pipe good, ho can get plenny pilikia. So I gotta check up on all dose tings. One of da worst is methane gas, C-H-4, one carbon, four hydrogen, plus one spark, and boom, you gone. Like one bomb. Ma-ke, die, dead. Goners. Ass my job. Make sure nobody die."

"But howcome Russo call you da fut checker? He said you da fut guy."

"I going slap your bruddah's head. Of all da tings I tell him, he remembah dat one. Naw, I one safety engineer."

"Hah?"

"Your fut is da same kine gas. You know how when you get one coming, j'like you going explode? Same ting." He laugh. "So you bettah watch it. I da fut checker, no try sneak one by me."

Uncle dig in his briefcase and show me one meter wit one small tube connected. "You know long time ago coal miners used to die because dey went breathe methane gas. Poison dat. J'like one ghost, no mo smell, no mo color, no can tell if you breathing um until you dead. Mo terrible den one *oni*, wit claws and wild hair and fangs and horns, carry one iron club with spikes. . . ." Uncle getting carried away.

Auntie call from da kitchen, "Eh, no tell dat kine story, he going get nightmare."

"Das okay Auntie, I like dat kine story."

"Anyway," Uncle tell, "da miners had one birdcage, wit one canary inside, I donno why gotta be one canary, but if da canary ma-ke, dey gotta get outa dere 'cause da canary went breathe da gas first."

"So you like da canary?"

"Yeah, I guess so. Early warning system." Uncle look out da window and start singing, "Meow, meow, meow, meow. Meow, meow, meow, meow. Meow . . ." like da Meow Mix commercial. I look at him funny kine and he wink at me, "Here comes Auntie Kat-a-rine Chow! Chow, chow, chow!"

Auntie Katherine Chow get red hair, fake I tink, and da kine cat glasses wit da jewels on top and da eyeglass cord so dat she can hang um like one necklace. She get long red fingernails every one perfeck. Everytime I see dat, I wondah how she pick her nose. Russo always tell me, how she wipe her ass? And den he sniff his fingah. Eeew. She get something wrong wit her skin so her face and her arms get pink places and get regular skin places. Sometimes look like one map.

208 | DARRELL H. Y. LUM

One continent or one state, maybe Illinois or Maine. She Auntie Violet's friend from small kid time, so I guess she can do what she like.

Auntie Violet tell, "Oh I gotta go wash my hair." And she hurry up go to da batroom.

I no catch but by den Auntie Kat jes open da back screen door and walk right in da kitchen. Auntie Katherine not one real Auntie but she jes walk in da house like she one real Auntie. She ack like she stay her own house: walk inside, open da refrigerator put one bunch green onions inside, open da Tupperware fo see what get, read da medicine bottles on da kitchen table. "What is urinary tract infection? How come Violet gotta take dis? Too much suk-suk, eh?" And she laugh, laugh, laugh until she start coughing. Smell like cigarettes. I donno what is urinary tract infection and I donno what is suk-suk, but probably stay something bad, especially since she stay poking her finger into her uddah hand. I know what *dat* is. Uncle no say nutting jes sing, "Meow, meow, meow, meow. Meow, meow, meow, meow. Meow . . ." like he calling da cat but he look at me and wink again.

Uncle and Auntie get one cat, Neko. I donno if das really da name or if da cat no mo name and dey jes call um neko 'cause das Japanese fo cat. Neko no come when Auntie Kat come their house. Kinda funny, yah? Maybe Neko smell her coming: not stink but old. Combination perfume and baby powder. And maybe mothballs and dust.

Auntie Kat still try though. "Where Neko, maybe he come if I give him food. She pick up his bowl from da corner and shake um so da food rattle den she put um down by her feet. Neko hiss from behind Uncle. Uncle still singing meow-meow. Auntie Kat shaking da bowl, da food rattling. She making kiss-kiss mout like she love Neko. Uncle pointing to da bowl and telling Neko, "Cat chow, cat chow!" I not sure if he telling da cat Auntie's name or if he telling him go eat his food. Auntie pick up da bowl and bend down, try wave da bowl right in front of Neko, making kiss-kiss sound. Uncle still going, "Meow, meow . . . cat chow, cat chow."

And den Neko, he scratch at her face. She jump back, spill da cat food. Back out da door. Da screen door slam: bang, bang, bang. Can hear her muttering, "Stupid cat." Uncle tell, "Ai-ya, no mo cat chow!"

Auntie Violet came out from da bathroom, hair all in curlers, "She went home?"

Uncle tell, "You went miss her. Neko went try scratch her."

"How come? You tease too much I tink. Neko know you no like her."

"I nice to her. Neko no like Kat Chow. Da cat know when he smell someting stink coming in da door. He get one early warning system." Uncle wink at me. 🐾

SECURITY QUESTIONS

On their first lunch,
what dish did your mother notice your father relishing?
    Chicken feet

When your parents started dating,
what were the surnames of the women your father lived with?
    Lee

If your parents were seeing each other after work,
what was their default meeting place?
    Hong Kong Hotel

From the very beginning,
what perk did your mother provide for your father?
    Haircuts

Strolling on the pier at night,
what did your father discover your mother could recite by heart?
    Chinese poems

After meeting your father for the first time,
what did your maternal grandmother give up?
    Smoking

What did your mother see in your father?
    Her green card

What assets of your mother's attracted your father?
    Her fixed deposits

Where did your mother and father share their first kiss?
>   None of my business

What was your mother's bride price?
>   19 suckling pigs

At the wedding of your parents,
what did your maternal grandfather say?
>   No refund

Atop the building where your parents first lived,
what cure did the neon sign advertise for?
>   Stomach ailments

I FELL

off our two-step ladder
trying to rearrange a box of files
on the top shelf of the cabinet
behind my desk. The ladder
is made of aluminum, and so
fairly light, and my foot must
have been too close to the edge
of the top platform so that when
I shifted my weight slightly
the ladder somehow tipped
out from under me. I remember
suddenly falling and hitting the
floor. It seemed like I was
floundering for a moment as I
landed under my desk. By the
time I got to my feet, others in
my office had come in having
heard, I suppose, the clank of
the ladder's fall. They asked
me how I was. But somehow I
was still trying to digest what
had happened, and then got
self-conscious that I probably
appeared too slow in responding,
making them think I had really
hurt my head. So I assured them
that I was fine—even though
there was some soreness in my
hip, my right elbow, and the
bottom of my palm. I tried to

get back on the ladder. But they
told me firmly not to, which I
was about ready to disregard
until they pointed out how one
of the ladder's spreaders was
now bent outwards. (I think
they were also worried I might
still be dizzy and could fall
off again.) So I relented, not
wanting to make a public fuss
out of all of this, my pride also
having been bruised as well.
They brought in a taller, sturdier
ladder to use since I was insistent
on continuing my filing. After
I finished, I put the ladder back
in the workroom. Everything
was back to normal except for
the throbbing in my wrist bone.
Later, though, I was bothered
even more so with how flustered
I had gotten when faced with
such a small unexpected accident.
I thought then when death
arrives and I lie stunned, blind-
sided, as we all will be, the
skin under my nails turning blue,
my legs cool, my breathing
bewildered and unpredictable,
I will still be fumbling, trying
to gather my wits together, and
everyone will think that this
just means I will now
                    go quietly.

THE DEAD DON'T KEEP QUIET

Let the dead keep their dead. I'm not wanting to excavate any of them. I don't need their secrets. And yet they are whispering to me like they can be heard. I hum a tune to drown them out. They become insistent like yellowjackets, buzzing in my sugar water ears. I cough to scare them away. They merely chuckle. Ah, what are they wanting from me? For the dead are dead, and I was taught they resided far, far away, tamped underfoot by years and forgetfulness. But every year, I went with Mama to clean their graves each November. We lit candles, and my grandfather, whom I never met, was still the prankster, the candles blowing out again and again despite no wind. He watched over me as I sat on the tombstone and listened to conversations between the dead and the living. I understood none of it. For what did I care? All of it was boring and grown-up as I flicked disrespectful ants from the painted stone. The dead are crying, "Love me! Love me!" It is so annoying when I have to run from their cloying pleas like a reluctant pied piper. I don't want their bones of sadness, their runny guts, their airy spirit tears. I want none of it. And I won't fall to my knees and cry for them like yesterday. The past is past. And the present is all there is. Tonight I will wrap myself in blankets and tell them to be quiet and let me sleep. Maybe they will yield to silence. Or only prayer, but I am not willing. Not yet. Not yet. Not yet.

JENNIFER SANTOS MADRIAGA

SISTERS: AWAKE AT OUR GRANDPARENTS' HOUSE

Pangasinan, Philippines

My sister and I lie awake in bed side-by-side
for the first time in years. Again, we become
children with unwelcome chaperones as my
parents sleep in the next room.

The air conditioning unit is noisy and
does its job too well. All night, we flip the switch
on and off to find the right temperature.
And the right mix of hot and cold never happens.

At four in the morning, my sister sighs,
shuts the unit down. Even then there is no quiet
as we listen to the neighbors herding goats down
the driveway, along with the diesel rumble of tricycles.

We were never close growing up. We bruised each other
with fists and slaps, inflicted scars with long fingernails.
Childhood was a continuing exercise in survival,
a nonsensical battle over who could be the golden child.

We are grown now, and we can speak in civil tones
about the weather and flight delays and crazy cousins and
how much we miss our children, but not about her hatred of
our mother or my divorce, which means she now has more money than me.

We know each other's secrets but don't ever relish
their telling like other sisters do—that is what I imagine.

While our arms touch in a way that I can feel the lingering
goose bumps on her skin, we cannot know each other.

It is too early to rise, so my sister turns over,
places the pillow over her head so that
she can muffle the noise of the still-dark world.

JENNIFER SANTOS MADRIAGA

DAY XX AFTER THE WORLD HAS ENDED

The world as I know it has already ended, and yet I'm alive and kicking, sucking in dust and diesel fumes in my father's hometown, sopping wet in the tropical heat despite the climate appropriate attire of tank top and shorts and slippahs. My younger sister leans against me, and my mother sits across in the tight shell of the tricycle cab as we bounce over potholes and past the greening paddies, not yet lush with height. We are three peas in the fragile metal pod as we skid past semis with bad brakes and buses with passengers hanging out windows as the driver speeds without conscience to keep the schedule— pedestrians and dogs and small children be damned. My arms are empty without my son, and I am still a mother but no longer a wife, and the alternate existence I thought would never happen is my new reality. This is just one wave of the few coherent thoughts strung together but drowned out by the mere need to survive the tricycle ride from home to market. I am in the pure element of id, living in a world immune to precariousness as the family of five rides by on a motorbike—mom, dad, two toddlers, and infant son huddled together like a human sedan on two wheels, holding on literally for life as they speed by. But at least they are one tenuous unit in contrast to my own frayed nucleus. Their full-speed-ahead declares that fear is passé because living trumps all. Because it has to. 🐚

POINT TO POINT

my two hands
on the lei
pinched and
placed points
of lau niu
in a taut braid
of beach fiber
balanced
between fingers
in a line
past my toe
and out to sea
like one long canoe
riding the current
past the point
where surfers
charge the cliff
or paddle
out to larger
swells

they pulled
in unison
going somewhere
hunting fish
or hooking islands
guided by wind
clouds
sharks
landmarks

and Guy Hagi's
weather report
followed by
the same
old news:

maddas
pop tents
in places
the no sit
no lie law
is enforced
like paved
taro patches
and lawns
near the
palace
the church
and
the capitol
plus braddas string
blue tarp homes
in the limbs
of thorny trees
right off
the road to
the house-less
shelter

not just to
make
their bodies
make
the case
that native

lands
are priced
out of
native hands,
but to

be

under sky
in the breeze
still fighting
the rip
round
this
point

TAMARA LEIOKANOE MOAN

THE AVON LADY

I was six watching my mother
at her vanity, its mirror top lifted
to reveal the well below
with its rows of brushes,
tweezers, puff balls,
blush, mascara, eye shadow,
and lipsticks.
She used an eyelash curler,
crimping down as she leaned in
to examine every detail.
She teased her hair
and blew a cloud
of hairspray to hold it fast.

The Avon lady waited
on our doorstep,
her smile brilliant and unending.
I loved her case
laid out on our couch,
all its compartments
colored like spring.
The lipsticks were small
like tight rosebuds.

I was seven, then eight.
My mother grew her hair out long
and showed off her legs in short skirts.
When I turned nine
I received a book with biographies of Amelia Earhart,
Margaret Mead, and Madame Curie.

To me they were as magical as the Avon lady,
arriving in my mind
with their gifts of intelligence and nerve.
I wanted to be all of them at once.

TAMARA LEIOKANOE MOAN

GARDEN OF NEGLECT

My potted plants
languish beside the front step,
weed-ridden, parched,
placed so prominently they cannot be ignored
yet I ignore them each time I pass.
Today I move slowly enough
to acknowledge we all need care.
Like the rosemary and oregano
that require light, water, and love
to grow their delicate
flavor and smell,
I need rest and nourishment
to thrive.
I crack a brittle pot open,
dig deep into exhausted soil
and dry roots.
Old leaves and dead bugs
fall away.
I place the herbs
in their new pot gingerly, patiently,
refreshing the dirt
in which we all grow.

APRIL 15

I tried, tried, tried
to do my taxes.
I wanted to tie those numbers
to the tabletop,
hammer them into order,
into terrible columns of reckoning,
but I reached for the telephone,
talked with five friends,
changed my T-shirt
three times in case that might help,
tempted the dog with a fresh bone,
and then left for the movies.
The big screen was comforting.
In that dark room
I followed a jewel thief
through mansions in France,
into the beckoning arms
of conniving women,
past undercover cops,
to a clever world of
secure bank accounts
and sunny beaches.
But there is only so much
running you can do
and it all leads to the same place,
that deserted bankrupt dead-end alley
between death and the IRS.

HAKU LELEIOHOKU

Pua ka wiliwili nanahu ka manō. "When the wiliwili blooms, the shark bites."
My love, it's true that when Leleiohoku blossomed, his immaculate stanzas and
insurmountable quatrains haunted my imagination, like rows of glistening
shark's teeth.

Yes, it's true: the lines I gave you, the ones you loved so dearly, were forged in
another man's heart. I approached their lyrical brilliance like a shark circling in
ever-tightening circles. And then, I committed the penultimate sin: plagiarizing
a former student's work.

I do not deny that I have always possessed this shark-like nature.

But I defend my larceny with platitudes: Don't the best poets steal? And isn't
everything fair in love and war?

Who was Leleiohoku? He was the wiliwili blossom, a rare flower born
upon the dry, unyielding slopes of Makakilo. By an act of fate or the foresight
of ambitious parents, he and his three siblings had inherited the names of
the royal composers: David Kalākaua Freitas, senior and scholar-athlete-in-
chief (being both student body president and captain of the football team);
junior Lydia and sophomore Miriam, accomplished synchronized swimmers
and National Merit Scholars (who would one day dedicate their Olympic
silver medals to Senora Hill, an indelible source of inspiration). And then
there was William Pitt Leleiohoku Freitas, the youngest of the four, a shy,
unpresumptuous freshman who, unlike his older siblings (and to his parents'
private disappointment), cared little for formal accomplishments, but who
was perhaps the most gifted of them all.

Collectively, they were bestowed the lofty title of "Na Lani Eha," the year all
four were Song Contest Directors. Beneath the bright lights and a mountain
of fragrant leis, each Freitas mounted the pedestal and summoned forth their
respective army of angelic voices: green then blue, red then purple, 400
synchronized voices crescendoeing and decrescendoeing with each sweeping
gesture into the shape of church bells and brave voyages, and a thousand
inconsolable emotions.

It is hard to describe the small miracle of Leleiohoku's performance. Beneath pitch-perfect thirds and each meticulous modulation trembled an untamed energy. It rolled over the crowd like a winter swell traversing the Pacific Ocean, carrying the birth and death of a violent storm in its liquid memory. Through the second miracle of broadcast television, it was pinged up into space, up through the tropo-strato-mesosphere into the oxygenless realm of satellites and seraphims orbiting earth; and then it came crashing back down again, filling our TV sets with its alien beauty.

When all was said and done, three of the four judges produced identical scorecards. The fourth judge, a petulant man who despised the idea of ties (believing them antithetical to excellence), anointed the Senior class victors by the slimmest of margins. All left that night recalling Leleiohoku's brilliance.

From day one, a radiance emanated from Leleiohoku's poetry. It was the product of an infinite imagination and an unnatural appetite for verse. The young prodigy consumed canons with impunity: Basho for breakfast, Li Po for lunch, seven Shakespearean sonnets before supper; a fortnight of Keats was followed by an anahulu of Auden; and when time would allow, a nightcap of Neruda the hour before drifting asleep. His intestinal depths delighted in this moving feast, digesting the swirling poetic stew of continents and centuries, mapping the luminous geography of the human heart. Inevitably, a spontaneous inspiration would take root, and something new and brilliant would emerge (perhaps he was the shark and the poems were the wiliwili blossoms).

His singular passion was love poetry, which he composed with a fierce urgency. Its inescapable truth was arrived at through the unyielding knowledge of his ill-fated predecessor: imagine young Leleiohoku standing before the crypt of his royal namesake at Mauna Ala, imprisoned in thought. A gentle rain falls, touching everything with the promise of life. What dissonance for such a poetic soul!

To escape the specter of death, he occupied his mind with Sisyphean tasks. Over and over, he reanimated the haunting love songs of his predecessor into the bodies of impossibly difficult poetic forms. The exquisite corpse of "Ke Ka'upu" became a Petrarchan sonnet before being reincarnated as a sestina. "Nu'a o ka Palai" through careful labor was reborn an elegant ghazal. With each arrangement, the young prodigy conquered death for a fleeting moment. Or rather, through love, he quelled his fear of death. He wondered how one could ever truly love with complete sincerity, yet its sheer impossibility confirmed its truth. And so, perhaps in his imagination, Leleiohoku viewed himself as the fragile wiliwili blossom.

To return to those singular love poems. I have been accused of theft by my enemies. In truth, they were a gift, a poetic hand-me-down given to me after serving their original purpose. A poem is a vessel that carries many lives and many secrets. The poems I have given you were born on a warm Wednesday afternoon, in chapel, from the loins of Leviticus 18:22.

"Thou shalt not lie with mankind, as with womankind: it is abomination." The kahu repeated the words once more, hoping to secure it in the hearts of his young congregation. His voice, as always, was filled with eternal warmth. Leleiohoku, meanwhile, tried his best to fan away the stifling heat. Or perhaps he was fanning away the kahu's words, for Leleiohoku had known for a long time that he was just such an "abomination." Once upon a time, he felt shame in it. But that was long ago. Instead, the stifling heat triggered an equal and opposite reaction in him. He began to lay out his vision for a PRIDE Club at Kamaha'o Schools. The school's namesake, after all, had male aikāne; and there were countless verses describing Christ's boundless love for the least among us. The next week he presented his arguments to the Administration, but the uncompromising spirit of the Old Testament prevailed. Leleiohoku's proposal was rebuffed by the headmaster, who always deferred to the spiritual counsel of his kahu.

The following week, a sealed envelope arrived at the kahu's door. It was early morning. When he opened it, he found a folded poem nested within. It was a love poem. It seemed harmless at first, resting there in his hands. His heart, through years of pious devotion, had wholly committed itself to God: what little space remained had been faithfully committed to his loving wife. Still, he delighted in the unexpected adulation. For an hour, he folded and unfolded its contents in the privacy of his office, imagining who his secret admirer might be. Perhaps it was Ms. Thompson, the cheerful math teacher who always sat in the front row, just within his field of vision. She always nodded appreciatively at his sermons. Or perhaps it was one of the many young souls who filled his

pews each week; a shy student who, in her impressionable youth, confused
his passionate preaching with the more worldly manifestations of God's love.
Regardless, it was a sign of a job well done.

Each morning a new envelope arrived, greeting the kahu with its precious
cargo. To his disbelief, the second poem was twice as beautiful as the first.
Its couplets conjured into existence two white terns soaring high above
Kawaiaha'o Church. Kahu floated in its luminous presence all morning: how
surprising the way a handful of words could invigorate his entire being: that
afternoon he gave an inspired sermon, perhaps the best of his career. That night
he carried his wife to bed with the same youthful industry of his wedding night.

It was the third poem that troubled him. Yes, it was even more beautiful
than the first two combined. But a subtle slip of syntax in the last stanza
revealed the gender of his anonymous paramour. He read and reread the poem
to be absolutely sure. Each time his eyes collided with that innocuous line of
two lonely ships passing in the middle of the night, his heart trembled, pierced
by the sharp reef of truth submerged beneath the surface. Poor kahu. He began
to take on water and sank deeper and deeper into despair. Kneeling before the
chapel altar, he called out to God, begging Him to banish the poems from his
imagination. *I ka 'ōlelo no ke ola, i ka 'ōlelo no ka make.* Yes, these words had the
power to destroy him. He repeated Leviticus over and over as if the words were
an antidote that could inoculate him from his deepest fears. But the poems
were filled with such undeniable truth that when the fourth envelope arrived,
he could not abstain from opening it. And as he read the poem, somehow even
more brilliant than the last, he felt, against his will, his heart soften. The words
reverberated through his body like the trumpets at Jericho. It shattered his
fortress heart. Within a week, he had fallen hopelessly in love.

How was this possible, you may ask? How could this reviled seed take
root in the guarded chambers of the kahu's heart? My love, such miracles have
always occurred in our islands. According to our best botanists, it occurred
with the clockwork efficiency of once every 98,000 years. The primal seed that
survived doldrums by clinging to a piece of flotsam, or overcame the dark night
of a tern's stomach to arrive on these shores, is living testament to this truth.
Why are we surprised when love, the most powerful seed of all, takes root in the
human heart?

For weeks, the kahu battled the demons in his heart. And yet he found himself arriving to work earlier and earlier each morning until one morning he looked up and found himself in the crepuscular darkness before the chapel door. The sealed letter would be there waiting for him. The kahu fretted. He lost sleep and began to skip meals (which worried his faithful wife). At night, he locked himself in his study and reread those intolerable poems. God saw him and his trembling desire. The knowledge of His omnipresence further tortured the poor kahu. And yet, when he walked around campus, everything reminded him of the poems, for the world and his heart existed within them: the moon, the birds, the wind passing through the trees, the burning warmth of the sun. He mumbled the verses like prayers; through sheer repetition, he committed entire poems to memory. Sometimes a rainbow would appear, reminding him of his broken covenant with God. Other times he thought he noticed birds eyeing him hungrily, having detected the forbidden seeds in his heart. For forty days and forty nights, he wandered in his desert without reprieve.

And then one morning, the letters stopped. The kahu sighed with relief. He had survived God's test, he told himself. For the first time in forty days, he slept beside his wife with profound peace. But the following week, a new desperation took root, infiltrating the fabric of his dreams. They were haunted by monstrous rainbows that hovered and arched above his head like horrifying halos wherever he went.

This was the state of poor kahu the day the last poem arrived. The kahu's heart raced. He looked sheepishly to his left, then to his right; he glanced over his shoulder. When he opened the envelope, he let out a sigh of relief: it was not a new poem, but a familiar verse from "Kāua i Ka Huahuaʻi," the original Leleiohoku's most famous and well-recognized song. It was unadorned and unembellished by his captor's touch.

That afternoon, on the last chapel service of the year, kahu introduced Leleiohoku Freitas, a quiet freshman who had been selected by his peers to speak before the class. He ascended the pulpit and nodded kindly to the kahu. Then he smiled at his peers, who responded to his quiet confidence, just as they did the night of Song Contest.

"I am humbled to be here with you in this house of love." Even when speaking, the boy's voice was a thing of beauty, a joy forever.

"In John 4:16 it says, *And we have known and believed the love that God has for us. God is love; and he that dwells in love dwells in God, and God in him.* I believe in the greatness of God's love. It exceeds our imaginations. It is the foundation of my faith. God is love, and our ability to love is what brings us closest to Him. From time to time, I have tried to express my thoughts and feelings in words. They are far from perfect, but I would like to share several of my failed attempts with you today."

Leleiohoku began to recite his words. The kahu's dismissive smile evaporated when he recognized each of the lines from the poems he had memorized. Perspiration assailed his forehead. His tongue cracked, his ears pounded; slender fire burned under his skin.

"I would like to end with a song from a poet much greater than I. It comes from my namesake, who lies near our beloved Princess at Mauna Ala."

Leleiohoku began to sing. With each verse, his voice ascended the four octaves like a cool fountain:

> *Kāua i ka huahuaʻi*
> *E ʻuhene lā i pili koʻolua*
> *Pukukuʻi lua i ke koʻekoʻe*
> *Hanu lipo o ka palai*

The girls sighed. Ms. Thompson cried, nodding her head approvingly.

All at once, the seeds that were poems blossomed in kahu's heart. A garden of wiliwili emerged. Other flowers bloomed too, until a rainbow of breathtaking flowers filled the chambers of the kahu's heart. Poor kahu. He was, in that moment, the wiliwili blossom, and Leleiohoku, the shark.

I went home that day thinking of the miraculous garden of poems. It made me think of the difficult journey of our own love, how we too have been collecting seeds in our hearts. With each fight, each reconciliation, our love has grown through doldrums and darkness. We have drifted from time to time on the precarious flotsam of our lives, waiting patiently for our love to bloom.

> *Kāua i ka huahuaʻi*
> *E ʻuhene lā i pili koʻolua*
> *Pukukuʻi lua i ke koʻekoʻe*
> *Hanu lipo o ka palai*

My love, I have always desired you, the way the shark desires the wiliwili blossom. ✿

LIMITED ESCAPE

What you remember in the middle of tragedy
are the same mundane things that break the surface
of your ordinary days; like at your kid's soccer game
you realize today's your mother's birthday
or while imitating the yoga instructor
doing sun salutation it hits you:
your Costco membership expired.

No one fed the dogs. That's what came to her,
a little after Dr. Park explained it was unlikely her husband,
who an hour ago fell from the fifth step of a ladder,
would ever walk again, a little after her gasp
eclipsed nearby conversations about OxyContin
and incontinence in the crowded ER waiting room.

Skittles and Randy she says a little too loud
the dogs, the ambulance left so quickly,
we live alone, no one's there to feed them—
her eyes scanning ours for a door or a window
any way to escape this slow judgment;
but all we have is a travel-sized box of Kleenex
and a consent form that needs her signature.

Unwilling to acknowledge the paper
she looks away when I cover her hand with mine,
We'll take good care of him.
A bewildered cry—more animal than human
contorts her mouth, bruises her voice and damages us all.

This is the wreckage too. Suddenly I recall
leaving my coffee in the x-ray department
cold now, bitter.

22 REASONS I WILL NOT ANSWER YOUR PHONE CALL

1. Because your rent is due

2. Because I know your goddamned rent was due two months ago when Jackie, your landlord, called me asking where you were

3. You put me as a reference on the rental application, you fucking dumbass, and didn't tell me. You used the number I told you not to give out, the number I didn't even want you to use unless you were in an emergency like if you got hit by a truck, or if you got cancer of the brain. I knew I shouldn't have given you my number

4. You still owe me four hundred from the last time you borrowed money from me, when they repo'd your car, begging me *please please please, I pay you back. My tax refund's coming in the next two weeks*

5. Jackie's not only asking about the money, she's saying the neighbors been grumbling about your friends, honking their car horns at all hours of the night and those fuck ups are parking in your neighbors' stalls. Everybody's *concerned* about the loud arguments coming from your side of the wall and say your kids are running wild. *No adult supervision* she said while they race remote control cars in the parking lot and piss on the side of the building between the dumpsters

6. I'm listening to Jackie list off the complaints and I'm thinking some complaints are legit and some are lame, but it's clear, people want you outta there

7. Because I know the arguments, late night parties and uncaged kids means you are using again no matter what kind of bullshit story you tell Jackie or your social worker

8. I heard all your stories; you hurt your back or your leg or your neck so you been off work for a while, your kids need new shoes, field trip money, books—whatever kids need and you cannot get from Costco with food stamps. You have no shame. Worst of all: *my mom is sick, she cannot work so I'm helping her with the rent*

9. Mom is sick, but you're not helping out. Not with the doctor visits, the pills, the bathing, the vomiting. Nothing. I can't remember the last time you came over to the house

10. When she first got sick, I thought I needed you to pull it together, to be around more. The house was so damn big with Pop gone and Mom was so small and she kept getting smaller. The whole world was disappearing in slow motion. Like those movies where the hero's fallen off the train and he's trying to get back on but he can't. And he's running and he's running and the train keeps getting farther and farther. He reaches out his hands but you just see the smoke—he reaches out his hands, then it's just the long road ahead

11. I'm stronger now

12. We took down your pictures in the house, all of them. The wedding pictures, graduation photos, all of them

13. She stopped asking about you

14. You even lie, straight-faced about Darcy, right in front of the kids. That's their mother for Chrissake. You'll say she's taking you back to court for custody of them so that's costing you, but the kids know that's not true. Darcy doesn't give a shit about them, she doesn't even know what day of the week it is. She's high all the time, lost plenty weight, still hanging out in Wahiawā even though she quit her job at Pearl's. Kids haven't heard from her in months. I saw her on the bus, wearing long sleeves, trying not to twitch, *Sis you can lend me a few bucks?* Long sleeves? In the summer time? I should have told her pull up her sleeve first, then I give her one twenty. But I already know. And what about you, what you wearing today?

15. Or are you still just sucking on that pipe?

16. You and her, you have kids. You have kids

17. Even Jesus had to draw a line in the sand

18. Remember Mrs. Yoshizaki from Sacred Hearts Sunday School? She was short, round, and instead of a cross, wore a white dove pendant on a thin gold chain. She brought vanilla cupcakes with rainbow sprinkles every Sunday to class. We would eat them outside on the picnic table in front of the Virgin Mary statue. We had to wipe down the table first with wet paper towels to clean off the dirt, even though me and you didn't care if it was clean. We just wanted the cupcakes, because cupcakes, not counting Sunday School, only came for us on our birthdays. I would eat mine real slow even though you gobbled yours so fast that you were done before everybody else, sometimes even before Mrs. Yoshizaki started the story. You would make these small whiny noises and a sad face at me so I would share the rest of my cupcake with you. Most of the time I did, and when I did you would smile, sit closer, and put your arm around my shoulder. *Thanks sis*

19. I'm remembering stuff like that more and more

20. It was me. I'm the one who took down your pictures

21. I thought it would be hard to put away the picture of you leaving for the Army; you got the camo greens on, duffle over your shoulder, and the sunlight is at your back. Even though you are not smiling, your eyes, and the way you are holding your head shows a confidence that was rare for you. In the background, your friend Jon is in the driver's seat of a brown Camaro waiting to take you to the airport. Waiting to take you to another place, a place where you can redeem yourself, a place so far away that we even begin to think you will make it, that you'll leave the drugs behind. The drugs that even way back then already had a grip on you. That was many years ago, nothing was left behind

22. Except us.

THE ROAD TO DAMASCUS

The walk to the psych unit is in the back of the hospital, away from the inpatient units, financial offices, ER, cafeteria—basically everything and mostly everyone. If you are walking down this corridor, it's to the locked unit, and that's it.

The corridor is about half the length of a football field and does not maintain the same façade as the rest of the hospital with its hardwood floors, and sepia photographs on the walls of old Hawai'i. It's white polished concrete floors with bare cinderblock walls painted a dark teal that was popular in the 80s. The overhead pipes are exposed and the ceiling is low so if you are looking up, you get an old factory feel: you are made small here. There is no warmth in this corridor, but it's not cold either; it leads you simultaneously into and towards, like judgment.

Staff working in the unit deal in behavior modification, so we're called for the medical issues. You can't really prepare for what you'll find on the locked unit. The last time I was there, the patient was having a bona fide heart attack: chest pain, difficulty breathing, the usual. The call before that, the patient had acute abdominal pain and sudden deafness after the staff stopped her from masturbating in the main dining area.

Marc's with me on this call; we're walking side-by-side. He has a funny limp, bum-knee-from-college-ball, which makes for a strange echo of our footsteps like a call-response spiritual: Get *up*, Get *up*, Get *up*.

Marc's telling me the latest about our boss, when midway, a shift in tone: *Remember to keep your back to the wall, don't let anybody get behind you.* I nod. He must still feel bad about what happened to Ruth. *And don't lose sight of the door, don't go into a room without me.* Ruth got pinned in a corner when Mark stepped out to get an IV kit. *I think only get chicks on staff tonight.* It took security seven minutes to get there, another four to get the patient off Ruth. For Marc, it's *that place* and *threat* now, but despite everything, I think of them mostly as unintentional, like lambs. I know I am right. I know someday I will be proven wrong. *Stay behind me* as we reach the end of the hallway,

Marc is already puffing out his chest, the bum knee goes straight. We turn right, and squint at the blinding light from the nurses' station coming through the protective glass up ahead. In my mind, I hear that old adage *Fool me once* . . . Marc pulls his ID badge over the keypad and the metal lock clicks open, *Fool me twice* as I follow him through the doorway.

CRAIG SANTOS PEREZ

ODE AND APOLOGY TO THE CHAMORRO RESTAURANT IN THE DIASPORA

Your grand opening is a celebration
for all Chamorros. For those on-island,
you're a sign that we've arrived, safely,
and settled into our destination.
For those off-island, you remind us
culture can be served from any kitchen.
But when I read your Yelp reviews, I burn
with anger at how diners fail to appreciate
your complex flavors. They say you're
a confusing mix of Mexican and Filipino dishes;
they question the combination of coconut,
chicken, lemon, hot pepper, and onion;
they describe your marinade as part Texan,
part Asian; they call you "inauthentic"
and claim L&L Hawaiian Barbecue is real
Pacific Islander food. I've heard all this before,
since ever since my family migrated to California.
I say to you: si Yu'us Ma'ase, *thank you*, brave
chefs, for believing in our cuisine, for the
shine of your red rice, the tang and depth
of your kelaguen, the spice of your fina'denne.
Si Yu'us Ma'ase for proudly displaying our flag
and printing the Guam seal on your menu.
Dispensa yu, *I'm sorry*, for not visiting you
more often, but home still tastes bittersweet,
and it turns my stomach knowing that lack
of business will force you to close soon,

and you will be forgotten, just as our islands
have been forgotten. I'm sorry that you,
like all diasporic Chamorros before you,
will choke on this bony truth:
there's no recipe to make our culture
visible and digestible to the world.

CRAIG SANTOS PEREZ

ISLAND BOYS

No matter
how tall or big or old
we grow
our parents and grandparents
and aunties and uncles
will call us
"boy"

not because they see us
as innocent children
but because they want
to raise men
who know affection

because they know others
will say "boy"
to shame
and discipline us
into men
who deserve
nothing
more than
violence

FLOWERS FOR MY FATHER

Thirty-two days after the funeral, the remnants
of wreaths still lie upon my father's
unmarked grave from foot to crown;
as below, so above is a mirror
spill of hundreds of roses, carnations,
orchids, and daisies plucked and set
upon his wooden casket.
Among the denuded bramble,
are the blue of dyed
daisies and the gold of embossed
ribbons. I pick out the purple banner
of the wreath I bought—one of my last
public acts of filial love.
I resist my magpie impulse to tug
free the yard of Tyrian and calligraphy.
I leave it mired in the foot-deep mound to be
discarded when the groundskeepers
lay down the cut sod and polished
marble and bronze marker,
where then the only place
for flowers will be
a small bronze vase.

SAAN NAK-A BALIKBAYAN

My tongue remembers the simple greeting, *"kumusta"*
—the corrupted *"como esta"* of Spaniard overlords.
It even remembers the gratitude but not the health in *"salamat,"*
from seafaring Arab merchants.
This is my meager Tagalog vocabulary.

Still, I never forget how to be Filipino when embraced
by the cool still air beneath green bamboo groves and the long
tumbling thunder of summer storms.

When I fly from one archipelago to another, I soar
through an invisible blue over liquid teal, which I'm not
friends with because of the turbulence
guarding me from my parents' native land.

My flight is a wash of navy and indigo through the window.
I wave farewell to the green flash on the horizon.
The sun has fled the Pacific for the continent. Lagging
behind, we are swallowed by the following dark.

Manila city lights are strings of dirty ice chips
strewn on asphalt. I yearn for Isabela, the province
still a nine-hour Nelbusco ride away.

Under the starried sky of a new moon night,
air swelters, wet with humidity.
Such suffocating warmth would be welcome
in the refrigerated darkness of the bus
where we huddle, shivering in jackets or sweaters.

With each gradual rise, the bouncing bus headlights
sweep the mud and gravel curves and hairpin
roads of San Mateo. No streetlights contour
this mountain municipality.

Nearing midnight, we rumble through the quiet
roads of the *baranggay*, Old Centro Proper, to the station yard.
Light rain keeps the grey as slick mud and not dust
rising around *trisykels* laden with passengers, boxes, and baggage.

I cross a bamboo bridge onto a muddy yard.
As we slough toward a lit window, my grandmother
is silhouetted by spilling light as she opens the door.
For the next ten weeks, this once more will be home.

LATENT TUBERCULOSIS
PART I: ISONIAZID

One millimeter was one too wide;
upon my skin, the red welt
told in two days what I had not known
for five years—I had been exposed.

Later that day, bare-chested,
I paced across green
linoleum to stand chilled between
suspended metal plates and wait
for an exposure to a short x-ray pulse.

I shiver on a Naugahyde bench,
fear has stolen feeling and warmth
from fingers, hands, feet, and toes.
On the radiograph, there is
in my right lung "a spot of some concern."

Before bed, a single white pill of Isoniazid
made me dream of an army of red
ants nipping at my skin, raising
little red welts with an insistent prickling.

I would wake: blanket thrown off;
my shirt rolled into binding
across my chest, wedged into armpits;
my clipped nails scratching the rash into red
welted skin that plagued
my waking and dreaming worlds.

LATENT TUBERCULOSIS, PART I: ISONIAZID

Upon my skin, this galaxy
of red stars and systems
told in seven days the doctors
what I had known by two:
I was allergic. Violently.

Before bed, there would be no more
swallowing a single white pill.
Isoniazid was no longer the way.
Instead, I would imbibe a pair of red capsules.
Rifampin would take up the second
chase into my lungs.

ERIC PAUL SHAFFER

THE LAUREATE AND THE COCKROACH

We listened from the edge of light beaming down
on his gray locks and lowered lenses, and into the circle
bright on the stage crawled an enormous cockroach.

The day was chilly. The insect labored and paused,
heavily and often, antennae waving like batons in the fists

of a deranged conductor directing the grave tempo
of a poet's notes. Together, we crossed three hundred lines
and a long hour of creeping from the dark and crossing

the cold. Laboring over the boards, the cockroach had nearly
reached the far edge of shadow when the words were done.
From the poet's gracious nod, we knew he did not know

the difficult journey we had made before him and his work
that day. Stepping from the podium, books and papers

in hand, fumbling glasses, he stood before us on the stage.
Looking down, he quickly crushed the insect with his shoe,
and with a brief smile, he bowed, accepting our applause.

ERIC PAUL SHAFFER

PERSEID METEOR SHOWER, O'AHU

For the last three nights, I've urged friends into darkness
to see stars fall from the night. Not one of us has seen a streak,
      a spark, or a flicker. The moon swells as the days pass,

and the stars themselves dim in the reflection from that steady,
serious, gray and white face. And then, from the coast, the clouds
      trail the wind, crowding the stars into thin cobalt canyons

and coming between us and the quick vision of rock and flame
we seek, lying back in the grass with only us between the planet
      and everything else. I expect a lot from the sky, I guess,

and I want to give the universe every chance to come through
for us, yet I awaken to rain and a sky blank with clouds glowing
with the light we cast against the night. Not all that falls burns

or brings light, nor is all above clear to us, waking or dreaming.
      We rise to walk through rain and sky, abandoning the stars
we cannot see to the night and the long, lovely business of fire.

TRACI'S SUNSET

for Traci Winegarner, 1959–2016

That evening, we sat in the cellphone lot. The low rumble
of the pickup idling beside us throbbed through the glass.

      Aunties in the cab laughed and cooed over a baby
whose crying pierced reggae and rock from radios clashing
in the dusk. In our silence, I named this one Traci's sunset
while day faded over black mountains. When the sun rose
this morning, she was petting cats, sipping coffee, making
a shopping list for the barbecue, and watching an upcountry

      morning awaken. Now, that same sun was sinking
into the waves, and the last day she had ever seen was done.

Airliners and egrets emerged from the glow on the runways
and disappeared over the darkening island and darker sea.

      On the orange horizon, silver clouds were turning
pink, pink flushing to rose, rose to purple, purple thickening
to black, and the blue over all deepening until the first stars

      shone their long, thin light into our eyes. The racket
of traffic beyond the fence was blurred, and the chain link

      diamonds between us and the last of day sheared the sky
into a puzzle. At that moment, far behind us, shadows trailed
the rays of the sun climbing the slope of Haleakalā, gleaming

      once at the peak as the Earth turned away from the light.

ERIC PAUL SHAFFER

MY LAME SUPERPOWER

I glow. That's all I do. All the time, night and noon, I emit constant rays
that scientists agree are equal to a thousand watts. In daylight, I shine
with a golden nimbus, a halo that makes me gleam like a Renaissance god

on a ceiling. In moonlight, I bring the blush of the sun. Moths worship
my every step, circling me as I blaze beneath stars. When I sleep, I am

my own night-light. When I can't, I'm a lamp to read by. Among all
my fellow heroes, I am the least. For the mighty, striding the comic-book

pages of the world, I'm a figure of fun, the one with no costume, brilliant
and naked in my illumination. These brave defenders of truth control wind
and weather, fire and ice. They surf the airless void and breathe underwater.

They retrieve revolvers with magnetic hands. They have respectable names,
like Wolverine, Storm, or Mr. Fantastic, and I am flippantly known as Glow.

They say, "Flame on!" or "It's clobbering time!" What can I say? "Keep on
glowing"? "Let there continue to be light"? Yet these heroes allow me
a seat at the council table, though I am little use for the colossal battles

between good and evil they plan for themselves. I sit beside the Invisible
Girl, whose power is even more ironic than mine. She's already a woman,

she once joked, who needs to be invisible? We stifle our laughter within
the lofty halls. We whisper during meetings, snort and giggle helplessly
at nemeses and evil plots we have no power to confront, oppose, or defeat.

While the stalwart champions of justice strategize, we invent silly names
for ourselves: Glass Gal, Glimmer, Pane, Sparky. Yet she keeps me honest

about myself. If superpowers can be simple, she says, mine is. Where I am, darkness has no dominion. I lead the lost through the night surrounding us.

Where I look, there is nothing I can't see. Shadows flee when I approach. My light is neither charge nor reflection, for I shine from within, inexplicably and inexorably radiant. I illuminate the way for all. If you seek, follow me.

CATHY SONG

THE ART OF HEALING

Ching Ming surprised the two sisters every April, arriving like an old relative to a party they had forgotten to invite as they made plans to visit their mother's grave on her birthday. This year was no exception. Her birthday fell in the middle of the Chinese days of remembrance, a time for families to honor the dead. Since their mother's death twelve years ago, the sisters had begun to do their own version. Bearing a simple bouquet on that first birthday without her, the sisters had noticed other families huddled around graves, performing elaborate rituals that produced plumes of smoke and loud, crackling noises. What they brought had seemed meager by comparison. Over the years, their own version of Ching Ming grew haphazardly, mimicked from those around them or dimly reconstructed from the past. The two sisters were the elders now. They had no one but each other to rely on.

"Have you got the paper money?" Catherine inquired over the phone.

"Yes," Alexandria said, "plenty left from last year. We won't need to go to Chinatown. I've also got lots of incense."

"What about the whiskey and the shot glasses?" Catherine realized she was having her sister supply everything. Quickly, she added, "I've got a lighter."

"Glasses, yes. Whiskey, we'll get on the way as well as the oranges and flowers. Anything else? Oh! Do you have a coffee can we can burn the money in?"

"I'll find something," Catherine assured her sister. A coffee can was the least she could bring.

It was the same conversation every April ever since they had assumed the responsibility of taking care of the dead. It was the same way they put together family potlucks; somehow whatever they each brought to the table, it always worked out. There was never too much or too little of one food group. They preferred the spontaneous menu, the impromptu feast, as if they already knew what the other would bring. They couldn't bear the weight of planning anything too far in advance. They couldn't bear planning anything alone.

Alexandria, after discussing the matter over the phone with her younger sister, looked in the garage for the cardboard box, having not given it another thought after putting it away last year. The cheap floral vases and shot glasses had not been properly rinsed, and the candle stumps and bunches of incense were netted with cobwebs. However, she was glad to find the paper money—those heavenly notes for the dead to spend in the afterlife—still crisp as if newly minted in half-opened packages of cellophane, squares of gold and silver window-leafed on the thinnest paper.

Surveying the supplies and the stash of unspent notes, Alexandria felt dismayed. They should have been more generous. They should have burned the whole damn stash last year.

That was the problem. Alexandria and Catherine were the elders now, but they had not received proper instruction. They didn't know how many bundles of heavenly notes to burn, how many candles and sticks of incense to light, how many oranges to offer. They didn't know the sequence of such offerings, when and how to bow, which Daoist incantation to mumble, what kinds of flowers to choose, and if any of the things they thought to do or bring were meant to be done or brought at all. There was no one left in the family to consult.

"It's the intention," Catherine said, "that matters."

Alexandria agreed. "Our hearts are in the right place."

They were especially uneasy about the whiskey. The first Ching Ming they did by themselves found them hesitant, doubtful. Maybe they were recalling the prodigious flow of whiskey at weddings. They served the dead alcohol anyway, later, substituting sake instead. Would their grandparents be offended? Had their grandparents been alive to read about the Japanese Imperial Army killing, raping, and mutilating thousands of their Chinese brothers and sisters in the siege of Nanjing, they would have long since settled on a faraway island in the Pacific, and the Pearl River Delta would have receded into the distant shore of memory.

They were the elders now and two heads were better than one. Piecing together what they remembered from the pilgrimages they had made as children accompanying their mother and her three sisters to the Chinese Cemetery in Mānoa to visit the grave of long dead parents, Alexandria and Catherine gave themselves high marks for intention. The rest they made up.

Even as a child Catherine had sensed that the circle of women who spent most of the visit telling each other what to do and arguing about where they would eat lunch afterwards ("Nothing too salty!") were performing the ceremony half-heartedly. Many years later, during the one time she had witnessed as an adult her mother and her aunts go through the motions of being dutiful daughters, what she had long ago suspected was confirmed. The eldest aunt took Catherine aside and, in a hushed voice, confessed that lest Kitty had any doubts about the heathenish things they were about to do, she, Eve, child of God, had already taken it upon herself to receive clearance from above. The Lord had granted her special dispensation, for their poor, ignorant parents had never had the chance to know the Lord and to accept Jesus Christ as their savior. They remained in the dark. He knew that as Christians they were not worshipping, God forbid, their ancestors. He knew they worshipped only Him-Almighty-through-His-Son-Jesus-Christ-Our-Lord-Amen. Catherine's head spun as if suddenly struck by heatstroke. She was tired and hungry, and in looking back, angry. It didn't help that her normally frail aunt clutched her right forearm, squeezing it as she grew more agitated at the utterance of His Name. At lunch—her mother and her aunts had finally agreed upon Asia Manoa for the Hong Kong-style shrimp wonton mein—Catherine looked down at a trail of crescent moons etched into her skin.

Awareness of the spirit realm came to the two sisters late, well into middle age, the lifting of the veil coinciding during the time of their mother's descent into dementia. It happened suddenly. It happened slowly. It happened depending, they came to realize, on how closely you were looking. One day she was shopping, eating, laughing with her daughters. One day she was caught wandering into traffic. Cries of distress from their usually self-reliant father rallied Catherine and Alexandria to help him watch her. She could no longer be left alone. They took turns during the day to free him to run errands—it was too risky to take her along—but the nights were his. When he appeared ragged and sleep-deprived having had to lock her in the bedroom by installing a latch from the outside to prevent her from cooking eggs at three in the morning only to slip out with the stove ablaze to knock on the doors of strangers, his daughters gently released their father's hold on her.

A barometer to her parents' well-being in happier times, Alexandria being the eldest, prospered, having them all to herself for four years until her sister's arrival. She witnessed the adoring look of her mother whenever her father, confident and jaunty, entered the room. She witnessed his ability to extract from her pretty mother a girlish self-consciousness. She was aware of her mother becoming aware the moment he stepped into their presence. It was his presence alone, Alex observed even as a young child, that could elicit such a flutter. Her mother betrayed herself at these times, her inability to hide her good fortune.

Over the years, the look gave way to one of distraction, a blurring, a mixed crossing of signals that left her mother looking worried. The face fell, drooped, held in place by a mesh of lines. The eyelids seemed hooded, heavy. The burden of worrying about so much happiness had made her miss most of it.

Alexandria wanted assurances. Her own happiness depended upon the happiness of others. Such happiness depended upon her mother and father. If all was well and right with them, then all was well and right with the world.

Anxious about the recent palpitations clamoring inside her chest, Alex picked up the phone and dialed her sister's number. Catherine's answering machine clicked on. Pick up the phone, Kitty, Alex muttered. Cold and forbidding—Please leave a message!—her sister's voice challenged the intrepid caller to leave one. Kitty was probably right there at the kitchen table, writing the morning away, making up stories about their deprived childhood, the perceived hurts, the disappointments.

Several hours later, the palpitations resumed. The anxiety would not be relieved until she had talked to her sister. Alex tried calling her again. This time Kitty picked up.

"I'm worried about Mom and Dad." Alex wasted no time in unburdening herself. She heard Kitty sigh on the other end of the line. "We need to do something. I think we should try some alternative healers, you know, maybe like massage or acupuncture. What do you think?" Sensing her sister's hesitation, she added, "We can't let them continue like this. They're killing themselves and each other."

What it was that she wanted from her sister, Alex couldn't say. Help sounded feeble, yet help was what she wanted. Help in the form of alleviating the pressure, the psychic weight of having to think about their parents. She wanted Kitty to think about them as much as she did. And since it was obvious Kitty didn't think about them as much as she did, she wanted to share her thoughts about them to her sister. Every day. Talking to Kitty helped to relieve some of the mental pressure building up, amassing like the clouds over the Koʻolau mountains every afternoon. Kitty listened with patience and sympathy, her own form of convoluted guilt, guilt for not bearing her share of the burden.

Near School Street, on Lusitana, in a rundown block of old storefronts, they found Cal's place, a martial arts studio where he told them he also practiced his healing art. Just before their appointment, he had turned on the air-conditioner, a wall-unit that seemed capable of blowing only hot air. The dark interior suggested a cool refuge from the afternoon glare, but within minutes after introducing themselves, Catherine felt claustrophobic. The room was stuffy and airless and the healer himself was glazed with sweat. He was wearing a tank top and swim shorts, minimal yardage that revealed a powerful, muscular body. Around his waist, he wore a bulging fanny pack that held his special ointments.

Eleanor remained standing obediently between her two daughters. She waited to be told the next thing to do. She wanted to sit, but she remained standing. She wanted to go out the door, but she stood still.

Cal led her gently to the vinyl-padded table in the center of the room. He helped her to lie down. Eleanor obeyed, stiffly, wordlessly, her eyes conveying apprehension. He removed her sandals and began to talk to her, putting her at ease. Her daughters stood on either end of the table. She could see them. Still she looked worried.

"I'm Chinese, too," he said, trying to make her feel comfortable. "Your daughters tell me you're Chinese."

"You're Chinese?" Alex blurted. "You don't look Chinese."

Cal laughed. "I'm the Portuguese-kind Chinese. From Macao." Turning back to Eleanor, he asked, "And what about you? Where are your folks from?"

"Canton." Alex and Catherine were surprised by her response.

"Canton? You mean, Guangzhou," Cal corrected, good-naturedly. "Nobody says Canton anymore. Only the old futs, but you not one old fut, yeah?"

"Canton," Eleanor repeated, the word sounding more like a phlegm-filled cough.

"We're originally from Wahiawa," Catherine offered quickly. She could sense her mother was barely enduring the humiliation of being there.

"No Chinese in Wahiawa," Cal joked. "Only Filipinos, roosters, and a few Koreans."

"That's us," Alex said. "Our father is Korean."

"Oh, yeah?" Cal unzipped his fanny pack. He took out an unlabeled plastic squirt bottle and squeezed a generous amount of liquid into his palms. "Kimchee temper-kind?"

The sisters laughed.

"Except he thinks he's Irish," Alex added.

Cal was rubbing his hands together. "Oh oh, what kind of mix-up confusion is that?"

"Maybe he should see you," Alex said, enjoying herself. Catherine gave her a look. She was afraid her sister was saying too much.

"Maybe," Cal said, taking a long look at Eleanor. "I'll straighten him out." He began to rub Eleanor's hands, examining each crooked finger, each knotted knuckle. "Isn't that right, Mrs. Park?"

The healer and the sisters fell silent after a while. The healer, sitting on a stool, appeared to be in deep concentration as he worked his hands along Eleanor's right arm. He spent a long time at her elbow, bending it back and forth like a hinge.

Alexandria, uncomfortable with the silence, began talking again. "So, are you finding anything?"

Cal smiled and said softly, "Just a lot of goodies."

"Excuse me?" Alex felt caught off guard.

If he heard, Cal didn't answer. He brought his stool around to the other side to begin working on her left arm. "Yeah, you got a lot of goodies, Mrs. Park. You've been holding a lot of goodies for a long time now. Time to give them up. Open the drawer. Give them to me. No need hold them anymore."

Eleanor struggled to get off the table. Catherine and Alex watched her stoop to pick up her sandals. She sat down on a stool and started to buckle the straps.

"It's not time to go yet, Mom," Catherine said. "Cal's not finished working on you."

"I want to go," Eleanor mumbled. "Yes, it is. Time to go."

Cal took her hand and led her back to the table. Once again, he removed her sandals, slipped them to the floor. "Almost done, Mrs. Park. Just a little bit more, okay? I'll take good care of you. Just relax. Your daughters are here." He held her feet with one hand while the other hand searched inside his fanny back. The plastic bottle came out again. He started to work her toes, examining each toe as he had each finger.

The sight of their mother's feet pained both daughters. The once beautiful high arches, narrow heels, and delicate bone structure had over the years become swollen and discolored. The toes, sprang and curled in various directions, as if the joints were screaming in agony.

"Painful, yeah?" Cal said with complete understanding.

"Why are her feet like that?" Alex wanted to know.

"Goodies," Cal said, "all those goodies she won't let go."

"Can you fix it?" Alex wanted to know.

"Depends on your mother."

For a second time Eleanor struggled to get up. Before she could slide off the table, Cal gently guided her back. "See," he said, "she doesn't like it."

"Like what?" Again, it was Alex who wanted to know.

"Like being touched," her sister answered.

"That's right," Cal said, "and I'm hardly exerting any pressure."

"Too painful?" Alex asked.

"Too painful," Cal agreed.

Once again, the healer and the sisters fell silent. The grumbling of the air conditioner and Eleanor's palpable agitation didn't seem to distract Cal, who had stopped the massage. He was no longer even touching Eleanor but seemed to be listening for something, a pulse or a vibration. His eyes were closed, his head hanging down. He could have been sleeping.

Alex wanted to know but waited.

Catherine was aware of being uncomfortable and hot. Eleanor was looking at her. Her eyes were saying letmeoutofhere.

Then Cal woke up. "Quick! Get the incense in the can—over there—the can, in the corner on the desk—grab seven of them. Light it quick!"

Catherine responded first, fumbling for the bright pink sticks and a lighter.

"Light them—and walk around the room—now—quick! And you," he motioned to Alex, "Grab the phone, dial Walter in Kalihi. Eight-three-nine-nine-four-nine-four. Walter Kunimura, the healer."

Alex dialed and redialed, using the phone on Cal's desk, her fingers not working fast enough to match Cal's frantic tempo.

"Wait," Alex said. "Why am I calling him?"

"He can help," Cal said, visibly shaken. "I'm not at that level."

"What level?" Alex was starting to feel as uncomfortable as her mother and sister. The call was put through. "Hello? Hello? Is this Walter . . ." she paused.

"Kunimura," Cal filled in, holding Eleanor's hand. Eleanor looked as though she had had enough.

"Is this Walter Kunimura? Oh, hello. Yes. I'm with my mother, we're with Cal. And he wanted me to call you. Wait, just a minute." She handed the phone to Cal.

He refused to take the phone. "Ask him about your mother."

"Oh, hello. Yes, Cal wants me to ask you about my mother. She's here with Cal, and he wants you to tell him something about my mother."

Catherine, waving the bunch of incense around the table, paused by her sister. "This is weird. Never heard of a healer needing a consult during a session."

Alex shot her sister a look. "Yes, yes, okay, we'll bring her by. Okay. Cal knows where you live. Okay. Tomorrow. We'll come by tomorrow." The phone went dead. She placed the receiver into the cradle and looked at Cal for an explanation.

Eleanor sat up. No one stopped her as she started to put on her sandals. She was out the door and soon, Catherine was too, still holding the pink sticks of incense like a decomposing bouquet. She wanted to know why Cal couldn't help their mother, why they had to seek another healer. This Walter what's-his-name in Kalihi.

Alex threw a wad of cash at Cal and, in exchange, she was given two addresses—Walter in Kalihi and Collin in Pālolo—and a thick bunch of incense to burn at home.

"I didn't like that man," Eleanor said in the car. "He gave me the creeps."

They strapped their mother in. The click of the seatbelt buckle sounded like a padlock. Alex took the driver's seat and Catherine crept into the back, sitting behind Eleanor. She noticed her mother's hair, flat and matted, how much her mother needed a comb through it, some light fluffy teasing.

On the freeway heading east, Alexandria steered the Volvo expertly through the afternoon rush hour. They rode in silence. Catherine wished for a stick of chewing gum to dispel the odd pressure in her ears like a sudden drop in altitude.

"You're just going to have to accept it. This is the way I am. You're just going to have to accept it," Eleanor burst out.

"Like hell I will," Sung Mahn snorted at his daughters' request that according to Cal's instructions he was to light seven sticks of incense for the next seven days. Light them in the apartment, carry the burning sticks from room to room, preferably at twilight.

Sung Mahn had been downstairs in the lobby of the condominium, waiting for his girls to return his wife to him. He had taken the elevator down to the lobby entrance fifteen minutes early. He must have been nuts, he scolded himself, for allowing the girls to talk him into letting Eleanor go with them for the day.

At first, the prospect of a break from caregiving sounded like a good idea, but as the hours dragged on, he found himself unable to concentrate on anything. He tried to watch television, something he couldn't do anymore with Eleanor roaming around the apartment, removing her clothes, turning on and off the lights. In no time, he threw down the remote control, unaware that he himself was roaming from room to room, sprinkling each empty doorway with sighs, missing his wife. He tried scrubbing the shower, something else he had wanted to do but hadn't been able to as Eleanor's condition worsened. He couldn't leave her unattended. He was exhausted and yet, he could not relax. He could not close his eyes and nap, not even for a few minutes. He made himself an early lunch, a tuna sandwich, which he ate without joy. No matter how many times Eleanor threw her napkin onto the floor, no matter how many times she stumbled to the toilet, pulling down her elastic shorts in the hallway as he lurched after her, calling her to come back, he missed her.

"Don't ask, just do it. Will you please?" Alex shouted out the car window. "And have Mom ready tomorrow at eight o'clock."

As they drove off, Catherine turned to wave. Their father stood looking long and hard at them, bewilderment flushing his face, astonished that he no longer had the last say. Eleanor, hunched toward the building, was already gone.

Through the revolving glass door of the condominium, Sung Mahn guided Eleanor into the elevator, into the apartment, and into the clean shower. He entered the shower with her, wearing swim trunks, and scrubbed her down. Careful lest she slip, he instructed her to hold on to him as he worked down her legs, calling out for her to lift one foot, then the other. She lifted, and shifted slowly. He soaped around the distended belly, the sagging breasts. He soaped her with the efficiency of a zookeeper in a stall with a docile beast.

Through it all, Eleanor remained mute, obedient. Once she was showered and changed into fresh underwear, T-shirt, and shorts, he guided her to the recliner, flicking on the television. He then had three minutes before she started to look for him. In that time, he pulled from the freezer two Lean Cuisine frozen meals and had them zapping in the microwave. When she wandered into the kitchen, he was ready for her with a head of lettuce to tear. She liked tearing lettuce.

Tonight he remembered the incense. He lit the seven sticks as instructed and, holding Eleanor's hand, they went together into each room, sweeping passes of burning scent, like children waving sparklers at New Year's. He had an inkling that what they were doing was a kind of cleansing. Of what, he had not a clue. His crazy girls. But since he had come to a point where he had nothing to lose, he decided to make an effort. He wondered if he should be murmuring an incantation. He began to recite the only one that came to mind, "The Lord is my shepherd. . . ." He recited over and over as they went from room to room, "The Lord is my shepherd. . . ." Eleanor mumbled the four words she would say that night, "I shall not want."

Sung Mahn had Eleanor ready at ten minutes to eight the next morning. He could have had her ready the moment they dropped her off the afternoon before, so profound was her confusion that he could have turned her back around, called out to his daughters to wait, and strapped her into the car. She would have stared out the car window, giving him that look of helpless pleading.

They entered Pālolo Valley and stopped at the Pālolo Higashi Hongwanji for directions to the Chinese Buddhist Temple, the one with the red door. Cal had been adamant about the red door and a man named Collin who resided behind it.

The old ladies looked up from their quilting when Catherine entered the side hall of the temple. Alex waited in the car with their mother. Bright colored squares of material were being pinned in place for patchwork blankets the ladies were piecing together for the homeless.

"Getting real cold now," muttered one of the ladies. That was the answer to Catherine's second question, the first drawing no results. None of the ladies knew of any Chinese Buddhist Temple in the valley. Not even one with a red door. Try the Korean Temple, farther in, on the side of the mountain, the one with the big tiled roof, they suggested, or the Chinese Old Folks Home. "Get plenty Chinese over there. They might know what you looking for."

Catherine felt reluctant to leave them. They seemed content in the selfless task, enjoying what was being given them at that moment, the sound of mourning doves in the cool valley light, the opportunity to get together and make use of their still able hands.

They found their way to the nursing home, following the long driveway to the entrance. Once again, Catherine ran out to inquire while Alex and Eleanor remained in the car. She found the common room where a dozen or so residents dozed in wheelchairs. Finding no one to help her, Catherine ran outside, shaking her head to her sister, who thrust her face forward over the dashboard looking annoyed.

"May I help you?" a kitchen worker on a smoke break called out from the side of the building. She had heard about the temple with the red door. "Around this hill, take a right and another right into the road that leads to the back of the valley. It's there. A lot of people come driving up here looking for it. A lot of people need help."

Eleanor said nothing as her two daughters called out, "Turn here. Try this road. Shit. Turn around. Try the other road." When it seemed they had crisscrossed every street, they saw it. The red door at the end of the valley. They had been searching for a more substantial structure, a real temple with an ornate gate, a garden, banners, the drone of chanting monks, not an ordinary house. Disappointed, they entered the red door, flimsy as a curtain. Eleanor stumbled between them as they passed as if through a stage prop into a carport that had been converted to a waiting room. Even the cloud of incense was an illusion, more like burning coils of mosquito repellent.

A couple, sitting very close, sat on one of the two benches. Catherine wondered what sort of help they sought—blessings for an imminent marriage, assurances for the birth of a healthy child, guidance for an elderly parent.

Before greetings could be exchanged, the couple stood up, called through a side doorway by someone who remained unseen on the other side. Bowing slightly, the couple went through the door.

Alexandria inched along the bench, craned her neck, and peered after them. "Must be him," she whispered.

"How much do you think we need to give?" Catherine reached into her purse.

"I don't know. Twenty? Thirty?"

Catherine fumbled for the envelope she had prepared earlier in the car. Inside was a crisp twenty-dollar bill. She suddenly felt insecure and plucked another twenty from her wallet.

Eleanor sat staring at the ground, the cement floor of the carport swept clean but stained with oil patches. Alex never saw the couple leave. It didn't occur to her to wonder if they had left by another door until as in a doctor's waiting room, Eleanor's turn was called.

A shadow passed through the doorway. "Okay?"

Catherine looked up, embarrassed to be caught putting more money into the envelope, like an afterthought. Bowing, she handed the envelope to the man whose shadow fell across their mother's feet.

The envelope disappeared into the folds of a gray robe.

Alexandria guided Eleanor by the elbow, and the three of them entered the next room, behind the man who had yet to introduce himself. He led them up three steps into another garage, one that had been converted into the main temple hall. Alex wasted no time in describing Eleanor's condition to the man who remained imposing in his physical height and emotionless expression, a neutrality Catherine interpreted as bored and, worse, condescending. He had heard it all before.

Catherine had to admire her sister's sincerity, saying too much too soon, as though this stranger were the family doctor and, if she could recount the story of their mother's descent into depression with enough conviction, he could make Eleanor well again.

Catherine regretted adding the extra twenty-dollar bill to the envelope, feeling shortchanged as they stood at the elaborate altar festooned with an assortment of Daoist gods and lavish offerings of sweets and fruits resembling a window display in a Chinatown gift shop. The gods from their great height looked down and scowled.

Opposite the altar was a view of the valley, the humble houses they had passed to find this place.

Alexandria rattled on about Eleanor's deterioration. The list of ailments seemed to move the man in the gray robe in no visible way. He almost seemed irritated, as if she were telling him the very things he was planning to reveal for a fee.

Moving his head in a succession of quick nods, which Catherine interpreted as yesyeslet'sgetonwithit, he held out a fan of fortune sticks to Eleanor. He could just as well have offered her a handful of cigarettes the way she stared at them dumbly.

Apologizing, Alex chose one for their mother. The man lifted his chin to indicate she should pick a few more. Catherine watched her sister's fingers pull at the long sticks the way they did when they were children playing pick-up-sticks. So competitive were the games, the sisters dared not breathe on the other's turn. Chin to floor, they eyeballed the nest of sticks to make sure not a single quiver occurred as each stick was deftly extracted. The stakes were always high.

"Okay," the man said, meaning that's enough. He took the sticks from Alex and placed them in a bamboo container. He shook it like a bartender mixing drinks.

"What's your mother's name?"

Alex answered.

"Write it down." He thrust his jaw toward a notepad and pencil on a small table covered with a green cloth.

Alex wrote it down.

He added Eleanor's name to the cocktail and continued to shake the bamboo container. Great, Catherine thought, all we need are some tiki torches and paper umbrellas.

If he was praying to the gods behind him, he gave no indication. No spine-tingling mantra came tumbling out. After a few more rattles—was he actually counting, Catherine wondered—he threw the sticks onto a small table.

The sisters stepped closer.

With a quick glance, he studied the cryptic arrangement of sticks. "Okay," he pronounced, satisfied. Once again, he thrust his jaw in the direction they should follow, toward a set of stools and a card table. Eleanor had already started to drift there.

They sat down. Eleanor looked miserable. She was probably hungry.

"Your mother," the man began.

Catherine felt herself retracting as Alexandria leaned closer to hear the reading. Her eagerness seemed to cause him to lose his train of thought.

"Yes?"

"Your mother," he began again, "has high blood pressure."

"Yes?" It was Alexandria's turn to indicate tellmesomethingIdon'talreadyknow.

"...and..."

"...and?"

"She's disappointed." The man's relief was evident at this last pronouncement.

"Disappointed?" the two sisters repeated in unison.

"Yes," Collin said, staring over their heads at the view of the valley.

"I don't understand," Alex said, crushed.

Returning his gaze to the women at the table, he made his final assessment. "Yes, she's disappointed the way her life turned out. She's tried very hard and can't understand why things didn't work out the way she wanted." His eyes came to rest upon Eleanor.

"So...." Alex said as a cue for more.

"So, is there anything we can do?" Catherine pushed aside her sister's politeness.

"No," Collin said, standing to his feet, a sign that the session was now over.

Catherine had to control herself from demanding a full refund.

"No hope, no cure, nothing," Catherine ranted as they marched Eleanor to the car. "A big fat zero."

"What a waste of time," Alex agreed, opening the door for Eleanor, who looked miserable.

"And money!" Catherine snapped. "What was that all about?"

They sat in the car, fuming for a few minutes before they drove away. Catherine wanted to shake her fist out the window, spit something vulgar at the man who was probably still watching them from his lofty carport. She didn't think he was capable of activating any spells, but the thought of the scowling gods made her control herself.

"I feel we've been had," she muttered glumly.

"We've still got Walter," Alex ventured.

"I don't know," Catherine said, discouraged. "It's just this silly wild goose chase. What do you think, Mom?" From time to time, they remembered to include their mother.

Eleanor didn't answer.

"Let's try Walter," Alex said, taking control. "Then we can have lunch."

"Mom looks tired and hungry. Are you hungry, Mom?"

Eleanor didn't answer. They decided to find Walter in Kalihi.

They found Walter easily enough in dilapidated, junk-filled squalor around the corner from the Golden City Chop Suey Restaurant. They had the distinct feeling he had been expecting them for when they arrived at the front door, he saw them first through the grimy picture window, smiled, and waved them in.

Barely.

They had to remain standing near the door in order to fit in Walter Kunimura's living room. Piled with chairs and tables and overflowing cardboard boxes, it seemed as if once upon a time he couldn't decide whether to move in or move out. Defeated by the two directional pulls, it was easier to live in the La-Z-Boy recliner and have the world come to him.

"I know you! I know you folks!" He grinned, his teeth as messy and dingy as the surroundings. "Come inside! Come inside!"

Catherine had the impression Walter spoke in repetitive couplets. She was going to make Alex pay this time.

Not for lack of manners did Walter not get up to greet them. There was simply no clear floor space for him to stand. Catherine shuddered at the image of the sprightly man coming toward them like a monkey, balancing on the precarious piles, lunging from table to box to chair.

"Excuse the mess! Excuse the mess!" He hadn't stopped waving since the moment he spotted their car.

Brave Alex began to speak. Catherine braced herself for the litany of ailments.

"Never mind! Never mind! I know, I know . . . Cal told me. He told me already. Your mama . . . it's your mama. . . . Try wait, try wait. Elsie! Elsie! Where you stay?"

From the dark airless kitchen, a woman of indeterminate age hobbled out, stopping short at the boundary between the linoleum floor of the kitchen and the mustard-colored carpet of the living room. She stood waiting for instructions.

"Get the stone! Get the stone!"

She bowed once and disappeared.

Walter turned to his guests and offered them treats: dusty pieces of peppermint in a koa bowl. Catherine unwrapped one for Eleanor. Her mother grabbed it and stuck it quickly in her mouth as if she was afraid it would be taken away from her.

"Take more! Take more! She look hungry! She look like one hungry ghost!"

Catherine, having already decided they were on another wild goose chase, chose to ignore what this second charlatan just said. She gave her mother a second peppermint.

Elsie returned, weighed down with a rock. She stood at the edge of the linoleum.

The sisters looked at each other. They wondered who was going to retrieve the rock. It was obvious Elsie would go no further. To their surprise, Walter jumped out of the recliner. Nimbly, he climbed over several boxes and stood on top of a coffee table. As he reached to take the rock from Elsie, he almost slipped on a mountain of magazines.

"Watch out!" Alexandria cringed.

The weight taken off of her, Elsie retreated into the dark airless kitchen.

"Sit down! Sit down! Anywhere alright. I go put the stone on your mama. I go put the stone on your mama's belly. Okay? Okay?"

Eleanor, upon receiving permission to sit down, promptly did so on the nearest cardboard box. Empty, the box collapsed. The swift downward pull extracted from her a loud cheerful fart.

Alexandria cringed. Catherine vowed once again that this time her sister would certainly pay.

"That's what I told Cal!" Warren hooted, standing like a mischievous monkey on the coffee table, the rock like a coconut he was about to hurl. "No need the stone! No need the stone! I already know what her problem! I already know!"

"Excuse me?" Alex and Catherine reached to help Eleanor to her feet.

"Your mama! She get gas! She get too much gas!"

The sisters swore off healers. They were all kooks, they agreed. They found
a care home in the valley near the Chinese cemetery, which seemed like a good
sign, that their mother would be close to her parents whom she had lost so early
in life. They gently released their father's grip, telling him it was all right. He
could rest now. The real professionals would take over and make sure she was
safe and comfortable. He had done all that was humanly, husbandly possible.

When they brought their mother to the care home, it was the last time
Eleanor walked unassisted, entering the gated garden infused with the dappled
light of late afternoon and the sound of water trickling from a fountain
surrounded by a grotto of ferns and orchids. The sisters knew their father's heart
was breaking as he led his wife into the large room that served as a dining area
for the residents, six of the seven seated at their own small round tables, waiting
in wheelchairs for the noon meal. The smell of chicken and ginger simmering in
a large pot filled the room. A few of the residents turned disinterestedly at the
commotion of the new arrival shuffling toward an empty table. Their mother
glanced at their father, turning her whole body the way an injured person with
a neck brace would, stiffly, looking it seemed for permission to sit down. One of
the attendants went to get a wheelchair. It was if she was his child and the three
of them were dropping her off at a new school where a birthday party was taking
place. The other guests scratched their heads and rubbed their eyes, each one
brightly bibbed as though they were wearing party favors: the bibs—red, blue
and yellow—the color of balloons.

What disturbed Alexandria the most was the way her mother's face,
once soft and tender, hardened. The effect for those who knew her when
the life force coursed through her being was chilling. Eleanor stared at the
ceiling, the bed an extension of her confinement, staring at nothing, staring
at everything. There was no way to know. The swollen flesh around her eyes
made her look mean; the bloated jowls dragged down the sides of her mouth
into a scowl. "She was really a nice person," Alex felt compelled to tell the
staff. "She was really the sweetest mother." The sweetest mother had stopped
speaking the day she walked unassisted into her new home, sinking into
the wheelchair that the attendant adjusted, strapping her securely with a
Velcro-belt. She never looked at her husband. She never looked at her two

daughters. Once the meal was served, she fed herself that first meal, slurping the chicken soup with loud smacking sounds. It seemed to the three of them as they let her go, the gate shutting quietly behind them that she could finally rest. She didn't have to be cheerful for any of them anymore.

Knowing that their mother was being well cared for and that their father could spend his days by her side—feeding her, combing her hair, holding her hand—and leave to return the next morning after a good night's sleep to repeat the loving attention brought Catherine and Alexandria a measure of relief.

That relief was short-lived. Not long after their mother entered the care home, Catherine noticed that whenever she put on a T-shirt (paired with jeans, her uniform), an indentation would appear between her breasts as if an invisible finger were pressing down on the sternum. When it first appeared, she was unaware of it until her youngest child cried, "Eeew! Uji, Ma! What's that on your shirt?" She looked down, agreed that it was indeed uji, her children's go-to word for anything odd, amiss, inappropriate. She stepped in front of the bathroom mirror, shrugged, and changed into another one. The same thing happened. The indentation appeared, blooming right before her eyes. She thought it was a defect in the cotton fabric and went through her stack of standard-issue GAP Favorite T-shirts. She ended up trying on the entire collection of T-shirts. With each new T-shirt, the indentation appeared like a mysterious stain.

After the morning's upheaval of getting the residents bathed, medicated, fed by noon, and settled back into their rooms for the long siesta, Alexandria could hear the shuffling of papers as the nurse and the two attendants on duty retreated to their stations, portable desks tucked amid the warehousing of wheelchairs and crooked stacks of formula and diapers for the elderly. The endless minute-by-minute updating of medical files, reports that charted the fastidious progress of decline had the same effect on her as the sound of lids being peeled back from plastic lunch containers. The sound and the immediate burp-like smell of egg salad sandwiches made her feel sad. The nurse and the attendants on duty sat on stools, penciling in numbers, chewing soft tired bites, seeking nourishment from homemade sandwiches before the next deployment.

Staring at her mother as she lay in bed, asleep or awake, Alexandria was no longer sure, she had stopped feeling intrusive. Whether her eyes were opened or closed, her mother seemed unaware of her presence. She had left, she was gone, and no matter how hard Alex tried—reading to her, holding her hand, massaging her swollen legs—she could not call her mother back. Whatever that essence was that only recently and valiantly flickered recognition, amusement, weariness, and love had fled. Alex couldn't help but feel that her mother willed her own escape, that if she had wanted to stay she would have. There was something almost triumphant in the way she lay, solidifying right before their eyes, their tears hastening the process, resistant to the claims each of them made on her, beseeching her to come back, smothering her with attention.

Her feet, encased in skid-free, rubber-soled socks, were the last bony extremities left of her body. They fit into Alexandria's palms as she massaged them, the feel of the high ballerina-arch familiar; the toes, curled as though all her life her mother had worn shoes too small, still slender and pliable. Like a landscape altered by a lava flow, the rest of her mother's body had lost the finer undulations of hip and breast, clavicle and neck, hardening into an almost undistinguishable mass of flesh. It wasn't that she had gained weight since becoming bedridden, rather she was sinking under the weight of her own physical matter. She lay hard and frozen, the result of an internal collapse.

Her face, once so friendly in its openness, inviting others to approach without fear, seemed fixed in paralysis. Of all the expressions that had visited her face, Alexandria thought how unfortunate that the last one that remained would be one of fear, as though she had witnessed something dreadful. Whatever it was that she had seen, it stuck. It was hard to look at her mother.

It was hard to look at her, but Alexandria felt compelled to visit every day, during the brief hour when her father went home for lunch. She didn't need the added pain of watching him attend to her, stroking her arm, combing her hair, loving gestures he rarely exhibited when she was well. She felt she was coming closer to understanding that look on her mother's face. She had seen that face before. It wasn't until she was looking through old photographs that she discovered how much her mother in her present condition resembled her own father, their grandfather, in the last photograph taken shortly before his untimely death at the age of fifty-three. She felt she was coming closer to making sense of things that had happened in the past, things that no one had time to piece together in the rush of years and deaths, how her mother and her sisters had scattered after their parents had died within a short time of each other, scrambling to find other living arrangements in order to survive.

Alexandria called Catherine. She needed help.

The first thing she saw was the strange mark on her sister's shirt.

"I know," Catherine said. "It looks like an invisible finger is poking me. The kids say it's uji."

"I think it's someone trying to tell us something."

Catherine dismissed what she heard. "Oh, no. I refuse to seek the help of any more healers. There's nothing to uncover. No magic cure. Mom has dementia. End of story. Sad but true. At least we got Dad to agree to get her into a place where she's safe."

"But that look on her face, Kitty. It's not natural."

"It's what it is, Alex. We can't all look gorgeous at the end."

Alexandria took out the picture of their grandfather, the last one taken before his death.

Catherine took a long time with it, holding it up to the window. They were in Eleanor's room. Her eyes were closed, but that didn't mean she was sleeping. "I have to admit," she said, putting the photograph back into the album, "there is a weird resemblance."

"Resemblance? Kitty, it looks like his face has morphed into hers."

"What are you trying to get at? That our dear old grandfather's spirit has entered into Mom?"

Eleanor stirred in bed. The sisters lowered their voices. "No, but I was looking at all the photos and figuring out the dates. Grandpa's first wife, Uncle Guy's mother, died in China."

"And then he married our grandmother."

"Yes, but you see, after the three of them went back to China and Grandpa's first wife died there, Uncle Guy couldn't have been more than a few years old. We'll never know why they went back to China, but the thing is," Alex took a deep breath, she could feel her palpitations starting up again, "he married our grandmother so soon afterwards. Like he knew her while his first wife was still alive."

"They were probably from the same village. Maybe even family friends, distantly related. You know in those days everyone was related."

"I mean real soon after because when I looked at the date when Auntie Evie was born, it was the same year his first wife died."

Catherine seemed to need a moment to absorb her sister's detective work. "Still possible without being immoral. First wife could have died in January. Grandpa, already knowing our grandmother through village connections, marries her as early as the next month or so—still possible for Auntie to have been born that year."

"But Auntie Evie's birthday is in August," Alex said ominously.

All Catherine could say was "oh."

They went to the Chinese cemetery after the hour with their mother. They left before their father returned to take up his usual position in a chair beside her bed. Although they knew it wasn't nice of them to leave without at least waiting to see him, they had too much on their minds. They drove separately, not wanting to leave either car behind should their father recognize one of them. It would get his hopes up. He would expect to find them with their mother. He would look forward to the company.

Under the ever-blossoming pink plumeria tree, the sisters sought the graves of the grandparents they had never known. A feeling of neglect pervaded the site, littered with soft petals and large brown leaves. No one had been there for a long time. Maybe not since the last time years ago when they had come with their mother and aunts to perform the ritual of Ching Ming. The time Auntie Evie had grabbed Catherine's arm, invoking the name of Jesus over and over as if that would dispel the superstitious practice of paying respect to one's ancestors.

Catherine decided that that wasn't such a bad thing to do. To pay respect to one's ancestors was a way of acknowledging the hardships they had endured. She knelt down to pray to her grandfather and grandmother. She was grateful they had left China seeking a better life for themselves and the grandchildren they would never know. If she had been born in China, she probably would be dead. She had read that those who came of age during the Cultural Revolution, if they survived, would be street sweepers and refuse collectors, having been denied years of schooling. She was grateful for all the years of school she had been given.

Alexandria knelt beside her sister. "Let's pray to Grandpa's first wife, Uncle Guy's mother. I feel sad that she was left all alone in China. After all, she gave birth to Uncle, and he was a good brother to all his sisters. He was so young when he was left as head of the family, left to take care of his stepmother and all those sisters. Remember Auntie Evie said that after Grandpa had died, Uncle worked in the kitchen at a Chinese restaurant, how he would bring home the leftovers in a little tin for them?"

The two sisters fell silent as they sat under the plumeria tree that graced the grave of their grandparents with a never-ending shower of blossoms. They didn't need to tell each other what they prayed for. Although the valley was bright with sun, a light rain began to fall. They didn't need a healer to tell them it was a blessing.

EATING BITTERNESS

I was born deprived. The shelves nearest the cash registers at our family market were lined with a mouth-watering array of chips and candies, but I was forbidden to eat most of it. No shrimp chips. No Fritos. No M&Ms. No Almond Joy.

My mother deemed all those deep-fried snacks and chocolate goodies—*nyet hai*, creating an intolerable imbalance of yin and yang in your body, making you ripe for a cold, the flu, or even more serious illnesses.

"Chinese people strive to maintain their health, whereas Western medical practice is more often based on treatment, not prevention," she said.

But to my brother Tommy and me, the literal translation of *nyet hai* was "tasty food," as in Leonard's malasadas or the Colonel's Kentucky Fried Chicken.

As we perused the snack section of the market, my mother allowed us to select some items: haw flakes, dried persimmons pressed into flat nickel-sized circles; sweet sour plum seeds; and Tomoe Ame, Japanese candy made from gelatin and coated with sticky edible rice paper. Everything else was *nyet hai*.

After all, the family business was built on the motto, *Live Longer—Eat More Fruits and Vegetables*. It was imprinted on the back envelope flap of every customer's monthly charge account bill, and right under the name Chow Hoo Market in the newspaper advertisements announcing weekly specials.

"You are unbelievably lucky," my mother said. "If it wasn't for Kung Kung's hard work, we might all be just another starving peasant family in China, better dead than alive."

She often recounted the story about my grandfather, who at age fourteen left his home in Chung San, China. Promised payment of three dollars a month, along with housing, food, and passage to Hawai'i, he arrived to work in the sugar plantations as a contract laborer. Fulfilling his stipulated three years, he began to peddle fruits and vegetables up and down the affluent neighborhoods of Mānoa, Makiki, and Nu'uanu.

With a sturdy bamboo pole on his slight shoulders, he balanced baskets filled with mangoes, bananas, and bitter melon. Many customers would buy the heaviest items like pineapples and taro first, to ease his burden.

Then, he would continue walking, calling out in pidgin, "Splecial froot for sale. Papaya, balala for sale."

Soon he would open a series of shops, first on South Hotel, then on Kekaulike Street, before becoming one of the only wholesalers of fresh fruits and vegetables to restaurants and institutions, and the exclusive supplier of produce for military post exchange stores at Fort Shafter, Schofield Barracks, and Hickam.

My mother pointed to a photo of Kung Kung on her desk as proof. "See, here he is on the slopes of Wilhemina Rise, where he experimented growing pineapples."

I looked at the image staring straight back at the camera lens, thinking how Kung Kung must have cursed the fields as a young man, red dirt collecting underneath his fingernails, the cuffs of his shirt sleeves, and pant legs. By the time the photo was taken, however, he owned entire fields, whole plots of rust-red dirt.

But it was because of this legacy, from an empire built from fruits and vegetables, that my brother and I had to suffer. Our after-school snack was discolored brown apple slices, peeled and quartered.

And on Halloween, my mother would never distribute candy, only whole apples. "Too much *nyet hai* at Halloween time," she said. "All the parents will be happy that someone was thinking smart." Indeed, the entire neighborhood got smart, as everyone skipped our house.

The Chow Hoo Market was one of the first supermarkets in the islands. Eventually, a shopping plaza was built alongside. On opening day, a traffic jam was created on Nuʻuanu Avenue and School Street. There were lines of cars waiting for parking spaces and lines of people waiting to order cheeseburgers, saimin, and root beer floats at the Chow Hoo Drive Inn.

Paying no heed to the customers ahead, my mother barked out her order from the back of the crowd.

"Three hamburgers, one order French fries, and three hot waters."

Tommy and I looked at each other in disbelief. French fries? This was no doubt a special occasion. With excitement, we followed my mother to a place behind the public eating area. It was a stock room filled with cardboard boxes and Formica tables for employees and the family to use.

My mother distributed the hamburgers and then carefully blotted each thick-cut French fry with a paper napkin before giving it to us. Even if we had to peel a little bit of napkin stuck to the steaming fry, it was still delicious. She then ordered us to drink some hot water.

"Can't I have a Coke instead?" said Tommy.

"No, you have to flush down the oil with boiling water. Get that grease out of your system."

"Okay, I finished the hot water," he said. "Now can I order a Coke?"

"No, Tommy," said my mother, as she whipped out a wax paper bag filled with sliced apples.

Strangely enough, Coca-Cola was reserved for when we were really, really ill. My mother would drive us to Chinatown to see the herb doctor. As she would describe our symptoms of a dry scratchy throat or a cough with mucus, Dr. Wang would check our pulse. With his dull pallor, skinny frame, and filmy eyes, he wasn't the "picture of health" himself. I almost felt better when he turned his back, opening and closing a myriad of minute drawers, row upon row filled with herbs and animal parts.

Occasionally, he would turn around and dump any number of delicacies— ginseng, licorice root, dried twigs, leaves, cinnamon bark, dried seahorses, and other indeterminate items—on the counter. Using a small scale, he would measure each ingredient and divide them between several squares of brown paper. The papers were folded in thirds and tucked in on one end to form a packet, each one equaling a dose.

Next, Dr. Wang used an abacus to calculate the amount as my mother negotiated the price in Cantonese. Whatever amount, it was way too much for what looked and smelled like gathered dead leaves. After my mother mixed the packet with water, the *hu cha* boiled continuously, permeating our house with an earthy aroma, smelling just like Kapi'olani Park after a heavy downpour.

After many hours, the liquid became darker and more bitter, "more healing" my mother was convinced. However, seeing our grimaces facing the *hu cha*, she knew we would never down the brew without a sip of soda in between gulps.

But three servings of vegetables and an apple a day couldn't keep the doctors away when my mother, in her seventies, suffered chest pains and was rushed by ambulance to Queen's Hospital.

Surrounded by monitors and machines in the emergency ward, my mother, too weak to speak loudly, signaled my brother and me to come closer.

"I . . ." she faltered. "I sh . . ." she started again, short of breath. Her pallor matched the hospital walls and bed sheets, but she was determined to finish speaking. "Sh . . . should have. . ." she struggled, her eyelids lowering.

"Should have? Should have what?" repeated Tommy.

"Eat-en . . . more . . ." then she paused before gasping, ". . . Ch—ips."

Suddenly, the tracings on the cardiac monitor produced no rhythm and flattened. "Code Blue" was announced over the hospital P.A. system, and a cardiac arrest team streamed into the room. As we contemplated her final words, the medical personnel attempted to vigorously pump her heart alive, but to no avail.

We were in a stupor planning my mother's memorial service and consulted with Uncle Kam Sung, the family's authority on Chinese tradition. "It is customary for every mourner to receive a *lai see*, a red packet containing a nickel, besides a piece of candy," he said.

"Why candy?"

"The candy serves to 'sweeten' the sorrow. And the coin must be spent to buy something with sugar to counteract the bitterness of death."

Eight months later, on her birthday, Tommy and I visited the Buddhist temple in Nu'uanu to pay our respects and bring offerings. Locating the niche where both our parents were inurned, we cleared a place directly below on the altar table.

I arranged several oranges on a paper plate, while Tommy added a couple of apples. Our aunt had cooked *jai*, a vegetarian specialty, and I uncovered the lid of the plastic bowl containing a heady stew of dried mushrooms and lily buds, black fungus, fresh water chestnuts, and snow peas, all combined with fermented bean curd paste and oyster sauce. Tommy set a pair of wooden chopsticks and a bottle of Coca-Cola nearby.

As I bowed down three times and scanned our offerings, all sensations of taste rushed through my head and engorged my heart: Salty. Sweet. Bitter. Sour. However, something was missing, just one element. I reached into my straw tote to present the final contribution, saving the most satisfying—a bag of Lay's Potato Chips, for the end. And upon opening the package, I smelled flavor, at last.

BORN SILENT

I was born silent. The rules of conduct in our home were the proverbs—
Children should not speak unless spoken to and *Children should be seen and not
heard*. Or as my mother needlessly reminded me, "Don't talk too much. You'll
sound stupid. Too many people yak yak yak and say nothing."

No one could accuse me of being a chatterbox. I was so bashful growing up
that I didn't even want to be visible. I found comfort clinging to my mother,
trying to hide my shyness in the voluminous folds of her skirts, barely peeking
out to see whom I was trying to avoid.

I grew up shy. I grew up quiet. Even so, my mother would warn me not to
speak. She needn't have worried. Throughout elementary school, I never had a
desire to speak up. Whenever my first-grade teacher Miss Stewart said, "Okay,
children, time for Show and Tell," I would sink a little lower in my chair, trying
to hide my discomfort.

Typically, my cousin Lincoln would leap from his seat, waving both hands to
declare, "I'm going to be a doctor, a . . ." and he always spelled this out, "G-Y-N-
E-C-O-L-O-G-I-S-T, like my father. This is a pair of forceps. He uses them when
he has a difficult time delivering a baby." Or "This is a speculum he uses for
internal examinations of the pelvic area," triumphantly displaying yet another
glistening sterile object borrowed from his father's medical bag.

It was my cue to disappear. Raising my hand only a few inches above my
shoulder I mumbled, "I need to go to the bathroom." Miss Stewart pursed her
wrinkled persimmon lips and barely nodded, too enthralled with Lincoln's
detailed explanation.

Since going to the bathroom was just an excuse to leave the class, I usually
grabbed something from inside my desk—a pink eraser or a shiny pencil cap—to
take with me. I proceeded to the bathroom stall and sat on the toilet and waited.

Waited, while my feet dangled above the damp cement floor, until someone
else entered the bathroom. Then I would drop whatever object I had with me
into the bowl and flush the toilet, pretending that I had just finished.

However, I was not good at judging when "Show and Tell" was over and the next lesson was to start. Oftentimes, I returned to the classroom just as Miss Stewart was placing the large green flannel clock with the cut-out felt numbers and long and short hands back behind her desk. And it wasn't until sixth grade that I had the courage to ask my brother to explain why the long hand pointed at the "3" and the "9" positions was called "quarter after" or "quarter to."

Unfortunately, my speechlessness was responsible for placing me in more than one uncomfortable situation. In third grade, I had a crush on my brother Tommy's classmate, Winston, and at my brother's command, my mother drove to Winston's house.

"Mom," said Tommy, "since Susie invited Merle over to swim in our pool this afternoon, let's stop off at Winston's to see if he wants to go swimming, too. Susie would like that, wouldn't you, Susie?"

Merle's parents had just returned from a podiatry convention in Palm Springs. Aunty Bea brought us back our first bikinis—hot pink with chartreuse polka dots, and Merle made me vow that we'd wear the matching suits that afternoon. Even though mine was too tight, I was too timid to disagree.

In the backseat of the car, I prayed, "Please say, 'No,' Mother. Please say, 'No,'" and had thoughts of the last time I went to Donna Lin's home for a sleepover. Donna's mother decided at the spur of the moment to take everyone to the beach, but none of the girls had packed a swimsuit.

"No problem," said Mrs. Lin. "Donna has so many suits. You can all just borrow one of hers."

As I struggled to get into a shirred, but thankfully, expansive faded orange one-piece, I overheard whispers of "It's going to be permanently stretched out." And when I caught a glimpse of myself in the full-length mirror in the bathroom, the sight was horrifying. The suit crinkled in the most unflattering places. I looked like a giant Vienna sausage, fried plump and wrinkled.

What a humiliating prospect that Winston might actually see my chubby form in a bikini. My brother had no right to include Winston in my plans.

As Tommy and Mother laughed with gusto, our car whipped around and changed direction up the Pali Highway, and like a hurricane picking up momentum, nothing was safe in its wake. It was useless to say anything.

Difficulty speaking up was a recurring problem. There was an instance in fourth grade when our teacher Mrs. Ziffrin asked, "Children, who can tell me something about volcanoes?"

Lincoln couldn't have answered fast enough. "According to *Webster's Dictionary*, 'a volcano is a vent in the crust of the earth from which gases and molten rock called magma escape.'"

"Correct," said Mrs. Ziffrin, "anything else?"

"Our islands are volcanic in origin. Every Hawaiian island was formed by at least one volcano, and some islands are composites of more than one."

"Excellent, Lincoln. Isn't volcanology the topic you've selected for the Damon speech contest? Such an impressive representative from our class, you'll be!"

I could have spewed forth like Kīlauea, one of the most active and continuously erupting volcanoes on earth, that volcanoes considered extinct could prove unpredictable, and it was possible for some to erupt after a long cessation of activity, but the facts, like Haleakalā, lay dormant, deposited deep within me.

As usual, I kept quiet, my voice still.

Only once did it pay to keep mum. I was definitely offered a part in a movie because of it.

During one summer in eighth grade, I took painting classes at the Academy of Arts. The instructor, Mr. Pohl, announced that a casting director was planning to visit, but to pay no heed.

Almost immediately, Kathy Waterman, Leilani Morris, and Susie Shea rushed to the bathroom to comb their hair and primp. When they returned, they became very talkative and animated in an effort to call attention to themselves. It was annoying because their antics made it difficult to concentrate on the still life that Mr. Pohl had arranged on a colorful Mexican serape.

All of their jabbering was for naught because at the end of the hour, the raven-haired woman with the wiry curls, handed me a note with her name and phone number. Trying not to distract the rest of the class, she mouthed, "Call me," while clenching her hand, holding it close to her ear as if it were a receiver.

When my mother picked me up that day, I resisted the urge to tell her that I was going to be a movie star. After all, how many average girls are selected over the likes of Susie Shea and Leilani Morris? Instead, upon arriving home, I got up the courage to phone the director, Shirley Kandell, first to make sure that she didn't make a mistake.

"Hello," I said. "This is Susan. I'm in Louis Pohl's art . . ."

Not letting me finish, she said, "Yes, of course. I think you'd be perfect for the role. I'll tell you all about it during our interview. Can you come on Saturday morning?"

"I think so."

"Great. My office is at the State Hospital. Come at ten o'clock and use the intercom to enter."

When I asked my mother to drive me, she said, "The State Hospital—in Kāneʻohe? The mental institution?"

"That's where her office is."

"What part do you have?"

"She's going to let me know on Saturday."

"Well, my symphony rehearsal isn't until the afternoon. There should be enough time to drive over the Pali."

Without delay, my mother picked up the phone to dial her sister, Aunty Waynette. "Guess what, Way? Susan's been picked for a role in a movie. She doesn't know yet. Yes, yes. Need more Chinese actors and actresses. *Flower Drum Song*, just a disgrace. All the stars except Nancy Kwan—Japanese. No, no! Jack Soo's not Chinese. Changed his name from Suzuki. And wasn't Miyoshi Umeki's Japanese accent ridiculous? Yeah, they think we're all alike. Okay, I'll call you."

My mother's conversation prompted me to search for our record of Rodgers and Hammerstein's soundtrack from *Flower Drum Song*. I placed it on our hi-fi and turned up the volume so I could hear it from my room.

When the song "You Are Beautiful" played, I pictured dreamy James Shigeta, as Wang Ta, singing to me, as I replaced Miyoshi Umeki in the role of Mei Li.

I would be the first Asian to win an Academy Award. A Chinese actress playing a Chinese person. Not Luise Rainer, who accepted the Oscar in 1937 for starring as O-Lan in the movie version of Pearl Buck's *The Good Earth*.

Uncle Chew Fat had told me that silent movie actress Anna May Wong lost the major role to Rainer and didn't get the part as the concubine either. It would be different for me.

After a sleepless night, fantasizing about my trip to Hollywood, pondering over my Oscar acceptance speech, thinking about how to get away with saying nothing, deciding that since my work would speak for itself, a "Thank you very much, members of the Academy" would suffice, I dressed in a simple skirt and blouse, careful not to appear too flamboyant.

Following my mother to the car, we drove past the Pali Lookout, where warriors jumped to their deaths to escape capture by Kamehameha the Great, our car clinging to the curvy road, down into the depths of the valley.

A barbed wire fence encircled the hospital property with a few automobiles caged in the parking lot. As I opened the car door, my mother said, "I'm coming in with you, Susan. I want to hear what leading role you'll be given and help with the negotiations. You have to ask for first billing, you know?"

"Oh," I said, wondering how many film stars went to interviews with their mothers in tow.

We walked up a long stairway to reach a door with a discrete sign— "Kaneohe State Hospital—AUTHORIZED PERSONNEL ONLY—Please ring for admittance." I rang the button. Through an intercom came a curt "Yes?"

"We're here to see Mrs. Kandell," my mother shouted back.

"Okay, I'll buzz you in. Go straight down the corridor to the second set of double doors and press the bell between each locked entry."

Proceeding down the hall, I noticed no open doors. There was barely any light, only the filtered light of day that seeped from under the doorways to the floor, burrowing into the linoleum cracks. It was eerily quiet.

After two long hallways and two sets of double doors, Mrs. Kandell sat at a metal desk, her back facing a window.

"Hello, I'm Mayette, Susan's mother. So what's her part?"

"Actually, I would prefer to talk to your daughter alone."

"I can speak for her. She's a minor. I'm her mother; I know what's best."

Mrs. Kandell politely motioned towards the door, "Why don't you have a seat in the hall?"

My mother didn't budge. "I've heard too many stories of actors and actresses being taken advantage of in Hollywood."

In a clipped manner, Mrs. Kandell said, "We're in Kāneʻohe. This won't take too long." She pointed towards the door again. "There's a chair out there."

"Well, then," said my mother, "I'll just wait for you in the car, Susan," leaving without giving so much as a glance.

Unruffled, Mrs. Kandell looked at me directly, "Sit down, dear. You must be curious about the film. I am the producer, director, and writer, and your role is a non-speaking one."

What luck, I thought. Maybe I can be the new Anna May Wong, but my first starring role wouldn't be like hers in the 1922 film, *Toll of the Sea*. In that movie, Anna, as Lotus Flower, was forced to tell her son that she was not his mother, but a Chinese nanny, and then was coerced into giving her son to her haole lover and his haole wife. Out of desperation, Lotus Flower eventually committed suicide.

I nodded for Mrs. Kandell to continue.

"In the first scene, you will be sitting in front of a piano." She looked down at my stubby fingers and asked, "By any chance, do you know how to play?"

I indicated "yes" by bobbing my head up and down, for to be a true silent movie star, I thought I should act the part.

"Good. While playing the piano, you will suffer a breakdown. Then, running outside by a stream, the one that runs just beyond this property, you try to commit suicide."

I gasped, but said nothing, thinking the story line was creepy, remembering Uncle Chew Fat's comments about Anna May Wong's decision to move to Europe. Portraying characters that were always killed off by murder or suicide, she purportedly said, "I left Hollywood because I died so often."

"Are you okay with that?" I nodded again, suddenly noticing the view behind her, a forest of wild ferns and maile vines strangling trees with abandon.

"Good. Your father, who will be played by Duke Kahanamoku's brother, will rescue you and bring you to the hospital for rehabilitation."

I sighed at the thought of starring with a relative of the famed Olympic gold medalist.

"We just need your parents' permission. Take this contract with you, have them sign it and mail it back. Filming will start next month."

I returned to the car and my mother's interrogation. "So, what are you? The ingénue?"

"Not exactly."

"Tell me, so I can tell Aunty Way. I need to phone her with the news when we get home. You know you will be the only Chow Hoo to star in a movie."

I hesitated before rapidly saying, "Mrs. Kandell wants me to play a mental patient who is suicidal."

"What! Are you crazy? Is she crazy? You are not allowed to play a lōlō. *Dai Gut Li See*. Heaven forbid! And suicidal! No! No! No! It's nuts, just plain nuts!

What did you tell that woman anyhow?"

I shrugged my shoulders and looked down.

"Answer me. You didn't say anything? What's the matter with you? Why didn't you speak up and tell her that you are not going to play a crazy lōlō? I knew I should have stayed with you in that room."

"But Mom, you always tell me not to speak so I won't sound stupid."

"I know. I know," she said, gripping the steering wheel, the veins on the back of her hands straining. "But if someone is asking you to *be* a lōlō, then you have no choice but to say 'No!' dummy," she screamed, shaking her head in disbelief.

Then, losing some of the anger in her voice, she said, "Don't worry. I'll call that Mrs. Kandell as soon as we get home, before I phone your aunty. We are not lōlōs."

Upon returning home and my bedroom, I snatched a postcard that was propped up on the mirror of my dresser. It was sent by Uncle Chew Buck, the only one of my mother's siblings who didn't live in Hawai'i, but in California. Facing me was an image of the whitewashed "H-O-L-L-Y-W-O-O-D" sign. I flipped the card around, revealing Uncle Bucky's postscript: *Wish you were here!* Me too, I thought, before setting it back down.

JOSEPH STANTON

THE NIGHT OF THE ʻAʻO

Young shearwaters fledge on clear nights,
flying off their nested places of birth,
seeking the brightest part of the sky.

In olden days that would aim them
towards moon and stars,
astronautical ambition leading them always offshore

to commence careers feeding on high seas.
But now our night-time electrifications
sometimes confuse their flights

so that fledge-night birds descend
on backyards, on shopping malls,
on all our lighted night places.

Some autumn nights flocks of shearwaters
rain down suddenly
on a high school football game,

making it seem a scene by Hitchcock,
the horror mostly in the hearts of the birds
who cannot lift off from level ground

and need to be,
by the kindness of strangers,
carried to the sea.

AT COFFEE MĀNOA, CLOUDS RISING

Dark French roast,
the steam rising and drifting
from the white cup
with the green picture
of the volcanic cliffs
that rise green before me,
as I sit drinking and looking.

Some days it's so quiet
it's as if everyone
has been gone
a long, long time.

Clouds whiter than the cup
rise and drift.
Dark birds draw lines of flight
against them, rising
above the parked cars, the trees
bright green in the bright
late afternoon light.

I am watching
the cliffs on the cup,
the white clouds rising.

THE LAST KAUA'I 'Ō'Ō

In 1983, in the highest branch of a tree
in a deeply forested place
a male 'ō'ō called and called to his mate—

ringing tones echoing, echoing—
far and far, a quarter-mile at least
his yearning bell tolling

the remains of wild Kaua'i.
In the pauses between the calling,
he was gathering,

building the nest his mate would need,
building it stronger, building it better,
building towards her return.

At least once every year
he was seen to try his song—
his cry eerie, penetrating.

In 1987, his song soared one last time
and then arrived the silence,
and he was known to be, at last,
the last of his kind.

THE MAIN EVENT

Undercard

Front and center was a cage where men would soon punch each other for money. Seats inside Seoul's cavernous Olympic Hall wrapped around it on two levels: cageside VIP tables for the type of people who wear suits to a cage fight, and open-seating above it for everyone else. Behind the cage was a ramp that led up to a theater stage set up with rock band equipment. Above, a jumbo screen showed silent highlight videos of older matches on loop.

A pre-fight promotional video started. Clips of knockouts played as the lights dimmed. Band members crept to their positions through the shadows while the video showed mean-mugging men holding up their fists. The video culminated with resounding, ear-splitting English: "Top FC! Fighting! Champion!"

The screen went blank. A row of mortar-like pyrotechnics shot flames upward from the edge of the stage, and the band started screaming over the sounds of their instruments. They sounded like the kinds of bands most kids listen to in high school but are now embarrassed to think about—except Korean.

It was exactly the type of campy, weird high-production values that I wanted, but as the music pierced the on-stage flames and echoed through the auditorium, I didn't quite feel there. I didn't quite feel anywhere.

There were no students in the halls when I left my classroom to make the short walk to go watch the Korean mixed martial arts promotion, Top FC. Teaching on weekends doesn't feel odd to me anymore. That's how education works in Korea; learning never takes a day off. What never ceases to feel strange, though, is the silence after kids leave. Not having something to block out becomes more distracting than any group of screaming, laughing middle-schoolers could be. Absence itself is a thing, a phantom punch.

Top FC puts on fight cards only a few times a year. A handful of Korean fighters have graduated from Top FC to the UFC, but for the most part it's regional-level talent: think NFL Europe compared to the NFL, or the NBA developmental league compared to the real thing. The appeal of watching Top FC is not the possibility of seeing high-level prospects or to witness exciting fights—though both of those do happen—so much as the guarantee that there will be something charmingly goofy to occupy my attention. It's something different to do, a way to break up the routine.

The walls of my classroom used to be decorated with colorful posters my students made, but for no apparent reason they were torn down and thrown out one night after I went home. They were drawn too well and stuck to the walls too purposefully to think throwing them out could have been an honest mistake, but regardless of who did it or why it feels more like a hospital than a classroom, the walls like visual white noise. It fits the monotony of Korean cram-schools, or *hagwons*, where students come to study for several hours after they finish regular school (or on days when they don't have school). There's something empty about it all. It's nice to teach dedicated students and, contrary to how I taught stateside, I have yet to feel the need to break out my "please don't go to jail" lesson. Still, this wasn't exactly what I had in mind when I decided to come here.

If I had a dollar for every time I've been asked why I moved to Korea from—"of all places!"—Hawai'i, I would have enough money to pay off my student loans and move back home. Debt is a conversational downer, though, so I usually blame some other millennial pathology, like existential angst or wanderlust or feeling too young to settle into a long-term career. All of which is true, even if those reasons are secondary to debt.

Living and working in Korea was a way to check off all boxes. I make more and spend less than I did in Hawai'i, I travel around Asia easily, and living abroad on a temporary work visa guarantees I won't be doing this forever, endowing the future with a sense of possibility.

What I didn't expect was the antiseptic walls, the one-day weekends, the repetition of drill-and-kill test prep. For all the excitement living abroad can provide, it can be just as boring and tedious as life was back home when my time was spread across multiple jobs that barely covered the bills.

Main Card Fight #1

"My dream is to become champion and get into the UFC."

"I just think fighting is fun."

The first fight is a matchup of two different personalities: an ambitious and professional fighter vs. one nicknamed "Drunken Hong." Ambitious Professional walks

out to a kind of generic gothic dubstep, Drunken Hong comes out to "Zombie" by the
Cranberries.

The ring announcer grabs the mic. With gel-haired swagger, his voice booms
through the auditorium in English: "We are live at this time! Only the strong survive!
Featherweight special match!"

He announces that the fight will be five 3-minute rounds. The people cheer, not
noticing he meant to say three 5-minute rounds. The opening bell dings.

Ambitious Professional is clearly a grappler, stocky with a low crouching
stance. Drunken Hong is a kickboxer. The crowd goes silent and for a minute the
only sounds are the thuds of feet bouncing on the mat and the interruption of
skin-on-skin thwacking.

Drunken Hong nearly kicks Ambitious Professional in the groin. They both
instinctively back off and bow. I scream "HWAITING, DRUNKEN HONG," which
translates into "FIGHTING, DRUNKEN HONG," the generic "go team" cheer for any
and all Korean sports, but especially pertinent here. People in the crowd look around
and laugh when they see that a foreigner said it.

It isn't exactly an action-packed fight, but it's watchable enough. Drunken
Hong stays back and throws strikes at a comfortable range. Ambitious Professional
follows a formula: he showboats by shuffling his feet and putting his hands down,
eats some punches and kicks for his troubles, resets, and then does it all over again
until the end of the fight.

The scorecards are a strange, nearly random assortment of numbers: 30-28, 29-
27, and 28-29. The referee announces Drunken Hong as the winner by split decision
while he lifts Ambitious Professional's arm. He realizes his mistake and quickly pulls
it down to raise Drunken Hong's arm. As a group of four ring girls approaches him for
post-fight pictures, the winner doesn't seem to notice the error.

Living in Korea isn't terribly difficult. It's cheap, it's safe, it's convenient, the
food is good, and you don't even really need to speak any Korean; one of the five
biggest industries in the country is private English education, so most people
in Seoul can meet you halfway. Unless you're living somewhere distinctly
non-urban, there aren't many big cultural adjustments to make to feel
comfortable.

What is hard is the aggregate of the little everyday things. The walking
smartphones with people attached who stride squarely into you; the crowds
in front of elevator and subway doors who don't wait for people to exit before

they walk in; the *ajeossi*'s, the old and usually drunk men who cough on you and touch your face; the *ajumma*'s, the old women who push and elbow their way to cut in line; the size Large shirts that are really Mediums. It's stupid and doesn't seem like much, but those minor annoyances—the awkwardness, the obliviousness, the drunkenness—add up, to nothing.

Main Card Fight #2

"From Korea! Playboy!"

Fog machines puff oscillating smoke as a Korean alternative rock song plays. Playboy emerges from behind the curtains. It's his professional debut and the crowd cheers. The next fighter comes out to "Gangnam Style," but the crowd is silent, like they know something I don't.

"From Japan!"

The audience's silence fills the arena as heavily raining boos. The 35-year Japanese occupation of Korea ended in 1945, but some wounds—forced immigration to work in Japanese factories and fight in the Japanese military, abduction of Korean women to serve as sex slaves for soldiers, political and cultural oppression—take longer to heal.

The stillness lingers as the fight starts. Playboy picks up From Japan and slams him to the mat. The crowd erupts. He then smothers From Japan, hitting him with short elbows until they tangle themselves into a Gordian pretzel. They remain locked together for another minute and a half until the referee cuts in.

There are no chants for the hometown favorite, just stubborn silence consciously funneled toward From Japan. Playboy drags From Japan to the mat and sprawls across his wriggling foe. He delivers more short elbows, carefully advances position, and stifles his opponent's ability to move. The referee stands them up, rinse and repeat.

In the third round I yell "PUNCH!" No one in the crowd reacts, but seconds later Playboy throws a straight right and scores a knockdown. You're welcome, Playboy. This is the moment everyone has been waiting for, something sudden and violent and more immediately gratifying than the slow grinding dominance of top-position wrestling. It isn't a clean knockout, but it's enough to be the definitive highlight of the fight. The crowd applauds.

Playboy ends up winning a decision. For his effort, he is awarded a phallic-looking glass trophy. He takes his time bowing again and again in all directions as he exits the cage, the repetitive motion a polite aftertaste of how he performed inside of it.

When the laundry is drying is when my apartment feels most like a shoebox.

If dryers exist in Korea, they have long been extinct in my apartment building. My fiancée and I use a drying rack, which covers roughly one-third of the floor space and takes roughly way fucking longer for clothes to actually dry. Between the two of us and our dog, laundry days feel very much like the trash compactor scene from the first *Star Wars*, the open space of our room closing in on us until the clothes are all put away.

I've never needed much space indoors, though. I've always found reprieve outside, among trees or in the ocean. Over the mountains from my hometown on Oʻahu is Town, capital T, the *other* side of the island defined by loud crowds of tourists. I never went Townside unless I had to be there for work or school. It always made me the worst tour guide to visiting friends who wanted to see Waikīkī and experience nightlife outside of my favorite dumpy dive bars. I'd turn down the wrong one-way streets, drive past parking garages, and generally not know where I was going. That claustrophobic tropical metropolis of Honolulu is home, I guess, in the same way that distant cousins are technically family. It's familiar enough, but not the same. No matter what, I always knew how to get out of Town; just head to the mountains and sooner or later I'd be back Home.

Seoul is Town magnified by ten condensed into less than half the land mass of Oʻahu. Only there is no escape road over the mountains, no away, only snaking subways and bumpy taxis to another identical part of itself.

Rinse. Repeat.

Main Card Fight #3

Either a moth or a slip of paper flutters in the spotlight above the cage. Figuring this out is by far the most interesting part of the fight. The fighters beneath the moth/paper obstruct my ability to solve the mystery—as if I need another reason to begrudge them.

The action, if you can call it that with a straight face, is functionally no different than choreographed shadowboxing. The two men mirror each other like two skittish puppies, prancing ever-so-slightly into range then hurriedly dashing out again. They might as well be exchanging butterfly kisses; their so-called "strikes" are almost exactly as damaging as eyelash tickles. I cross my fingers and hope that they somehow knock each other out at the same time. It's the end all parties deserve.

The Korean fighter who walked out to Bon Jovi's "It's My Life" realizes it is our lives he is wasting and at the end of the third round mercifully smashes his fellow Korean into the mat with ground and pound, preventing me from pounding my head into the ground and sparing us another godawful ninety seconds of twinkle-toed pugilism.

On his way out, the winner bows repeatedly to the audience in all directions.

At least he knows when he needs to apologize.

Birth and death are obverse sides of the same coin: you leave the only world you know, alone, usually to the sounds of someone crying nearby. Life, then, is the grand distinguisher, the invigorating in-between that gives those criers reasons to wail and those lonesome acts of birth and death a sense of meaning.

And yet, we have done an exceptional job at putting what matters in long quarantines. Modern life has been whittled down to *birthschoolworkdeath*. Daily monotony knows no culture and obeys no borders.

When I talk to friends back home, they tend to think I'm off on some Big Adventure, looking the future in the eye, facing the horizon with my right knee perched atop a mountain, pointing my finger defiantly outward and piercing the unknowable expanse of destiny.

In reality: Monday through Friday I wake up make coffee walk the dog shower go to work go home eat dinner watch TV drink tea go to bed.

Saturday: Wake up make coffee go to work go home take a nap wake up walk the dog eat dinner watch TV drink tea go to bed.

Sunday, my one day off: I wake up, watch people punch each other in the UFC, walk the dog take a nap go out to dinner with my fiancée, watch a movie or read while I drink my tea then go to bed.

Multiply by 130, my life in Korea.

Main Card Fight #4

"I'll bring a trophy home for Thanksgiving," says the first fighter, boasting a record of 0-1-1. Chuseok, Korea's three-day thanksgiving holiday, is a few days away.

"I'll make him retire from MMA," says the second fighter, nicknamed Lucky Guy. He has a thick tattoo scrawled across his chest that says "EfforTempeR" with an angel-winged cross on his sternum bridging the two words. Incoherent tattoo aside, Lucky Guy has thus far been unlucky more often than not as a professional fighter: his record is 1-2.

The first round is exciting and evenly matched and surprisingly technical for two sub-.500 fighters. In between rounds, Thanksgiving sits on the ground while Lucky

Guy is on his stool with his legs propped up by his coaches like he's going into labor.
He knocks out Thanksgiving early in the second round, and everyone is off their feet. I
check the time. The thought of three more fights makes me preemptively tired. I shift in
my seat, waiting for the reason I came to be done with already.

I lied.

My weekly schedule times 130 hasn't exactly been my life in Korea. More
like times 126. Every year earns me two weeks of vacation. Over the course
of the past two years, I've thus far spent them with my fiancée in Cambodia,
Indonesia, Hawai'i and California. The latter two trips were not my choice
destinations; two of my brothers were getting married and I was obliged to go.

Obliged. As if going on vacation to see family and get away from work and all
my irrational annoyances is a bad thing, a thing I have to do and don't want to
do. It's not like those trips were a bad time, either. I stuffed my face with all the
food I've been missing in Korea, I enjoyed all the nature that's absent in Seoul,
I saw my niece and nephew become walking talking humans when previously
I had only known them as fleshy baby lumps. All of those are good. Still, it's
hard to reason out of kneejerk responses. It felt foolish to move to Asia and then
spend all my vacation time going back to places I used to live.

Most expats have a common personality trait, a desire to see new places
and experience new cultures. That desire becomes an expectation once you've
actually planted some roots in foreign soil. The first year in Korea met those
expectations. My fiancée and I had momentum, we made plans. We knew life
in Korea was temporary and that we'd be back in America sooner than later. We
wanted to make the most of our geography while we're out here. But that's not
how things worked out.

I really have nothing to complain about, and yet I complain. Feeling
frustrated by visiting family is much worse when you know you shouldn't
feel that way and you do anyway. Spending time with people you love is what
matters—maybe the only thing that matters. The monotony of adulthood has
at least taught me that much. Yet I still can't help but feel let down, like I
blew opportunities to be with my family even though I *know* being with my
family itself was the opportunity.

It's aggravating to feel and exhausting to not feel.

Main Card Fight #5

"This guy is a kickboxer!"

Despite competing in the third-to-last fight, Takenori Sato is the most notable name on the card. The Japanese fighter had a pair of bouts in the UFC, but is best known for getting knocked out in both of them before getting cut. But before that he was the six-time defending welterweight champion of Pancrase, a legitimate and respected Japanese MMA promotion. Sato walks out to a Japanese hip-hop club jam, his hair highlighted with bleach-blonde frosted tips. His 36 professional fights make him look older than 31.

His opponent, a buff, baldhead Korean guy runs past the cameras to the cage. He is stopped and reset by the cameraman so they can film his walkout for the folks at home.

Sato gets slammed onto his back almost immediately, but scrambles back up the cage. An advertisement sticker on the fence starts peeling off and sticking to Sato's face. The ref steps in without calling time and peels it off while Buff Baldhead clinches against the fence. He pummels his arms underneath Sato's to gain dominant leverage. They separate, and with seconds left in the round, Buff Baldhead delivers a thunderous kick directly to Sato's crotch. The men in the audience reflexively put their hands between their legs.

Sato writhes in pain while Buff Baldhead sits in his corner. Sato tries to prop himself up with his elbows, but he keeps falling flat to the floor. A team of doctors enters the cage and inspects the affected area on the spot. On the jumbo screen the camera zooms in voyeuristically as the medical crew holds towels up to cover any potential indecency.

As men huddle around his lower torso, Sato's head sticks out. He covers his eyes with the backs of his hands, but it's apparent he's grimacing in pain. Surely most of it is physical pain, but the scene itself is painful in its own way.

Sato winces as he tugs his shorts back on and crab-crawls to the fence. The fight is called. The official decision is a No Contest, but as both men exit the cage—one walking and the other limping, one thinking of where to go out tonight and the other questioning why he came—there is a clear winner. Or at least, a clear loser.

When I'm on stage with the CEO of my company—*hagwons* are private education companies, not proper schools—I try not to think about my immediate situation. I stand on stage doing nothing, a piece of décor for the boss to parade in front of parents or business partners, while a meeting in Korean unfurls. Usually they are in the three-to-five-hour range. My mind wanders.

Something I've noticed: those who question themselves the most tend to be the ones who don't need to question themselves. This is especially true in teaching. Good teachers often get down on themselves, worry they aren't doing a good job. Lesser teachers don't have that anxiety. Their confidence spawns from not caring enough to worry.

I am a good teacher. I taught Special Ed for four years back home, at every level: kindergarten, elementary, middle school, and a summer of high school. The only subject I'm not "Highly Qualified" to teach—and that's a DOE term, not mine—is math. The only qualifications needed to teach in Korea are a college degree and a willingness to live in Korea.

I'm a good teacher I'm a good teacher I'm a good teacher. I tell myself like I tell my dog he's a good boy. He really is a good boy.

My mind stops wandering somewhere in the second hour. That's when my back starts to hurt from standing. Later it will move down my legs and to my feet, but as the meeting continues and I think about where I am and where I've been, the pain suddenly feels more acutely debilitating.

Main Card Fight #6: Co-Main Event

Heavyweight fight between a Korean guy with a sumo braid and a guy from Guam draped in the flag of his homeland. Guam Flag makes his way to the cage and his walkout song skips to the next track. It restarts as the cage door closes.

The announcer introduces the fight as three 4-minute rounds, ending a four-fight streak of saying the correct numbers.

It's a slow, plodding match, spent mostly in clinch pirouettes with both men taking turns pushing each other against the fence. The first round ends and they're both exhausted. So is the crowd; these minutes aren't normal minutes. It's as if, like a black hole, the sheer mass of the men has distorted time itself. When the second round starts, it feels like it should be the last.

Guam Flag starts to take over, sort of. He presses Sumo Braid against the fence and unleashes a barrage of hammer-fists to the thighs. Somehow, a small cut opens on the face of Guam Flag, and the "action" stops. The crowd leaks a collective groan as the medical staff examines the cut to see if Guam Flag is fit to continue. He is, unfortunately, and the fight resumes.

Everything is in slow motion. I no longer know what minute of what round it is.

The two men take turns pushing up against one another on the fence, over and over, with only the occasional punch to Sumo Braid's thighs to let us know that time is still moving forward. It is an awful fight, but for some reason it sucks my undivided attention and I can't stop watching.

With heavy steps and heavier breaths, the bout limps to the final bell. Sumo Braid can barely hold himself up after the big brother-style Charlie horses his thighs endured. For a fight announced as three 4-minute rounds, it felt like ten 20-minute rounds. At least there was a clear winner. I think.

"Majority draw!" The announcer raises both of their arms at the same time.

The fights took place on September 11th. I tend to think of 9/11 as the moment that thrust me into a consciousness higher than my childhood's, when I realized that events going on in the world were real. I was 13. This night was the fifteenth anniversary of 9/11, yet I completely forgot about it; it was just the night of the fights.

It's easy and comforting to forget that the rest of the world continues without you. There is simply too much going on to keep up with, and we're bombarded by so much information that it is tempting to just forget about it all and focus on ourselves. It's like that anywhere, but especially out here when you're isolated from everyone and everything you know. The catch is that the world does keep spinning, regardless of your consent or awareness.

I often forget that I've been living in Korea for three years. In that time, friends and family members have married, moved across the country, changed careers, had kids, continued on with their lives—and I've been gone for almost all of it. What should have been my memories and my experiences have been stolen from me while I was busy going through the same old rounds I always do. I feel stuck, spinning around in circles on the same plateau, telling myself I'm actually moving forward. Only when I come up for air and see the world outside of myself do I realize how long I've been here, and how little I have to show for it.

I forget that I—or anything, for that matter—exist outside the walls of my classroom and my apartment. Everything else feels interstitial. The rest of the world happens at a sanitized distance. Time moves slowly, then all of a sudden it's three years later and nothing has changed except everything else.

Main Card Fight #7: Main Event

A face-melting 80s style metal band introduces the challenger for the Top FC

featherweight championship, Choi Seung Woo. Gnarly guitar solos fill the room as the
singer screams "Korea! OooohYEAH!" The same screamo band from the beginning of
the show introduces the defending champ Lee Min Gu.

"Ladies and gentlemen, men of the world, only the strong survive! The final two
finals! We shout together! It's rEEal!" The announcer's voice cracks; it's realer than
he thought.

The opening bell dings. A woman in front of me screams for what seems like
ninety straight seconds as the fighters trade heavy leg kicks. It's annoying, but I
don't blame her; the first round is exciting, so much so that I'm no longer keeping
score. I'm just watching.

The crowd is fully immersed. Anxious cheers and attentive silence ebb and flow.
Lee and Choi are perfectly matched, mirroring each other's movements in violent
choreography. When one throws a strike, the other reacts almost flawlessly. One can
never expect to go untouched in a fight, but both men avoid eating any flush shots. It
really is beautiful.

Midway through the fourth round, Lee slips right into Choi's fist and crumples
instantaneously. It's hard to tell if Lee made a mistake or Choi made an adjustment,
but the result is undeniable. Choi's team rushes the cage and tackles the new
champion. Lee is still out cold, surrounded by trainers and doctors. For a moment,
there are two piles of men in the cage, for very different reasons. Choi walks out with a
trophy and a championship belt, Lee is carried out on a stretcher.

I lingered outside Olympic Hall after the fights finished. Excited chatter
buzzed around me, none of it in English but all of it understood. The pure,
visceral charge of a good fight knows no language, needs no explanation. It's
something to be experienced. It's something you feel.

I took my time walking back to the subway station. Cool, crisp air trickled
through the leaves and coalesced into a light breeze, the kind of breeze that
whispers hints of winter but is unwilling to forget the summer. The kind of
breeze that is caught between two worlds but is exactly what it is.

It was late enough at night, and I was far enough away from the road that the
brushing of the wind through the trees was all I heard. Somewhere behind those
trees loomed Lotte World Tower, the fifth tallest building in the world–just
forty-three feet taller than One World Trade Center. It was nice to not see it, to
be in the company of trees.

The trees gave way to a small, circular flower garden. At the center of the garden, thousands of wind chimes were arranged in a large spherical *taeguk*, the red and blue design at the center of the Korean flag that represents balance between negative and positive forces of the universe. The breeze stayed with me and danced between the chimes, allowing a few more moments of peace before I would have to leave it behind and walk across the highway. Those moments are hard to pin down exactly, except to say they felt right. I walked weightlessly, in a place as foreign as it is familiar, and everything was where it was supposed to be.

Korea has been good to me. The hardest part about living here has been seeing myself under new strains and seeing how poorly I react to them. If it has taught me anything, it's that getting hit is inevitable. How you get hit and what you do after—that's everything. I haven't yet figured out how to respond to the punches thrown at me out here. But I did for a night, and at that moment, what was there and what wasn't there was perfect.

I am a good teacher. I really am. 🐢

SUSAN LEE ST. JOHN

FAT LEONARD

My goal: in ten weeks I like weigh 300 pounds.

The lady teach say, *That not one goal.*

Look like one goal to me. It get components like one goal. It get doable steps you can measure: I gain five pound a week. I eat all da Spam rice and Portagee sausage I like before I barf. I no do nothing to make me lose da weight, like walk all the way from the caf to this fricking class on the second floor of A building.

This is Health class, the lady says. *We want healthy goals.*

Fifty pounds in 10 weeks is one healthy bugga weight gain, lady.

No one wants to be fat, she says.

Being fat is what I good at, I say. The whale stay my 'aumakua. I work my strengths.

It's not good for you, the lady says.

Yada, yada, yada. Your heart gotta pump the blood a couple of extra miles, you no can breathe because all the fat cells stay clog up your lungs, no one like sit next to you 'cause you overflow like that.

Just give me one pink slip, lady. I no care. Why I like stay here? All hot and no screens on the louvers. Half the louvers no open anyways, the handle stay broken and dangling, like one broken chicken wing. The floor all scuff-up, the janitors no buff 'em. Back wen like World War II time, the linoleum like fake green marble. Now just cloudy and brown scratch-up with uku-million fat kids itching da chairs back and forth.

Watch me walk, lady. I one wide-load coming through, but I cool, I like slam da back of the heads, but I cool. I crab walk through the aisle—Michelangelo's to the front of me, da Vinci's to da back. Precious art, man.

Benny Malapit, that pilau flip, wen stick his foot right in front me, like trip me. I wen crush him, no bother me, like stepping on one soda can.

What that noise, wah waah wah. Get soft, get loud, da kine Doppler effect, the sirens all night long going up and down my street.

He broke my foot, Malapit say.

Aw, I say. *You like me take you to the nurse? No bother me, it's on my way.*

Fuck no, Malapit says.

Goodie, I say. *Cuz I never like do you no harm.*

I stay wait for my pink slip. Da lady look at me, look at the class, look at Malapit, look at the pink paper, run through her vocab list, tinking, tinking of jus' da right word. O.K. I no bother. I let her compose the best pink slip ever.

I look out da door, look at the metal railing outside.

Da metal railing look like made in World War II shop class. It fat and round like flagpoles welded together. Like jail. Da last paint job beige, and it all flakey already.

I like come up hea and peel paint. Some kids start one peel where it all chip off and uneven. But you get nothing but little flakes like dat. I start where it bubble, one air pocket, you pop 'em and you get one long big peel. Beige, den puke green, neon green, jaundice yellow, dried blood red. Like archaeology, like da guy Schliemann, digging up one Troy, den one more, den one more after dat.

Past the railing, just dried up brown grass. Red dirt. Jus' flat. Den one tall chain link fence. Den the ocean.

Wide and blue, you can spock one end of the bay to da other end. Da smell of raw fish ride on da trade. Wen you hear a little splash, you know a school of fish stay turning jus' under da water.

Eh, Captain Cook. You like land hea? We geev 'em to you. 🐚

SUSAN LEE ST. JOHN

TRADE SECRETS

My mother worked in the school cafeteria.
All through elementary
I rode to school at 6 a.m.
Did my homework
at the stainless steel prep table
between the two walk-in refrigerators,
squinting in the dim light which
seeped through the back screen door.
Before the first bell, I would slip out
and go to homeroom,
just like any other student.
But one day, the cook—hunched Mrs. Kong—
noticed me. I began folding dish towels,
then aprons. Then carting trays
of unbaked yeast rolls into the refrigerators.
The cafeteria ladies had their secrets:
where you get those big ca-ca-roaches for your
science collection—
the government cheese in the pizza is past due—
Mrs. Kong drops raw meat and does not
wash it when she picks it up.

Mrs. Kong motions me into
the refrigerator where a naked block of butter,
big as an armchair, sweats on a pallet.
She hands me a butter knife and, as an
afterthought, a food handler's glove.
Scrape, she says.
Under the light of the single bulb, the surface of
the butter shivers. The greasy satin is pock-

marked with patches of electric-lime mold.
Even through the thin plastic, I feel
the soapy cerumen
cloaked in the morning dusk-dark.
The refrigerated air is citrus and pepper.
I feel no disgust,
even when Mom sees me and says
Don't tell your friends

ICE, ICE CUBE

One
In the early morning light
he rails against the row of fences shut tight.
Where's my dog? Who has my dog?
Ice Cube! Here boy! Ice Cube!
The man's wobbly orbit churns restless
around the suburban street, circling the lake.

Two
I am standing by the kitchen sink
staring out the back window
when he lets himself in through our side gate.
He is barefoot, jeans hanging low.
His open shirt flaps as he strides
through the yard onto our dock.

Three
The man whistles, and it echoes across the lake.
Your dog's not here, I say through the window.
He's here, I know he's here. He presses against the glass.
Abe, our terrier, barks angrily—*there is no other dog here,*
get out of our yard.

Four
In the golden hour of dusk, a tawny, round nose hound
emerges from the dark waters. It shivers on our small dock.
It is wet and hung with threads of sea grass.
Rivulets of brackish water track through its fur.
Abe gives chase. The hound trembles, then bounds
over the stone wall and slides into

our neighbor's dry fishpond.

Five
I'm not going in there, the cop says.
He might be vicious. If you are worried
about leaving him there for a couple of
weeks, you can go in if you want. I can
shoot him, but I'm not going to get him.

Six
The neighbors on the loop:
He lives in that abandoned house.
He beats it.
What a name for a dog—Ice Cube.
The social worker just drops him off—
she should get fired. He siphons electricity
from our line. It's swum up to our house too.
After you take care of that dog, do something
about that black one that poops on our front lawn.

Seven
The abandoned house is boxed in
by untrimmed yellowing panax.
The street gutters are clogged with debris,
water pools in the driveway, a large stagnant reserve.
The walls sip the corrosive waters and bleed
rust. Deep in the emptiness, a single light: a headlamp.

Eight
I'm not his girlfriend, the woman with the headlamp says.
Her long black hair is matted and greasy.
She wears the sad fat of low-income distress.
He came in this morning shouting, "Where's
the silverware, where's the silverware?" He
shattered something and the dog ran off.

She leans over our stone wall.
Here Iceberg! Come here, Iceberg!

Nine
The dog will not come. He is not a variety of lettuce.

Ten
The panax has been bulldozed over, the gutters swept clear
of rotting clutter. A contractor's sign and the bones of
a two-storied mansion rise from the wreckage.
It will be listed at 1.3 million.

DELAINA THOMAS

TENCHIJI-AMACHIJI UTAKI

Nakijin Castle grounds

is this all the Noro needed to pray
no temple no fortress no stained glass window
just a running stream or spring
a tree for shelter
a half-circle of stones

I have lived half my life
I've come from thousands of miles away
and I brought no incense with me
no tangerines or rice
not even some water
for a small depression in a stone

I've lost everything I thought I had
thought I meant to someone
there's no credit from the gods for the loss
I didn't surrender what was taken

that boulder must be sacred for where it is
at the apex of the semicircle
it's wrapped in so many roots
like a heart muscle bound with veins
how old is the tree
is anyone going to stop the boulder from toppling
someday

my hair is lifted by a slight wind
time is slower between these trees
the air seems denser

did something appear
or disappear between those trunks

standing here who would hear me
ancestors whose names I've never known
in this land where I was not born

the plaque says men were prohibited from this place
women made offerings to the gods here
for good harvest
progeny
and safety from invaders to the kingdom

the Noro priestess and her attendants
wore white robes and headdresses of leaves
I'll never see their summer rituals
Upu-Uimi and Gusuku-Uimi
centuries ago

this stone I've been running my hands over
is something coming out of it
I must be imagining it it's just a stone
but what is this warmth
without heat
coming into my hands

I lift my hands up
and put them back on
it's starting again
spreading into my arms

is that you ancestors
are you here

be with me

in this time that is breaking me
be with me in the night of my forest
I cannot speak your language
but you left it in the stones

ELEGY FOR UNCLE KAZU

You were not my uncle and you had little to say to me,
Recent stranger in your long life, married to the niece
You adored, whose brother used to pedal his bike
To your gas station on Kūhiō Avenue, where you kept
Your arms deep in grease and your smile quietly left
Upon tourists who asked you to pump gas, directions
To Ala Moana or where they could find good eats.

Your nephew, Gary, skin nearly as dark as the asphalt
In Waikīkī, would keep his surfboard in your office
For those times when you stopped whatever repairs
You were making for Keoni Chang or Mits Oka
And drive him to Queen's Beach, your arms only
Slightly free of those dark smudges mechanics
Wore as badges of their trade. Then after many years,

Your service station long replaced by a nameless condo,
You and your wife, childless and suddenly helpless
Had to go to a nursing home. Gary was the one who
Found a home in Pālolo, cleaned your house, sold
It to pay for your care and visited you after your quiet
Smile had been lost to all but us. Those trips to Queen's
Beach gave us directions for what now endures of you.

JEAN YAMASAKI TOYAMA

RHODODENDRON/ HYDRANGEA

That's the one Jichan planted forty
years ago, rododendron,
I think, my mother says,
pointing her trowel at a shriveled bush.

Rododendron, I tell myself so I can
remember: rodo, rodo,
dendron, dendron,
rododendron,
rododendron. I snip off
the dying branches, toss a
few grains of fertilizer around
the roots, wondering what color
flowers will bloom.

Back home I Google the word,
rododendron.
Oh, I spelt it wrong. *Rho* not *ro*,
but the leaves in the image
don't match the leaves on Jichan's
plant.

Mom, you know that
plant, it's not
rhododendron.

No? Wait, what did Jichan call it?

He planted it with Baban, right there.
I can see her holding it in her palms.

What did they call it, Mom?

Let me think, think . . . *Aji*, *aji*,
that's it, *ajisai*. I remember it
had something to do with
taste: *aji*. Do you know what that is,
ajisai?

No, Mom.

Back to Google . . . restaurants, so
many restaurants, *Ajisai*. There
it is, so many pictures of hydrangea.

Hydrangea?

Hydrangea is *ajisai*. You remembered
the Japanese word, Mom.

Ajisai is hydrangea. It almost died,
but now, look, so green, the leaves.
You paid attention.
You know its name.
So many flowers,
so dark, the blue.

JEAN YAMASAKI TOYAMA

IN THE SHADE

Under the shade of the jabon tree
she sits. I watch the lights on her face
traced by the movement
of the breeze in the leaves.
Few lines around the eyes
looking through space.
She says, "We used to sit like this side by side,
Jichan and me. He'd rip off the skin
with his thumb stuck in
like this and tear it off
with one hand. Like this,
see?"
She hands me a crescent of fruit.
"See how juicy?" and wipes her
mouth with her T-shirt.
She looks at me,
"Hard to believe
I have a daughter
over seventy years old."

We taste the sweet
and bitter of it all.

MAUI

I am sitting at the crossroads of Makawao
population 2500
where Baldwin Avenue meets Olinda Road
which sweeps steeply uphill
for the town leans like splintered siding on the slope of Haleakalā "House of the Sun,"
an extinct volcano
on the stillness of Sunday, fled
to a vacant beach
despite the shade of musty leaves
and monkeypod trees.

The rock & rollers I teach call Makawao
Hippy Town
of surfers, craftsmen, farmers, entrepreneurs
from Newport, Boston, Canada, Missouri
from elsewhere from long ago
like some of their grandparents
in rusty pickups and four-wheel drives
in shacks and pole houses
breeding orchids on their back porch
or pot in forest pockets
where maile grow
on the shoulders
of ghosts.

It's really a town of Portuguese cowboys of

      mainland steaks
      and Hawaiian fish

MAUI

ono
uku
mahimahi,

of barnyard nights at Longhi's Saloon
where the men are grizzly   dusty
leathery as jerky or a chaw of tobacco
where the women are horses, saltier than the men
who need no Colts or bullwhips
to kill each other.   Alex
known as Geek
was already bustin' broncs at 17
while Derek
back from U of Davis makes
Maui wine   and Suzanne
turns English into Spanish
for the Sandanistas.   —Ahkoi?
she simply chucked the whole thing
went back to the peninsula
wraps laulau with her own taro leaves
dances ancient hula
under purple shower trees
and jacaranda.

I teach up Olinda Road, through a tunnel of eucalyptus
across Oskie Rice's Rodeo. Take a right
between two rows of cypress trees
across a rattling cattle guard, through the gate
which opens
upon

the lettuce-green campus
the chapel
the West Maui Mountains
the ocean
a pasture of drifting cows

It is dusk
and in the vesper light
you can almost hear.

JOE TSUJIMOTO

LUCKY COME HAWAI‘I

As an American
with an Oriental face
whelped in Manhattan
in subways
to school in the Bronx
or fixing teletype machines on Broad St.
next to Wall
I've been asked "What country you from?"
"What language you speak?"
and my eyes cloud over
like concrete. So I say
"What country you from?
What language you speak?"
since everyone in New York speaks with an
accent.

Here, in the islands
I am invisible.
Till I speak.
Then "Eh, brah,
you one katonk, yuh?"
"Yeah, brah. Married one local girl
who wen grad from
Parrin'ton High Schoo.
That kind."
Smiling, he looks at me
with dolphins in his eyes.

Across the flight line of the Maui airport
I walk from the plane

reading *Lonesome Dove*.
Eyes following mine.
They appear at the baggage carousel
to my left. Knowledgeable eyes
in a middle-aged,
mainland face, perhaps from Texas.
He smiles over our secret
nods in approval at my
perseverance.
The local boy learning to read.

I sit in the lobby of the old
Kaiser Hospital
my newborn baby warm in my arms
next to two old ladies—very old
who coo "Oh, how adorable!"
"An angel from heaven!" "Look at those cheeks!
They're like sunshine!" "You must be
the happiest parent!"
when I stand to introduce my wife
newly come from signing documents. "And
here's the mother," I say.
Hair flashing, they look at each other
aghast—
when one says
"But we thought you were the mother."

DRIVING HOME

I am driving down an empty road, toward home; my son
David, three hours ago, took flight from Honolulu to Haneda
on Hawaiian Air, having had, I think, fulfilled his cravings
for local fare, us, and friends, a week was enough fuel for a year
and a subsequent visit and celebration, meal after meal, night
after night. It should be my turn to visit him in Saitama, but I'm
afraid of being bored in his new apartment, distant from
everywhere. Here, I have what I want and need. I mean, I can
drive to Koko Head Theaters, see *Ghost in the Shell*. Feel, for a
moment, fear.

ALICIA UPANO

COACH, 1937
at the First Annual Duke Kahanamoku Outdoor Swimming Meet

Listen to me, kid. Don't let those Frisco boys get in your head.

I saw you looking at them when we first arrived. They were fresh from first class on the mainland steamer and made us feel like the ragtag group from Maui. You looked at their bodies, their swim trunks, and their goggles, and I imagine you thought, That's what winners look like. The tall brunette's a long-distance champ out of Stanford and the stocky blond's a sprinter with the silver from the Berlin games. They cleaned up with medals the first night and spent the last two days tanning and sauntering around the natatorium as if that trophy's already theirs. Just the sight of them punctured a hole in your confidence. "What do you think, Coach?" you asked, but it was not a question. What have I told you, over and over again? In the water, we're all the same.

Who thought, when I first saw you splashing in a sugar ditch, that we'd be here at the best pool in the Pacific? One hundred meters long, forty meters wide. The tank filled with Waikīkī's seawater. I see you fidgeting on the block. So what if you're a boy in a men's event, two heads shorter and a hundred pounds lighter? So what if you don't have goggles and your woolen water-logged trunks were donated by those nice church ladies on Maui? I'm telling you, you belong.

It's my job to look at those Frisco boys. Focus, kid. Feel your body, watch the water, and wait for the gun. I'm watching that trigger. Right now and for 400 meters, the only thing in the whole world is your lane and your body. There's the shot, go!

Those Frisco boys reach ahead of you with their larger bodies, their perfect technique. No matter. Every time you breathe, hear your teammates. Hear those local kids sitting high in the hau trees for a free look at the meet. Even the Oʻahu kids who don't know your name want you to win. "Go, Maui," they say. "Maui, Maui, Maui."

Years ago, I found you kids in that filthy irrigation ditch after school. Despite the barbed wire, the lunas who would whip you if they found you, or the occasional dead animal floating down the waterway, you couldn't resist the cool of the water and I don't blame you. In the relentless heat of thousands of acres of cane, there's no other relief. The beach is a day's walk and the pool on the plantation is for the haoles. You're workers' kids, and I'm your teacher. It was the happiest I'd ever seen you all, who usually roll your eyes at my science lessons and my admonishments that you speak straight English in class so you can go somewhere, far away from the plantation. I don't care where you go or if you go, what I care about is that you've got a choice.

You got as far as this moment, turning at 100 meters. You're a body's length behind the blond sprinter and the distance champ's way ahead of you both.

Remember, remember: *Steady, steady, steady.* The haoles say I work you kids too hard, but if your parents can work hard in the fields, then I know you kids can work hard in the water. We moved to the paved part of the ditch—no more scrambling up slippery banks—and I turned the valve to cut off the current. People got opinions, so many opinions. They said the same thing about me that they say about you kids now: We're dreamers, deep down we're soft and lazy. Who was I, a schoolteacher who can't swim, to teach you about swimming? But then who are you, any of you sugar kids, to think you can be Olympic-level swimmers?

Think about it. Who are you? Are you just that boy whose father drinks what he earns cutting cane, that what he doesn't drink, he loses at the Filipino billiard hall? Are you just that kid burying the pet pig your mother beat to death? I said nothing when you came to practice with bruises the shape of a woman's fist, but I ask you, as you come up on 200 meters, is that who you are?

Steady, steady, steady. Yeah, the Stanford champ's turning and there goes the Olympian too.

Last Sunday, I sat in church with Mary and the children. She says I spend too much time at the ditch, running around the island for donations, and I'm full of Olympic dreams, and so Sunday mornings are for my own 'ohana. As I sat there, head bent in the Lord's Prayer, I thought of you, swimming a mile, stroking as if that ditch will lead you out to the ocean, as if your body is a plane that can fly you anywhere. Amen.

This is your moment, kid. Pull that water to you like it's your life.

Mary once asked me why I love swimming so much, and I couldn't say.

All I know is that when I saw that picture in the paper of those Japanese boys with the gold in Berlin, I thought of you, Keo, and Halo, Pachi, Shangy, and the rest. At practice, I held the photo up to your faces. I wanted it to be a mirror of greatness. Before the Filipinos came, they hated us. "Japanese and Dogs Forbidden," the signs read. My Pops couldn't get a haircut 'cause they wouldn't touch us. The haoles didn't respect us, and the other workers said we were taking their jobs for less. They called us scabs, but really we were hungry and far from home. Who else would leave Japan for shitty work on a Hawaiian plantation where everybody hates you? Maybe those times have passed on, but I think of you kids in the water, not just happy, but free. Free from your family's journeys to the plantation and not yet part of the bosses' plans for you, their new young, workforce.

Think about how far you've come. You started with speed-floating and, at the makeshift Friday races after school, you kids made such a ruckus that the camps complained you were louder than the No. 8 sugar train. Remember how I turned the valve and the current rushed toward you, and still, you swam upstream? That's life, kid. We're always pressing against the current.

You may have lost those first races to the sugar bosses' kids who could do push-off turns 'cause they practiced in a real pool with a wall to push off of. But in that second year, as the haoles drained and cleaned the pool you kids competed in, we came home with their medals. That's when I saw that you had found the fight inside of you.

Now I see it. The blond Olympian falters. It's just a sloppy quarter stroke, but he's a sprinter after all. At 200 meters, you're just warming up. Go, go, go! Slide past him. There's his knees. There's his elbow. You're on him, kid. On this Sunday in Waikīkī, you're taking on these goddamn Goliaths.

You've still got the Stanford champ ahead of you. I see your tired arms above the water, I hear you gasping for air, but you're starting to remember who you are. He's turning at 300 meters, and there you are, right behind him.

You want to know what I think? When we're from where we're from and you swim like you swim, that trophy's yours. You've been swimming upstream all your life, waiting for the chance. There it is: the wall. Four-hundred meters, almost close enough to touch. Let's finish this. Reach out, kid. Reach out and grab it. *Show them*. Show them who we are. Show them who *you* are. Reach that arm above your head and take what's always been yours.

AMY UYEMATSU

FROM A BOOK OF FOLD-OUT BOATS

—for grandson Tyler

At three, he discovers ocean liners, only wants
to study the detailed two-page illustration
of the massive ship. Speedboats, kayaks,
barges, and pirate ships will be put on hold
as he points out and names the decks labeled
A through G, thrilled that an entire lower level
can store so many cars and even trucks.
He asks me to read the words, "boiler room,"
locates a library, kitchen, swimming pools.

When we get home, he wants to build his own
ocean liner in the upstairs den, where
a couch, bed, chair, and blankets
will house different decks.
Passengers will be a stuffed bear,
Ugga the monkey, a souvenir Mickey Mouse.
We two will be the captain and crew, taking turns
steering the ship and cooking meals
with his brightly colored plastic food.

Our route matches all the places
he knows—from hometown San Francisco
to his other grandma in Saratoga
and me in Los Angeles.
He's been to Hawai'i and London,
two more ship destinations,
and we travel to Taiwan and Japan,

the two countries he's been told
he comes from.

He's not quite sure what a ship's captain is,
but there's no question he directs
the whole operation. *Time to take a shower—*
we rush to the light blue quilt
where there are bathrooms and beds.
The passengers want to read—so we carry
monkey, mouse, and bear to a sofa cushion
library. *Now let's build an airplane—*
no time to lose.

WHEN THE WORLD AGREES ON NOTHING

Even the Chinese elms
that line my walk at dusk become
a weary long-armed tribe
whose ragged branches crowd the twilight sky,
their limbs in disarray.

Inside this corridor
there's an oddly comforting
sense of chaos, the noise
of a car rushing by
can't penetrate the stillness.

Before the last light dissolves,
dozens of invisible birds burst out
like dark, silent buds
from trunks and upper branches
to flee into a starless night.

I recall a little girl playing
with her sister, their arms outstretched,
as I witness this outbreak of voiceless birds
in a sky so brittle that all the trees
contort in greeting.

AMY UYEMATSU

SISTER STONE

i

These are the stones that sing to me
　　　not the granite boulders
　　　　　　transported from canyons
　　　or rocks the size for hurling
　　　　　　like those thrown at Grandpa
　　　　　　　　　when he came to America

The stones I choose are washed in by the tides
　　　their ocean sleek skins
　　　　　　polished by current and time
　　　the sheen of wet black
　　　　　　on these pebbles I save
　　　　　　　　　like treasure

ii

A wise man says, "The stones cry out,"
　　　and even the most ordinary rock
　　　　　　carries a history
　　　rapturous as the stars
　　　　　　bursting sky and mountain
　　　　　　　　　with longing

iii

My early ancestors built gardens of gravel
　　　the dry landscape a place
　　　　　　for meditation

our monks tending to
seas of white stones
with rakes

At Manzanar issei and nisei inmates
searched the Sierra bajadas
for bedrock
to create barrack gardens
camp ponds and parks
for solace

And I have long called myself
a stone lover
somehow knowing
my unfinished story is also carried
in the wordless stones
that fill my path

FROM

i.

They say that cats and very small children know where we're from. In time, the children forget; cats never do.

This story, which is not about cats, was told to me by my friend Bernard. You don't need stories, he says, if you don't forget.

It is set in Zim where he grew up. Perhaps a holiday or coming home; both his parents have long since passed. But everyone else is gathered— grandmother, sisters, uncles, aunts, the children of grandmother's children. Small angers have been put away, stomachs filled with food.

Someone brings out a drum, the singing starts. Soon everyone's dancing—even the smallest boy, who's just turned three. His elders laugh—their large selves perfected in a tiny mirror.

But as the small form sways and stamps, gyrating hips and flashing limbs, the laughter hushes. This is no mirror, but an open window to something very old from far away.

Child, his grandmother asks when the dancing stops, where did you learn to dance like that? He shrugs, Before this, where I came from.

ii.

The 13th Dalai Lama has passed. Someone dreams of a child. The landmarks of the dream are noted, and a search party is dispatched.

When the child is located, he is shown a collection of objects, among which are possessions belonging to his former self.

Without hesitation the child selects a walking stick, a pair of spectacles, a circle of prayer beads. "Mine!" he calls out at each object, in delight.

And so it's confirmed that the dream is true, and word sent forth that the 14th incarnation has been found.

Now, when he is reminded of this story and asked what it is like to carry the memories of one life into the next, His Holiness shrugs, then smiles. "I have forgotten," he says.

Bamboo Shoots

Selections from our online writing community

DOREEN B. BEYER

A SPOT OF SERENDIPITY

She loves the look of her newly purchased composition book, blank lines inviting the scratch of her just-sharpened number two pencil. "See Spot Run," she writes in careful print, mindful of the spacing between words. "Run Spot. . . ." Frowning at the less-than-perfect fullness of the "o" in "Spot," she scrubs vigorously with her eraser to make "Spot" disappear. The effort wins her a small smudged puka through the paper. Her face crumples and she fights back tears. An idea blossoms, composing her face. With regained confidence, she grasps hard at the pencil and begins anew: "Run (puka) run!"

A BEGGAR'S CHRISTMAS, 1947

East Bremerton was called Manette back then, and it had the same relationship to the Navy town of Bremerton as Brooklyn has to Manhattan: Inferior. Also, a tall bridge over tidal water connected them.

Manette featured several World War II-era barracks-style housing projects, still occupied by holdover military families. Those were the good neighborhoods, well-maintained by the government, as the homes of heroes should be. We lived in one of the civilian districts, among the quonset huts and tar paper boxes that sheltered shipyard scrabblers, evangelists, hookers, Okies, Irish, and Swedes.

For all that, it did not feel to us like a dangerous neighborhood or a dangerous town. First graders walked to school accompanied only by other young scholars a full mile through sometimes inclement weather and always varied streets and alleys. Armed with good advice—walk fast; don't talk to strangers—there were never problems. Strangers apparently got the message and showed no interest in us.

Each Saturday Leonard Seifers and I would meet at the Perry Avenue bus stop, then ride, all by ourselves, across the Manette Bridge to downtown Bremerton for the Saturday Matinee at the Tower Theater. After feasting on Jujubes, Tootsie Rolls, and Big Screen Serial Adventure with a lot of other kids our age, we'd catch the Perry Ave. bus and head home, hours later, still all by ourselves.

So there was really no sense of foolhardiness or irresponsibility on either my or my parents' parts when I as a second-grader was allowed to take the bus to Bremerton to do my Christmas shopping. It would be an adventure, to be sure. I'd be all by myself this time, not with a buddy.

"Are you sure you can do it?" my mother asks, her head bent forward so she can look squarely into my eyes. "You won't get lost or lose your money? Will you?"

"Of course not."

"Don't be afraid to ask a policeman for directions."

"I won't."

"Don't be afraid to run away if somebody talks to you mean or looks wrong at you," adds my father, standing straight up behind Mom. "Find a cop if you need help."

Although I hadn't any idea what looking "wrong" meant, I assumed that if it happened I'd know it. "I will," I reply.

I don't know how much money I had or how I carried it. Did I have a coin purse? I'm sure I didn't have a wallet. Maybe I had my money tucked away in a tobacco-fragrant Bull Durham sack?

Crossing the bridge all by myself in the front seat of the bus where I looked straight down at the pavement through the stairwell windows, riding poised within inches of falling-off-straight-into-the-water far below, I imagined how I would get out of the upside-down bus from underwater. And then how I would save my fellow passengers, modestly flaunting my remarkable, Saturday-serial-honed courage and resourcefulness to reporters afterward. Wasn't it cold and wet? Wasn't the current dangerously strong? How had I managed to save that frail old man, that helpless woman with her baby? Honestly, I'd protest, I'd just done what any other boy on his way to buy Christmas presents for his family would do. And if you'll excuse me, I've still got some shopping.

Soon I was off the bus in the middle of holiday-festooned Bremerton, the streets decorated with evergreens and colored lights, Salvation Army bell ringers on every corner, people dressed up for the holidays moving quickly from store to store, diesel and gasoline fumes clouding the air, overlapping Christmas carols from unseen sources: "round yon virgin mother still we see thee lie right down Santa Claus Lane." Everything and everybody was suddenly much bigger than it had ever been before. Was it already starting to get dark? Did I remember where to catch the bus home? If I needed a policeman, where would I look? Was it cold enough to snow?

Probably not coincidentally, Bremerton's main drag runs south toward the shipyard's main gate. Stopping at an intersection, I plotted my mission quickly. Two-thirds of what I wanted was waiting for me at the Bremerton Sport Shop and at Woolworth's, directly across the street.

The Salvation Army bell ringer was especially lively there, ringing and gesticulating and nodding from the waist to one and all celebrants of the nativity to the strains of "Hark! the Herald Angels Sing" and the sounds of shifting gears as traffic lights mandated.

First the Sport Shop, where I'd get my dad the trophy I'd first spotted through the window weeks ago. I just hoped it would still be there or that they had more than one. It was pleasantly warm inside and smelled vaguely of tanned leather. That would be from the Wilson and Spalding baseball gloves on display against one wall and the footballs and basketballs in bins.

On the wall behind the cash register hung a cluster of small wooden shields on which were mounted artistic renderings of golf clubs, baseball bats, and bowling balls in miniature. None of those would appeal to my dad, but among them was something that stood out from the rest: a rainbow trout suspended forever at the curved apogee of its graceful leap. My dad was no more a fisherman than a golfer or bowler, but he liked animals, and who could resist so achingly beautiful an object as a perpetually leaping fish?

"I'll need six cents more for the governor," the man at the cash register said. "He gets mad when he doesn't get his cut."

I understood about state sales tax and even had a few tokens in my pocket. They were made of aluminum and had a hole in the middle so you could string them. I handed the man three tokens and a nickel. "The governor thanks you," he said, rapping his furry knuckles on the counter. I tried to catch some sign of sadness or regret at having to give up so beautiful a possession as the leaping trout, but found none.

"It's for my dad," I said. "For Christmas."

"I'm sure he'll like it," he said, smiling too broadly it seemed to me.

O'Neal's Shoe Repair was right next door, and you didn't have to go inside to catch the strong cowhide smell that hung about the entrance. They displayed a black, high-topped leather shoe, an enormous item made for the world's tallest man, shown in a black-and-white photograph wearing a pair of shoes exactly like it. Even my six-foot-three Uncle Ben did not wear shoes anywhere near that big. The world's tallest man was over eight feet tall. What did it feel like to be that tall? What could you do to get that tall? Just eat a lot, I guessed.

My next stop was Woolworth's, and I passed through the entrance without even giving the bell ringer a tax token. Maybe on my way out, if I had enough to spare. Woolworth's had a popcorn machine that gave the store a pleasant smell and an over-warm ambience that I liked.

They'd moved things around since the last time I was there, no doubt making room for Christmas ornamentation, and at first I couldn't find what I was looking for: the pre-Barbie fashion dolls, costumed to appeal to little girls like my sister. She already had three or four displayed on her side of our shared bedroom, still in their white boxes with cellophane windows like the objects of art they assuredly were. For reasons I couldn't fathom, my sister still didn't have a platinum-haired doll, but now she'd have one, thanks to me.

"It's for my little sister," I told the lady cashier.

"I didn't think it was for you," she laughed.

"Did I give you enough for the governor?" I asked.

"Three cents to the dollar," she said. "Just the right amount."

It felt so good to make such progress that I dropped a nickel into the bell ringer's red kettle on the way out, an impulse I immediately regretted. I could be running short and still had no idea what to get my mom. I should have looked around Woolworth's, but I didn't want to go back. Besides, it was definitely getting darker now, and colder. People's breath was plainly visible now and cars spewed rich clouds of exhaust. I'd go to Kress's and see what they offered.

Kress's felt like Woolworth's low-rent cousin, stripped down to the open-bin essentials. Maybe Mom would like a spatula or a pair of salad tongs? Not very Christmassy. Then how about a headscarf or perfume? But what fragrance, what color? Anyway, Kress's didn't look like a very likely place. Woolworth's would have been better.

Then how about Sears? They might have such items, and it was on my way to the bus stop. Overhead, the evergreen garlands strung on poles and across streets were illuminated by brightly colored lights, and the music seemed ever louder. City sidewalks, dressed in holiday style.

They'd gone all-out on the main entrance to Sears, a big manger scene with all the trimmings just inside the glass double doors, complete with its own sound system, set up to compete with the holiday cacophony outside: Silent night, holy night.

Beautifully inspirational though it was, I realized I didn't have time to stop and appreciate it. Where could I find ladies' scarves and perfume? Or candy? Was candy a good Christmas gift? Perfume would be better. Or a scarf.

Just off to the side of the manger scene were shelves of smaller mangers and Marys and Wise Men and babies Jesus and lambs of God and so forth so you could build your own manger scene. And on one small shelf, off to the side and all by its lonesome, the most gorgeous piece of sculpture I had ever laid eyes on. Tall and graceful and green, it had to be the most stupendous Christmas decoration ever conceived. A tree, you might guess. But no.

A camel. But not just any ordinary camel. It was a big, tall, broad, chalk replica ship of the desert, painted a kind of bright avocado green and shown best in profile. And I loved it and wanted to buy it and give it my mom for Christmas. But I didn't have enough money.

So I stopped to ponder a bit about the Christmas season and people giving to bell ringers and just feeling kind and generous. And, to make a long ponder short, why not?

Standing just outside the main entrance to Sears, but away from any bell ringer, I hunched up my shoulders and held out my hand. Lo and behold, some people put money in it. Others asked what I needed money for, and when I told them I needed bus money to get home to Manette, they put money in it too, money that I quickly transferred to my now-bulging front pocket.

Before long I had enough money to buy the camel, so I did. But I discovered that after giving the governor his cut, I didn't have enough left over for the bus, which sent me back to the sidewalk with my hand out.

A well-dressed guy and his beautiful wife walked up to me. I remembered them well. And they remembered me. "Hey, I thought you needed bus money?" the man said.

"I did. I still do."

"I gave you a quarter. You said that was all you needed."

"I counted wrong."

"How much do you need? This time?"

"A dime is all. Sir."

"Here's another quarter. Don't count wrong this time." His beautiful wife smiled but looked vaguely worried.

"Thank you, sir. I won't. Sir."

And I didn't. I found my way to the Perry Avenue bus stop and finished my day by walking home in the dark to my parents, who said they were beginning to worry.

At Christmas everybody liked their gifts—especially my mom. She loved the camel as much as I did, and maybe more. She adored it, displayed it with great pride all the rest of that Christmas season. When visitors called she'd say,

"Well you know he did his Christmas shopping all by himself. Took the bus to Bremerton and came back with presents for everybody."

"All by himself. My my."

And that was the last I saw of the camel. Apparently it got misplaced somehow when we moved out to Bear Creek. Oh well. My sister and I had our own bedrooms there, and my dad generously let me hang the leaping trout on my very own wall, where I admired it for many years.

The first portion of this story was posted in the Bamboo Shoots section at www.bambooridge.com on December 24, 2014, and was published in Bamboo Ridge *Issue #108. The conclusion appeared online in Bamboo Shoots on December 10, 2016. The story appears here in its entirety.*

CROOKED PINKY

This wacked-out little finger?

It was third grade,
he was Melvin,
she was Irene,
and I was in the way.

To Melvin I was.
Nobody asked Irene.

Irene had dark eyes,
raven hair,
a quiet smile.

Melvin wanted to see me at recess
to bend my fingers backward.

I didn't know that's what he wanted
until he grabbed my hand.

"Hey, that hurt!" I yelled,
balling my hand into a fist
and slugging Melvin's bony chest,
hard.

"I'm glad Melvin's crying," Irene whispered,
running cold water over this very finger,
which stayed cheerfully purple and swollen
for over a month.

WHERE FOR WATCH WAIPAHU NEW YEAR'S EVE, 2010

"Why're we stopping?"

"This the best place."

Skeptical, Esme opened the door, careful of the guardrail. There, she stood in the narrow space between.

They had parked just before the exit curved down, merging with Farrington Hwy. The high school was visible still, but the neighborhoods. . . .

There were no houses or streetlight poles, only shingled rafts and creosote pilings surfacing from a smoldering sea. Coloring the smoky depths, streetlamps glowed; sparklers and morning glories flared. Far away, the firecrackers' staccato ebbed and flowed. Chromatic streaks, there and there, breached the surface to ascend and, at apex, bloom violent.

"It is. . . ."

NORMIE SALVADOR

THE LION WEARS SNEAKERS

—for C, B, and their little C.

Caleb clutches his mother's leg.
With the clash, crash, and boom of brass
gong, cymbals, and drum, the white lion dances
closer. Its head whips out at the circling
crowd. His mother's outstretched hand
holding a folded dollar bill
disappears into the lion's gaping
maw. Eyes shut, Caleb screams
into his mother's thigh. A hand settles
on his head, coaxing and comforting.
Blinking through tears, Caleb raises
his head, reaches for his mother's fingers.
As the lion dances away, its rising
flank exposes black pant legs and sneakers.
The dancers beneath are a revelation
to Caleb, washing away his fear.

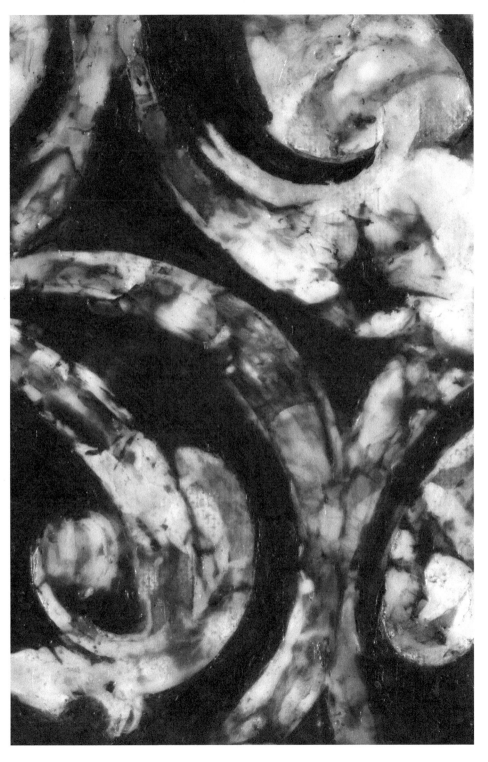

Winged Energy of Delight (detail), by Noe Tanigawa, encaustic with Kahakuloa beeswax, 12 x 15.

Contributors

Amanda L. Allison: In my 31 years of living in Hawai'i, I have had the pleasure of learning about the people and the land from many wise kūpuna. Their lessons have been a continuation of those taught to me by my own 'ohana in my hometown of San Diego—lessons of the ocean, the land, and what it means to be family. From all of this wisdom, my geographer's soul was born and nurtured. I am an instructor at Kapi'olani Community College and spend my free time walking my dog and writing. "Diving Lessons" is my first non-academic print publication.

Nalani Mamoali'ialapa'iha'o Ano's poem "Hawaiian Blood" was published in 1997 in the University of Hawai'i Women's Center's *La'i La'i*. She was the 2005 recipient of the James A. Vaughan Award for Poetry for "Wana" and "Night Dive"—published in the *Hawai'i Pacific Review*—and has been internationally published with the Society of Women Writers and Journalists (UK) in *The Woman Writer*. She is currently writing, editing, and illustrating her first collection of poetry entitled *Iwi in the Closet*.

Nicholas Becher is an MFA candidate at Florida Atlantic University. Previous work has been published in *Noise Medium*, *A Sharp Piece of Awesome*, and *Hawai'i Pacific Review*.

Doreen E. Beyer writes to escape the jackals, the high horse, Pooh bears, and other impressionistic characters of her workplace. She thanks Bamboo Ridge for the light it casts and for the much needed reality check to Paradise Found.

Sally-Jo Keala-o-Ānuenue Bowman first learned literary rejection at age 9, in a form letter from *Jack and Jill* magazine. She has since had more rejections and many acceptances, some of the work winning awards in Hawaiʻi and the Pacific Northwest. She is a 1958 graduate of Kamehameha Schools. A holder of BA and MS degrees in journalism, she taught writing at the University of Oregon for 20 years. Currently she writes and records songs in both English and Hawaiian. She grew up in Kailua, Oʻahu, and now lives in Springfield, Oregon, with her husband, David Walp.

Amalia B. Bueno's poetry and stories have been published in various local, national, and international journals such as *Hawaiʻi Pacific Review*, *Bamboo Ridge*, *Hawaiʻi Review*, *Tayo Na*, and *Cha*, among others; and in books published by Kore Press, Philippine American Literary House, and Moria Poetry. She is pursuing a PhD in English and teaches composition and creative writing at the University of Hawaiʻi at Mānoa. Her research interests include Pilipinx poetry, creative writing pedagogy, and Asian American literature.

Donald Carreira Ching was born and raised in Kahaluʻu and graduated with his MA in Creative Writing from UH-Mānoa. His short stories and poetry have appeared in local, national, and international publications. His début novel, *Between Sky and Sea: A Family's Struggle*, was published in December 2015 by Bamboo Ridge Press. He is currently working on his second novel, *Who You Know*, and a collection of short stories.

Jacey Choy was born and raised in Honolulu, Hawaiʻi. She left the islands for the Midwest when she married and has now returned as a some-of-the-time resident. Jacey's writing reflects her life and the world around her, although so much of her writing seems to find its way back to Hawaiʻi, either tangentially or directly. She tries to write about things that really matter to her and speak from her heart because she feels that is when her writing is strongest. More than anything, Jacey cares fiercely about her family—the family she has and the family she carries with her.

BC Chun-Ming lives in Wahiawā, was fortunate enough to study poetry with Dorianne Laux, and is in the process working on several writing projects when not playing music with SBIV.

E. Shan Correa is a former university professor who has written fulltime since 1980 for both children and adults. Her middle-grade novel, *Gaff*, has won national honors, as has her story, "O," published here by Bamboo Ridge. Among other publications, her poetry and prose have appeared in *Writer's Digest*, *ByLine*, *HONOLULU*, *RSVP*, *Ranger Rick*, *Aloha*, *Jack and Jill*, *Spider*, *Cricket*, and *The Pen Woman* magazines; in the literary journals *Time of Singing*, *American Poets & Poetry*, *Japanophile*, *Rain Bird*; and in anthologies *Caring Stories*, *Christmas Talk Story*, *Toasts*, *A Loving Voice*, *The Book Group Book*, *Wedding Blessings*, and *Sunset Inn*.

Brian Cronwall is a retired English faculty member from Kaua'i Community College in Hawai'i. His poems have been published in numerous journals and anthologies in Hawai'i, Guam, the continental United States, Australia, Japan, France, and the United Kingdom, including recent publications in *Bamboo Ridge*, *Chiron Review*, *Hawai'i Pacific Review*, E*kphrasis*, *Pinyon*, C*olere*, *The Santa Fe Literary Review*, and others.

Marie Hara . . . still writing, still feeling lucky about the now that I live in. For you the reader, I wish everything you might like to read from local writers in Hawai'i. Can forty years have passed so quickly? We are still here.

Jim Harstad: A circa 1965 Pacific Northwest transplant, Jim Harstad is proud to be included in this important issue of Hawai'i's most avant publication. T'anks, eh, Bamboo Ridge!

Jennifer Hasegawa is a poet and performance artist. She was born and raised in Hilo, Hawai'i and lives in San Francisco. Her poetry manuscript, *La Chica's Field Guide to Banzai Living*, received the San Francisco Foundation's Joseph Henry Jackson Literary Award in 2014. She has curated the Altered Barbie Spoken Word series and her work has appeared in *Tule Review*, the *San Francisco Bay Guardian*, and *Transfer*. She currently ponders paranormal phenomena, including alien encounters, Marian apparitions, and Sinéad O'Connor.

Jeffrey J. Higa: My father was the kind of ballplayer that teams built their defense around. As his firstborn, I was destined for the diamond. Any talent I inherited, though, was given to me slant. I could throw but without grace. I could hit the ball but irregularly. My fielding was adequate but my feet were slow. I stopped after being unable to see a pitched ball. Disappointment settles, father and son move on. And yet, somehow, the game has more to teach him, and so the son sometimes returns to mine the legacy that had once been offered to him. Jeffrey Higa has been published in *Zyzzyva*, *Sonora Review*, and *Bamboo Ridge*. He can be reached at jeff@jeffhiga.com.

Ann Inoshita was born and raised on Oʻahu. She is author of a poetry book *Mānoa Stream* (Kahuaomānoa Press), and she co-authored *No Choice but to Follow* and *What We Must Remember* with three other poets (Bamboo Ridge Press). Her short play, *Wea I Stay: A Play in Hawaiʻi*, was included in *The Statehood Project* performed by Kumu Kahua Theatre and published by Fat Ulu Productions. Her creative works have been anthologized widely in local and international journals. She teaches at Leeward Community College and is host of *The Reading Room*, a series of author interviews and readings: http://leewardccreadingroom.weebly.com/

Sabrina Ito lives in Honolulu with her husband, Victor, and her son, Xander. An International Baccalaureate (IB) teacher in Kailua, Sabrina also enjoys writing, cooking, spending time with family, and is at her happiest in or near the ocean. Sabrina's poems have appeared in *Clarion Magazine*, *Slipstream Press*, *Coachella Review*, and *The Cossack Review*, among others. A Pushcart-nominated writer, Sabrina's first chapbook, *Witches of Lila Spring*, will be published in 2018 through *Plan B Press*.

Dina Wood Kageler lives in the upland rainforest on the island of Hawaiʻi, in the village of Volcano. She works as a visual and performing artist and arts educator, and is an aficionado of old-style slack key guitar. She has been a *haumana* of Cyril Pahinui and is honored to have had many opportunities to learn from him in the old way, by watching, listening, and imitating. She is a collector of stories and images of life on the Big Island. Some of these stories she weaves into poems and songs celebrating the uniqueness of place.

traci kato-kiriyama is an award-winning artist, community organizer, and cultural producer based in Los Angeles. She has served as Teaching Artist-in-Residence for Grand Park, Artist-in-Residence for the AARC at Pomona College, and guest lecturer for the Claremont Colleges, with a focus on art and community-self care in radical wellness and healing processes. She is an actor and principal writer for PULLproject Ensemble, and has received two consecutive awards from the Network of Ensemble Theaters. Her writing and commentary have been featured by numerous print and online publications including Elle.com, *The Hollywood Reporter*, *Entropy*, and *The Rafu Shimpo*; and in publications from Regent Press, Heyday Books, Tia Chucha Press, and Chapparal Canyon Press. Her forthcoming book will be released by Writ Large Press.

Zeke Kearns grew up in Mānoa, and graduated from ʻIolani School in 2013. He currently lives in Vancouver, British Columbia, and spends most of his time missing his family (and, secondarily, Zippy's chili).

Scott Kikkawa grew up in Hawaiʻi Kai, where the only culture was Yick Lung commercials and Kikaida on the Zenith in the family room. He writes detective noir stories set in a Honolulu where cops still wore coats, ties, and hats and Kakaʻako was a Japanese ghetto.

Milton Kimura was born and raised on Oʻahu. After retiring from the Hawaiʻi DOE, he moved to Pittsburgh in 2012, where he searches among penguins and pirates for the perfectly played Mahler's *Symphony of a Thousand*, the perfectly danced *Giselle*, and the perfectly sung *Aida*.

Juliet S. Kono: Happy Anniversary Bamboo Ridge Press. Thank you for the years!

Brenda Kwon co-edited *YOBO: Korean American Writing from Hawaiʻi* and is the author of *Beyond Keʻeaumoku: Koreans, Nationalism, and Local Culture* and *The Sum of Breathing*, which earned Honorable Mention for Excellence in Literature in the Hawaiʻi Book Publishers Association's Ka Palapala Poʻokela Awards. In 2015, she won the Cades Award for Literature. She teaches Language Arts at Honolulu Community College and yoga at Open Space Yoga. She hopes to retire sometime soon and open an animal sanctuary.

Karen An-hwei Lee is the author of *Phyla of Joy* (Tupelo 2012), Ardor (Tupelo 2008) and *In Medias Res* (Sarabande 2004). She authored a novel, *Sonata in K* (Ellipsis 2017). Her book of literary criticism, *Anglophone Literatures in the Asian Diaspora: Literary Transnationalism and Translingual Migrations* (Cambria 2013), was selected for the Cambria Sinophone World Series. The recipient of a National Endowment for the Arts Grant, Lee lives in San Diego and serves in the university administration at Point Loma Nazarene University.

Jeffrey Thomas Leong is a poet and writer raised in the San Francisco Bay Area. He earned his MFA degree at the Vermont College of Fine Arts, where he began to translate the poems that are found in his book, *Wild Geese Sorrow: The Chinese Wall Inscriptions at Angel Island*. His writing has appeared in *Bamboo Ridge*, *Crab Orchard*, *Hyphen*, *Spillway*, and other publications. For over twenty years he worked as a public health administrator and attorney for the City of San Francisco. He lives with his wife and daughter the East Bay. For more info, please visit him at www.jeffreythomasleong.com.

Darrell H. Y. Lum: 40 years! Who knew? It is with respect and gratitude to the editors for including my work in this issue. And humbling to participate in the process of submitting and anxiously waiting for a decision. What is particularly satisfying is to see fresh voices and new leadership carrying the BR mission forward, one issue at a time. Congratulations to all!

Wing Tek Lum is a Honolulu businessman and poet. Bamboo Ridge Press has published his two collections of poetry, *Expounding the Doubtful Points* (1987) and *The Nanjing Massacre: Poems* (2012).

Jennifer Santos Madriaga resides in Durham, North Carolina, and is a native of Honolulu, Hawai'i. Her fiction and poetry have appeared or is forthcoming in publications such as *North American Review*, *Bamboo Ridge*, *Hawai'i Review*, *The Bellevue Literary Review*, *Crab Creek Review*, and others. She has completed several residencies at the Vermont Studio Center, Byrdcliffe Arts Colony, and the Virginia Center for Creative Arts, including the international location at the Moulin á Nef studios in Auvillar, France. She is a recipient of the Durham Arts Council/NC Arts Council Ella Fountain Pratt Emerging Artists Grant in Literature.

Prana Joy Mandoe's husband says she is the best wife. She likes to work hard on the computer, in the books, and teaching school. She writes day and night, playing with words, finding each poem's heart. She loves to sit by the ocean weaving lauhala and watching her husband carve pahu while their kids surf and turn cartwheels. She most recently published in *Buddhist Poetry Review*, *Hawai'i Pacific Review*, and *SlamChop! Journal*.

Tamara Leiokanoe Moan is a writer and artist who lives in Kailua, O'ahu. Her nonfiction has appeared in local and national-circulation magazines. The last few years her writing has focused on memoir and poetry. She teaches art at the Honolulu Museum of Art School and exhibits her own work regularly throughout Hawai'i.

Ryan Oishi teaches at Kamehameha Schools and enjoys writing short stories that help to deepen his personal definition of love. He is proud and immensely grateful to be published in *Bamboo Ridge*, an important source of inspiration for him growing up.

Derek N. Otsuji teaches English at Honolulu Community College. His work has appeared, or is forthcoming, in *Poet Lore*, *Sycamore Review*, and *Threepenny Review*. He is near completing his first book of poems, tentatively called *The Rabbit in the Moon*.

Lauren (Kalani) Nicolle Padilla is a student of English and Visual Narratives at Whitworth University and a recent alumna of the Los Angeles Film Studies Center. "Waimaka" is coincidentally her first short story and the first of her works to be featured in a non-student publication; it is her voyages into the liminal place—between her homes in Mililani and Spokane—that form the beating heart of these first vocational pursuits.

Christy Passion is a critical care nurse and poet, author of *Still Out of Place* and co-author of two collections of linked poetry, *No Choice but to Follow* and *What We Must Remember*. Her work has appeared in *Crab Creek Review*, *Haight Ashbury Literary Journal*, *Blue Collar Review*, and *Mauri Ola*. She has received the James A. Vaughan Award for Poetry, the *Atlanta Review* International Merit Award, the Academy of American Poetry Award, the Hawai'i Book Publishers Association's Ka Palapala Po'okela Honorable Mention for Excellence in Literature, and the

Cades Award for Literature.

Craig Santos Perez is a native Chamorro from the Micronesian island of Guam. He is the co-editor of three anthologies of Pacific literature, and the author of four collections of poetry. He is an associate professor in the English department at the University of Hawaiʻi at Mānoa.

Normie Salvador teaches composition and creative writing at Kapiʻolani Community College and freelance edits on the side. Since 1990, he has published short fiction, poetry, essays, and articles in literary magazines, journals, websites, and newspapers. He has a poetry chapbook, *Philter* (Tinfish Press). During summer and winter breaks, he paints Warhammer 40K miniatures, posting pictures of them to Instagram.

Eric Paul Shaffer's seventh book of poetry *Even Further West* was published by Unsolicited Press in 2018. Previous books include *A Million-Dollar Bill*; *Lahaina Noon*; *Portable Planet*; and *Living at the Monastery*, *Working in the Kitchen*. Over 450 poems have been published in national and international reviews. Shaffer received Hawaiʻi's 2002 Elliot Cades Award for Literature, a 2006 Ka Palapala Poʻokela Award, and the 2009 James A. Vaughan Award for Poetry. In 2015, he was a visiting poetry faculty member at the 23rd Annual Jackson Hole Writers Conference. Shaffer teaches composition, literature, and creative writing at Honolulu Community College.

Cathy Song is the author of five books of poetry, including *Picture Bride*, recently listed as one of the "50 Essential Hawaiʻi Books" by *HONOLULU Magazine*.

Susan M. Soong dedicates her work in this publication to the Chun Hoon clan, and thanks Lois-Ann Yamanaka and Mel Spencer of Naʻau for their encouragement and support. The stories are excerpts from a manuscript entitled "Princess Wo Fat." In 2008, she received the James A. Vaughan Award for Poetry and in 2012 won First Place for Fiction and Poetry in the Lorrin Tarr Gill Writing Competition. Her most recent writing is inspired by her mother-in-law's life in China. *Bamboo Ridge* included "The Blooms of Shanghai" in issue no.104.

Joseph Stanton's five poetry books are *Things Seen, Imaginary Museum: Poems on Art, A Field Guide to the Wildlife of Suburban Oʻahu, Cardinal Points,* and *What the Kite Thinks: A Linked Poem* (co-authored with Makoto Ooka, Wing Tek Lum, and Jean Toyama). More than four hundred of his poems have appeared in such journals as *Antioch Review, Bamboo Ridge, Cortland Review, Harvard Review, New Letters, New York Quarterly, Poetry,* and *Poetry East.* His other books include *Looking for Edward Gorey, The Important Books: Children's Picture Books as Art and Literature, Stan Musial: A Biography,* and *A Hawaiʻi Anthology.* He is a Professor of Art History and American Studies at the University of Hawaiʻi at Mānoa. He occasionally teaches poetry-writing workshops, such as the "Starting with Art" workshops he has recently taught at the Honolulu Museum of Art and Poets House (New York City).

Eric Stinton is a writer and a teacher from Kailua. He has written short stories and essays for various outlets including *Harvard Review Online, Honolulu Civil Beat, Summit Magazine,* and *Vice Sports.* You can find his work at ericstinton.com. He has been living in Seoul with his fiancée and dachshund since 2014.

Susan Lee St. John teaches at Windward Community College in Kāneʻohe, Oʻahu. Her work has appeared in anthologies published by Calyx Books, Mutual Publishing, and Bamboo Ridge Press. Her short plays have been produced by Honolulu Theater for Youth, and she has received the James A. Vaughan Award for Poetry. She resides in her hometown of Kailua with her husband, Robert. They are the parents of three grown children.

Delaina Thomas has returned to Honolulu where she is a caregiver for her father.

Ken Tokuno was raised in California, mostly in the Sacramento area. Learning how to write poetry late in life at the University of Washington, he has now published poetry in *Seattle Review, The Bellowing Ark, Hawaiʻi Review,* and other magazines in addition to previously in Bamboo Ridge. His collection of poems, Orchard was published in 2007. He now lives in Kāneʻohe, Hawaiʻi with his wife, artist Diane Nushida Tokuno.

Jean Yamasaki Toyama is professor emerita of French and former Associate Dean of the College of Languages, Linguistics and Literature at the University of Hawaiʻi at Mānoa. Her latest books include a volume of poetry, *Prepositions*, and one of short stories, *The Piano Tuner's Wife*. Her work is included in two collections of linked poetry, *No Choice but to Follow* and *What We Must Remember*.

Joe Tsujimoto has published two teacher texts, *Teaching Poetry Writing to Adolescents* (NCTE/ERIC) and *Lighting Fires: How the Passionate Teacher Engages Adolescent Writers* (Heinemann). He also published a collection of short fiction, *Morningside Heights: New York Stories* (Bamboo Ridge Press), was awarded the 2008 Elliot Cades Award for Literature, and was a finalist for the 2010 William Saroyan International Prize for Writing.

Alicia Upano is the 2016 fiction winner of the *Poets & Writers* Maureen Egen Writers Exchange Award Hawaiʻi. Her creative work has appeared in the *Asian American Literary Review* and *Hyphen*. Her family's history in Hawaiʻi began at the sugar plantation in Puʻunēnē, Maui, home of the Three-Year Swim Club, the inspiration for the fiction piece in this issue. To learn more, check out Julie Checkoway's *The Three-Year Swim Club: The Untold Story of Maui's Sugar Ditch Kids and Their Quest for Olympic Glory* (Grand Central Publishing, 2015).

Amy Uyematsu, a sansei poet and teacher from Los Angeles, is grateful to *Bamboo Ridge* for publishing so many of her poems, going back to 1986, and delighted to be part of this 40th anniversary issue.

For most of the year, **Sylvia Watanabe** lives and teaches in Ohio, a condition of perpetual transience. But, like all cats, she has never forgotten where she is from.

CANE HAUL ROAD
HONORS
BAMBOO RIDGE
40 YEARS OF RELEVANCE